JONATHAN HARVEY

The Confusion of KAREN CARPENTER

PAN BOOKS

First published 2013 by Pan Books
an imprint of Pan Macmillan, a division of Macmillan Publishers Limited
Pan Macmillan, 20 New Wharf Road, London N1 9RR
Basingstoke and Oxford
Associated companies throughout the world
www.panmacmillan.com

ISBN 978-0-330-54439-9

1 3 5 7 9 8 6 4 2

A CIP catalogue record for this book is available from the British Library.

Typeset by Birdy Book Design
Printed and bound by CPI Group (UK) Ltd, Croydon, CR0 4YY

Visit **www.panmacmillan.com** to read more about all our books
and to buy them. You will also find features, author interviews and
news of any author events, and you can sign up for e-newsletters
so that you're always first to hear about our new releases.

For Lee Anderson

ACKNOWLEDGEMENTS

Last time I had a book published, the acknowledgements were longer than *War and Peace*, so this time I'm keeping it brief. Ish. So. To my hairdresser, Chantay-Oolay at Jeffrey Soubriquet – you're a star and take years off me. Can you squeeze me in at two?

Oh okay, I'll be serious.

Continued thanks to my agent Gordon Wise at Curtis Brown for his belief and encouragement. Thanks to Wayne Brookes, Camilla Elworthy, Jeremy Trevathan and everyone at Pan Macmillan for making me laugh so much, and for publishing my books, and correcting my punctuation. Also to Michael McCoy and Alec Drysdale at Independent for keeping me employed and employable the rest of the time.

In respect to this particular book, I owe a debt of gratitude to many people who helped me with research. Thank you to Mark Winnock for answering my questions about working on the London Underground. Thanks to Dr Lesley French for discussing Karen's state of mind and the therapy she explores later in the book. Thanks to Jojo Moyes for giving me honest feedback on the first book and telling me to dig a bit deeper this time. And thanks to Angela Sinden for being a great sounding board when I got stuck on a story point. (A painful place to be.)

I used to be a teacher, but it was a very long time ago, so thank you to all the teachers I have spoken to in the last year at parties and on buses who answered such questions as 'Do they still have registers?' and 'What's an interactive whiteboard?'. Thank you also to Mike Christie and Andy McKenzie for sourcing me some DVDs of *Educating Essex*. It brought a million memories flooding back.

To all the kids I used to teach who are now in their 30s and yet still call me Sir. Thanks for that.

Hilariously huge thanks to Kate Tobin for bidding a lot of money in aid of the Sussex Beacon to have a character named after her in the book. The Sussex Beacon is a specialist hospice and care centre for those living with and affected by HIV/AIDS. In Sussex, believe it or not.

And finally, thank you to anyone who bothered to contact me after the first book via Twitter, Facebook etc. to tell me you'd enjoyed it. I am buoyant with gratitude.

ONE

Hello.

There are two things you should know about me:

1. My name is Karen Carpenter, and
2. Last month my boyfriend left me.

I'll get on to the boyfriend in a minute, but first let me tell you that having the same name as a 1970s pop star is no barrel of laughs. You may be thinking I'm as skinny as a rake, with poker-straight chestnut hair, sallow, sunken cheeks and dark brown eyes. You might also assume I have a voice like velvet and know my way round a drum kit, and on top of that you might presume I'm a dab hand at Solitaire. (Well, it's the only game in town.)

Sadly I am none of these things and have none of these skills or attributes. If you could actually see me, you'd probably be disappointed. I'm no fat old sow, but neither am I a Belsen-esque size-zero skinnimalinx. I can hold a grudge, but I can't hold a tune, and my favourite game's *Bullseye*. I've never actually played it; I just like watching the reruns on TV. My hair is mousy with blonde highlights and a tendency to frizz, my eyes are blue with a tendency to squint when I'm really,

really tired, and the nearest I get to playing the drums is when I have to hit one of my radiators a few times to get it working. (Temperamental radiators are the bane of my life. Or they were, till Michael left me. Oh damn. I said I'd get on to him in a bit.)

I don't want to mislead you. Although I may not slip into the skinny-minny category, I'm not a complete and utter minger. I once found a piece of paper at school that Yusef, one of our year tens, had written on. It was a top ten list of all the female teachers he wanted to shag. (It was called, coincidentally, 'Top Ten Teacher Shags'.) I was number three. Number one was Constantine, the French teacher, who wears hot pants and low-cut tops, and is always dropping her folders on the main staircase like a damsel in distress so that the lads hurl themselves at her to help her out, so I'm not surprised. More unexpectedly, number two was Dorothy from religious education, but I think that's because a rumour went round a few years ago saying she'd got drunk on a French trip and fellated a wine bottle for the amusement of the other staff. Complete rubbish, of course, but you try telling the kids that. So number three ain't that bad. If it was in my nature, I might even take a bow. Of course, happiness, as I've discovered, is fleeting – when I told Danny from English about the list one day, he chortled into his polystyrene beaker of tepid coffee (our staffroom drinks machine is pants: you could bath a newborn baby in any of our 'hot' drinks) and pointed out that Yusef is blind in one eye.

I later tried to verify this hypothesis by catching said eye in class when I thought no one else was looking. I carefully mouthed the word 'Help!' with an expression of panic on my face. I regretted it instantly. Yusef frowned, looked around and then said, 'Is you OK, Miss, man?'

I returned the frown and made out I had no idea what he was talking about and demanded he please get on with his work. I know. The *shame*. But at least I was able to tell Danny that he was full of crap when I saw him next.

Back to my name. Think how many times you have to give out yours over the phone. Now imagine what that might feel like if it was vaguely ridiculous. Every time I ring the bank, or the satellite-TV people, or the gas, or the electric, they ask for my name, and when I give it, there's always a pause. Or a giggle. Or a wisecrack. 'Oh, I thought you were dead!' is a common one. Or 'I hope you've had something to eat!' And only last week the woman in the call centre at my bank wondered if my password was 'Sha-la-la-la'. It's not.

I know the name Karen Carpenter is quite a mundane one, erring on the humdrum. If it wasn't for the fact that it was *her* name, it would definitely be dull. But if this doesn't sound too bad to you, imagine this scenario. A woman moves in next door. You go round with a bag of sugar (because you're like that – you're delightful; I can just tell) and you say to her, 'I'm —' (insert your name here) and she goes, 'Oh, hello, I'm Dolly Parton.' Or, 'Hi. I'm Beyoncé Knowles,' or, 'Hi. I'm Lulu.' Admit it – if you didn't perhaps laugh, you would definitely crack a smile. And I wouldn't blame you. But that's the sort of thing I've had to put up with all my life.

Growing up in Liverpool, where everyone's a comedian, was where the rot originally set in, especially when I hit my teens and got myself some puppy fat. When the hard kids at school rechristened me 'Skinny Bitch', they argued to the teachers that their nickname was not an ironic reference to my size, but to my namesake. Thankfully the teachers banned it, so they reverted to calling me 'S.B.' instead, which of course sounds completely innocuous to those not in the know, but to me, a whispered 'S.B.!' during double geography would make my skin burn with shame and give me the full-on horrors.

I used to dream that I had a normal name, like all the other girls in my class. Colette Carpenter or Tracy Carpenter. But Karen? *Karen?* What were my parents thinking? Well. Their hackles rise if I so much as challenge them over it. You see, Karen was the name of Mum's sister, and she died in a car crash when Mum was pregnant with me, so of course when Mum gave birth, the family was so uproarious with joy that she decided to name me after my dead, car-crashed aunt. Forgive me if that sounds cold and uncaring, but really . . . didn't someone think to say to Mum, 'Val, I know you're knackered and you feel like you just pooped out a block of flats, but please . . . remember your surname. Call her Colette'?

Hmm?

No. Apparently there were tears of happiness in the Oxford Road Maternity Hospital, and my nan kept saying, 'It's like she's still alive. It's as if our little Karen's still here!'

I like to think she stopped for at least a second, adding, 'Just a shame she now has the same name as a woman who's known for two things: a fabulous pop voice and not eating her dinner.'

I hope by now I have convinced you of some of the embarrassment involved in sharing a name with a recording artist. Oh God, I sound like a complete teacher, saying that. Like I'm doing a lesson plan and recapping to check everyone's up to speed with me. If I was doing a lesson plan right now, it would have two aims: to illuminate the issues involved in having a silly name, and to establish that I am newly single.

Single. Oh heck. That. I said I'd get on to Michael leaving me. Suppose I better do that now. Here we go.

Michael and I were together for nearly twenty years. That's a lifetime, if you're twenty, and it represents a lot of haircuts/crow's feet. It's the section in my life from ages sixteen to thirty-six. Help.

Michael's an affable chap who won a 'Who Looks the Most Like Bart Simpson?' contest at Butlins when he was fifteen, which will a) date him, and b) give you an idea of what he looks like. Or looked like at fifteen. Except he didn't really look like the cartoon character. People assumed he'd dusted himself down with yellow chalk, whereas in fact he had gone that colour overnight and was later diagnosed with hepatitis C, from which he nearly died and spent months in hospital.

Things had been great between Michael and me, mostly. He really was the full package: decent, caring, could put up a few shelves and was drop-dead gorgeous. I know he's gorgeous because whenever I've put pictures of him on Facebook, people who don't know him post comments such as: **God, Karen, your man is well tasty. LOL.**

Or: **OMG, Kagsy, well jel.**

Of course, the unspoken subtext of sentences like that would be: **And what the hell's he doing with you, you fat knacker?**

Or even: **Punching above your weight there, you hefty bitch. LOL.**

I'm not really fat, of course. It's just when your namesake's synonymous with anorexia, every time you look in the mirror you see Mount Vesuvius staring back.

I once got very jealous when I saw that some woman he worked with – Laura – had written on Michael's Facebook, under a particularly nice shot of him: **Were U born that handsome? Stunning eyes.**

I really wanted to write underneath it: **Hands off, bitch – he's mine.**

Luckily Michael talked me out of it. Well, laughed me out of it, saying that this Laura was away with the fairies and was on another planet. Which, thinking about it now, wasn't that reassuring, bearing in mind she's a safety officer for London Underground. You see, Michael is a Tube driver. He works on the Jubilee line. I'd never given much thought to the men and women who drive the trains beneath the streets of the capital before he started driving. Now that he's left me, I wonder if I'll ever be able to bring myself to get on one again.

Being a Tube driver just about sums him up really, and by that I don't mean that he is deep. (Even though he is. A bit. He is into Leonard Cohen – does that count?) I don't know if you know many people who work on the London Underground, but having spent so long with Michael, I do. And if you think about it, their jobs and lives revolve round helping people. Helping people get from A to B, with no snobbery – there's no class divide on a Tube. We, the paying public, are their number-one priority, so they put others before themselves. And while transporting us from A to B, our safety is paramount, so they need to be lean, clean transportation machines. Consequently Michael rarely drank, never took drugs and always put others before himself. You might think that makes him sound like a boring bugger, but actually he is a laugh and can get pissed as a fart when he fancies it. Just not the night before he starts a shift at four in the morning.

I know I've made the entire staff of a rather large organization sound like a heavenly host of angels – and I'm sure the next time you cross a surly cleaner on the Northern line, you'll be thinking, Jesus, Karen, did you never meet *this* one? – but generalizations are like clichés: there's a large grain of truth in there somewhere.

The one thing Michael did that wasn't exactly angelic was leave me. He did so just over a month ago. Three weeks before Christmas to be precise. Perfect timing. I came back late from school one evening. We'd had a departmental meeting and then

I'd slipped to the local pub, the Who'd've Thought It?, for a dry white on the way home with some of the English department and got in to find an envelope Sellotaped to the kettle. In that envelope was a letter.

> Dear Karen,
>   I'm sorry but I can't do this anymore. You know I've been unhappy for a while. I think the only way I'm going to be happy is if I go. I'm sorry I'm such a coward I can't tell you to your face. Don't come looking for me, and don't worry about me – I'll be fine. And you deserve better anyway.
>   Michael

What stung the most was not the content – that after nearly twenty years he was throwing in the towel – but the fact that he'd not put a kiss after his name. I'd noticed he'd stopped putting kisses on his texts about six months earlier. I'd attributed it to him being busy with work, but now that this might well be his last ever communication with me, and still no kiss . . . well, I burst out crying. Daft, eh? Not even really crying for the fact that he had left me, but that he had cared so little about me that he'd not even put a kiss.

He'd not thrown in the towel at all. He'd dropped it limply at his feet and grunted in a fashion that conveyed the meaning of a sort of 'Make of my towel-dropping what you will.'

The next few hours were a bit of a blur, but I went and lay on the bed, staring at the wallpaper, staring at the fake sunflower Michael had 'planted' in a tub by the window. I must have lain there for hours, catatonic. The next morning I was still lying on my side of the bed, still staring. It was as if I hadn't blinked once. And all night long the thought had been trapped in my head.

Michael had left me.

A thought so huge it was beating the shell of my skull. A manic thought in the padded cell of my mind, desperate for escape but unable to find a way to break out. A thought growing bigger and bigger until it would become too much for me and for the umpteenth time I would burst out crying.

Michael had left me.

And throughout the weeks that followed the thought was very rarely absent. Unlike Michael, it never left me. My only respite was the mornings when I'd wake and, for a few fleeting moments, not remember. But then of course I would. I always would. And slowly but surely I'd start to sink.

One thing I've learned to do over the last month or so is zone out. Thinking about him leaving makes me sad, so I have become very adept at turning my mind into a sort of Internet browser, clicking on link after link after link, zooming off in opposing directions from the place I started, thinking of more and more things that move me away from the sadness. The downside to this is I spend so much time in my head that I'm often unaware of what I'm doing physically.

Like now.

I appear to be in a park. This happens a lot lately: I find myself in a place with scant recollection of getting there. It's dark. The moon is piercing the trees and it's reflected in the puddles. Peering through the leaves, I can see what look like low-level multicoloured stars beaming out. Blues, reds, yellows. Christmas lights from the crescent of houses circumnavigating the park. They make me think of home.

Home.

Where is my home now?

I have to think for a second, and then I remember.

Well, there's the house I shared with Michael. Better head there, even though since his departure it's not felt like home. I leave the park, retracing the steps I must have taken, heading to the place that used to be warm, the place I used to love returning to, but that now just leaves me feeling cold and sad.

God, I sound miserable and sorry for myself, don't I?

I tell myself to cheer up. Mind over matter. If I make myself smile, then I will feel unmiserable and happy. And the world will smile with me. And I will never feel depressed again. It works for about two minutes. I get some funny looks from passers-by, as I am clearly grinning like the madwoman who escaped from the loony bin. Then all of a sudden I am caught up short, winded. A red neon circle, slashed by a blue line.

I am outside a Tube station.

Why do they have to have so many Tube stations in London? Don't they know I am suffering? Don't they realize that every time I see one it's like a slap round the face?

I freeze at the entrance. I could go down there. I could go down there and get on a train and find him. I could work my way through every single Tube until I found him. I could climb into his car, slap him round the face and say, '*Why?* Why did you leave me? What did I do that was so bad that you couldn't bear to share your life with me anymore? I don't buy this "it's not you, it's me" bollocks. Tell me. Please!'

Because the weirdest thing about him going was that he offered no explanation. He didn't tell me why. Nearly twenty years down the pan and nothing. Zilch. Nada. I tried phoning him to ask – in fact, it was the first thing I did after reading the letter on the kettle – but the minute I called his mobile, I heard it ringing in the kitchen drawer. He'd not even taken it with him. I had no idea where he'd gone. I have no idea where he is. I don't know if he's run off with someone else. I could find out. Ask his friends, his mum. But I simply don't want to know.

And yet if I just went down these stairs, if I just went into the hot draught of his subterranean world, I might find him, confront him, discover. For some reason, though, I don't want to.

I turn. I hurry on. It starts to rain and I feel like I'm running through one of those smudged pastel drawings of night-time London that they sell in the tourist shops, the sort that look like they were drawn in 1968. London looks so much nicer at night, lit up like a Christmas tree all year long. In the day, though, especially round here, it's just grey, grey, grey. As I run, I am overcome by waves of sadness. I know why. For years I have sent waves of affection and love out to someone else, and I still send out those waves, but because he's not here anymore to receive them, they just spray back and engulf me.

In the end I run out of breath. I take a bus to our street.

My street. It is my street now – I have to remember that.

I am bedraggled. Everyone on the bus is. We sit alongside each other, squelching every time the bus judders, puddles collecting at our feet.

I let myself into the house and the first thing that strikes me is that it's freezing. It's been quite a mild Christmas, but the central heating's been playing up and I'm not brilliant at sorting out practical stuff like that. That was always Michael's domain. I head to the boiler and click it off and on again and hope for the best. I take off my coat and put on two cardies and a woolly hat with flaps. I try the tap in the kitchen and am briefly excited that, for the time being anyway, the hot water appears to be working. I hotfoot it upstairs to the bathroom and run a bath. I have to go back to work tomorrow, and at least if I can have a bath tonight, I won't be too embarrassed if there's no hot in the morning. If I can grab one now, I won't be too smelly for school.

I feel a little wave of dread roll over me as I luxuriate in the hot water. Much as I am looking forward to the start of the spring term and having lots to take my mind off my current predicament, I am not relishing the prospect of the sympathetic looks in the staffroom, or the loaded questions.

'How was *your* Christmas?'

'How *are* you?'

'How're you getting on?'

The last thing I want to do is get emotional by the photocopier. Everyone knows what's going on. Not everyone will care, mind you, but enough people will feel they have to say something, see how I am. Which of course on one level is lovely, but on another I find cringeworthily mortifying. Everyone knows because I took a week off before we broke up for the Christmas holidays and bad news travels fast. The morning after getting the Letter, I phoned in sick and pretended to have flu, but word soon got round after I told Meredith from PE in Tesco. Well, she asked how I was and I burst out crying in the Home Baking aisle and before I knew it, I had the head Skyping me and telling me to take as much time off as I needed. Our head, Ethleen, is very into technology. In fact, she says technology is her 'thang'. I hate it when she says 'thang', but she's OK once you chip away at the psychobabble and her insistence that the kids aren't pupils or students but 'learners'. If you ignore all that, she's a bit of a laugh and her heart's in the right place.

I have a little panic.

The first thing that will happen in the staffroom tomorrow will be that we have our Monday-morning briefing. Basically this means that Ethleen comes in, claps her hands to get our attention and then fills us in on anything we need to know.

I am worried.

I am worried that she'll say, 'OK, guys, it's a welcome back to Karen Carpenter. Sadly Karen's partner, Michael, left her a few weeks ago. No idea why – I've not gone into details – but obviously what she'd really like is if each and every one of you could go up to her, hug her inappropriately and ask her lots of questions about it. Is she rubbish in the sack? for example. That kind of thing. She's doing OK to good-ish, I'd say, as her newfound misery has clearly not stopped her eating. The fat moose.'

I snap myself out of this reverie. There's no *way* Ethleen would say something like that in a staff briefing. Although when Kirsty in humanities had that miscarriage, Ethleen did say something like, 'It's lovely to have you back, Kirsty. Hope everything goes smoothly for you.' Kirsty went beetroot and picked imaginary fluff off her imaginary cardy (she was wearing a puffa jacket) and didn't know where to put herself, while all the blokes shuffled from foot to foot, and the women all looked at Kirsty and smiled sympathetically and slightly patronizingly. Apart from Gina from science. Basically, if you've got a headache, she's got a brain tumour, so she sucked her teeth, gave an ironic laugh and nodded in the direction of Kirsty as if to say, 'I have had twenty-three miscarriages, babe. Do *not* get me started on mass mourning.'

I am just toying with the idea of missing out on the Monday-morning briefing altogether and hiding in my office with two Fruit Pastilles in my ears when there is a noise downstairs. A key in the door. I hear the front door open. Footsteps. What sounds like a bag being dropped onto carpet. And I just know. I do, I just know.

Oh my God.

Michael has come home.

TWO

The salmon-pink swing coat I see slung over the banister as I run down the stairs and the casually discarded Ugg boots in the hall tell me that maybe it's not Michael who's just let himself in. And when I hear a croakily contraltoed 'Fly Me to the Moon' coming from the kitchen, I realize with a crashing blow that it is of course my mum.

How? How have I forgotten that she is staying? Am I going mad?

Mum appears in the kitchen doorway with a box of Findus Crispy Pancakes in one hand and some broccoli in the other and looks confused. (Huh. *She's* confused? I'm the one who's forgotten she's even staying.)

'I think you've got rats in your loft. I can hear a real scritch-scratching tonight,' she says, perturbed.

Oh well. Beats bats in the belfry, I suppose.

'You all right, love?'

I nod, smiling, as if to say, 'Why shouldn't I be?'

She looks me up and down curiously, as if to say, 'Well, you're the one stood in a fluffy pink dressing gown, fresh from the bath, no towel, dripping water on your parquet-effect flooring that you got for a knock-down price in the Ikea sale, if you please.'

I hurry back to the bath.

Mum came to stay last week, convinced that since the split I'd be wasting away to nothing and would only get through this with the aid of her good old-fashioned home cooking, which in her book is a vast array of frozen produce mixed up with fresh green veg. Yes, Mum really *has* been to Iceland. It was the day before Christmas Eve, and she breezed in laden down with three matching fake-Gucci travel bags and a two-thirds-sized artificial Christmas tree. She likes things that are two-thirds their normal size. My dad is known as Pint-Sized Vern down the Legion, they live in a house called Val's Cottage (it's not a cottage – it's just a two-up, two-down terraced house with antwacky latticed windows, but the ceilings are so low a dwarf would be claustrophobic), and her favourite Disney song is 'It's a Small World (After All)'.

She claimed she'd arrived because she couldn't bear to think of me being on my own over the festive period, but I was all too aware of the real reason. She'd clearly had a row with Dad and wanted some space, as well as some time to explore one of her favourite cities. Mum has long had a habit of suddenly texting to say she's just got off a train at Euston and would be arriving at the house in half an hour. She will then appear, bedraggled, on the doorstep, in a cloud of excuses and Tweed by Lentheric, claiming she's had another 'fight' with Dad and *had* to come to London or else she'd be 'serving an eighteen' in Holloway. My mum is prone to exaggeration. Dad has never laid a finger on her in his life; in fact, she's more likely to clobber him. The thing about my mum is, she has to have drama wherever she goes. She likes to be the eye of the storm. As my dad succinctly and precisely puts it, 'She could start a fight in an empty room, that one.'

I think part of the reason I'm quite shy and retiring – on

the surface at least – is because my mum is so loud and 'out there'. Everything about her has volume: her hair, her voice, her clothes, her stature. As a child, I wondered if she was the lady upon a white horse that they rode to Banbury Cross to see in that nursery rhyme, as my mum did always appear to have rings on her fingers and bells on her toes – she wore that many bangles, anklets and so on that she only had to take one step across a room and she sounded like an epileptic wind chime.

When I was a kid, she sold Marks & Spencer's seconds on a stall in Garston Market, so was used to and comfortable with the sound of her own booming voice. When I was about eight, she got bored on her market stall and decided to mix it up by introducing a little 'friend' to help her sell the misshapen duvets and pillowcases. Her little friend was a cuddly teddy bear that she had customized into a ventriloquist's puppet, and sometimes she would speak to the customers through him. Or Cheeky, as he became known.

Let me get one thing straight: Mum was no Roger De Courcey. She made no attempt to disguise the fact that her mouth was moving when Cheeky was speaking; nor did she alter her voice when doing the voice of Cheeky. Cheeky, in fact, sounded just like Mum. What she did to hide her moving mouth was hold Cheeky up in front of her face whenever he 'spoke'. It is not the best technique in the world, you have to admit.

However. This didn't stop a lot of people at Garston Market telling Mum what a character Cheeky was. How funny he was. What sparkling repartee he had. Crowds used to gather to wonder at the hilarious stand-up act of performance art that went on at the Marks's seconds stall three times a week. I say crowds, but I never saw them, though Mum described them as ten deep on occasion. (As I said, prone to exaggeration.)

Anyway, the upshot of all this attention was that Mum decided it was high time to pack in the market stall and pursue a career as a ventriloquist. Which was a great idea, except that:

1. She couldn't speak without moving her lips, and
2. She couldn't speak without moving her lips.

That certainly didn't stop her having her van resprayed with 'Val Carpenter and Cheeky the Liverpool Bear!' on the side. She took an advert in both the *Stage* and the local paper, the *Echo*, announcing that 'due to popular demand' she and Cheeky were now 'available for bookings!!!'

And yes, she did put three exclamation marks. And she had professional photographs taken at a studio on Allerton Road. For months afterwards her huge portrait adorned their shop window, Mum smiling so hard she looked like she was trying to expel something, and holding Cheeky up as if to say, 'Look – I've found the elixir of life, and he is a foot-high teddy bear in a shell suit top. Share with me my discovery, my joy!' A bright orange star had been cut out of cardboard and attached to the corner of the portrait. On it, in marker pen, someone had written:

Local celebrity Val Collins and Peeky the Bear

Which got Mum's blood boiling and she went in to complain, insisting they change it to 'Local celebrity Val Carpenter and Cheeky the Liverpool Bear.' Although she knew it would be a challenge to get that on a small bit of cardboard, she was sure they could *if they really tried*.

She must have rubbed them up the wrong way, though, because instead of altering the star, they removed the photo from the window altogether, claiming it had 'made them a laughing stock'. Mum just wasn't as famous as she liked to think she was. Or, as they put it, 'You're no Edwina Currie.'

In order to 'up her profile' – as she explained she was doing one night to Dad over a high tea of fish fingers and mashed potato, easy on the peas – she decided she was going to 'crack the schools market'. Dad looked slightly alarmed, but I thought no more of it.

Until a few weeks later during assembly at school when our headmistress, Mrs Girvan (who had a gold tooth), announced we were going to learn all about road safety. Nothing amazing there, but then she added, 'With none other than Cheeky the Liverpool Bear.' I froze. What fresh hell was this? The doors at the back of the assembly hall swung open, a tape of a piano started to play, and Mum walked in wearing a pillar-box-red safari suit and carrying Cheeky, singing a song that went along the lines of:

> *Look left, look right.*
> *Only cross if it's all right.*
> *Look back, look ahead*
> *If you wanna make sure you're not dead.*
> *Find a zebra or a pelican*
> *If you don't wanna be a skeleton.*
> *Do not dawdle. Do not bop.*
> *Do not hit the lollipop*
> *Lady . . .*

Anyway, this room full of approximately two hundred under-elevens knew this song was complete *rubbish*. A few kids looked round to gauge my reaction.

One boy leaned in and said, 'Isn't that your mum?'

I shook my head.

'It is, Karen. That's your mum.' Another voice, more insistent.

'How can it be my mum?' I blustered as Mum carried on singing her way to the front of the hall. 'My mum's . . . *dead!*'

Whoops. No one was going to believe me, were they?

'Liar!'

'Yeah, you lying bitch!'

I blushed. They were on to me. Something, possibly, to do with my mum singing into a head mic at the front of the assembly hall right now, a teddy covering her face, as our headmistress was tapping her foot in time to the 'beat'. But then I heard a girl whisper behind me, 'It might be true. My mam said someone else is working on the Marks's stall now.'

I saw various mouths drop open in shock and eyes watering in sympathy. I didn't care that I had lied, because when I looked ahead and saw Mum jigging about with the shell-suited teddy, I wanted to kill her.

I know I shouldn't have said it. I know it was really bad of me. Lying's always bad, and this was one lie that would be pretty hard to keep going, right?

Wrong.

I kept it up for almost a month. It was amazingly easy to do. I suppose because, looking back, children will believe anything. Or they did in those dim and distant days, even if the obvious was staring them in the face. A bit like if I now said to some (admittedly young) kids at school, 'See this wall? Although it looks white to the naked eye, it is in fact blue. It's an amazing new blue that appears white but is in fact blue.'

After a while you might say to those children, 'What colour is this wall?'

They would look at this white, white wall and answer, 'That wall is blue.'

So as long as I had the odd pretend cry at school and said things during the dinner break like, 'God, this chicken à la king with mash really reminds me of my mum. I wish she wasn't dead,' and as long as I didn't take them back to the house, then no one would really know the difference.

But of course Bryony Cathcart had to go and spoil everything in class one day. Mrs Tipping was asking us to bring in photos of our families for a project, so Bryony put up her hand and said, 'Miss? What should Karen do, Miss? 'Cos her mum's, like, dead.'

Mrs Tipping frowned, glanced at me, then shook her head at Bryony. 'That's not very grown-up, Bryony. And not very nice. Get on with your work.'

'No, it's true, Miss.' Debbie Fontaine was backing her up.

Mrs Tipping glanced at me. This didn't look good.

'She died in a freak tornado at Rhyl Sun Centre while she was there on a Dooleys tribute weekend.'

Why? Why had I said that? Why couldn't I have just said she died peacefully in her sleep like a normal person? Why had I had to have her blowing away in a cyclone at a North Wales holiday destination?

'She's not dead, Debbie,' Mrs Tipping said calmly.

'She is, Miss. Her funeral was at the Protestant Cathedral,' Debbie argued.

'Well, she had half of it there,' added Bryony, 'and the other half at the Catholic Cathedral.'

Now Mrs Tipping was looking quite scared.

''Cos she was halfy-halfy,' explained Debbie.

Again, why? Why had I said that? Why had I described such an elaborate funeral? What was I thinking?

I screwed up my face in a 'what the frig are they on about?' look.

'Then they went on to a really nice synagogue, Miss,' added Jamie-Lee Morton, ''cos she was really into Jews.'

Oh. *God.*

Mrs Tipping was not happy. When she gave Jamie-Lee, Debbie and Bryony detention, I knew my days were numbered. You see, it's one thing lying to other kids – they'll swallow anything – but grown-ups are a different matter entirely. I was quite convinced that grown-ups were part of a club and they all knew each other's doings. So if my mum and dad had a row on a Tuesday night about a colour scheme for scatter cushions to go with the three-piece suite, I quite expected Mrs Tipping to have an opinion on the decision the next day. So it completely stood to reason that Mrs Tipping *knew full well* my mother was alive and parading herself round as a ventriloquist of dubious repute in the schools of south Liverpool, and of course if she had died in a freak act of God, then surely she would know.

My assumptions were right.

'Why did you tell everyone Mum was dead, Karen?' asked Dad that night, following a very long pause as we ate a tea of chicken Kievs and green beans.

I shrugged. I couldn't tell the truth, could I?

'Well, isn't it obvious?' asked Mum, who was taking this far better than I thought she would. She even had a chuckle in her voice. Dad looked at her.

Oh God, she was going to say it: *The child is embarrassed that I am such a dreadful ventriloquist. I hang my head in shame and hang my fistable teddy on the back of the bedroom door, never to be seen in public again.*

No such luck. Instead she said, 'You've let her watch too many Hammer House of Horror films, so she's got a morbid fascination with death.'

She said it almost proudly, like it was something to brag

about, something that made me different and interesting. Beguiling, bewitching. I was almost won over.

'Ergo . . .' she continued – I had no idea what or who Ergo was – '. . . she has chosen me, the most important person in her life, and wondered what it would be like if I was . . . a goner.'

Dad rolled his eyes, and I wasn't surprised. I'd watched about two movies and hated them both. Mum just hated him watching them. That's what this was really about.

'Don't roll your eyes at me, Vernon.'

'Nothing to do with Cheeky, then,' Dad muttered under his breath.

'Vernon!' snapped Mum, as if he was the one being cheeky.

We continued to eat in silence.

To maintain the pretence that I was indeed obsessed with death, I took to watching more horror movies, reading the death announcements in the *Echo* and mysteriously circling some of them with red pen. I also claimed to want to be an embalmer when I grew up. Mum loved my new fascination and actively encouraged it. This culminated in her taking me to look round the local undertaker's and chapel of rest.

As we gazed on our fourth corpse, Mum leaned in and said, 'This one's been garrotted. I think it's drugs-related,' and I realized I was starting to feel faint.

I looked up at her and said, 'I think I'm over my obsession with death.'

She looked down at me, rather disappointed.

And then I really did faint.

The other kids at school were slightly more tricky to shake off. After word spread that I was a liar, liar, pants on fire, because I'd claimed my mum was dead when she wasn't, I did a counterattack with, 'Well, you'll never guess what. The police came to our house and said they'd made a terrible mistake. It wasn't my mum who was blown away by the tornado. It was just someone who had the same snood as her.'

It was the 1980s.

'And now she's home and it's amazing. I've got my mum back again.'

'Where's she been?'

'I can't tell you. It's top secret. Well, I could tell you, but then the secret police would come round and kill you.'

'Which secret police?'

'I can't tell you. It's a secret.'

And guess what? It actually worked.

So what did I learn from this little experience?

Lying works. Kids will believe anything.

I lie in the bath, contemplating my navel. Literally. The water has gone cold, but it's OK, as miraculously the central heating appears to have come on. Maybe Mum has the magic touch. Or maybe she threatened to bring Cheeky out of retirement unless the boiler sorted itself, so it did.

Thinking about this lying-to-kids thing, and how easy it is, I wonder if I ever do it now I am a fully grown-up grown-up. And lying there in the bath, I think (and I must be feeling bitter now) that yes, I do. I stand up in front of them every day, at school, and lie to them. I say, 'Work hard and you can achieve. Settle down and listen to your teachers and the world's your oyster. You can do anything with your lives. Why, you could even be a future prime minister, or . . . or . . . president of the United States!'

Whereas really maybe I should in fact be saying, 'You're screwed. Really screwed. You live on a shit estate. You have zero prospects. Half your parents don't care, and if they don't, why is it my responsibility to improve your life? I wish you well, but, you know, maybe you should go out with the local dealer and have kids at sixteen. There's far more likelihood of that than you becoming the next Barack Obama.'

Then I hate myself for even thinking that, because someone might have said that to me once upon a time, but they didn't. And I've done all right for myself.

Or have I?

Thirty-six years of age, abandoned by my boyfriend and having to have my mum move back in with me to make sure I'm OK. Over bloody Christmas.

Oh yeah, Karen Carpenter, you've done really well for yourself.

I dry and change into my nightie and dressing gown, then decide to choose an outfit for tomorrow, to save time in the morning. I open my bedroom wardrobe and two things sadden me, just when I'm trying to feel positive about tomorrow's fresh start.

The first is Michael's side of the wardrobe. His clothes hang there neatly, untouched. For the millionth time I wonder why he didn't take them with him. Has he gone and joined a naturist commune? The thought, ridiculous as it is, stings me. He never particularly enjoyed being naked in my presence. Why has he changed so much, hmm? Is he having some sort of mid-life crisis? And if he is not at a nudey commune, then what on earth is he wearing? Is he just wearing the uniforms he keeps in his locker at work? Has he, in fact, been squirrelling away outfits without my knowledge over the last few months, readying for the day he'd leave, so that he would be spared the effort of carrying a case with him? Rather than letting my mind boggle with these useless, fruitless worries, I slam his side of the wardrobe shut and open mine.

Which is when I see the second thing.

What looks like a thin ivory satin shift hanging from the rail. My wedding dress. Michael and I were planning on getting married in the summer. June, to be precise. But that dress didn't just represent a future full of hope and opportunities; it also represented the tantalizing prospect of the day when I wouldn't be Karen Carpenter anymore. I would be Karen Fletcher. No more anorexia jokes. No more 'Calling Occupants of Interplanetary Craft' gags. Normality. Mundaneness. Banality. Bring it on.

But not anymore.

I run my fingers over the thin, delicate material, thinking of what might have been, thinking of the day I would have worn it. How I might have felt. The person I was going to become.

I sigh and close the wardrobe door, and decide I can choose my outfit tomorrow.

Just then I hear Mum calling me down for my tea.

THREE

I want to live in suburbia. I want to live in a nice street of nice houses and nice neighbours. I want to have a car in the drive with pink fluffy dice that announce me as girly. I want to get in said car every morning and drive to school listening to Chris Evans. As well as the dice hanging from the rear-view mirror, I would also have an air freshener hanging there too. Each time I'd get into the car, I'd sniff and sigh contentedly, secure in the knowledge that my car smelt nice. Nice. Such an underrated word. Why can't my world be nice?

Sadly I don't live in Suburbia. I live in East Ham. Also, it's so impractical having a car in London. Driving to school would take approximately three and a half weeks. On a good day. The Tube is the most practical way of getting from A to B, where A is my house and B is my workplace. Speed is of the essence, of course, but the downside is that when you travel by train, you don't have the luxury of a boot or a messy back seat, just the inconvenience of having to carry everything. So each day I look like Fatima Whitbread as I juggle scores of exercise books, lesson plans, pencil cases, etc., on public transport. (NB I don't really look like Fatima Whitbread. I was just trying to give the impression of a muscly-lady-type person lifting large, clunky items.)

In my fantasy version of driving to school, I would arrive calm, centred and more fragrant than Pippa Middleton's thong. In reality, after battling the rush-hour throng, I will usually arrive bedraggled, sweaty, runny of make-up and in a general state of fumingness that working in a school does little to alleviate.

Today I am nervous as I swipe my Oyster card over the magic eye as I enter the Underground. As the partner of a Tube driver, I get free travel all year round, but this is the first time I have used the Underground since Michael went and I am worried he will have cancelled this and my card won't work. I am fearful that when I scan it, an alarm will go off and a big, flashing red sign will appear above the escalator screaming:

DUMPED LADY TRYING TO GET FREE TRAVEL!
DUMPED LADY TRYING TO GET FREE TRAVEL!

I check the red sign. It says:

NO REPORTED INCIDENTS

Am I soon to be an incident?
I swipe. I check the sign. Nothing. Still:

NO REPORTED INCIDENTS

The gates open and I am allowed through. My card still works. I sail through unhindered. Well, as unhindered as you can be with three bags and a clutch of hardbacks. As I descend the escalator, I worry. How long will it be before Michael remembers? How long will it be before he's at work one day and his boss says, 'Oi, Mike, you know you've still got your free partner pass?' and Michael swears quietly and tells his boss to delete me from the system?

Actually, that is what has happened to me: I have been deleted from Michael's system. I am no longer important to him. Whereas once upon a time I was the centre of his universe, now I am nothing.

You're nothing to me. That's what they say in movies all the time, when the teen heroine ditches the hero at the prom or something after she's caught him necking the class slut. *You're nothing to me.* In fact, what she really means is: 'You mean a great deal to me, which is why your slut-necking saddens me, but no way am I going to give you the satisfaction of showing you how much I care, so instead I will say, "You're nothing to me."'

Whereas actually if Michael said that to me now, he would mean every word.

As I sit on the Tube, I realize I am thinking about him and so my mind automatically darts off to different places to avoid the numbness or pain, to avoid the tears, to avoid the anxiety. I find myself pinballing between the latest Jessie J video I've seen, Meryl Streep in *The Iron Lady*, the fact that I need to get Toilet Duck and wondering how many people on the planet are starving. I pinball so much I almost miss my stop.

Depending on the weather, and how much I am carrying, it is either a fifteen-minute walk or a five-minute bus ride from the Tube station to Fountain Woods School. As it's the first day back, it looks like rain, and I am armed with hardbacks, I plump for the bus. Sometimes the bus is a bad move, as I have to share it with students, but today I have got in nice and early, thus avoiding all contact with them just yet. I stare at the driver from my seat. The back of his head, the flash of his eyes in the rear-view mirror.

Drivers. I'm not sure whether, as a breed, I like them anymore.

I wonder if he left his girlfriend over Christmas, and if so, why? I wonder if he left his clothes and his phone and reinvented himself somewhere else, with a whole new wardrobe. I wonder if his ex-girlfriend got on at the next stop, whether he would apologize, offer an explanation. I am almost tempted to go and ask him these hypothetical questions, but then it is time for me to get off.

Oh well. Probably for the best.

Fountain Woods School is ugly. There are no two ways about it. Whichever architect thought that breezeblocks and concrete slabs with porthole windows and carport-style covered walkways would make kids' hearts sing as they came to school each day and therefore want to work harder as a result was very much mistaken. If this building was a human, it'd be a tattooed seventeen-year-old lad hanging around outside the off-licence giving you evils. Once you got to know him, he'd be a laugh. He'd have a heart of gold, in fact. He'd probably love his old nan, but the first impression would be pretty scary. I cross the near-empty car park and head inside.

The first thing you see when you come into the foyer is a six-foot-high poster saying, 'Welcome to Fountain Woods School.' Embroidered on the left of the poster is a fountain and on the right some woods, despite there being neither in the local vicinity. Between the fountain and the woods is a string of people. All colours, heights, abilities. Two are in wheelchairs. One appears to be a drag queen. Our message is loud and clear: all are welcome here.

I am distracted by what sounds like machine-gun fire to my left. I know what it will be even before I turn my head to look. Behind an oversized serving hatch sits our chief secretary,

Rochelle. She has hair like a 1970s porn star, and a face like a boiled sweet. She's one of those women who looks about seventeen from the back and seventy from the front. The machine-gun fire is the sound of her nails on the keyboard she is typing on right now. As she types at approximately three hundred words a minute, it's quite a sound.

She looks up at me and, without stopping her nails from clattering on her keyboard, asks, 'Have a nice Christmas, Karen?'

OK, so she is pretending nothing bad has happened. This I can deal with. This I prefer.

'Yes, thanks, Rochelle. You?' I smile.

She nods. 'Yeah. I went to Cornwall. It was lovely.'

'Lovely,' I say, and move on.

Rochelle is odd. I know for a fact that her husband left her a few months ago, and I know for a fact that he left her for another woman. Another woman who lives in Cornwall. I know this because I was told by some of the dinner ladies. Basically, if you want to know anything about what's going on in a school, ask the dinner ladies. They know everything. I could probably ask them where Michael is and they'd know.

I'm relieved that Rochelle chose to pretend everything was OK in her world and mine too. It means I don't have to go into any of the gory details or 'what if?'s. The only downside is that every time I see Rochelle, I am reminded of the thing I don't like to think about: what if Michael left me for someone else?

It is feasible. I mean, come on, it would make sense. Over the last few months he has become more and more distracted, more and more distant. There was a gradual removal of affection towards me, a gradual removal of intimacy. I would come in from school and put supper on, and he would get back from work and, rather than talk to me, go on the phone and chat endlessly to his mates, or his mum, or whoever, his supper on his knee, chomping away between sentences. I'd wait in vain for the calls to end, hoping we might talk, catch up, share anecdotes about our working days, but no. Phone down, he'd stretch his arms, yawn and say how knackered he was and how bed was calling. Other nights he'd be chatting with friends on Facebook, wrapped up in his online world, taking little notice of me.

Maybe he was chatting with a new lover.

Maybe I need to hack into his Facebook account and find out. I can pretty much guess what his password is. I could do it easily. I could do it tonight.

Something stops me getting excited about this, though, and I know why.

I am scared of what I might find out.

I am walking towards the staffroom now, but part of me wants to turn round, to run back to Rochelle and say, 'What is it like? What is it like to know your fella's off with someone else? How does it feel? How do you reconcile that? Only I think my fella might have done the same, but I am too scared to confront those feelings, petrified of how it might make me feel. And so I am pretending that everything's OK, but it's not, Rochelle, it's not.'

I know what she would do, though. She'd just stare at me, then turn her back on me and start typing again, for Rochelle has been in denial ever since her husband left her. I only know she's been through this heartache because of Claire who does the custard. Custard Claire lives in the same road as Rochelle, so has her finger on the pulse. Looking at Rochelle, you'd never guess she's been dumped on from a great height by some bastard of a bloke. She just goes about her business with a big smile on her face, teeth gritted, and if you ask how she is, she just goes, 'Fine!'

Or if you ask after her husband, you'll get a 'Really well!'
And it doesn't make sense.

Because Custard Claire reckons Rochelle's fella's been shagging anything in a skirt for years; it's just that Miss Cornwall is the first one who'd have him.

Poor Rochelle. It must be awful to be in denial.

I go and hide in one of the cubicles in the ladies' toilets. I am in no mood to be the recipient of pitying looks or gossipy 'Oh my God, I hear Michael left you's. I will wait in the toilet till a quarter past eight.

The start of our Monday-morning briefing is heralded by the arrival of Rochelle clapping like a demented seal to get our attention. Three steps behind her is our fragrant headmistress in a powder-pink Chanel suit and big hair. As the buzz of the staffroom dies down and Ethleen goes about welcoming us back to another important term, I look around the crowded staffroom – it's standing room only – and see a few people staring at me. One is Gina from science, who – I have no idea why – is wearing a neck brace. She winks at me and nods, then winces. She has obviously done something to her neck, though in her case it wouldn't surprise me if she'd done nothing to her neck but just wanted to give the impression she had for sympathy or attention. I also see Mungo, my ginger-bearded head of department, who mouths to me, 'Are you OK?'

I mouth back, 'I'm fine.'

And he smiles and gives me a thumbs-up, which makes me feel a bit nauseous as he is double-jointed and his thumb bends right back. Having said that, most things Mungo does make me slightly nauseous. Like his habit of licking his moustache when he's thinking. Or the way he wears his watch the wrong way round so he has to do an elaborate gesture with his bony arms in order to check the time. Or the way (and this is unforgivable) he wears open-toed sandals with grey socks underneath. When people ask what is the most surprising thing about teaching, I am often tempted to reply, 'The fact that my HOD doesn't get his head kicked in by the kids on a daily basis.'

Ethleen is welcoming a new member of staff and I strain to see her standing beaming by the coffee machine. She is wearing John Lennon glasses, a sensible bob and a rabbit-in-headlights smile.

'I give her five minutes,' says Meredith, the PE teacher, under her breath, leaning in to me. I can't help but chuckle. Meredith has a habit of invading your personal space. It gets on some people's nerves, but personally it doesn't bother me. It's not like she means anything by it. I think it's just because she's from New Zealand.

The new teacher looks over, as if my laughter was directed at her. The smile freezes on her face and I worry that she thinks I'm being bitchy and laughing at her, so I wink at her, to show I am her comrade in arms – all for one and one for all – but instead of garnering the grateful wink back I expected, she turns and looks quickly away.

Why? Why did she do that? I look to Meredith, who is red-faced with mirth.

'She thinks you fancy her,' she whispers, barely able to contain her glee.

I roll my eyes. OK, so a great start to the new term this is turning out to be. Not only has my boyfriend left me, but now the new teacher thinks I'm a lesbian who's after her. Oh, joy of joys.

Just as I am contemplating scrawling a sign on the back of one of my books saying, 'Relax. Me Not Lesbian,' and holding it up to show her, I realize that Ethleen is saying something about me. I've missed the beginning of it because I was doing my lesbo mortification routine in my head. And then I miss the middle of it because Mungo is sneezing loudly into what looks like a Starbucks serviette, then checking the contents of said serviette. I turn back to smile at Ethleen, who has cocked her head on one side and is looking at me sympathetically.

Mortified.

I am mortified. There is no other word in the English language for it.

Since when did splitting up with your partner merit being brought up in the Monday-morning briefing? So what if he didn't give me any warning? So what if he stuck a letter to the kettle and didn't take his phone or clothes? (He did take his laptop, bizarrely.) So what if my Christmas was probably a bit/ lot more crappy than yours was? So what if I am so inept at dealing with stuff like this that my mother has to come and stay to make sure I don't do anything daft? It doesn't need bringing up now. It has no bearing on my performance in school or the education of our learners. Why, oh why, do I have to work in a school where the head likes to see herself as touchy-feely? I feel a thousand eyes on me and can tell I'm going the colour of some scarlet scanties. Just as I'm hoping the ground will open up and swallow me, five pips sound over the tannoy, announcing it's time to head on up to registration.

I am a special needs teacher. Fountain Woods is a mainstream comprehensive school, so my job usually involves sitting at the back of other people's classrooms, helping the slower kids with the task the main teacher has set. Sometimes I withdraw small groups of kids to work in another classroom. Sometimes I have groups of ten or so, say in GCSE year, where I give them extra help with their coursework on other subjects. (Let's face it, you can't *learn* special needs, I don't think.) The only times I really have full-sized classes are when I'm teaching media studies (about which I know nothing, but it was in the curriculum and no one else was free that period) and when I'm with my own tutor group.

I love my tutor group. They're year sevens, which means they're either eleven or twelve and this is their first year at Fountain Woods. Each tutor group takes the first and last letter of their tutor's surname, so my group are 7CR. They're a lovely, lively group who keep me on my toes, make me laugh and are generally at the school to learn and improve their lives. For now. I'm sure all that will change when they hit year nine. Then they'll want to get pregnant or be drug dealers, but for the next eighteen months or so it'll be a halcyon time.

I have this little routine whenever I enter a classroom. I stand at the door with the wastepaper basket in my hands before letting the kids in. As they pass, if they are chewing gum, they are expected to spit it out into the bin. Bizarrely they seem to enjoy this ritual. It brings out their innate sense of competitiveness, so they like to spit any gum out as extravagantly as they can and with the utmost drama. It's like *Dancing on Ice* with gobbing, but that's pre-teens for you. I collect the gum, then return the bin under my desk, power up my electronic whiteboard and log in to the register on my laptop.

Before I can begin calling out the names, I am inundated by several kids calling out, 'You OK, Miss?' and, 'You feeling better, Miss?'

Oh good. They think I was off before Christmas with some kind of sickness. Excellent.

I reassure them I'm fine. 'Heaps better. Best Christmas of my life. Ever. Loads of presents, yeah! Loads of booze, yeah!'

'Loads of drugs, Miss?'

'Don't be clever, Inderjit.'

'Did you, like, get off your nut, Miss?'

'OK, settle down, everyone.'

'Miss, was you like seriously off your face on pills, Miss?'

I really need to get on with this register.

Elizabeth, one of my better-behaved girls, is approaching me with an envelope.

'Miss? Connor's dad asked me to give you this, is it?'

'Thanks, Elizabeth,' I say, and rip open the envelope, not thinking, calling out to the class to settle down for registration.

I'd not even noticed Connor wasn't here. He never misses school, yet I didn't even realize he was off. Is that bad?

I glance over the letter. And then reread it.

Oh God.

The handwriting is neat, considering it is written by a man. It is written in fountain pen, which I find at once sweet and beguiling. No other parent I know writes absence notes in fountain pen.

> *Dear Miss Carpenter,*
>
> *Sorry Connor isn't in school today. Sadly his mum passed away last week and I am going to keep him off till the end of the week, as it's the funeral on Friday. Hope this is OK with you. If you have any work you think he needs to do, then please call me on my mobile.*
>
> *All best wishes,*
>
> *Kevin O'Keefe*

I knew Connor's mum was ill with cancer – she has been ill for some time – but still the information shocks me. I see a quick video montage in my mind. Connor holding his mum's hand as she takes her final breath. Connor's dad breaking down as the doctor says she's gone and they can't bring her back. Father and son eating beans on toast, missing a woman's touch. Sombre visits to the chapel of rest. Kevin ironing Connor's school shirt for the funeral. Family descending. Invasion of space. Men having to deal with emotions more easily associated with women.

I realize I can't really remember what Connor's dad looks like. I've only met him once, at parents' evening. Although he's written lots of letters about his wife's illness, and made lots of phone calls, I can't really remember what his face is like. So I imagine him, in this movie version, as being played by Michael Fassbender.

Dream on, Karen!

I look back at the letter. The writing is smudged near the end. The word 'mobile' is fuzzy. I wonder if it has been smudged by Mr O'Keefe's tears.

The letter brings me up short.

There was me wallowing in my own misery through the Christmas break when all along one of my students was going through the experience of losing a parent. The letter is like a slap round the face, like a sharp waft of fresh air in a stuffy room. Usually letters like this would upset me, but this one makes me feel I don't even know I'm born. There was me thinking the worst thing ever had happened to me.

God, Karen, get over yourself. Your boyfriend left you. So what? You have your life. Your family. Your friends.

OK, so you also have a wedding dress you no longer need, but *it doesn't matter.*

Nobody died.

I put the letter in my bag and look to the class and smile.

'Happy New Year, 7CR!'

And I start to call out their names.

*

As I am having my lunch later, Custard Claire sidles over, her eyes aflame. I saw her earlier, when she'd offered me her sympathies about Michael leaving. She'd then quickly changed the subject, saying she had *major* gossip on Rochelle from the office and she'd tell me at lunchtime.

So here I am, sat in the salad room. She sits opposite me and says, 'Well, have you heard about Rochelle?'

'What about her?'

'Went off up to Cornwall over Christmas. Well, you know who's in Cornwall, duntcha?'

I nod. 'Her ex.'

She nods. 'Her ex and his fancy piece. Anyway, two days she's gone, and guess what time she gets home?'

I shrug, and don't guess.

'Three o'clock in the morning,' says Claire dramatically.

Behind her I see the new teacher standing with a tray full of food, wondering where to sit. She clocks me and moves to a table in the far corner.

'No one gets home at three in the morning,' Claire continues, 'unless some major shit's gone down.'

'What d'you think she was doing in Cornwall?' I ask.

Claire shrugs. 'Vera reckons she was after a threesome, but I reckon she went to beg him to come home, only he never.' She shakes her head disparagingly and repeats it like it's the most heinous thing in the world. 'Three o'clock in the morning. I ask you. Silly bitch.'

And I can't help but laugh.

Heading back from the salad room to the staffroom, I pass through the foyer. Rochelle is still typing through the lunch hour, the rat-a-tat-tat of the keys echoing round the reception area. I walk by, but she looks up, and this time she stops typing.

'Karen?' she says, a smile in her voice.

I look over at her. 'Hi, Rochelle,' I say, like it is a surprise to see her there, when actually it would have been a surprise to see her anywhere but there.

'I was so sorry to hear about Michael. It must be awful.'

Bless her.

'Oh. I'm OK, thanks, Rochelle, but I appreciate you saying it.'

Rochelle smiles and returns to her typing. So I risk it.

'And I was sorry to hear about . . .' which is when I realize I don't know her husband's name '. . . your husband.'

She looks up. Her hands freeze. 'What about my husband?'

She looks murderous. I immediately realize I've said the wrong thing.

'Oh. I thought you'd . . . split up with . . . your . . . husband.'

She smiles, shakes her head. 'No, Karen. Some of us are able to hang on to our men. Geoffrey would never leave me.'

Ouch. Touché!

Again she smiles and it throws me off balance. Is she completely mad, or has Custard Claire been making things up about her?

I go to apologize, but Rochelle butts in. 'Did you want something? Only I've got exclusion letters to write.'

'I'm sorry, Rochelle. I must've got the wrong end of the stick.'

Rochelle's eyes widen and she just nods sarcastically, as if to say, 'Yes, you silly mare. Won't make that mistake again in a hurry, will you?'

I nod back, then hurry off to the staffroom, feeling strangely unnerved.

The afternoon passes without incident. Well, that's somewhat of an understatement. No afternoon passes without incident in an ex-ILEA school. There are the usual near-violent exchanges, and actual violent exchanges; two girls call me a 'cheeky bitch';

one boy calls me a 'rasclart'; practically my whole media studies group find their way on to unapproved websites; plus there is an unexpected fire alarm caused by someone vandalizing the boys' toilets by the PE block. Apart from that, it is generally a pretty quiet afternoon.

I'm vaguely aware of a passing siren as I'm supporting in Danny's English class, but this is a busy estate – you hear sirens all the time. Then half an hour before the end of the final period I get an email from the head popping up in my inbox marked, 'Urgent.'

From: Ethleen Butterly EButterly@fountainwoods.org.uk
To: All Staff
Re: Emergency Staff Meeting 15.40

Dear all,
    Please come to the staffroom immediately school finishes for an emergency staff meeting.
    Many thanks,
      Ethleen

How odd.

There is an excitable buzz of anticipation as we all crush ourselves into the far-too-small staffroom. I look around and see practically every member of staff there. Meetings like this are only called in extreme circumstances: a child has stabbed another; a teacher has dropped dead in the car park, that kind of thing. When Ethleen walks in without Rochelle in front of her doing her seal impression, I feel a hand of ice grip my neck. Something is seriously wrong.

Ethleen clears her throat. 'Thank you all for coming at such short notice,' she says, with the warm, efficient professionalism of a young Harriet Harman. 'I'm sorry to keep you back when you no doubt have better things to do with your time, so for that I apologize. Anyway, something happened this afternoon and I had to share it with you.' She takes a deep breath. 'Rochelle from the office has been arrested, for suspected murder.'

There is an audible gasp. It dances round the room like a Mexican wave.

'It transpires that recently her husband left her and moved to Cornwall.'

'Cornwall?' says Gina incredulously, like that's a really bad move. Which is kind of missing the point, I think.

'And Rochelle heard that he had met someone else. Anyway, it looks like last week Rochelle drove to Cornwall and . . . well . . . ran this woman over. So they've taken her in for questioning and I'm not sure she'll be coming back.'

Gosh.

'Cornwall?' Gina is saying again. 'I've been to Cornwall.' Like it gives her inside knowledge.

I roll my eyes and tap my foot.

'Now, obviously this is quite a newsworthy story and I've already had some press phoning up about it. If there are journalists at the gates, or approaching you here, or in the Who'd've Thought It?, please, please, *please* just say, "No comment." Thank you.' She sweeps out, leaving us all reeling.

As we mill out, exchanging incredulous looks, I overhear some bright spark commenting, 'Thank God I never complained about her typing.'

FOUR

'Are you going to go to the funeral?' my best friend, Wendy, asks me that night as we share a bottle of wine in my lean-to.

'The woman Rochelle ran over? I didn't know her, and Cornwall's such a long way.'

'No, the boy in your class, his mum.'

'Oh. Well, I didn't really know her either. I mean, he only started last September and she's been ill since before then.'

'Right.'

'Why? D'you think I should?'

'I dunno. Do you want to?'

'Not really, no.'

To be honest with you, I've not given it much thought. I look at Wendy and know why she is here. She's come to check that I didn't freak out at school, that my first day was hitch-free and that going back today was the first step along the way to becoming my normal self again. My normal single self, that is.

Why do people think I can't cope? Am I that much of a wuss that I fall to pieces when left to live alone? Then I remember finding myself in the park last night, unable to remember getting there. I think back to forgetting that Mum is staying. Am I having some sort of breakdown? Am I in fact going mad and no one has told me? Everyone seems to be behaving as if this is the case.

Wendy is talking about something – I'm not sure what as I've zoned out – and I interrupt abruptly with, 'Wendy, do you think I am going mad?'

She looks surprised, stares at her wine, then shakes her head. She looks back suddenly, worried. 'Do you?'

I shake my head, then shrug. 'I don't know. It's just . . . well, you come round more than you did and . . . Mum seems to think I can't be left alone.'

Although she was quite happy to nip out to a Zumba class once she heard that Wendy was on her way over. I don't even know what Zumba is.

'I just came round 'cos it was your first day back at work and . . . well . . . usually you'd've had Michael here to chat to. About how it went. What happened. Just thought it might make you feel a bit less . . . alone.'

She's great, Wendy. We've been mates since our first day at uni together. Nearly eighteen years later she always manages to know me inside out, anticipate my needs and generally be an all-round good egg. Not sure what she gets out of our friendship, but she really has been like the proverbial rock to me. Particularly over the last few weeks.

OK, so maybe I am not going mad. That's good. And as my best mate she'd know. She'd be able to see the signs. Like, say I was standing in Tesco with a bowl of spaghetti on my head singing 'I (Who Have Nothing)' – that would not be good. And I know for certain I've not done that. Yet.

'Why do you think Michael left me?' I ask, sounding more like a petulant child than I mean to.

Wendy gives a sigh as if to say, 'It's the million-dollar question.'

'I don't know, darling. I certainly don't think it was your fault.'

I've heard her say all this before. It still helps, though. It's still a balm.

'I guess he had his own demons.'

'But not his own clothes!' I want to say, but it feels inappropriate. She's being nice and serious and everything a best friend should be when you ask them a proper, grown-up, serious question. Something I rarely do out of school.

Demons. Not sure I like the sound of those. I picture Michael driving underneath the ground, dissecting London in his toilet-roll-shaped train, garden-gnome-sized devils dancing about his shoulders. Some of them even have red forked fishing rods. No. Demons are bad for anyone, never mind someone who has public safety in his hands. I shudder.

'Babe,' Wendy is saying, fixing me with one of her encouraging looks. Wendy works in telly, so she knows a thing or two about communication. Well, I say she works in telly – she is a PA to a producer at the BBC in Shepherd's Bush. It's still telly, though. She's met Pam St Clement. 'Babe, the past's not that important. What's important . . . is the future.'

I nod. She's said this before too. I realize now she's a bit tipsy. Never mind – she's not driving. She's probably not eaten. Telly people probably don't. Too busy meeting Pam St Clement and the like to worry about grabbing the odd snack.

'I think,' she continues, 'and I know you don't agree, but I think they're going to be queuing round the block for you, Kagsy.'

This too she has said before, and I still don't agree with her. Just because Yusef at school thinks I'm the third fittest teacher doesn't mean I can now take my pick of men. I'm about to argue with Wendy when she butts in with a swift 'I mean, look at you. What man in his right mind wouldn't want a dollop of what you've got to offer? You're gorgeous, and funny, and clever, and witty, only you just don't know it.'

What man? What man wouldn't want any of this? Michael. That's who, Wendy. But I don't say it. I get the feeling with Wendy that she has consigned Michael to the history bin. She speaks of him only in the past tense. In her eyes there is no hope with Michael. Michael has literally been shredded.

Whereas I am not so sure. He left unexpectedly. Ergo (yes, I know what it means now, thank you) he might reappear unexpectedly. Why shouldn't he? If I'm as fabulous as Wendy says, why shouldn't he? In fact, if I'm as fabulous as Wendy says, he'll *definitely* be coming back. Quick, I better go and get changed!

'Mark my words,' she reiterates, 'they'll come crawling out of the woodwork for you.' But then Wendy giggles and says, 'God, I'm pissed. Sorry. I haven't had any tea.'

'Were you with Pam St Clement?'

She looks at me like I'm mad, and I am really, to blurt that out without censoring myself.

She shakes her head.

'I could order a pizza or something,' I suggest, although I know Mum will return soon with something frozen and something fresh.

Fortunately Wendy looks horrified. 'God, no. We're all doing the Dukan at work,' and she takes a large glug of her wine.

'Dukan not be serious!' I joke, and we both chuckle into our Pinot.

'Karen, you do know I'm not friends with Pam St Clement, don't you?'

I nod, but she has met her.

'I've said about two words to her, so you don't need to go round telling people we're best mates or anything.'

'I don't!' I gasp, affronted, even though I do.

'She came in to meet my boss and I fetched her a glass of water and that was the extent of our relationship. I have told you this.'

I nod. Can we change the subject? Jeez. Anyone else'd be thrilled that they'd met her, not insist on downplaying it in my lean-to every time she comes round.

I like my lean-to. Michael built it with his own bare hands. Well, his bare hands and his builder mate, Jay the Builder. It is one of the many nice things he did for me. He always said he wanted us to sit in it and listen to the rain fall on the roof while we had a takeaway and a can. It was built for romance.

It was a few years ago now, mind.

It's raining again. Only softly, but there's the unmistakable pit-a-pat thud of rain on corrugated plastic. Like cats scampering across. Or a load of impatient people drumming their fingers on it. This image unnerves me.

I turn back to Wendy, but the sofa beside me is empty. I look round and she is on her mobile, phoning a cab.

It's funny. I met Michael and Wendy around about the same time. I put all my energy into hoping and praying that my relationship with Michael would run and run and run and that we'd grow old together, and smell of wee together in an old folks' home (while still having loads of amazing sex, putting all youngsters to shame with our agility and zest for new positions in the shared TV lounge). I didn't really hope, however, that my relationship with Wendy would run and run and run and that we'd be bezzy mates for ever. You don't tend to do that with friends, and yet with lovers you're planning a life time.

The irony now, of course, is that things didn't run and run and run with Michael, but they did with Wendy. To name-check the pub the teachers go to after school, who'd have thought it?

I pack Wendy into her taxi when it arrives. People in telly take lots of taxis, I've noticed. It's only half ten, but she can't face the Tube. I think she thinks it's beneath her. Mum is long back from Zumba and watching *Borgen* on the iPlayer. She's got her big glasses on and is sitting really close to the computer screen so she can read the subtitles, and she is munching on a Danish pastry, possibly to help her get in the mood. (Well, I guess it's either that or some bacon.) I tell her I'm going for a bath and I head up, hoping the water's hot, and eventually luxuriate.

The grouting needs doing.

I remember saying it to Michael the day before he left.

'The grouting needs doing, in the bathroom. Have you seen the state of it?'

And he nodded and carried on eating his toast.

I now know what he was thinking. He was thinking, Your grouting is nothing to me. Your tiles are nothing to me. Your bathroom is nothing to me. Tomorrow I'm outa here. You want that dump regrouting? Do it your fucking self.

I'm making him sound surly and arrogant and twatty and a bit like Stanley in *A Streetcar Named Desire*. He isn't. He's more like Stanley Baxter. He certainly never swore at me.

Again, there it is: the past tense. It still feels odd that he's part of my past. I am thirty-six. I am thirty-six and newly single. I met Michael when I was sixteen. Childhood sweethearts. I can't really remember a time without him. I have certainly not lived any of my adult life without him. Thirty-six is a shit age. I hate thirty-six. Thirty-six, I spit on you. Why do I have to be newly single now? I'm too old to be young and not old enough to be really middle-aged. It's an in-between age, but in between what, I don't know. Fun and full-on senility possibly. No matter what Wendy says, I'll be on the shelf for the rest of my life, I just know it. I know my place, and I know my future. It'll be ready meals for one. I'll get a cat and talk to it, spend my evenings doing jigsaws of Westminster Abbey on the dining table. I can just see it all spreading depressingly in front of me. My future.

I met Michael at my local youth club. Our eyes met across a ping-pong table. Chesney Hawkes was belting out of a crackly sound system, and I had the taste of overly diluted orange squash on my lips. He asked if he could walk me home. We got chips en route. The next day we decided we were going steady. Life didn't come more simple than that.

It was almost my seventeenth birthday and Mum and Dad had gone away for the weekend to Blackpool. As I'd be going off to university before we knew it, I'd promised Michael we could finally have sex as long as he brought a condom and a bottle of Bulmer's cider. He brought Woodpecker and I giggled nervously when he said, 'I'll be pecking your wood tonight, girl.' I thought he was incredibly cool because he had this really unusual track-suit that (he claimed) no one else in Liverpool had and he tucked the bottoms of it into his socks, which he considered quite artful.

We started off in the lounge, on the couch, necking for England, then decided to move to my bedroom. Then, audaciously, Michael suggested we move to my mum and dad's bed, seeing as they were away and it was double the size. We lay on the bed and started downing the cider. Suddenly he shoved his hand under my T-shirt and started squeezing my left breast.

'Jeez, not much there, is there?' He winked and I didn't feel too embarrassed because he said it with such a twinkle.

'Two aspirin on an ironing board or what?' was my retort, and he pissed himself like it was the funniest thing he'd heard in ages, his life practically. He leaned in and started snogging the

face off me, which he was actually quite good at. He took my hand and put it over his crotch and I could feel he'd got a stiffy through the nylon of his trackie bottoms.

He whispered urgently in my ear, 'Look what you're doing to me, Karen,' and I went, 'Michael, what are you like?'

And he was laughing again and then he pulled me over so I was sitting on his lap, and he was still snogging me. Anyway, just then I had a little panic because I was suddenly thinking, I don't want to lose my virginity in my mum and dad's bed. It doesn't feel right.

So I said to him, 'Have you ever seen When Harry Met Sally?'

And he was like, 'Yeah, it's boss.'

And so I started writhing around on him, joking and making little orgasm noises, and he started joining in. And we were getting louder and louder till he was shouting, 'Jesus, you dirty bitch!'

And I was shouting, 'Shove it in me, Michael La'!'

And it was just the funniest thing imaginable and we were being very *loud. Like* really *loud. So loud in fact that I didn't hear footsteps on the landing and then a voice saying, 'Karen?'*

I swivelled round. It was my mum.

Shit.

It was my mum, stood in her own bedroom doorway, gobsmacked because she had discovered what looked like her daughter losing her virginity in her own bed, and because I was wearing this massive *gypsy skirt, she couldn't see what was really going on, which was nothing.*

'I thought you were in Blackpool,' I said, hoping to God that under the gypsy skirt she couldn't see that my legs were either side of Michael.

'Your father couldn't find anywhere to park, so he turned round and came home. You know what he's like.'

I nodded. Like it was perfectly normal to be straddling my boyfriend on her bed.

'Who's this?' She was nodding her head in Michael's direction.

'Michael.'

'Michael?'

'Michael Fletcher,' Michael piped up. 'I go to St Margaret's.'

Mum held out her hand and Michael shook it.

'We were just re-enacting a scene from When Harry Met Sally. *You know when they're in that restaurant . . . ?'*

But Mum was giving Michael a funny look. As well she might. And he was staring at her, mortified. But Mum then chuckled, gave a flirty shake of the head and went, 'Yes. It is me.'

Michael's eyes narrowed, unsure what she was on about.

'Val Carpenter.'

Again more narrowing.

'Of Val Carpenter and Cheeky the Liverpool Bear fame.'

Michael smiled blankly, clearly having no idea what on earth she was going on about.

'Anyway . . . nice meeting you, Michael.' She shook his hand again.

'You too, Mrs . . . Thingy.' How mortifying. Michael had forgotten my surname.

Mum turned out of her own bedroom and I heard her rushing down the stairs, calling my dad with a chuckle in her voice.

Why didn't I just stand up? If I'd stood up, she'd have seen that Michael still had his trackie bottoms on. I was my own worst enemy sometimes. Michael was now pissing himself with laughter, so I got off his lap and slapped his face. He looked surprised.

'What was that for?'

I shrugged. 'Go home.'

'*Karen, you fridge!*'

Charming.

Mum said nothing when Michael had gone. I thought I'd got away with it, but then a few days later I overheard her on the phone to one of her friends saying, 'Yes, and he was quite clearly penetrating her, Sheila, on my best Marks's king-size duvet. The one with the poppies? I mean, it's not an ideal situation, is it? Meeting a prospective son-in-law when he's got his doodah inside your daughter. How's your arthritis?'

Even now I am embarrassed when I think of that. More so when I remember trying to convince Mum that nothing had happened. Even more so again when she was having none of it and started to get all inappropriately pally about it and asking if he'd brought me to orgasm. I had to draw a line somewhere, and that was it.

I have not discussed sex with my mother from that day to this.

Well, not sex involving me anyway. She occasionally divulges secrets from her and my dad's bedroom, which no offspring wants to know.

'I'm a woman with needs, Karen. I have a high drive. Sometimes your father can't keep up, bless him. He tries – God knows he tries – but I'm a twenty-first-century gal. I've seen *Sex and the City* and I am entitled to my orgasm, Karen, entitled to it. Or them. Why speak in the singular?'

'Because it's Dad you're talking about?'

'It. You're absolutely right.'

I lie on my bed, unable to sleep.

Careful what you wish for, I think – you used to moan the bed wasn't big enough for you and Michael. Well, it's too big just for you now. I stretch out my arms and legs so I am making a starfish and wonder if I'd get cramp if I fell asleep like this. I then wonder if Rochelle has as much room to spread out, wherever she is. Would she be in a police cell or a prison cell? I have never known anyone arrested for murder before, so have no idea. I have only procedural crime dramas in my head, the sort that Wendy's boss is involved in making. I can only picture someone affecting a cockney accent and telling her, 'You'll go down for this. You will. You'll do bird.'

I fear Rochelle will go mad. Not because of what she has or hasn't done, but because her manic fingers no longer have an outlet for their kinetic energy. If only they could give her a dummy keyboard, I think she would sail through the experience unscathed. Instead her digits will be twitching, no idea what to do with themselves. Desperate to spell out words, sentences, but without any to make.

I contemplate what she has done.

Word on the street/in the classroom/according to Custard Claire is she did it and she'll go down for it. She may not even contest it.

I wonder if I am the mad one, not her, for not wanting to know what has become of Michael. If he is living over the brush with some slut in Cornwall, I do not want to know, but maybe I don't want to know because I can't quite believe it of him. I try not to think about it because when I do, a name pops into my head.

Asmaa.

I don't know anyone called Asmaa. He does. It's a name he mentioned often a while back. It is someone to do with his work. I remember her name because I thought he was talking about having asthma and he corrected me.

Part of me knows. This has got something to do with her.

Whether he is with Asmaa now or not with Asmaa, I just know – and I'm not stupid – his departure has something to do with her.

I realize now that I am not like Rochelle, and do not want to be. Whatever Asmaa has or has not done, I do not have any desire to get into my non-existent car and run her over. I wouldn't even hire a car to do it, or borrow someone else's. Not for fear of damaging the car, but because no matter how much someone has hurt me . . . Well, I'm not saying I don't want to hurt them back, but killing them is a step too far.

Anyway, my gripe should not be with Asmaa. It should be with Michael.

I realize I am laying a lot at this Asmaa's feet, and she is really just someone he mentioned a few times a while back. Still, it was someone he mentioned enough to make me wonder what was going on.

I know deep down that if I really want to know what is going on with Michael, I can find out easily enough. All I have to do is go to his depot and wait for him. All I have to do is ask some of his friends from work. I realize now that I probably need to find out. Or else how many more nights will there be when I can't sleep? How many more nights, days, months of not understanding why he went? How many more times must I lie on this bed and try to picture what this Asmaa looks like?

And so I decide that by the end of this week I will find out. I will go to his depot and ask him. It is Monday now. I will find out by Friday.

FIVE

The atmosphere in my local supermarket is one of seething menace. I would love, for once, to do my weekly shop in calm serenity, at one with my trolley and fellow shoppers, but that's impossible here. I have never witnessed a knifing or particularly violent crime, but I always feel I'm about to in these aisles. Everyone looks thoroughly pissed off, staff and customers, possibly because they pipe in muzak versions of things like 'The Birdie Song'. I often find myself apologizing to anyone and everyone if I perform the slightest misdemeanour: lingering too long deciding whether to plump for skimmed or semi, blocking the end of an aisle with my poorly angled trolley, asking a member of staff if they know where they keep their water chestnuts. (That was a night I was making a Chinese meal at home.)

The women who shop here look like they're about to venture forth to face the weekly beating from Him Indoors, and the men look as if they're just stopping off for provisions before heading off to rob a building society at gunpoint. The staff just look bored and hacked off that I have dared interrupt the enjoyment they were having shouting out to each other what they plan to do after they get off. With the advent of chip and PIN, they appear to have lost the ability to tell you how much money you have to part with for the privilege of standing at one of their tills. They wait glumly while you enter your PIN, then don't even bother to say, 'Thank you,' when ripping off your receipt and shoving it at you. Every time I come, I have to bite my tongue, for fear of saying, 'Hello. I am here. I am a human being. A human being who helps to pay your wages. Be nice to me or I won't come here again.'

I will come here again, though. I will always come here again. I have no choice – it's the easiest shop to get to, and after a hard day at the coalface/interactive whiteboard I can't be bothered to get two buses to the other one.

Basically I'm screwed.

As is this trolley. There must be hundreds of trollies in this store, so why do I always manage to choose the one that has an automatic tilt to the left? Pushing it is like taking part in one of those 'Strongest Men in Britain' things you see on TV on a bank holiday, in which burly blokes push trucks laden with really heavy things made of iron. I nearly put my back out attempting to steer to the right to keep it in a straight line. Navigating this store is like sailing single-handed across the Atlantic. With a 'Birdie Song' soundtrack.

I am not having a good time. And everyone, *everyone* appears to be giving me daggers.

So imagine my surprise when I accidentally crash my left-lurching trolley into someone else's as I roll awkwardly into one of the frozen-food aisles and gasp a quick 'Sorry!' only to have one gasped back at me with less than a millisecond's delay.

'Sorry!'

It's a man's voice and I turn to smile, relieved to find someone else with manners here. Possibly the one person in the whole store who doesn't want to knife me. He has a kindly face, I see. Rugged but gentle, and he looks harassed. He is leaning over one of the freezers, weighing up the choice between two packets of something.

Imagine my surprise when he frowns, then emits a wry smile and says, 'Miss Carpenter?'

He knows me!

'Yes?'

Oh God, he recognizes me and I don't recognize him. He must be a parent from school – who else would call me 'Miss'? Unless he's a throwback from a costume drama and has arrived on a white charger, sodden with rain. A quick check of his work overalls tells me no, I was right first time.

'I'm Kevin. O'Keefe? Connor's dad.'

He smiles again, and God forgive me if I don't find myself thinking, You're awful jolly for someone who's just lost his wife.

I know. It's shocking, isn't it? I'm being terribly judgemental about someone who is just trying, let's face it, to be nice.

'Mr O'Keefe! Kevin! How's it going?' I immediately regret it.

I know how it's going for him. It's going badly. He's probably going through the worst week of his life and here I am chirruping away like a roving reporter for a local news station, jumping in on someone's grief with a big smile and asking for a comment.

Mr O'Keefe! Karen Carpenter, East London News! I know your wife's just died a long, painful, drawn-out death, but any comment for the viewers? No?

I see Kevin grimace, which makes me feel even worse.

'Crap question – sorry,' I splutter, and he is laughing.

'No, no, it's just . . . Oh, I don't know. I'm running around like a headless chicken trying to get everything sorted for the funeral and I literally don't know which way up I am.'

He has an Irish accent. Why did I think he was a cockney?

'Well, if there's anything I can do to help!' I say, once more sounding like the crap reporter. There is nothing I can do to help. This is not my drama. Him losing his wife has nothing to do with me. I am just his kid's teacher.

I expect him to pull a face and comment on the weirdness of my statement, but instead he nods and says, 'There is, actually,' and he thrusts his packets in front of me, fresh from the deep freeze. I look. They're both party platters.

'Which one of these d'you think I should get for the buffet? I've no idea. Buffets and spreads were Tony's domain.'

I have no idea who he's talking about. Who's Tony?

I say it. 'Who's Tony?'

'Oh, my wife. With an "i" on the end.'

Ah, that explains it. Toni.

'Oh, I see. I'm sorry. Erm . . .'

I look at both platters. Round plastic trays with various canapés. Both trays are much of a muchness. I am about to tell him that but realize he'll probably appreciate some directness now.

Confidently I point to the tray in his right hand. 'I think this selection's nicer than that one.'

He looks, nods. He is in agreement. 'Good call.'

I like the way he says it and find myself flicking my hair back like I'm at a bar and we're chatting over a few drinks.

Which we are not.

This is a man in mourning.

This is the parent of one of my pupils.

Stop this now, Karen.

I clear my throat as he plops the chosen platter in his trolley and switch my tone to authoritarian, professional, slightly lezzy. 'This must be a really tough time for you all.'

He nods again, leans on the trolley, seems to suck in a load of air – his cheeks balloon – then sighs it all out of the side of his mouth. 'It's Connor I'm most worried about.'

I cock my head to the side as I have seen many do to me over the last few weeks. 'For sure,' I say. I never say, 'For sure.' It doesn't sound like me. It sounds like someone in an Irish film pretending to be Oirish, and failing.

'I was . . . Oh, this is going to sound daft,' he says.

'No, go on – it's fine.'

'I was going to invite you to the funeral.'

I find myself blushing, like he had been contemplating asking me out on a date.

Karen, stop this.

'You know, 'cos you've been such an important figure in Connor's life . . . *are* such an important . . . but then I figured it was probably not the done thing and . . . well, you'll be teaching anyway, right?'

'When is it again? Friday?'

He nods. 'Three o'clock. Fountain Lakes Crem.'

'Yes,' I say, 'I'm teaching till half past. Shame. I would have come, actually. I think it's really important the kids see that we care.'

He nods again.

'When I say "we", I mean teachers.'

His eyes widen. He looks really impressed. 'Well, you can always come to the do afterwards, but you're probably busy.'

I shake my head quickly. 'What sort of time?'

'Erm. Well, I imagine we'll be kicking off at four-ish. Why don't you come straight after school?'

'OK,' I say brightly, then remind myself it's not a date.

Stop this, Karen!

'I think that'll be really good for my working relationship with Connor.'

He nods. 'Me too. God, I can't tell you how much I appreciate that.'

'Oh, don't be daft – it's the least I can do.'

'It's brilliant, really brilliant. Anyway, don't let me stop you. You must get on with your shop.'

'Yes, I must.'

Must I? Damn!

I look down at my trolley and see that I have four bottles of wine and a copy of *Heat*. He looks too and giggles.

'That's my kind of diet,' he says with a dirty chuckle. A very nice dirty chuckle.

'Oh, I'm just off to get loads of fresh veg and salady bits. I'm really healthy. My body's a temple.'

Move away from him now, Karen. You are talking complete and utter gibberish.

'Toodle-oo, anyway!' I chirrup, and push away my trolley.

The swerve to the left makes me crash into the opposite row of freezers. I yank it with all the strength I can muster and try my best to move away from Kevin O'Keefe in a ladylike fashion.

Toodle-oo. I said, 'Toodle-oo.' I never say, 'Toodle-oo.'

On the bus home I hate myself. My boyfriend only left me a matter of weeks ago and the first man who speaks to me I have flirted with like some sad slapper.

Then I remind myself that he wasn't flirting with me; he was talking to me as some sort of spiritual guide for his son. He probably views me a bit like a nun. And that makes me feel better.

I tell myself that as long as I don't carry on flirting with him, I'll be fine.

I find that I am smiling and I realize that, for the first time in ages, I have returned from the supermarket with a smile on my face.

I phone Wendy when I get in and gabble the occurrences of the past half-hour to her.

'You did what? You flirted with the grieving father of one of your pupils?'

'Yes. I should be struck off. From the feminist sisterhood and from teaching. In that order.'

'Is he hot?'

'Yes. In a grieving-widower type way.'

'Grieving widower with pre-teen child unsure how to see a way forward. My God, if this was a movie, he'd be played by Huge Grant.'

'No fucking way!' I snap, showing I mean business. I, Karen Carpenter, rarely swear. Much.

'Aha?'

'It would have to be someone much more macho and swarthy than Huge Grant.'

'Firth?'

'Tch!'

'We're running out of bankable British heart-throbs.'

'He's Irish.'

'The other one. What's his name? Looks like Kevin out of *Coronation Street* . . .'

'Colin Farrell? No. He pisses on the Farrell. Wendy, he's un-castable. He's a one-off. He just is.'

She sighs, sounding disappointed, then says, 'I hope you're not giving yourself a hard time over this. It was one conversation.'

'I know, but I'm treating his wife's wake like a first date. I might even wear my wedding dress.'

'You're joking, right?'

'Right. But only about the dress. I am excited about going, and not for the moral welfare of Connor.'

'Then put a stop to that and start again. This is fine. He's just the dad of one of your kids and he needs your help with his son.'

'I flirted,' I insist. 'I did a flicky hair thing. I giggled. I was coquettish. If I'd had one, I would have fanned myself like something out of *Dangerous Liaisons*.'

She chuckles warmly, then says, 'Stop giving yourself a hard time. It's fine. It's cool. It sounds like he didn't notice anyway.'

She's got a point actually: I don't think he did, which in itself is a blessing and a curse.

'Kags, the thing you've got to remember is . . . you've not chatted to a guy for twenty years.'

Well, that's wrong – I speak to men every day. I'm not some kind of radical separatist hairy-lady person.

'I mean, flirted. One on one.'

Oh, what, so I've flirted in a group? I may not be a radical separatist hairy-lady person, but that doesn't make me a swinger!

'And, OK, so it's a non-starter with this Kelvin guy.'

'Kevin!' I correct her sharply. 'His name's Kevin.'

Oh God, I'm protecting his image already.

'But, you know, sooner or later you will get chatted up. And it's OK. You're single now.'

She's right. I am. And I find it utterly depressing.

As an image of a cat walking across a Westminster Abbey jigsaw looms into view, she continues, 'And let's be honest. You've felt pretty much single for the last few years.'

I wasn't expecting that: brutal honesty. Oh well, I guess that's what best friends are for.

'What do you mean?'

'Well, you know, Michael did you a favour in a way. You'd been looking for a way out for a while.'

I let the words hang in the air.

I don't like these words.

I have been hanging on to the idea that Michael was lovely and everything was hunky-dory. The concept kept me warm at night. The concept helped me grieve the relationship. I had a good thing, and now that good thing has gone. Therefore it's OK to feel sad.

'Sorry,' she adds softly.

I say nothing, taking in the enormity of what she has just said. She interprets it as offence and apologizes again and tries to explain what she meant, but I'm not offended. I am chastened. Chastened because it's the truth. And sometimes, oh yes, the truth hurts. And for some stupid reason, it's hurting now.

When I eventually hang up, I reflect on the bizarreness of the human spirit. How we can squirrel away information and not bring it out to cause us pain, and how we can feel a hundred kinds of vulnerable just by remembering, with sudden clarity, how we once felt. I attempt to bury the information again, for then it won't hurt me. Denial is a comfortably numb place to be. I see now why Rochelle coped so well.

Well, before she murdered her husband's lover. In Cornwall.

I find it hard to put the notion back in its box now, though. I see my heart as a big chest with lots of boxes, drawers and flaps, but it's hard to get the flap to open for this one. It seems to have wedged shut.

I tell Mum over dinner. We're having Arctic roll with fresh strawberries.

'Wendy says Michael going's a good thing,' I say provocatively, daring her to agree, but she is my mother – she won't. She will offer unto me succour. Or something.

'Can I be honest, kid?' Mum says, checking her teeth in the back of her spoon. She spots a lipstick stain and rubs it with her finger.

I nod.

She takes a deep breath. 'I didn't really like Michael.'

Oh God, they're all at it. I feel the axis of the earth shift. A seismic force has grabbed the house and swivelled it round twenty degrees. I'm surprised the furniture doesn't slide across the lino.

'Don't get me wrong, kid. He was a nice lad, and he was from a good home, but I thought he treated you something rotten towards the end. The last few years, I know he had his demons, but he wasn't exactly nice to you, was he?'

It's those demons. Someone else mentioned those recently, but for now I can't think who.

'He wasn't himself, Mum.'

'I know, love, I know. All I'm saying is . . . maybe Wendy's got a point.'

I sit stewing. Like an apple in a pot.

'I still think you've got rats, you know. Or maybe it's a trapped bird,' she sighs, thinks, then changes her mind. 'No. I reckon it's rats. This is London, after all.'

I roll my eyes and she looks hurt.

'Rita phoned me today.'

I bristle.

'She says she's left umpteen messages for you, but you never call her back.'

'I don't want to speak to her.'

Rita is Michael's mum. I don't want to rake over the coals

of the end of my relationship with her. I'm not ready for her sympathy.

'Anyway, I've phoned her back a few times, but she's never in,' I fib.

Mum nods.

I go and lie on my bed after dinner while Mum watches something else in Danish on BBC iPlayer. Surprisingly I don't mull over what Wendy has said, or Mum. At the moment I don't care. The only thing I care about is that . . . if things were as bad as they say, maybe Michael has gone for good. Maybe he won't just walk in one day, apologize and ask if we can start again. I realize now that I have, to some extent, been banking on that. That made it all just about bearable. Now, though, that possibility is vanishing into a fog of uncertainty. I close my eyes, wanting to see him. If I can just remember another nice thing about him, maybe he will return.

After a while I see him. He's there. Clear as crystal.

'See this green line here?'

'Aha?'

'Well, that's the District line, and you need to take that from here, Earls Court, all the way to here, Embankment. OK?'

'Yeah. Ish.'

I looked at Michael, huddled over the Tube map on the back of the A to Z that he'd laid out on the coffee table. We'd not yet bought a couch, so we knelt on the floor peering at the multicoloured lines that represented the transport system of our new city.

'Or . . .' he continued dramatically '. . . you can take the Circle line. That's the yellow one here.'

I nodded.

'Clear?' he checked.

'*As mud.*'

He sighed, trying not to get exasperated. '*And then when you get to Embankment, you have to walk up the street to Charing Cross – the big station – and get your next train from there.*'

My eyes were glazing over now.

'*Karen! Concentrate!*'

'*I am concentrating. It's just really hard. How come you understand how it all works and I don't?*'

'*'Cos I've been sitting here working it all out. Look –*' and his voice softened '*– why don't I come with you? Save you getting lost. How are you gonna educate a bunch of arl cockneys if you can't even get yourself to the school?*'

I smiled. My boyfriend was ace.

Everyone had said this relationship wouldn't work, but here we were living in London and – da nah! – still together. I was the only person on my course at uni who had the same boyfriend when she started the four-year course as when she finished. Detractors doubted our longevity for two reasons. One, he was living in Liverpool and I was in Hull. Two, I was doing a degree and he was working in an Italian restaurant. Apparently that made me his intellectual superior, which was just rubbish – anyone who met Michael knew that he was one of the brainiest people around. He certainly got a handle on the transport system quicker than me, with my BSc joint honours (2:2).

He loved me. He must have done: everyone said so. He'd even moved to London to be with me because I'd got a teaching job here. And listen to this – he got the train in with me every morning for the first few weeks to keep me company till I found my feet, and my way around the London transport network. You see, our first flat was in Earls Court and yet I was teaching in south-east London in a place called Thamesmead. Before we moved down, judging from the map, the commute looked OK –

long but OK – but in reality it was quite draining. I had to go on the Tube from Earls Court to Embankment, walk up to Charing Cross and take an overground train to Abbey Wood. I then had to take a bus from Abbey Wood to the school. This journey took an hour and a half on a good day.

So my days were long and tiring, but one thing that was sweet was that Michael got up every morning without fail with me at six thirty, made tea and toast, and accompanied me on my journey. Other commuters read books, papers; we chatted and ate toast and drank tea, making each other laugh.

A few times a week he even met me after school, to accompany me home, and sometimes we'd be really adventurous and get off the train at Greenwich to take a boat back to Charing Cross. I'd never really wanted to live in London – truth be told, it was the only place that had plenty of special needs jobs going – but now that we were here, it was our playground, our film set. Everywhere felt so familiar from the telly, and we had a ball as each weekend we explored a new part of the city we didn't know: Camden Market one week, Hampstead Heath the next; Columbia Road Flower Market one Sunday, a ride on the Docklands Light Railway the next. Cor blimey, strike a light, guv'nor! The world was our oyster.

He spent his days going to job interviews. Eventually he landed a job as a waiter in an Indian restaurant in Soho called Namaste Bombay. It meant we saw a lot less of each other. He'd roll in at one or two in the morning, smelling of korma and spilt beer, and we'd spoon for a few hours before I had to get up for my early start.

Sometimes, if he had a day off, he'd still come and surprise me at the school gates, waiting for me with a bunch of flowers, and we'd cross London together, but then, after a few months at Namaste Bombay, he announced that he wanted a change of *scene. At first I thought he meant he wanted to leave London. I argued we couldn't. We needed my job to pay the rent. He laughed, though, and explained he'd had enough of waiting tables. He said he wanted to be a Tube driver.*

A Tube driver. I couldn't believe it!

'D'you think I can do it, Karen?'

Did I?

'Definitely. You can do anything if you put your mind to it.'

And of course I was right.

I snap out of my reverie with a crashing realization. It was one of the first thoughts I had after Michael left: how on earth am I going to afford to stay in this house without Michael? How on earth will I be able to afford to pay the mortgage without his monthly wage coming in? I am a sensible person and so have some money put by to pay about three months' on my own, but after that I am royally screwed. How did I forget this? Did I *choose* to forget this? This is one conundrum I cannot put back in its box. This is one I will have to face head on. I am going to have to put the house on the market, sell up and move on.

What if no one wants to buy it, though? There is a recession on. Everyone is being cautious. Who will want to live in this tiny two-up, two-down terraced house in the wrong part of East Ham? Actually, come to think of it, is there a right part of East Ham? Panic rises in my chest as I fear I will become another statistic. Repossession is nine-tenths of the law or something. I will have to act, and soon. I must be strong, pro-active, forthright. I cannot afford to go under. I cannot let this happen.

Oh God.

SIX

'It's simple,' says Wendy the next day as I chat to her on the phone during my break duty outside the girls' loos. 'Take in a lodger.'

A lodger. Why didn't I think of that?

'Oh, Wendy, that's a brilliant idea.'

The relief. The relief is fantastic. After a sleepless night I now feel some energy seeping into me for the first time today. A weight is being lifted from my shoulders and I could float away on this icy breeze that's spinning round the playground.

'Or . . . move out for a few months and rent the whole house out. You're in a prime spot for the Olympics. You'll be able to rent it out for a fortune.'

She has a point. Thus far I have been dreading the Olympics happening, as everyone reckons it's going to clog up the local transport system. Everyone round here has a good old moan about it at the drop of a hat.

'To who?'

'I dunno. The Croatian curling team, or some Yanks who are really into sport or something.'

I have images of six butch women with curling sticks hanging out in my kitchen. It doesn't look right. (The image, not the kitchen. My kitchen's quite nice.)

'But the Olympics isn't for ages.'

'July. June. One of those "J" months.'

'And I need a solution quicker than that.'

'Do you want to move?'

'I dunno. Not really, but maybe it'd be good to get away from all my memories of Michael.'

I don't want to move at all. I am just trying to sound grown-up.

'Hmm, but some might say don't act rashly. You've had a big shock. Don't do anything as a knee-jerk reaction.'

'The only thing it's a knee-jerk reaction to is the fear of being repossessed.'

Just then I see Ethleen on the other side of the playground. I shouldn't be on the phone when I'm on break duty, so I quickly make my apologies and hang up, adopting a stern 'don't mess with me – I am Toilet Tzar' face. I even cross my arms and shoot daggers at all the girls heading in for a wee. My look is steely and says, 'Don't even think about having a fag in there. And if I catch you so much as attempting to shoot up heroin, you'll be for the high jump. *Mark my words, missy!*'

They can see I mean business. Although I have to say, in all my years of standing outside these toilets, I am yet to catch a recreational drug user or nicotine addict. I get the odd fight, a bit of name-calling – mostly aimed at me – but that's it.

Ethleen is heading over, smiling. She is head to toe in powder green. Short skirt and boxy jacket. A string of pearls hangs round her neck. She looks like she's off to Ladies' Day at Ascot, not running a comprehensive school. All she needs is a fascinator and she'd be hot to trot. I would tell her this, but it would appear frivolous, and frivolity has no place when you're on break duty.

'Miss Carpenter,' she says, professional in front of the kids swarming round us.

'Miss Butterly,' I reply, stopping myself from adding an 'Utterly' in front of her surname like the kids do. I try to sound approachable but stoic. I want her to see I take the duty she has entrusted to me seriously. My tone says, 'I cannot talk for too long, as I must at a second's notice jump inside the toilets and swoop on someone jacking up.'

I know. Ridiculous. Still.

'How are you?' she asks, and then looks round the play-ground. Hundreds of teenagers are running wild. The noise is deafening. It grants us some privacy at least.

'Good, thanks.'

'Oh good. Good. Work's a tonic sometimes, isn't it?'

'Indeed,' I say. My tone continues to be in the 'look, do we really need to do this? Toilet duty's reeeeeally important, you know' vein.

'Whenever things are going a bit tits up for me, I'm always grateful to get into the office and have my attention diverted.'

'Of course.'

'There's no greater distraction than working in a school.'

'Indeed.'

I am giving one-word answers. Surely she will go soon.

'Not that it's particularly healthy to run away from our problems.'

'Of course not, Miss Utterly. *Butterly!* Sorry. I don't know why I said that.'

I expect her to be crabby, but she has her head cocked on one side. I know what this means: sympathy, empathy, any '-athy' you want, really. She rubs my arm as she speaks. Jeez, she's going for the full whammy.

'How are you financially? Are you OK or in a bit of a mess?'

I freeze. How? How does she know? Am I walking around with 'Bollocks. Up shit creek without a paddle, mortgage-wise' tattooed on my forehead?

Hmm?

No. My forehead isn't that wide.

'Everything's fine, thanks, Miss Butterly.'

She nods, as if she didn't expect anything less. And much as I'm grateful to her for taking an interest, and much as it makes me like her even more that she bothered to ask, and that it entered her head, I still don't want to go there with her. She's my boss, after all. Unless she's about to offer me a promotion?

'Only I was thinking . . .'

She is! She's going to ask me to be head of year or something! OK, so it's not exactly winning the pools financially, but it'd be a help. And I'm good with pastoral care. I'd make a brilliant head of year!

'There's quite a lucrative market out there for private tuition.'

I look at her. Private tuition?

'A lot of rich people want their kids to do better, and sometimes it just takes someone like you a few hours a week to get them on the right track.'

Blimey. She wants me to moonlight. It's like an NHS doctor advising a colleague to go and do evenings at a private hospital.

'It's worth bearing in mind,' she says, now sounding embarrassed to have brought it up, interpreting my silence as offence. I must learn to speak more.

'I will. Yes, it's a good idea.'

Ethleen smiles. It's a strained smile. She's weighing me up, my mood. She prides herself on being able to read people, and I know today I am unreadable.

'If you're interested, I'm sure I can point you in the right direction.'

We all know that Ethleen's husband is Very Rich. He is a surveyor for an international building company and they live in Knightsbridge, or near Sloane Square or something. She drives a Porsche Boxster. She never dines out on this fact. She probably doesn't need to work as her fella earns so much, but for some reason it makes me respect her commitment to Fountain Woods even more. And of course she must have contacts. She must know loads of rich people with thick kids who need a helping hand.

I would never describe our kids here as thick, but rich kids? That feels OK. Is that bad? Yes, it is.

'Thanks, Ethleen.'

She takes my use of her first name as a cue to leave.

As she heads off, I picture myself in a Knightsbridge drawing room with a fourteen-year-old called Rufus. He's been kicked out of the school that Lily Allen went to for dealing marijuana. (Or maybe they encourage that there, I don't know.) He is sullen and spaced out, but over a matter of weeks I have him wanting to learn, and within a year he has got eighty-three GSCEs and they're all A triple stars.

God, I'm good. It's a nice image. I like their house, and Rufus is a treasure. He goes on to be an international rock star and takes me round the world as part of his entourage, claiming he never wants to stop learning.

'Terrible about Rochelle, isn't it?'

Someone is talking to me. I abandon all thoughts of Rufus and the gorgeous house in Knightsbridge, our trips to Mauritius, Mustique, Miami, and turn to see a stranger standing next to me.

Oh God, another new member of staff whom I don't

recognize. I really should pay more attention in Monday-morning briefings!

She is in her mid-twenties; maybe she's a student. I wouldn't necessarily know all the student teachers. Maybe she started before Christmas when I was off.

I nod. 'Yeah, shocking, I know.'

The other woman – she has the most amazing curly red hair cascading down her back, though I find it a bit Seventies and retro – has crease lines round her heavily lipsticked mouth that make me assume she's a smoker.

'Are you a student teacher? Sorry, I've been off for a while.'

'Yes.' She holds out her hand. Golly, official. 'Kate. Kate Tobin.'

I shake it. 'Karen Carpenter.'

Her eyebrows arch and I expect her to burst out laughing, but she doesn't. She shakes my hand firmly.

'Karen, I've heard a lot about you, yes. Lot of respect for you at this school.'

Which suits me just fine. Actually, I really like her hair. She's very pretty in fact, and those lines round her lips add character to her – stunning – face.

'What department are you again?'

'Special needs.'

She nods earnestly, like she's *completely* impressed. 'Such an important job. I really take my hat off to you. Sorry, are you on a duty? Do you need to . . . ?'

'No, I'm fine. I can talk.'

I wouldn't care if eighteen girls ram-raided the toilets now and set fire to it and themselves. Missy Red Hair is flattering me.

'So d'you think she did it?'

'Who?'

'Rochelle. What's the word on the street?'

'God, I don't know. I mean, Custard Claire reckons something fishy's gone on there, and Custard Claire knows everything.'

'Custard Claire?'

'Yeah, Claire. Dinner lady. Does the custard.'

'Oh. Of course. She's great, Custard Claire, isn't she?'

'Oh, I love her.'

'Was Rochelle ever . . . violent towards you?'

'Violent?'

Kate nods. 'Did she ever make you feel scared?'

I shake my head. 'I mean, she once dropped a hole punch on my foot, but that was a mistake. I really like her. She's very good at her job.'

Kate looks disappointed. I like her too, so feel a sudden urge to entertain and please her.

'Though she would give everyone daggers, and was always creeping up on you without you knowing it.'

'What, to freak people out?'

I shrug mysteriously. 'Will we ever know, Kate?'

Just then I see Ethleen coming out of the main teaching block. She is on the warpath. And heading our way.

'Here comes Utterly Butterly.'

Kate suddenly turns and runs. Her Titian locks flash round like an energetic maypole and lash me across the face. She is gone, off across the playground, heading for the car park. Ethleen gives chase.

What on earth is going on?

'Stop her!' Ethleen shouts to the children Kate is passing. 'She's an intruder!'

Some kids pounce on Kate.

I shout out, 'She's not – she's a student teacher!'

Just then Kate kicks the kids away and batters them with an umbrella. God, that's a bit severe, isn't it? She'll never get her teaching qualification doing stuff like that.

'Kate!' I cry out.

'Stop her – she's a journalist!' Ethleen screams as Kate turns a corner.

From nowhere Meredith appears in one of her tracksuits and runs like a thunderbolt across the playground, following Kate round the corner, but the squeal of rubber on concrete tells me her getaway car is whisking her far, far away. Not even mercurial Meredith can catch her.

Ethleen is looking at me. 'What did you say? What did you tell her?'

'Oh . . .' I fumble '. . . erm . . . n-not much.'

I don't sound convincing.

The pips go for the next lesson.

The next day I buy a tabloid I very rarely buy. On page eight I am mortified by the headline '**She Tried to Kill Me Too.**'

Oh God. I can't bring myself to read the whole article, so I skim-read it, my eyes jumping about the page.

The pretty young teacher, who wanted to remain anonymous for fear of reprisals by Ludlow's family, claimed she was attacked . . .

Wow. Kate thought I was pretty. And young. Oh my God, attacked?

. . . in an unprovoked assault in the school's offices six months ago.

Where did this come from?

'Rochelle looked at me with death in her eyes and asked me why I was giving her so much typing to do.'

Kate must have talked to someone else. I never said this.

'Then she took a hole punch from her desk and hurled it at me. I'm lucky to be alive.'

Who writes this crap? Oh, of course, Kate does.

'Rochelle is well known for creeping up on people and then screaming at them, causing them to jump, and I believe she confessed all to Custard Claire.'
    Custard Claire is the nickname of Fountain Woods dinner lady Claire Greengrass (pictured).

They have taken a picture of Claire parking her moped in the car park. Bizarre.

'Basically, if you want to know anything in East London, ask Custard Claire. She runs this manor with a rod of iron. She knows the truth.'
    As of yesterday Custard was unavailable for comment. A neighbour of hers commented, 'She seems such a lovely woman. She did a sponsored run last year for breast cancer. Just goes to show – never judge a book by its cover.'

I see the paper is shaking in my hand. I put it in the bin.

Custard Claire isn't speaking to me. She is the only member of staff who saw through my 'Journalists! Why do they make up this kind of crap?'
    I carefully chose the word 'crap' as so few of them have heard me use anything other than the Queen's English, but Claire wasn't sucked in by it.

'She can't have made that up,' she insisted as we sat together in the salad room earlier.

'She did.'

'Bollocks. You must've told her I said she done it. I never said she done it. I said there was something fishy going on.'

'I said she should ask you. I said you knew everything.'

'Are you calling me a gossip?'

'No! God, as if I would! It's just . . . Well, round here the only person who seems to have a clue about anything is you. You're so wise, Claire, that's all. I'm really sorry. I genuinely thought she was a student teacher.'

Claire didn't look impressed. 'All that stuff about me running this manor.'

'Well, I certainly never said that. You must believe *that* at least.'

She didn't look so sure.

'Look – my head's all over the place, what with Michael leaving me, but I know what I said to her, and I didn't say anything that she said I did in the article.'

'I liked you, Karen. I felt sorry for you.'

'I don't need your pity, Claire.'

'Do you not, darlin'?' she said in quite an arch way. She pushed back her chair, stood, looked down at me. 'Well, that's a matter of opinion, innit?' and she walked away. She's not spoken to me since.

What did she mean? *That's a matter of opinion.* Why do people have to feel sorry for me? Relationships break down all the time – what's so special about me? What do I have to do to get people to stop feeling sorry for me? Go out and murder someone? This is karma. This is payback for me being such a horrible cow when I was a kid that I pretended my mum had died. It's unforgivable and now my karmic chickens are coming home to roost. I should have been proud of my mum's achievements as a ventriloquist. I should have celebrated the showbiz arrival of Cheeky the Liverpool Bear. Maybe I can make amends by apologizing to Mum tonight, explaining to her why I killed her off to my classmates. Maybe that will make everything all right in the here and now. Maybe then Claire will forgive me.

I can't, though. I can't face saying that to Mum. I will have to make amends in some other way.

Anyway, I can't think of that now. It's Friday. Lessons have just finished. I am stood in the small office off my tutor room applying a bit of lippy. I've said I'll have a quick drink with Meredith in the Who'd've Thought It? before going to the wake.

This is not a date, I keep telling myself. This is not a date. You are going to be supportive to a young lad in your class and you will be representing the school.

So what if his dad's gorgeous? So what if you keep rereading the letter he sent in on Monday and thinking to yourself, Gosh, his handwriting's so neat for a man? Hmm. Once you're there, it will all be very different. You will be among a mourning family and you will behave with dignity and professionalism.

In fact, this is how you will make amends to the universe for screwing up over Cheeky the Liverpool Bear. This is how you will right the wrong of being flattered into spilling some beans to a journalist you mistook for a student teacher.

I rearrange my pencil skirt, cloud myself in Pulse by Beyoncé and head for the exit, my stilettos echoing on the parquet.

I bump into Constantine, the French teacher, on the stairs.

'My God, Karen! You look amazing! Going somewhere special?'

I wither her with a look. 'A funeral,' I say, and walk on.

SEVEN

The Who'd've Thought It? is a 1970s breezeblock construction painted in gaudy red and black with interiors to match that wouldn't look out of place in a Ken Loach film from the same period. Still, it's the nearest pub to the school, so some of the teachers venture in on the odd occasion, despite the inherent likelihood of bumping into POTBs (Parents of the Brats). Really it should be called the Who'd've Thought They Could Make a Pub So Hideous?, but the drink is cheap and the mahoosive telly boasts a variety of sports, mostly on grass, which ticks a lot of boxes with the male members of staff. And Meredith.

She makes me have two gin and tonics before I head to the wake. She does, she *makes* me, her rationale being that everyone else will be tipsy by the time I get to the do so I may as well play catch-up now. I find myself powerless to disagree. She sits in the corner booth and I thank my lucky stars, not for the first time, that I don't teach PE like her. I couldn't be seen out on the streets or in public places like this in a shell suit. I can't imagine getting up in the morning and thinking, Yay, another day. And another chance to rock the sporty lez look. Which actually is exactly what she is. And nothing says 'Sporty Lez' more than a shell suit and a tiny ponytail. Practically speaking, her hair's too short for a ponytail, but she always manages to yank it into one, giving her pulled, taut skin around the cheek area the same texture as a tambourine. I've never told her this, though three G&Ts and I might.

Meredith is my favourite lesbian (actually, one of the few I know. I'm not keen on Sonia from humanities – or Sonia from inhumanities, as we hilariously refer to her, as she wears a constant scowl and clompy Birkenstocks) and always looks like she's just dusted her cheeks and forehead with blusher. She's not actually wearing any make-up; it's just that she is permanently rosy of cheek and brow, having just come straight from the sports hall or playground after refereeing something lively and bracing. I suppose what she oozes is health. A foreign concept to me. She also has a whistle dangling round her neck. She's never blown it at me, but it lurks, like a warning. One day she might.

She's flipping a beer mat between finger and thumb impatiently, like she's waiting for some important news, when she leans forward and goes, 'You and I need a night out, you know, now you're on your own. We need to get out there and paint the town red,' she says, smacking her lips after a hearty swig of her G&T. (OK, so she looks healthy, but she's no Keep-Fit Hitler.)

Meredith understands my predicament. She recently split with her girlfriend of six years, but because they're not going to make any money if they sell their house at the moment, they're still living together. Or something. Or maybe the girlfriend is trying to buy her out, I can't remember. It's awkward, anyway.

'Oh God, what? You gonna be dragging me to your fancy lesbetarian bars up Old Compton Street and the like? Oh, I'm really gonna pull up there!'

She laughs. 'OK, we do a deal. One night out on the dykey side of the street and another night on Breeder Alley.'

That's what she refers to me as: a breeder. We share a chuckle.

'How you feeling?' she asks, and I gulp. I do – I actually gulp. I think the gulp is loud enough to make people stop what they're doing and look over. They don't, but that's how it feels.

I sigh and feel myself getting a bit emotional. Must be those two gin and tonics. Damn her forceful alcohol-pushing ways!

'I dunno. Some days are good; some days are bad. I just wish he'd told me why.'

She nods, taking this in, like she understands.

'Well, the main thing is –' she leans back, flips the beer mat into the air, catches it between her top lip and her nose, then removes it and replaces it on the table '– you shouldn't blame yourself. It was his choice, not yours.'

I nod and check my watch. I really should be going. I toy with telling her that I've decided to go and see Michael later, but I really can't be bothered getting into all that now. I can't let my emotions get the better of me today, not when I have a wake to go to. It's funny, I've not told anyone about my secret plan and I know it will remain precisely that: a secret. Why? Why can't I tell anyone? It's nothing to be ashamed of, is it? But something is stopping me. Maybe I fear people will think I'm being a bit desperate. *He's over you, Karen. Deal with it and move on.* I know this is what they'll say, so I don't offer the information. Job done.

Instead I politely ask what she's got planned this weekend. I'm not really interested, but I feign fascination really well as she explains about the netball team she plays for each Saturday 'just for a hoot' and how she's going to a mate's in the afternoon to watch *Mildred Pierce* with Kate Winslet. I get a bit confused at first – possibly because I'm not listening properly – and think she is going to Kate Winslet's house, but she soon explains my mistake. One of her mates has got it on DVD and a gang of them are going to crowd round a widescreen and watch their favourite icon pretending to open a chain of fast-food restaurants. Or something. Jeez, I think, there'll be enough oestrogen in that telly room to sink the *Titanic*. I don't say it out loud, but I do smile to myself at my apt analogy.

'You look a bit like Kate Winslet,' she says, oddly. For odd it is indeed. I have never, *ever* been likened to her before, and the reason for that is, I look nothing like her.

'No, I don't!' I argue, but in the kind of voice that begs for reaffirmation because secretly I am thrilled. Who wouldn't be?

'Don't be offended. She's beautiful.'

I'm not offended, and she is certainly beautiful, even when she's not airbrushed. Why can't I be airbrushed? Just for a day.

'I know, but I look nothing like her.'

Meredith shrugs. 'Just sometimes.'

There is an odd atmosphere between us I can't quite put my finger on. She seems a bit distracted as I gather my bits together to leave, but we're all smiles as she shows me out of the pub and wishes me luck with the task in hand.

Then, just as I'm walking through the doorway, she grabs my arm and says, 'Are you sure you're going to be all right? This evening?'

Why? Did I tell her about Michael? How I was going to— Oh. She means the funeral. Right.

'Of course. Why wouldn't I be?'

'Well, you know.'

'Meredith, I'll be fine. Thanks for the drinks.'

And I head off. Why shouldn't I be able to cope with a little funeral wake? Have I really fallen apart that much?

Oh God. I wish I'd not had those two whole glasses of gin and tonic. Urgh. And gin. *Gin* of all drinks. The one that makes you maudlin. Not a good choice today of all days, but . . . hey ho.

I hate the feeling of not being in control, and now that I'm tottering through the estate, I'm regretting it. It's not a fear that I'm going to be trollied and make a show of myself at the wake by jumping on the coffee table and insisting everyone join me in an out-of-tune rendition of 'Hi Ho Silver Lining'; it's more that in light of . . . recent events . . . I fear my emotions are going to burst up like a bubbling geyser and I'll sob hysterically in a corner to a distant relative of the deceased about the one who got away. And that's probably not the most helpful of things at someone else's funeral. The funeral, let's face it, of someone I never knew, or even met. I get flashes of myself stuttering, 'He just l-left a letter on the k-k-kettle,' and want to turn round and run away.

I can't, though. I promised them I'd go. Well, I promised Kevin. This isn't about me; it's about showing a grieving family the support of the school.

And OK, the dad is hot, but let's gloss over that.

If only there was a coffee shop nearby. I could nip in, neck a latte, take control and carry on with what I have to do, but then I remember the familiar moan of all the kids at school: there's nothing to do round here, nowhere to go. You have to get a bus to the nearest shop, and even the once-busy pawnshop closed down. So finding a Costa or a Starbucks is about as likely as turning a corner and bumping into Sigmund Freud.

I turn the corner and Sigmund Freud's at a bus stop, looking lost as he attempts to decipher the timetable.

Oh. OK. So where's that Caffè Nero?

But when he looks at me and asks, in a broad cockney accent, if I can help him work out which is the best bus to get to Bethnal Green, I realize he's just some old guy with a beard.

Bye-bye, latte.

After pointing the Sigmund lookalikey across the road to take a bus in the opposite direction, I give him the (Freudian) slip and totter round to Lorenmead, the road where the O'Keefes live. I wonder when streets stopped having street names, like 'street' or 'road', and turned into these one-word weirdnesses they have round here. Maybe it was an aspirational decision by whichever architects thought it was clever or cool to build a crisscross of terraces and flats that almost look like they belong in Toy Town. And they probably did when they were built, with their yellow bricks, gaudy royal blue railings and porthole windows. Aesthetically it's no better or worse than the drab row of greying terraced houses I live on; it just looks more like someone's idea of a joke, as the estate can only be about fifteen years old. And no one could seriously have thought porthole windows and navy railings were a look that was going to stand the test of time, surely?

There are matching satellite dishes on every house, in the same position, between the two upstairs windows. They must have been a job lot, all fitted at the same time, by the same company. I'm so lost in the visualization of scores of workmen up ladders fitting a hundred dishes at the same time that I completely miss the O'Keefes' house and find myself at the wrong end of Lorenmead. OK, aaand backtrack!

My phone rings as I retrace my steps. I clumsily drag it from my bag and see from the caller ID it's Rita, Michael's mum. I kill the call. Why is she so intent on speaking to me? I return the phone to my bag.

When I find number 29 – I don't know how I missed it: there's music blaring out, and the front door is ajar – I nudge the door open and enter an overpopulated hallway. It reminds me of the sort of parties I went to in my student days: people shoved up against walls talking (political then) bollocks, and distant-looking women on the stairs apparently three Prozacs away from a nervous breakdown. The only difference this time is the dress code. We may have worn black at uni, but here the black is of course a much more formal affair. I don't recognize any of these people, unsurprisingly, so squeeze past trying to cause the minimum of fuss, finally saying to Distant Woman on Stairs Staring into the Middle Distance, 'Any idea where Kevin is?'

She just shrugs and says in a kind of stoned way, 'Somewhere between heaven and hell?'

I nod.

Someone else leans in and adds, 'Think he's doing the barbecue.'

Barbecue. At a funeral. In January. But of course.

Still, at least it's a pretty good bet that the barbecue will be in the garden, so I force through some more people in the kitchen and head for the light at the end of the tunnel, which I take to be the back door. And – hey presto – I am proved right.

Well, it is a bright, sunny day, I guess, so why not have a barbecue?

I look down the long, narrow garden and see it's not Kevin doing the barbecue at the end of it, but Connor. He is wearing a white shirt and a black tie, perfectly appropriate funeral attire, of course, but with a shiny apron over the top with the body of a naked woman cartooned on it. There are even tassels swinging from the nipples. Real tassels. His face is red and sweaty from the heat of whatever he's cooking over the flames. Just then I feel a hand in the small of my back and a voice in my ear.

'Miss Carpenter, thank you so much for coming.'

The way he says it is more like 'tank' than 'thank' and I know immediately it's him. I turn and see those eyes again. And how dashing he looks in his smart suit and black tie, loosened at the collar now. I ignore this and shake his hand and say, 'How you feeling?' – head cocked to one side, slightly patronizing voice.

'Agh, you know. I've had better days.' He emits a throaty chuckle. 'Still, the service was lovely. Dead celebratory.'

'Oh, that's good.'

Well, you can't beat dead celebratory.

'There wasn't a dry eye in the house, though, when Connor read his poem.'

'He wrote a poem? Oh, that's brilliant!' God, I sound like a teacher. Rein it in, Karen!

'Yeah. And he insisted on doing a barbecue. It's something him and his mam did together, you know? So he wanted to do it for her today, even though it's not exactly barbie weather, you know what I'm saying?'

I do indeed know what he's saying, and I look again at the little boy at the end of the garden and feel a huge lump in my throat.

'Anyway. You. Let's get you a drink.'

You. I like being called 'You'. It's cheeky. It's— *Rein it in, Karen!*

For the next five minutes I feel like Kylie Minogue. That's not to say I'm five foot one and have an amazing backside; more that I am presented to the assembled throng like a latter-day VIP.

This is Karen, Connor's teacher.

This is Miss Carpenter, Connor's form tutor. Isn't it grand? She came to show her support.

No, this is Karen. Teaches up the school. Yeah, Connor's teacher.

And, very kindly, not once does he introduce me as Karen Carpenter. Huge brownie points. No sniggering. No one realizes and guffaws into their tinny.

I'm really sensible, and gladly so, because when Kevin offers me a white wine, lager or vodka, I turn him down and take a Diet Coke instead. Decorum will be my middle name. When he falls into conversation with the (female) vicar, I break away and trudge down the garden to wait in line for a paper plate of dark brown meats. Not sure what they are – they're all of the same hue – but I'm guessing the cylindrical ones are sausages, the round flat ones are burgers, and the ones like little fists are chickeny bits. I am proved right.

'You're doing a really good job, Connor.' Head up, direct eye contact, very teacherly.

He smiles proudly and tells me it's what he used to do with his mum.

'And how are you feeling, mate?'

I have a habit of doing this: I call the lads I teach 'mate'. It's not big, it's not clever, but they seem to like it.

He shrugs. 'Today's OK.'

And those two eyes speak volumes. They speak of wisdom beyond his twelve years. I could weep.

I don't. I just take a dollop of coleslaw from a side table of condiments and compliment his culinary skills. I use the words 'Jamie' and 'Oliver', in case you are wondering. Karen Carpenter knows how to keep it real. Blud.

I look up the garden and see Kevin deep in conversation with a bloke who looks very similar, but for a beard, whom I take to be his brother. Just then a blousy woman with an Eighties perm leans in to me.

'How did you know Toni?' she asks, sotto voce, as if it's a secret code.

I smile and see myself reflected in her very round Deirdre Barlow-from-the-1980s glasses.

'Oh, I didn't. I'm Connor's teacher, Karen.'

She nods, her eyes dancing. 'Handsome, isn't he?'

I blush. 'Who?'

'Kevin.'

I blush some more. Is she a mind reader? Her eyes dart up to the top of the garden; then she looks back at me expectantly.

'Well . . . I don't know. I mean—'

'Dirty old dog, though,' she interrupts.

I look at her, taken aback. What on earth does she mean? 'I'm sorry?'

'He's a dirty old dog,' she repeats. Then she takes a bite of a beefburger. Some grease rolls down her chin. After she chews for a few seconds, her tongue descends and licks the grease back up. Is she part woman, part lizard?

'I . . . don't really know him,' I fluster.

'I do. I live over the road, see.'

'Right.'

'I miss nothing.'

'OK.'

'Nothing. *Nothing* gets past me, you know?'

I have no idea where this is going, but it is making me feel uncomfortable.

She continues, 'And while poor Toni was ill up the hospital, he had a different woman in here every night. Music blaring out. Disgusting.'

I am startled, and my face must say I am startled, for she reads it and nods. I am clearly right to be startled and she has got the response she was after.

'God knows what poor Connor must have thought. I mean, he didn't even wait till she'd died.'

I don't know what to say. Gosh.

'So, like I say, dirty old dog. Watch that one,' she says with foreboding. 'He's not all that he appears.'

With that the woman sweeps away, puts her plate on a nearby garden chair and disappears into the house.

I look at Kevin again and give myself a bloody big reality check. I actually chuckle. Better not make too much of a habit of that here. Not the done thing to be a human laughing bag at a wake, but I realize now why I have felt so flirtatious with Kevin. He is clearly, to quote Deirdre Perm, 'a dirty old dog', a Lothario, a player, and I have only responded to an energy he was giving out to me. He probably doesn't even fancy me; it's just in his nature to ooze . . . I dunno . . . sexy stuff. Well, at least I am not going mad, I tell myself. And look which vicar he chose to take the service, stood there on the patio looking like Linda Lusardi in a dog collar. She is – she's wearing false nails, and her tits aren't half perky for a lady of the cloth. I'd swear she's wearing one of those pointy uplift bras from the 1950s. Look at her, laughing at his jokes and flicking her hair. Oh, he's a dirty old dog all right, and she's an embarrassment to the church if you ask me.

I look back at Kevin. He's right in the middle of Slutty Vicar and Practically Twin Brother, nodding in earnest at something they're discussing. He doesn't look like a man who's just buried his wife. He looks like a hunter-gatherer, out on the pull to nail his prey, then drag it back to the cave for some naughty games round the campfire. (Did cavemen have campfires? Damn, those gins have made my analogies a bit pants.)

That said, I don't feel too critical of him. Who knows what sort of conversations he had with Toni while she was dying at the hospital? OK, so it didn't look too good to the neighbours, but for all they and I know, Toni might have been encouraging

Kevin to find a new partner, grab some happiness and get a new mother for Connor into the bargain. You just don't know, do you? I remember my mum telling me how common she had found it that when people lose a partner and there are kids involved, they quickly find a new soulmate and move on. The gossipy types go into overdrive; the rest of the world doesn't even blink an eye.

Move on. I know this is something I need to do, and I remind myself of the promise I made earlier in the week. I promised myself I'd move forward, find some closure. I recall that before the night is out somehow I must find Michael and talk to him. The realization that I am going to do it excites me. I am going to get answers. Or if not answers, I am at least going to confront Michael and demand an explanation. And if he can't give me one, I will at least have tried. And I will at least make sure we set up another time, either via letter, or email, or a phone call, when he can tell me. Tonight might not be practical for him. Yeah, well, tough. Him leaving me via a letter on a kettle wasn't that practical for me either. A shiver of excitement runs up my spine.

Kevin ambles over. 'How's the food?'

'Lovely,' I say, sounding unnecessarily Irish. 'Connor's done a really good job.'

'Do you have far to travel after this? Do you live far?' Kevin asks.

I don't answer. I have the wind in my sails. 'I'm really sorry, Kevin, but I didn't realize the time.'

He looks confused. I've only just got here.

'I'm gonna have to shoot.'

He does a comedy eyes-wide face and says, 'You have a gun in your handbag?'

We chuckle.

'I've just got a bit of personal business to attend to.'

He nods, but does a 'that's a shame' face. That won't work with me, though, for he is the original dirty old dog. I see it now. He was a dirty old dog in the supermarket with his 'which platter shall I choose?' shtick and he is a dirty old dog now. I'm surprised he's not dry-humping my leg or suggesting we go for some sexy time in the bedroom. I know his sort. Well, I do now. I give Connor a hug and say I'll see him Monday. I compliment him on his food again. I shake Kevin's hand – he's still looking dazed. (Oh, what? Not used to getting turned down, hmm? Get back to your vicar, Shamrock Features, and put your tongue away while you're at it.) Then I head up the garden and into the house.

I realize I've only stayed about ten minutes when I pass Sigmund Freud still stood at his bus stop.

You know, I might get a cab to Michael's work. I might just live a little this evening.

EIGHT

He was taking me down a staircase. It was dark except for the light from his torch. It might have been the middle of the day, but the lack of light made it feel like midnight. That must have been what it was like down here all the time: permanent midnight. We giggled like school kids in an Enid Blyton adventure. Off into the dark, scary woods to solve a crime. Uncle Quentin and his missing lemonade, Aunt Fanny and her priceless ruby necklace. We passed a sign on the toffee-coloured brick walls – '31 steps to exit' – and an arrow pointing back the way we'd come.

'Where are you taking me, Michael?' I gasped between nervous giggles.

'You'll see in a minute. Come 'ed!'

Michael had been working on the Underground for about six months by now and had taken to it like a duck to water. Or, well, like a Tube driver to a Tube train. His uniforms hung in our wardrobe and received such love and attention, anyone would have thought they were ermine robes belonging to Her Majesty and he was the curator of an exhibition displaying the finest garb in the land. I was amazed he didn't have them in cabinets with halogen spotlights. It was fair to say he loved his job. He loved his new purpose, his new direction, which on the whole was forward, through tunnels.

Thank God I trusted him. Thank God I knew him. This felt like the kind of route a murderer would take his victim on in a horror movie.

'Come down this darkened stairwell, my lover. It'll be a laugh . . .'

OK, so I shouldn't be writing horror-flick dialogue, but I'm sure you get the picture.

Then suddenly we were in a room, a long, narrow room. It was icy cold. I could just make out my breath hanging in clouds before my mouth. The brickwork here was blacker, stained with lime; the odd stalactite hung from the ceiling. Michael turned round and did a three-sixty-degree circle with his torch, as if revealing Aladdin's secret cave to me for the first time. I had to admit I was confused. He had brought me metres underground to show me this? I wasn't quite sure what 'this' was.

'What . . . is this place?' I asked, trying to sound bewitched and beguiled, bothered even. This clearly meant a great deal to him, if not to me, and so, as his delightful girlfriend, I had to take an interest in his fascination.

He seemed to be looking for something. He seemed to find it. He walked to the corner of the room and did a 'Da nah!' fanfare noise, then said, 'Let there be light!'

He did something with his left hand in the darkness to the side of his torch spotlight and – hey presto – some lights came on.

We switched off our torches.

I looked around, my eyes adjusting to the newly lit surroundings. Yes, it was still the slightly dull room I'd thought it was. I still didn't get it.

'I still don't get it.' (See, I was no liar. In fact, you might have said I did exactly what it said on the tin. If a paint-based analogy works here . . .)

'This . . .' he said, fizzing with excitement '. . . is St Mary's Tube Station!'

And as if to prove his point, beyond the brick wall to my left I heard the deafening rattle of a Tube passing by. A blast of warm air seemed to shoot through the bricks. Had I been wearing a white Fifties-style dress, I might have done a Monroe.

'And we are on . . .' OK, his overexcited schoolboy routine was starting to grate slightly '. . . the old platform.' He pointed to the floor and walls of the room we were standing in.

'Right,' I said, and OK, that did pique my interest. Slightly. 'But it's all bricked in.'

Even with my ever-so-slight knowledge of my newly adopted home city, I knew I'd not heard of a station called St Mary's.

I knew where we were, as in I knew which part of London we were in: he'd not brought me here with a blanket over my head. I knew we were in the East End (somewhere), and I knew we'd got in via a door in the street and he'd had to use a code on a punch-pad. I also knew we weren't in an area called St Mary's. St Mary's sounded like a quiet hamlet, where Miss Marple might hang her panty girdle at the end of a long day's detecting. Or it sounded like a nice suburban church where your cousin Sue might marry her childhood sweetheart and you'd get a fit of the giggles when she got his names mixed up in the vows so it sounded like she was marrying someone else, or that she was a goer who'd get hitched to anyone. In fact, I knew that the area, now I came to think of it, where we actually were was an area called Whitechapel. Which was odd, as I'd not seen a single white chapel up there in the real world before we'd started our descent.

'That's because . . .' he went on to explain. God, would he ever say a sentence today without putting a War and Peace-length pause in the middle of it? '. . . it's an abandoned Tube station.'

Abandoned. Jeez, I didn't like the sound of that. How did a Tube station get abandoned? How did the poor Tube station feel about that?

Did the paying public just decide one day, en masse, that 'D'you know what? This Tube station's doing my head in. Let's abandon the boring Tube-station bastard. Come on – up those thirty-one steps!' Or did the station master give it roses and say, 'It's not you, it's me,' and then run off with some other station?

'Have a look . . .' here came that pause again '. . . round here!'

Then he headed off to a corner of the room, so I followed.

There was an archway in the corner I'd not seen till now, and he hurried through, like a kid at Christmas throwing himself through the gates of the grotto because Santa would be somewhere in there, and with him, some presents to take home. I followed, less enthusiastically, wondering what amazements lay in store.

We walked down a narrow corridor. There was less light in here. A rusting Coke can sat on top of an empty electric points box on the wall. Some pretty recent gang-style graffiti was daubed on the brickwork. Michael put his torch back on and pointed it towards the ceiling.

'See up there?'

I looked. Across the top of the walls was an imposing pattern of iron latticework.

'That's the old footbridge, linking the platforms.'

OK, so that was pretty interesting, but where were we going now?

'And look.' He shone his torch onto the opposite wall. A handrail dissected the wall, rising up like a ski slope against the brickwork. 'That's where the old staircase was.'

It looked like the set of an abstract play. A handrail you could *never grab on a staircase that was no longer. Or might not have been there to begin with.*

'And now . . .'

He turned the corner and led me into another narrow room. Not too dissimilar to the first we'd been in. Again he found a power source and switched on some lights. Low benches lined the walls. A rusty red wishbone-shaped ventilation shaft hung on one wall, the top of it disappearing into the ceiling. Something told me this wasn't a platform.

Michael started explaining, with the brio of a newly trained tour guide, that the station had been closed during the Second World War and used as an air-raid shelter. In fact, we were standing in the air-raidy bit right now. The benches were where the people used to sit when escaping the bombing raids on East London. The air vent was what kept them alive probably. I felt a shiver down my spine as he pointed to some poles on the walls, parallel to the benches, about four feet above them. Michael explained that these had held bunk beds, so they could fit more people in, and they could get cosy. Well, as cosy as you can when there are bombs going off above your head and you're bricking it that you might emerge to find your house mown to the ground. He continued that the station and the shelter were bombed towards the end of the war, and as a result the station never reopened.

Immediately I could see the scores of people huddled in here, trying to be brave as London was blasted to pieces. Ordinary people. People like me and Michael. The rousing camaraderie that must have existed between them all. Checking their ration books, singing '(There'll Be Bluebirds Over) the White Cliffs of Dover', cuddling their kids and telling them everything was going to be all right, once they'd beaten that bastard Hitler.

OK, so my imagination might have been slightly clichéd at times, but it was like they were there in front of me. The ghosts of the past lingering on. Maybe they were excited that Michael and I were here. They can't have got many visitors. Maybe we should stop, have a chinwag with them, tell them what life was like in the late twentieth century. Tell them about mobile phones and Anthea Turner. Or was that rubbing their noses in it? And come to think of it, would there really be ghosts if nobody actually died down here? I knew Michael would know if I asked him, but I didn't want to.

I didn't want to think that anyone had actually died here. I wanted it to be a place of safety.

I turned to see that Michael was pulling two cans of lager from the pockets of his trench coat. (He was going through his mistimed mod phase, complete with wannabe Paul Weller haircut.) He handed me one and cracked his open.

'Thought we could stop for a drink, princess.'

He'd started calling me 'princess'. He'd adopted a few cockneyisms since moving to London, which felt at odds with his Liverpool accent. I pulled back the ringpull on my can and took a glug. It was warm. His was too. We both pulled a face. Then he moved to one of the walls and licked his finger. In the grime on the wall he wrote:

$$MF$$
$$Ls$$
$$KC$$

and drew a heart round it, then turned to me, grinning.

'So everyone knows we've been here.'

His finger was now black from the grime. He wiped it on my nose and we laughed.

I felt so confident on my way here. I could have taken on the world, well, Michael and won, but now that I stand outside the gates of his depot, it's like someone has taken a pin to that balloon of courage and it is slowly deflating, leaving me a shrivelled scrotum of bleurgh. I am empty of all hope, bravery and the requisite amount of chutzpah to make me walk in there and ask to see him, ask if he's on duty, politely request an audience with him and then defiantly demand an explanation.

It doesn't help that it has started to rain and I didn't bring a brolly. Nor does it help that I am dressed for a wake in my best heels and skirt and with only the flimsiest of jackets. It certainly doesn't help that my hair, with its tendency to frizz when wet, is shrinking in curls around my face. Stand here any longer and I'll look like a Roman centurion with one of those tight-knit boy-perms you see on urns dug up from a burial site. Without even looking in a mirror, I know that what little make-up I am wearing will be dripping down my face in rivulets of unattractiveness. Basically, I look like a bloody mess. I just know I do. I can't move, though. Try as I might to actually turn and run away, I can't. And try as I might, I can't advance towards the entrance and go and announce myself either. I am catatonic with ambivalence. That is not to say I don't care – I do – but the competing parts of me, the 50 per cent that wants to run away and the 50 per cent that knows I've got to run towards, are competing, and in the fight, nothing is happening. That for me is the recipe for ambivalence.

But I know. I know if I do turn and go home now, I am in dire danger of kicking myself for the rest of the night. My incompetence will hang over me all weekend and I won't be able to think about anything other than how frustrated I am with myself.

The main door opens and for a second I panic. It may well be Michael coming out now, his shift over. The decision about whether to go looks like it might have been taken out of my hands. I am almost excited, but I'm anxious too. Then the decision is snatched away from me when I see it is not Michael but one of his colleagues, Laura.

Laura, the one who always fancied him. She's not the slimmest of ladies, and her shape is not ameliorated by the girth of her uniform topped with all-weather overcoat. Clevérly, though, she is wearing wet-look gel in her hair, so she will maintain a consistency of appearance in all weathers (like her coat). I am almost jealous.

Almost. Because then I remind myself that wet-look gel is hideous, particularly on a burgundy perm.

Did I really get jealous of this woman when she left flirty comments on Michael's Facebook? No wonder he laughed in my face when I suggested she was after him. I mean, come on, it's 2012 and she is sporting a burgundy perm with wet-look gel. She pulls a ciggie from her pocket and lights it quickly, so quickly I don't actually see how she did it (though I'm guessing a lighter must have been involved. I'm clever like that). I step back against a wall, shielding myself from her view, but she's not looking over anyway. She's too busy peering at something on her phone. A website about Eighties hairdos, perhaps, seeking inspiration for her next 'look'.

I put my hand in my bag and feel for the envelope inside.

You see, I have been clever. Oh yes, very clever.

It is miles from the Fountain Woods estate to here, so I had plenty of gin-inspired thinking time on the journey over and I came up with a rather marvellous plan.

I mean, what's the likelihood that what you want to happen actually happens? Just because I have decided that tonight is the night I will get closure of sorts with Michael, how realistic is it that because I turn up at his depot at six o'clock in the evening, he will be here too? And not on a train? And hanging around the mess room. And available to chat. And explain. And apologize. And beg me to take him back. And . . .

Getting a bit ahead of myself there.

So. Using the old adage 'Hope for the best, expect the worst', I got my taxi driver to drop me at Westfield, Stratford. Where – hoorah – Paperchase was still open. And I bought a jaunty card with a picture of a Jack Russell in a deckchair. And I have written him a note. It says:

Dear Michael,

Hope you are OK and finding some peace.

I would really appreciate the opportunity to have a chat with you sometime soon. I think after all our time together I deserve an explanation for why you left. Please don't worry that I'm going to kick off, or be a bitch. I just want to hear it from the horse's mouth, just want to hear what went wrong. I kind of know, but I need to hear you say it so I can find some closure and move on. Call me anytime. I'm still on the same number.

Karen x

I chose the dog in the deckchair because it is generic enough not to raise alarm. It is not a card with all hearts and flowers on it screaming, 'Take me back! I'm still besotted with you!!!!' Nor is it a gothic piece of artwork that threatens, 'Meet me or I will kill you, then myself.' It is anodyne and harmless and – judging by how relaxed the Jack Russell is – say, 'I am doing OK and getting on quite fine without you, thank you very much.'

I keep my hand in my bag as I approach Laura. I clear my throat and she looks up, ready to smile, then looks slightly panicked because I have my hand in my bag, as if about to draw a gun. She relaxes a bit when I pull out the turquoise envelope.

'Sorry. Er . . . is Michael Fletcher working tonight? The driver?'

She freezes, like she is suddenly remembering my face but can't quite place the name. She shakes her head slowly.

'I'm Karen, his girlfriend.' Then I quickly add, 'As was.'

She nods. 'Hi, Karen. Yes, I remember you from—'

I don't give her time to explain. I thrust the card into her hand. 'Could you give him this for me? Thanks!' Then I turn and run away.

I can imagine her watching me run and thinking Michael was right to ditch me, as I appear a bit unhinged, interrupting her sentences and running really fast towards a parade of fast-food outlets. I seek refuge from the rain in a Chicken Cottage. I manically order a chicken kebab with garlic sauce. It's only then I look back and see that, further down the street, Laura is no longer there. I wonder if the card is in Michael's pigeon-hole yet. She will put it there, won't she? I have no other way of contacting him. I could send him a message on Facebook, but I know he will ignore it. You see, I noticed just after he left that he'd deleted me as a friend on there. It was a painful blow at the time. I actually cried. So sending him a message on there will be about as useful as a ra-ra skirt made of chilli sauce.

Jeez, where did *that* one come from?

Oh. The bloke behind the counter is talking to me.

'Chilli sauce?' he asks, like he's said it six times before, which is feasible.

I shake my head. 'No, thanks.'

I rat-a-tat my nails on the stainless-steel counter, smile at the bloke, then cross my fingers that at some point over the weekend Michael will get my inoffensive card.

Of course, what I really wanted to write was:

Dear Michael,
You fucking bastard. EXPLAIN.
K
No kiss. See that, sunshine? Two can play at that game!!

But I know I'd never have heard from him again, so I had to tread carefully and be charming and lovely and . . .

God, this is exhausting. It is completely knackering me out, whittling away at my emotional core, thinking about him and his departure and my future and my house and my job and my history and my loneliness and my bruised ego and my hair and my . . . lack of Michael. I have to stop this. I have to do something that will give me some closure, just in case he never offers it to me.

But what? What can I do to erase him like he has erased me?

Then I hit upon something and I know what I must do.

I must sleep with someone else.

Is it madness? Have I lost the plot?

No. Actually, it's a genius idea. I must sleep with someone and *soon*.

But who?

I smile again at the bloke. He wipes sweat from his brow and I see his fingers are dyed red from an over-handling of chilli sauce.

OK. Maybe not him. But someone.

NINE

'So you want a new boyfriend?' Wendy asks on the phone the next morning. I am lying in bed watching *Saturday Kitchen*, I think it's called. Someone from *EastEnders* is telling us she isn't keen on rice pudding with all the reverence of one describing the time they stared death in the face. I've already filled Wend in on the debacle of the wake and the whole 'discovering Kevin's a stud' thing. We both did a noisy shudder, and now we've moved on to my new mission.

'No. A boyfriend is not what I want. A boyfriend is the last thing I want. I just want sex.'

I've not told her about my card for Michael.

'Like a one-night stand?'

I fear she will think less of me.

'Exactly. Although I could do afternoons. I don't want to be time specific. Though only at weekends. Or half-terms.'

Like I am desperate to get back with him, which I'm not.

'Right.'

I'm not going to tell anyone I've tried to make contact with him. It's my secret and I want to keep it that way.

'Although night-time might be good because it would help to have a few drinks first, so it's less embarrassing to be taking off my clothes in front of a complete stranger.'

'What about a half-stranger?'

And we chortle.

'You do still have to take off your clothes for sex, don't you?' I ask.

'Think so,' says Wendy, 'but then, what do I know? It's been that long.'

'Right,' I say, a bit disappointed. 'I was rather hoping they'd invented a new way of doing it where you could keep your coat on.'

'And not have to touch?'

'Even better,' I giggle. 'But actually, no. I think it's the skin-on-skin thing I need, to get over all this Michael stuff.'

'Careful. You're starting to sound like a 1970s porno film.'

'Hey, maybe I could become a porn actress.'

And again we are in mini-hysterics. I hear a click on the line and realize Mum has picked up the receiver downstairs and may be listening in.

'Yes, I may well become a porn actress,' I add, for Mum's benefit/shock.

I can just see it now. I'll go downstairs in a bit and find her anxious over her Cheerios, worried about my burgeoning change of direction.

'You will play safe, won't you, love?' she'll whimper, forehead creased with panic. 'Bareback is never an option.'

And I'll nod sagely, imagining all my awards at the Porno Oscars for 'Best Double Penetration' and the like.

The line clicks again. She has hung up.

'So how does one go about having sex these days?' I ask Wendy, sounding for the life of me like the presenter of a BBC2 documentary. A younger Joan Bakewell perhaps, or a less irritating Peaches Geldof. I certainly sound posher than usual.

'Kagsy, if I knew that, I wouldn't be sat here right now in my onesie wondering if I should have that extra waffle.'

'Wend, my motto in life, as you know, is to always have that extra waffle.'

And again, daft Muttley-like sniggering from the pair of us.

'Do I have to hang around wine bars, sitting on high bar stools, quoting *Sex and the City* one-liners and pretending to be all ballsy?' I wonder.

'Well, that's one option.'

'And the other?'

'Oh, there's more than one, Kags.'

I find myself sitting upright in bed, ready to take it in, and take it in I do.

These are my friend Wendy's rules for getting sex in the twenty-first century: 'How to get SEX' by Wendy Wolverhampton.

And yes, that is her surname. She, like me, has been socially crippled with a shit name. She says whenever she announced herself in her youth as Miss Wolverhampton, people assumed she was a vacuous beauty queen. I like to think it's how we became friends.

1. Go on a swinging website. I say swinging – that's the only way I can describe it. Basically, Wendy says there are websites you can go on to meet like-minded people who want to do things called 'hook-ups' for casual, NSA sexy stuff. 'NSA' equals 'no strings attached', apparently. She tells me the names of some of them. Essentially it sounds like www.ifancyashagbutnotadate.com or www.imaslagbasically.net.

2. Advertise your services as a high-class hooker. Then not only do you get sex out of it, you could possibly afford a

string of pearls afterwards. (She makes some joke about a pearl necklace. I don't get it, but laugh anyway.)

3. Come on to all of my single straight male friends – winking salaciously at them over a glass of wine, running my finger over the outline of my nipple when we're alone, that kind of thing. (I didn't even know my nipples *had* outlines. Maybe I've got freaky nips. Oh no!)

4. Hang around the local supermarket weighing the marrows suggestively (I can't do this. I may get shot) with a trolley full of lube and condoms.

5. Go to a meeting of Sexual Compulsives Anonymous and see if there's anyone hot there who fancies falling off the wagon.

6. Go clubbing. (For some reason, this one fills me with more dread than becoming a hooker!)

7. Become a contestant on *Take Me Out*. (Ditto. Plus not orange enough.)

8. Place an advert in the Lonely Hearts column of the local newspaper. (Not sure why it has to be local. Do men who fancy a fumble not like to go very far? Talk about shagging on your own doorstep.)

9. Put a status on Facebook saying, 'I wanna get laid. Inbox me if you're up for it.' See what happens. An hour later change status to 'Sorry. Been fraped. That'll teach me to leave my laptop on in school!' (Thus avoiding all your mates thinking you are desperate.)

10. Go and see Kevin O'Keefe.

Well, who would have thought there were so many options for getting some sex in Cameron's Britain. I hope he's proud!

Mum says nothing over breakfast about my prospective porn career. I'm a bit gutted, truth be told, as I'm sure she'd have some fascinating pointers, happy as she is to talk at length about any given subject, even if she knows nothing about it. Just last week she regaled me with the ins and outs of someone's life. Someone called Tim. When eventually I realized I had no idea who Tim was, and mentally ticked off all my relatives and cousins, double-checking I knew no one called Tim, I asked her who she was talking about.

'Tim Henman,' she said, displaying a slightly worrying over-familiarity with well-known tennis players with lots of teeth. Then she went off again, talking about 'Tim this and Tim that'.

Eventually I interrupted. 'Mum, how do you know all this stuff about Tim Henman?'

She looked a bit bewildered, then explained she'd read an article in one of her magazines. I asked how long the article was and she held up her thumb and forefinger about three inches apart and yet she was able to bang on for a good fifteen minutes about how she felt he felt about the state of British tennis, and what sort of orthodontic work she assumed he'd had. All from a three-paragraph article. I sometimes think I could leave Mum talking in the kitchen, nip out to the shops, get my hair done, take a cardy back to Marks's and have a row with the assistant, stomp out in a huff, run the London Marathon, come home exhausted and Mum will still be sat there in the kitchen discoursing on the same subject that I left her rabbiting away about earlier.

So. I am about to tell her I have no intention of whoring myself on camera when my phone buzzes.

Is it him? Is it Michael?

Has he got my card and is offering an explanation? I grab my phone and take it into the hall. If it is him, I don't want Mum to see me reading it, in case I get angry or upset or confused.

I sit on the second-from-bottom stair, still not looking at my phone, then take a deep breath and unlock it.

OK. It's not from him. It's from Meredith.

Meredith: **Hey, do you fancy coming to see *Mildred Pierce*? Might be fun if you've got nothing on.**

I chuckle and reply: **I am fully clothed. Shit.**

Meredith: **Damn! Come anyway?**

I deliberate. Oh, sod it, why not? Me and a houseful of lezzers? Bring it on!

Me: **Sure. Text me the address.**

Oh well. That's Saturday sorted.

Mum looks a bit wary when I tell her I'm going to Meredith's mate's for the afternoon.

'For what?'

'To watch DVDs and drink.'

'You won't be eating?'

'Yes.'

'What will you be eating?'

'Jesus, Mother. What do you expect me to say? Minge?'

She looks horrified.

'I don't know,' I continue apologetically.

'And how many lesbians will there be?'

'I don't know. We'll probably get a takeaway.'

Mum raises an eyebrow. 'Of lesbians?'

'No, of food. A Chinese banquet or something.'

'And what are you going to be? The main course?'

'Oh, for God's sake, Mother!' and I slam my pudding bowl down on the table and do a really good flounce up the stairs. I have a shower. Then, just to wind up Mum, I put on some clothes that make me look a bit more dykey than usual and scrape my hair back into a ponytail. I look like Sporty Spice on a pension. When I head downstairs, she is stood in the hall, arms crossed, tapping her foot passive-aggressively.

'Well, you can see why Michael lost interest!' she says, knowing it will rile me. And it does.

'No, he lost interest 'cos he had you as a mother-in-law!' I shout back.

She throws her head back and laughs. 'Ha, ha, ha!'

That's exactly how it sounds: ha, ha, ha!

'You weren't even married!'

I can't be bothered with her. I see her Uggs lying near the front door. I kick them, open the door, then head out, slamming it satisfyingly behind me. As I head down the street, suddenly self-conscious that I look like I'm going to a Spice Girls fancy-dress party, I hear my letter box fly up and Mum screaming, 'There's no need to take it out on my Uggs, Karen!'

I head for the Tube.

The Tube!

I stand outside the station, take a deep breath and walk in. A text comes through on my phone.

Mum: **Might go in the loft. Check for rats.**

Oh, for God's sake! I quickly delete it, take another deep breath, then head down, all the time thinking about anything other than Michael.

Rats. Rats. Rats. No, rats are horrible – think of something else, something nice. Er . . . Lily Allen's baby, Lily Allen's pram, Lily of the Valley perfume, *Valley of the Dolls*, 'Living Doll' by Cliff Richard, Max Clifford, Max Factor, *The X Factor*, ex-boyfriends. Oh no, Michael again! I try to delete the browsing history in my brain and start again.

As I rattle along the District line, surrounded by the usual Saturday commutership of shoppers heading for Knightsbridge (yes, even I know they'll have to change trains) and well-turned-out families heading for the museums of Kensington, I decide a makeover is in order. I take my scrunchy out and lose the ponytail. I only dressed like this to wind up my mum and now I feel a bit daft. If only I could be a bit more like Superman and do some rapid swapping of outfits, but as I've not brought a change of clothes, I can't. Meredith's mate lives in Chiswick. *Chiswick!* It's miles away. Still, when I get off at her Tube station, I pass a row of shops and am able to purchase a cheap but jazzy skirt, so chuck my tired old jogging bottoms in the bin. By the time I arrive at Meredith's mate's, I am looking more like a dowdy Baby Spice than Sporty.

I don't know why I am referencing the Spice Girls like this. I never even liked them.

The atmosphere inside the house is a bit morose at first. Put it this way – Emeli Sandé is playing when I walk in, and some vegetable crisps are being passed round in a Le Creuset casserole dish lined with paper napkins. Someone passes it to me and I almost drop it it's so heavy. My legs buckle under me and Meredith makes a dive to stop it crashing to the floor. Jeez, are all these women weightlifters or something? Everyone introduces themselves in such quick succession that I don't take in the names. It's like watching *Family Fortunes* and hearing the contestants' names really quickly but not having name badges to remind you who the hell these people are. Maybe I should suggest name badges. Or maybe I should just try and concentrate. I decide in my head to call them Dave, Dee, Dozy, Beaky, Mitch and Titch. Meredith is Dave, just to add to the confusion.

As the mood shifts when some Lady Gaga comes on, I decide they're a jolly lot, though this is the first social gathering I've been to in a while where everyone stands in a circle, as if to start playing a trust game in a drama class. I don't say much, just enjoy the ricocheting one-liners and retorts that can only happen in a gang of mates. Instead of feeling like an outsider, they're full of such bonhomie that I feel flattered to have been invited. When I do pipe up with the odd throwaway line, they all laugh heartily and give Meredith a look as if to say, 'Good work, Dave – you've brought a mighty fine filly into our fold.'

Because there is definitely something horsey about this crew. I even wish I'd worn an Alice band and a Barbour. It does my self-esteem the world of good and for the first time in yonks I relax and feel a weight lifting from my shoulders. Half of them are PE teachers (Dozy, Mitch and Titch, I think); two of them are partners (Dozy and Dee, I think); one of them's a lawyer (Dee, though I have a terrible feeling she said her name was Horatia. I could be wrong, and it feels impolite to ask); and they all, bar Meredith – sorry, Dave – have a whiff of the boarding school about them. I dread to think what japes this lot'd get up to after lights out. I bet it's a far cry from Mallory Towers.

Whoops. Turning into my mother there.

Mallory Towers. I wish I'd read those books now. I bet this lot have. I often find myself pigeonholing whichever group of people I am with by deciding which reading material they would have in common.

Ah, I'm among the Wolf Hall *brigade.* (Pseudo-intellectuals with a lot of time on their hands. Or compulsive liars.)

Ah, Harold Robbins, eat your heart out. (Mum's friends.)

Well, how many of you are familiar with the Lucky Santangelo trilogy, hmm? That's right. All of you! (Not sure, but they definitely sound like fun!)

So these ladies, for sure, have Mallory Towers in common, and probably a smattering of early Jeanette Winterson. Well, *Oranges Aren't The Only Fruit*, basically.

As we stand in the kitchen, it starts to rain. I look up to see that part of the ceiling is made of glass. The room darkens as clouds cover the sun and I am reminded of my own lean-to. And him. And as if they're reading my mind – oh God, telepathic lesbians, who'd've thought? – Dozy says, 'Meredith told us about your boyfriend. I'm so sorry.'

But I don't want to talk about Michael anymore. He has invaded my thoughts for so long I've had enough. I am exhausted by him and my concern about him. I telepathize this back with a strained look. Say, 'Thank you'. And with a sensitivity you might not get with Jackie Collins readers, say, the subject is dropped and Dozy grins and says, 'Shall we go and watch *Mildred*?'

I'm a bit worried that I'll hate *Mildred Pierce* and that we'll have to sit in hushed reverence, marvelling at the beauty of Winslet, like school kids on a trip to a cathedral, so that if one of us whispers something, someone else will do a librarian-esque 'Shhh!' and point to a sign on the wall that reads:

SILENCE. WINSLET ADMIRATION IN PROGRESS. FFS!

Fortunately there is no sign, and actually I am relieved to discover that these women like to chat all the way through an HBO mini-series, which is fine by me. Wine is poured; nibbles are passed round, then dumped tantalizingly on the coffee table. We are all hunched up on two colossal dumpy settees set at right angles, and the TV screen is mahoosive. Like really mahoosive. Like totally filling-your-field-of-vision mahoosive. Every time Kate W. comes on the screen there is a collective sigh of admiration, of satisfaction, like this lot are a gaggle of junkies and they've just had a spoonful of smack. (That's how you take smack, right?) And after a while I join in, which amuses them.

At one point Meredith says, 'See? Even the breeder likes her!' which makes them giggle, and I suggest getting myself a T-shirt printed saying, 'Breeder and Proud.' And when I offer Meredith some nibbles because I'm cramming a shedload of Chinese-style stuff that isn't potpourri (I mean, who has *that* anymore?) but looks like it, she insists the T-shirt should say, 'Breeder, not Feeder,' which again causes mirth.

Then somehow the chit-chat returns to me again, and with the fortitude of two glasses of wine, I share with them my plan of sleeping with someone in an attempt to move on. They're keen to fantasize about which bloke they'd sleep with if they had to, and their string of names is hilarious, if slightly scary: Eric Cantona, Dermot O'Leary, Peter Barlow from *Coronation Street* (mostly, it seems, as a way of getting to Carla) and Alan Carr (comedian, not stop-smoking guru).

Then, from nowhere, I ask a burning question that I don't think has been that burning but turns out to be. Maybe it's the drink, and maybe it's the fact that I get a text from my mum saying: **No rats in loft. PS I don't want you to be a hairy lebian.**

(I tell them this. They relish the new concept of lebianism and claim they will only refer to themselves as such from now on. And in case you're wondering, we pronounce 'lebian' so it rhymes with 'plebeian'.)

And so I find myself saying, 'Do you guys wax your pegundas?'

They look at me like I am mad. I have no idea where the word 'pegunda' came from, but they know what it means, and they take it seriously.

'Only, I've been in a relationship for so long that I've never done that whole Brazilian thing and I'm wondering . . . if I am going to get down and dirty with, say, Alan Carr or Dermot O'Leary, do I need to start a deforestation process on my . . .'

'Pegunda,' says Mitch.

'Pegunda,' I agree.

You see, this is where Mum gets it so wrong. She would now assume that the women in this room would argue that to come to a decision, I would need to get my pegunda out for them to analyse and then make a decision about whether to get the lady-gardeners in, but they don't. What they do instead is embark on a discourse about the waxing and shaving of the female pegunda. (Yeah, right, like males have pegundas. Jeez!) And sitting on our sofas, it feels like we're on a late-night discussion programme on Channel 4 from the mid-1990s. Any minute now Tracey Emin will rock up, call us all twats and then vomit in the fireplace. And I am surprised to learn that every single one of them has waxed her pegunda.

Every single one of them.

Fancy that.

I am a hairy freak.

Oh God. I will have to get it done.

I ask them where they go, which is a bit of a daft question in itself, as I can't imagine they go to the hairdresser's, sit backwards in the chair, chuck their legs skywards and say, 'Brazilian, please, babes. It's like bloody Center Parcs down there. Oh, and no perm solution this time!' A wall of silence surrounds me, though. They will not divulge, for they want me to be the one, the brave one. They want me to stand up for feminism and say, 'I will not be waxed. I will not be primped and preened. I will not kowtow to male oppression and gender stereotypes. We all get old and we all grow hair. I will maintain my Forest of Karen and ya boo sucks to anyone who finds that offensive. For I find *you* offensive.'

I agree with them. I nod my head oh-so-vehemently and I can tell they are impressed. I can tell they're proud.

But secretly I'm thinking, Sod that. I'm so getting my minge waxed.

I change the subject shortly after as I don't want to be a hypocrite. I guide them steadily back to Winslet, wondering if she is as smooth as a bowling ball, and soon my own pagunda is history, thank God.

I must have mentioned my mortgage crisis too, at some point, because when a few hours later Dave, Dee, Dozy et al have decided they want to head up west and parade around some ladybars and I decide to head for the Tube and my mother, Meredith says on the doorstep, 'They all think you're fab.'

I almost curtsy with pride.

'Oh, and Karen? Have a think, but I'm gonna be looking for somewhere to live soon.'

Really?

'You know I'm looking for any excuse to move out from being with Yvonne. She's really doing my head in.'

Yvonne? Oh yes, her ex who she still lives with.

'So . . . if you're in need of a lodger . . .'

Right!

'Have a think anyway.'

'Yeah, OK, I'll have a think.'

Then something crosses my mind and I lean in to her and I whisper, 'If you lived with me, and I waxed my lady bits . . .'

She nods.

'. . . you wouldn't tell Dee, Dozy, Beaky, Mitch and Tits, would you?'

Oh dear. I must be a bit tipsy. I said 'Tits' instead of . . . Actually, Tits is better. Tits I like. Though I better not tell Meredith that!

'Who?'

I roll my eyes. 'That lot in there.'

She chuckles. 'No, Karen. Your secret would be safe with me.'

Oh joy.

'OK, then I'll definitely think about it. See you, Da—
Meredith.'

'See you, Karen.'

We hug. She pecks me on the cheek. She lets me go and I skip
down the street towards the Tube. I then stop, remembering I
am thirty-six and a little bit tipsy, but then I miss skipping and
start again. I practically skip home.

TEN

'So, Karen . . .'

It's Wednesday. It's twenty-five to four, which means it's my departmental meeting. Mungo is once again wearing grey socks under Jesus sandals.

'. . . I've got a really interesting proposition for you.'

Oh God. He's going to suggest that thing. He wants to introduce that thing, that new way of learning to read. I heard them discussing it on Radio 4 the other day when Mum was peeling the potatoes and I was joining a group on Facebook called 'Bring Back *Bullseye*: get enough likes and we'll petition ITV!' Apparently there's this new way of learning to read where you do it phonetically and I immediately thought, Oh God, Mungo'll be well up for that. And I won't. I'll have to learn a new way of reading, then learn how to teach it, and I may as well be teaching Portuguese for all I'll really understand of it.

But Mungo continues, 'Today I thought we'd mash things up a little and head out for something to eat. What say you?'

What say I? Oh. Erm.

'I dunno really,' I say, which is hugely insightful, if true, though not particularly helpful.

So this isn't about phonetic reading, or whatever it's called.

It's about going out for something to *eat*?

It's just a bit weird. Much as I hate my departmental meetings, because there's only the two of us in our department, and the sight of peep-toes and socks makes my stomach somersault, and much as Mungo loves the sound of his own voice, and appears to hate that of mine, we are meant to be working. We are meant to be checking in on all the kids we teach and seeing if there's more we could be doing for certain kids, or if anyone else has come to note that we need to keep an eye on. And surely that can only be done round a desk in Mungo's office, the smell of his Paco Rabanne floating in the stale air.

'I . . . know you've been through it a bit lately . . . and, well . . . you know my background is in counselling. Let's forget about the kids for once and just build some emotional bridges. What say you?'

What say I? Again? I'd say I can't think of anything worse. I don't want to build emotional bridges. In fact, I'd quite like to draw up some emotional footbridges and slam down an emotional portcullis or two.

But of course I say, 'Brilliant. That'd be great.'

Mungo's car is weird. He tells me it's a Citroën 2CV when I ask with a tone of distaste, and he points out it's vintage, but all I know is the doors face the wrong way and opening the windows is like doing ten minutes on *The Krypton Factor*. Moving in it is even more disturbing. It's not often I've felt like I'm driving through the streets of London in a bumper car that's escaped from the fairground, but I do now. It's not that we're bumping into anything – Mungo drives far too slowly for that; we don't appear to go any higher than first gear, even on an empty road – it's more like you can feel every lump and bump in the road. And I wasn't aware that roads were that bumpy, to be honest. It feels like we're off-road and we're not; we're on-road.

The car's so old it has a cassette player in it. As soon as we set off, he had to jab a button very hard on the dashboard, and now we appear to be listening to Gregorian chants. Though it could be the Army Wives – I'm not sure.

Mungo gives a running commentary about our journey as if he is a driving instructor and it's me who's driving, not him, so he's saying stuff like, 'And at the lights we're approaching we're going to indicate when it's safe to do so and then hang a left.'

Fortunately he doesn't keep saying, 'What say you?' although I'm sure we're in for plenty of that when we reach the pub we're going to.

He's taking me to a little 'out of the way' place that he and Fionnula 'adore'. Fionnula is his wife. Bizarrely, she's seemed like a bit of a laugh on the few times I've met her. So God knows what she's doing with him. He always has a bit of lunch-time sandwich in his beard in the afternoon, and she clearly has no compunction to tell him that socks and sandals give the air of a paedophile . . . Not the best look when you work with children.

When I notice I've been in the car for a good half-hour, I realize that 'out of the way' means 'a long way away' (like Glasgow) in a normal car, so to be doing it in Noddy's car could mean we're in for a three-hour jaunt simply to get there. I'm just starting to fear we're morphing into Bing Crosby and Bob Hope in one of those interminable road movies when Mungo announces, 'And we'll take the third exit off this mini-roundabout and pull into the pub car park.'

And relax!

This pub is no easier on the eye than the Who'd've Thought It? so I don't know why we had to drive eighteen hours to get here, but then I spy the menu, which says, 'All you can eat for £5 before 5 p.m.', and I suddenly understand, as my heart sinks.

I will order a main, but I just know Mungo will go for the full three courses.

Which he does.

I do a mental calculation as to how long we are going to have to be here. It's not looking good. I may have to feign an attack of the vapours, invent a love of long-distance running and leg it home.

Mungo wants to *talk*, though. Why do people want to *talk* so much these days? Can't we just leave other people be? Some of us don't want to *talk*.

Oh, I don't mind a bit of inane chatter, pointless gossip, even important political discussions, but I spend so much time mulling over my feelings and being self-indulgent with my own thoughts that when I actually go to *talk* about it, the words run dry.

I'm monosyllabic as he eats his breaded garlic mushrooms and I daintily sip my orange and lemonade. Batting away his 'So how are you really?'s and 'How have you been?'s with grunts and noises that indicate 'Oh, you know' and 'Well, mustn't grumble', he starts telling me about how he felt after his first wife, Connie, left him. I stifle a giggle. I only thought people were actually called Connie in Victoria Wood sketches. Apparently he was bereft following her departure, didn't eat for weeks, and his family were worried he was developing man-orexia, but then he met Fionnula at a self-help group and the rest, so he says, is history.

Or geography, I joke, as Fionnula is a geography teacher.

He talks a lot about light at the end of the tunnel, and the black dog of depression. He talks about the restorative powers of exercise – in his case a love of Nordic walking he shares with Fionnula, or 'the Big F', as he's started calling her. I ask what Nordic walking is and he gets up and demonstrates, just as our waiter arrives with the mains. He looks at Mungo like he is mad. And maybe he is, for he is walking briskly across the pub, pretending to do a skiing movement with his arms, explaining that Nordic walking is a cross between walking and skiing, but you do it on normal roads, or in the countryside. He and Fionnula try to squeeze an hour in each night.

'You must come and join us sometime,' he says excitedly.

I tell him I have a lot on, what with my mother staying. I don't tell him she's always out at Zumba or watching BBC4.

As we tuck into our mains, when finally he has sat down – even doing a comedy mime of pretending to put his skis away, which did actually make me chuckle – I suddenly have a panic on. A guy comes in dressed in some DMs. No, he is not wearing departmental meetings on his feet, but Doc Martens, and they remind me of the reinforced shoes Michael has to wear to work in case a member of the public kicks off and he has to kick them back. Suddenly I worry, thinking, What if Michael walks in now, or anyone who knows me, and sees me having an all-you-can-eat-for-a-fiver meal with Mungo? They'd think we are . . . going together!

I try to comfort myself with the restorative powers of my tepid red prawn curry, but it's not working.

Then I tell myself I'm overreacting. Mungo is my boss. It must be clear to people. He might be boring as shite, but he is never inappropriate. He never oversteps the mark.

Famous. Last. Words.

For as he tucks into his veggie lasagne ('I've not eaten an animal since 1986'), he divulges the secret of his now twenty-year marriage to Fionnula.

Sorry. I hope you've not just eaten.

They have an open relationship. Yes, I heard it right. An. Open. Relationship.

I can't remember the last time I was this mortified. I have used far too often in my life the phrase about wanting the ground to open up and swallow me whole. In fact, I'd often do it in a cod Irish accent, so it sounded like 'swallow my hole', which I find particularly guffaw-worthy. But honest to God, I have never really known the absolute feeling of it. And I'm feeling it now.

It's the way he's talking. Like it's the most natural thing in the world. Like he doesn't think I'll be shocked. Like . . . like . . . every person I know must be in one too.

For the record I don't know *anyone* who is in an open relationship. Well, apart from Mungo and Fionnula. The Skinny M and the Big F. And I'm kind of going off her now, laugh or no laugh. In fact she's a bit touchy-feely for my liking now, the more I think of it. God, you can really go off a person. D'you know what I mean?

Open relationship. Open relationship. Does that mean they are . . . ?

'Are you swingers?' I gasp, though I really didn't mean to say it out loud, and in such a Disgusted of Tunbridge Wells tone. Though I did.

He looks offended.

'Sorry,' I say, then rather feebly comment, 'This red chicken curry's gorgeous!'

'It's prawn,' he points out.

'It is!' I agree excitedly. 'But don't the really posh food critics say that truly good food always tastes like chicken? It's lovely. *Try some!*' I jab my fork across the table, splattering red curry sauce everywhere, and realize I'm trying to shut him up.

He practically pushes his chair back, squealing, 'I'm a *vegetarian!*'

Resisting the urge to say, 'But you eat other people's wives!'

121

I apologize profusely, telling him my head's all over the place, and that actually I'm really cool with open relationships and swinging, and how my mum and dad were naturists when I was growing up.

Which of course is a bare-faced lie.

Why did I say that? Why did I try to compensate for my embarrassment by lying?

But he is fascinated. Natch.

'And did you . . . ever . . . ?'

'No. *No*. No, never!' I respond quickly, with the tone of someone who as a child wore a protective plastic rain poncho to jump in the shower, and he looks disappointed.

'Alternative lifestyles can be so empowering,' he says, and I nod eagerly.

I change the subject to some worky stuff. Recently a boy has arrived at the school from Eritrea, Bashir, and has literally no English, even as a second, third or fourth language. I have been taking photos of different things in the school and sticking them in a book with him, then drawing arrows to various things in the photos and writing out the words for him, then practising saying them. I've really enjoyed it. Bashir just gives me a look as if to say, 'Back home I am a thirteen-year-old brain surgeon and you think I'll get excited by the phrase "'Biro' can also be called 'Pen'"?'

Bashir is living with an auntie near the school and I ask Mungo if there's any news on his mother, who is meant to be coming over to join them in London, but Mungo says there is not. He is the subject of a child protection investigation because the social workers think there's something dodgy about why he is here, and how capable the aunt is at looking after him, and of course the poor lad is stuck in the middle of it all, not having a clue what is going on because he's still learning words like 'book', 'door' and 'interactive whiteboard'. It's important that if Mungo knows any more about the situation than I do, he should tell me, because maybe there are more important things I should be telling him, like 'You're entitled to three meals a day and your own bed', but Mungo claims he doesn't.

Over Mungo's lemon soufflé he tells me he and the Big F practise tantric sex. He tells me this with all the dispassionate casualness of someone mentioning, in passing, that they have a membership to the local gym.

I am no longer shocked by anything that comes out of his mouth. Though the image that flashes through my mind of what Mungo and the Big F get up to – positions, settings – isn't the most palatable stuff I've thought of lately, I am intrigued. As he's banging on about base chakras and the all-over body orgasm, I wonder how you go about being – as he calls it – 'emotionally monogamous but sexually promiscuous'.

How does that happen when you have a ginger beard with bits in it, the figure of a pencil and the old sandals-socks combo?

It gives me hope. Because if he can get a shag, then surely I can too.

Dare I tell him? Dare I tell my manager that I fancy a bit of the old sexy time to help me move on from Michael? He's told me about his sexual proclivities, hasn't he? So why don't I own up to fancying a shag as well? It's not like I'm nailing my colours to the mast and asking if I can come to one of his and Fionnula's swinging parties, is it? In fact, I wouldn't be seen dead or naked at one of those. I'm only after a bit of intimacy, getting something out of my system, being held, being touched, doing completely normal things. I'm certainly not interested in having an audience while I'm doing it. An audience who I fear might press *Britain's Got Talent*-style buzzers in the middle of it all if they weren't impressed with your technique. I'm only after a bit of fun.

I picture myself saying, 'Mungo, I really fancy having some sex. I don't want to do the whole swinging scene, but . . . well, I really think it would help me get over Michael. Is there anything you can do to help?' Meaning 'What are the tips of someone who's no Rock Hudson but gets their end away on a regular basis?'

Unfortunately I can just imagine him nodding, thinking, then taking out his mobile and saying, 'Let me text Fionnula, see if she can come home late tonight so we can frig for hours.'

I most certainly don't want that.

And actually, come to think of it, if I do sleep with someone, I'd like to think they hadn't slept with twenty-eight women this week already, frankly. So maybe he's not the right person to be going to for advice.

I will keep my powder dry. I will keep my counsel. Deifying Mungo with the role of sex guru is definitely a no-no.

Images keep flashing into my head: Mungo on top of me, pumping away (and missing the point of entry thankfully) and me looking around his spare room, bored and embarrassed, and then seeing his sandals and socks neatly arranged on a chair.

I look at my watch and say I think we should be making tracks.

Mungo puts a different tape on for the journey home. Enya. Everything he does now I feel is loaded with sexual innuendo. I keep expecting him to say, 'I like to make my own sweet music to Enya. She's so . . . tantric,' as we're driving, but he doesn't. When I see he is wearing driving gloves (why did I not notice them before?), I imagine him explaining how he likes to take them off and whip his naughty ladies with them, but he doesn't say that either. And the way he manhandles that gearstick? Well, least said, soonest mended.

Bless him, he very kindly drops me off at my house, which is sweet of him. Just before I get out of the Noddy car, he looks at me earnestly. I fear he is going to say, 'Shall I . . . come in for a coffee and a hot-finger massage?'

Instead he says, 'Karen, I have been quite open with you today.'

'I bet you say that to all the girls!' I giggle, but he looks stung.

'And I really hope I can rely on you to be discreet. I . . . would really like what we discussed in the pub to remain just between us. Not everyone is as broad-minded as you or I.'

Bless him again, he's worried. I put my hand on his on the gearstick and coo reassuringly, 'Don't worry, Mungo. Your secret's safe with me. I won't tell a soul.'

He looks so relieved. I squeeze his hand. Anyone else, I'd kiss them, but I don't want him to get the wrong idea. I don't want his tongue to come poking out of that ginger beard. I scrabble around trying to open the door. Five minutes later I manage to get out of the car. I walk round to the pavement and look back at him. He's opening his window. Another five minutes later he says, 'Thanks, Karen. Our secret.'

'My lips are sealed.'

He smiles, like I've made a joke.

I quickly shoot my finger to my mouth. 'These lips!' I gasp.

He nods, and I head inside.

Then I'm on the phone.

'Meredith, you'll never guess what! Mungo and his wife are a pair of dirty old swingers!'

'*No!*'

'I know. Can you *believe* it?'

'Excuse me while I *throw up!*'

125

'I *know*!'

'Swingers?'

'Well, they have an open relationship.'

'How the hell d'you know this? What did you find? Did you go snooping in his office?'

'No! I didn't find anything. He told me to my *face*.'

And I tell her about our jaunt out to the pub where they sell cheap food.

'Oh my God, he was so coming on to you.'

'Meredith, *don't*.'

'Was there a motel nearby? Was it a pub with rooms?'

'Meredith, change the subject! I wish I'd never told you! Let's talk about something different.'

'Face it, Karen. You only called to tell me that tasty morsel of gossip. We have nothing else to talk about. Did his hand brush against you while he was changing gear?'

'No! I pushed myself up real tight by the door.'

'Did he run his fingers seductively through his beard?'

'No! Well, he might've done.'

'Did he pick food out of it and lick it in a suggestive manner?'

'No! I did that for him.'

I hear her shriek. And I shriek. And Mum comes through from the kitchen, wondering what high jinks she's missing out on. She gives me an unimpressed glare, then heads back to the kitchen, where I assume she is making herself something to eat.

Meredith gets over her hysteria and sighs, like it's taken it out of her, then says, 'Oh, Karen, you have *the* most infectious laugh.'

I giggle nervously. Because it sounds a bit weird. Because she may as well have said 'adorable' and not 'infectious'. It sounds almost like she's making lovable doe eyes at me.

Which is preposterous and terribly arrogant of me. Meredith is my friend. Jeez, do I think everyone's coming on to me right now? Mungo? Now Meredith? I need to get a grip.

So I do, and grab the bull by the horns.

'So anyway, when are you moving in with me?' I say, half joking but half serious. I need some bloody rent money!

'Oh, Karen, I've been thinking about that . . .' and her voice trails off.

OK, she hates East Ham. She hates my house. She hates me.

'. . . and isn't your place two bedrooms?'

'Aha? And your point is?'

'Well, either I have to jump in with your mother or you.'

Ah. Good point. I'd not thought about that. I'd forgotten that Mum doesn't just squirrel herself away under the stairs like a certain junior wizard each night. She does actually sleep in my spare room.

'Oh, yeah,' I say. 'Duh!'

'So . . . I mean, I'd like to, but . . .'

'No, I'd love you to too, but listen, let me talk to my mum. I'm sure it's time –' and here I lower my voice, cupping my hand over the receiver '– she moved on.'

'Oh. Well, if she's heading back up North . . .'

'She will be. I'll tell her tonight. I'll get her on her favourite subject, the rats in the loft . . .'

'They're back?'

'Allegedly. I've never heard them.'

'I don't want to be responsible for kicking her out.'

'Meredith, she doesn't pay rent. You will be. It's not me kicking her out; it's my bank manager.'

'Oh.' Meredith's voice is small with disappointment. 'I'll have to pay rent?'

And again we giggle. Me, of course, with my infectious laugh. When eventually we hang up, I look towards the kitchen and realize there's no time like the present. I will go and tell her now. I get as far as the kitchen door, then turn and run upstairs. I might do my nails first.

The computer's on in my bedroom, and I'm logged in to my school email system. As I paint my nails 'Morello Kiss', I hear the ping of some mail arriving. I blow on my fingers and read.

From: Kevin O'Keefe Kevok75@hotmail.co.uk
To: Karen Carpenter KCarpenter@fountainwoods.org.uk
Subject: Connor

Dear Karen,

Thank you so much for coming along after the funeral last week. It was good to see you. We both appreciated it, and were glad you made the time to drop by. Hope you managed to attend to whatever it was you had to head off for.

I have taken this week off work and brought Connor to visit some relatives at the seaside in Suffolk. I'm just letting you know that he will be returning to school on Tuesday, as we are scattering Toni's ashes into the Thames on Monday. (She loved water.)

I was wondering if I might come in and see you after school one day in a few weeks' time to check on how he is getting on. Between you and me, he is being a bit quiet and withdrawn at home, and although I'm sure that's to be expected, I just want to check how his behaviour is in school. I can come in at any time to suit you, as my hours are pretty flexible.

Hope all's well with you and that you're having a good week.
    All best,
        Kevin

Once my nails are dry, I ping one back.

From: Karen Carpenter KCarpenter@fountainwoods.org.uk
To: Kevin O'Keefe Kevok75@hotmail.co.uk
Subject: Re: Connor

Hi Kevin,
    Sure. I can do most days after school except Wednesdays, when I have a departmental meeting. I run Homework Club after school every day, but that is usually over by half four. Drop by anytime.
    Let me know what suits.
      All best,
        Karen

From: Kevin O'Keefe Kevok75@hotmail.co.uk
To: Karen Carpenter KCarpenter@fountainwoods.org.uk
Subject: Re: Re: Connor

Great. I'll come in Friday of next week, unless that messes up your plans for a debauched weekend.
    Kx

From: Karen Carpenter KCarpenter@fountainwoods.org.uk
To: Kevin O'Keefe Kevok75@hotmail.co.uk
Subject: Re: Re: Re: Connor

If you come to the special needs department, I'll be the one most likely tied to a chair amid the debris of a riot. I'll attach the details of my next of kin to my blouse.
    KC

Well, I could hardly put a kiss, could I?

From: Kevin O'Keefe Kevok75@hotmail.co.uk
To: Karen Carpenter KCarpenter@fountainwoods.org.uk
Subject: Re: Re: Re: Re: Connor

Total LOLZ! X

And there he was again, kissing me. How dare he!

From: Karen Carpenter KCarpenter@fountainwoods.org.uk
To: Kevin O'Keefe Kevok75@hotmail.co.uk
Subject: Re: Re: Re: Re: Re: Connor

Not sure what the head would make of a parent putting kisses
on an email to a teacher!
    KC

From: Kevin O'Keefe Kevok75@hotmail.co.uk
To: Karen Carpenter KCarpenter@fountainwoods.org.uk
Subject: Re: Re: Re: Re: Re: Re: Connor

WHOOPS!!! XX

I thought it best to leave it there.

ELEVEN

I am quite proud of the way I handle Connor's return to Fountain Woods. As he's coming back on Tuesday morning, I have a chat with the tutor group at afternoon registration on Monday about how he might be feeling. I ask them to imagine what he must be going through, which is a nice idea in my head but does result in some of the girls having a competitive crying competition, which kind of drowns out the rest of the discussion. Keisha-Vanessa is almost hyperventilating when I eventually tell her to shut up, as any fool can see she's attention-seeking. She gasps, 'My . . . mum's . . . my . . . best . . . friend!' before legging it from the classroom, never to be seen again.

At least it lets the rest of the group reflect on and come up with suggestions for how they might support Connor if they see him upset. These mostly involve the lads proposing they tell him to 'cheer up – your dad's next girlfriend might be a MILF', and the girls say they'll offer him cuddles and a read of their *Heat*. I suggest that if they see him in a state of distress, they should tell whichever teacher is taking them for that lesson.

'But what if it's in the playground, Miss?' asks Elizabeth, thrilled, it would appear, to be catching me out.

'Then tell whichever member of staff is on duty,' I reply. With the subtext of 'And now shut up.'

'Yeah, but what if all the members of staff have been annihilated by a passing gunman?'

'That's highly unlikely, Elizabeth.'

'No, Miss, yeah, 'cos it happened in America, yeah? I seen it on Channel 5 and that.'

A murmur of apprehension ripples round the class.

'Yes, well, it's not going to happen here, so there's no need to worry,' I confirm.

'Miss, is you, like, a psychic 'n' shiz?'

'No. I'm just thirty-six and know more about life than you.'

Elizabeth tuts her affront.

'And don't say "'n' shiz" to me.'

Which makes the rest of the class erupt into laughter, some of them flicking their fingers towards Elizabeth, shouting, 'Rinsed, man!'

'Yeah, 'lizbeth, you is *well* rinsed!'

'Shaaaame, 'lizbeth, 'n' shiz!'

Elizabeth drums her false nails on the desk, staring at the wall, trying not to let their mickey-taking get to her, which is when she utters, 'Everyone's proper screwing me up, bruv.'

'Elizabeth, nobody is screwing you up, least of all me. Now face the front and join in.'

But she doesn't.

One of the lads shouts, 'Do what Miss says, 'lizbeth!'

She spins round. 'Why? Miss is a bitch anyway.'

I then point out that false nails are not allowed in school and send her to the Student Support Centre. I call down to let them know she's on her way, though whether she'll actually turn up is anyone's guess.

*

132

Tuesday morning and I meet Connor in the foyer as he arrives, looking pretty cheery, it has to be said. I take him to my office before registration and give him a pep talk about strategies for coping now he's back in school. I tell him that everyone in his class is aware of what he's been through, and although they won't be intrusive (fingers crossed, though I don't say that out loud), they will be happy to let a member of staff know if he ever feels like some time out. He doesn't say much, does a bit of nodding, clutches the sports bag perched on his lap and occasionally looks out of the window.

I am just extolling the virtues of how lovely and under-standing all our staff are here at Fountain Woods, and how many of us have lost our parents (little white lie there. Some of the teachers, mentioning no names, would go to pieces if confronted by a grieving twelve-year-old boy, but a school cannot survive on touchy-feely alone. Some teachers 'need to be bastards to get the fuckers to work'. That's a quote from a colleague. I would never be so coarse. Yeah, right) when Connor interrupts me with, 'Miss, is my dad coming to see you this week?'

I shake my head. 'Not this week, but he'll be in at some point.'
'Why?'
'Well, he just wants to make sure you're OK.'
Connor takes this in, nodding.
'Is that all?'
This throws me.
'Well, yes, that is all. Why, what were you thinking of?'
Connor shrugs, then gets his phone out and starts playing on it.
'And that stays in your bag, right?'
He nods, and continues to text someone.
My work here is done.

As I head back to my tutor room, Ethleen is hovering near the door to the corridor.

'Oh, there you are, Karen,' she bleats nervously, still hovering, like she's unsure whether to come in or not, like a snobby, disapproving mother-in-law from a 1970s sitcom, unsure of your décor.

'Everything OK, Ethleen?'

And she takes the plunge. She comes in. I'm not sure what she's worried about catching in here. I like my tutor room. I took down that poster of Rihanna that Janet next door claimed was exploitative, didn't I?

Ethleen has a small piece of paper in her hand, which she offers to me. I take it.

'Any thoughts on this?'

I look at it. It takes a while to decipher.

Dear Mrs Burtterly
　　Yesterday my Keisha-Vanessa got told by her teacher Mrs Carpenters that they had to fink about mums dying. And when my Keisha-Vanessa starts crying Mrs Carpenters wen told her to shuyt the fuck up. My Keisha-Vanessa is now very very fick, what wit her nerves. I wish to make complain bout Mrs Carpenters. I aint fotgot how that place treat me when I was there. I wanna now what you gonna do bout it.
　　Shirelle Pepper

I groan, roll my eyes and explain. I imagine if Ethleen could rip the letter up and chuck it in the bin right now, she would, but it will have to be put on Keisha-Vanessa's file, with a copy of her response via letter and any log of phone calls made relating to the matter. A silly amount of paperwork just because someone somewhere along the line got the wrong end of the stick. And that person wasn't me. I know Keisha-Vanessa and Mrs Pepper will be invited into the school to discuss the incident with myself and Ethleen if Mrs Pepper (even thinking her name makes me want to sneeze) is unhappy with Ethleen's comeback. The dread washes over me like a hot flush and I have to sit down to get my breath back. Maybe this is my fault. Maybe I wasn't clear enough when explaining what I wanted the kids to do. Maybe Keisha-Vanessa is too young to grasp the concept of empathy.

Or maybe she's a spoilt brat whose illiterate mother believes every word she says and assumes she will always be in the right and Fountain Woods in the wrong. Opposing sides of a boxing ring, slugging it out to prove who has her daughter's best interests at heart. At moments like this I could give up.

After Ethleen has gone, I sit there stewing. It's then that Connor puts his head round the door and practically whispers, 'Are you OK, Miss?'

There's a catch in my voice as I tell him I'm fine. This boy's not stupid, though. This boy's witnessed and felt raw emotions recently. He knows I'm not. He walks to the filing cabinet in the corner of the room and opens the top drawer. He pulls out my 'emergency paper hankies', which are nestled next to the 'emergency pantyliners' (for the girls, not me), and offers me the box.

Gosh. I didn't even realize I was crying.

'Thanks, Connor,' I say as I pull out a couple and blow my nose.

'Life's shit sometimes, innit, Miss?' he says, far too worldly-wise for his years.

I chuckle softly. 'Oh, you got that right, Connor O'Keefe,' I say, then reach out and ruffle his hair. 'Life is shit all right.'

He nods.

'But you didn't hear me say that.' I wink.

And he winks back.

I coast through the day on a cloud of detachment, my mind elsewhere, which is not a great idea when you're in charge of children. Fortunately today I spend most of my time supporting other teachers in their classrooms, sitting with the slower kids, helping them with their spelling.

The irritating letter from Mrs Pepper has annoyed me and thrown me because it has reminded me that we all make mistakes, that life has a habit of coming along and slapping you round the face when you thought you were only trying to do something good, something right. And of course it reminds me of Michael.

Not only that he has left me, but that he hasn't replied to my card. Every time the phone has rung, every time an email has popped into my inbox, every time there's been a knock at the door, every time the postman has dropped the mail through the letter box, every time a text has pinged through on my phone, I've been hopeful, then disappointed. It leaves me feeling vulnerable. Almost as vulnerable as the time when he first disappeared. Which is how it feels. He is a missing person, vanished from my life, with no 'why's or 'wherefore's as to why or where he has gone. Am I that awful? Am I such a monster that that is all I deserve? I've always been strong in my opinion that I am worth more than that, but as the days grew into weeks, and now almost months . . . well, I'm not so sure.

Is it because I've let myself go? I'm not exactly tipping the scales at twenty stone, but I'm heavier than when we first got together. That's natural, though, isn't it? I'm twenty years older, for goodness' sake. Which thirty-six-year-old looks like the sixteen-year-old they were? Nobody. Even people who've been lifted and Botoxed and peeled and waxed and pulled hither and thither look nothing like their youthful selves. They just look like Joan Rivers.

Is it because I got boring? Somewhere along the way did I lose my sense of humour? My zest for life? Is it because I once used to get pissed with Michael and dance naked with him in the back garden as the rain fell at midnight, and lately all I talked to him about was grouting? Or what he wanted for tea? Or why he couldn't make his own fucking tea as he wasn't the only one who'd been out at work all day? Did I start off unique and become a cliché?

Did I become sexually unadventurous? Probably. But then so did he. Gone are the days when we would make love with spontaneity. In a graveyard; in that abandoned Tube station. (Yes, that is what we ended up doing.) Am I just dull? Or is it because I was too wrapped up in myself to hear his cries for help as he clung to the sinking wreck of our relationship, waves surrounding us? I've certainly been wrapped up in myself since he left. Maybe I was like that before and that's why he went. Was I just living in my head and not in the real world? Had I made myself invisible to him?

He wanted a dog at one point. I said we couldn't because we were both out at work every day. He took me to Battersea Dogs Home and we spent hours looking at the quivering, matted wrecks behind bars. It broke my heart, but I remained resolute. Maybe there wasn't a heart there in the first place. Maybe I was – and am – just a heartless bitch.

I knew why he wanted a dog, though. It was because of Evie.

My breath catches even now when I say the name to myself. Evie. I told him this at the time and he disagreed. Maybe it wasn't about her. Maybe he just did, in fact, want a dog. I knew, though, in my heart of hearts.

I don't want to think about Evie. Which is terrible. But I can't. Not now. Surely I must have some marking to do. Surely there is something to distract me. School is such a wonderful distraction from my thoughts and feelings. But on the journey home, and then being home, there is less to take my mind off . . . well . . . me.

I know. I'll go downstairs. I'll go and tell Mum I want Meredith to move in and for her to move out. She'll be fine. She's been here ages. She'll understand.

I head downstairs. She's in the living room, watching *The One Show*. I come in, sit on the couch and look at her. She looks over and smiles.

'Mum, I've got something to tell you.'

'What is it, love?' she asked, head tilted to one side. She knew something was up, as Michael and I didn't come back to Liverpool that often and had suddenly arrived for the weekend with scant warning.

We were sat on her couch and she and Dad were sitting on the matching armchairs either side, the telly blaring between us.

'Turn that off, Vern. Is everything OK?'

As Dad fussed with the remote, at first turning it up to a deafening full pelt, which resulted in Mum throwing a cushion at him and screaming, 'Vernon!' he soon muted it and they looked at us again.

I turned to Michael. 'Will you tell them, or will I?'

'You,' said Michael, taking my hand. 'I wanna tell my ma and da.'

Mum's eyes lit up. She knew what was coming now.

'You're getting married!'

'No!' I gasped, horrified.

'You are *married! Oh God, Vern, they did it on that beach in Cornwall in the summer and never told us. I knew something like this had happened. You've been ever so wary with me on the phone lately.'*

'I'm pregnant,' I said, and waited. Waited for the champagne to come out, for party poppers to go off, for Mum to jump up and hug me.

Instead she looked dumbstruck, and it was not like Val Carpenter, former ventriloquist, to be lost for words.

'Beg pardon?' she said.

'She's pregnant, woman. What are you, deaf as well as soft?' Dad snarled at her.

'I heard full well what she said, Vernon. I just can't quite believe what she's telling me.'

They were now looking at each other as if we weren't even in the room.

'Well, I'm made up for her,' said Dad, 'for the pair o' them.'

'Thanks, Dad,' I pushed in, trying to take the reins back in the conversation, but it was no good.

'Well, you would be, but personally I'm mortified,' Mum said, then returned to her knitting.

'And why's that exactly?' went Dad.

Mum looked up from her knitting. 'Take. A. Wild. Guess.'

'Val, this is good news,' Michael said.

God, he sounded nervous.

'Let me tell you one thing about this family, Michael,' Mum said, not looking up from some very passive-aggressive cast-one-on-ing. 'There has never – till now – been a baby born out of wedlock.'

'*Valerie!*' screeched Dad. '*It's 2001. We're in a new millenni-thingy.*'

'*And your point is?*'

'*Jeez, you'd test the patience of a saint, you.*'

'*I see no saints here, kid, only sinners.*'

The pair of them. The pair of them still hadn't looked at us.

'*Val, we do love each other. This baby's gonna be born into a dead loving family,*' Michael pointed out, and he did indeed have a point. As an extra flourish he added, '*I love Karen, and Karen loves me.*'

Mum looked at him. '*Then marry her.*'

Michael gulped, then looked at me, panic in his eyes. I rolled mine.

'*Shall we go and tell your mum and dad?*'

He nodded. We stood. I looked down at Mum, furiously clacking her needles together like she was getting some coded message through to the French Resistance in the war.

'*I just want you to be happy for me, Mum.*'

She harrumphed. It was very annoying when my mother harrumphed.

'*I want, Karen, doesn't get.*'

I sighed.

'*I'm made up, love,*' said Dad, looking the epitome of apologetic.

'*Thanks, Dad. We'll see you later.*'

As we headed out of the house, we could hear raised voices, and Dad calling Mum an 'old-fashioned bitch'. We then heard what sounded like a load of knitting been thrown at a middle-aged man, but I could've been wrong.

'So, let me get this straight . . .'

'Aha?'

'You want me to move out so you can move your little lesbian friend in?'

'That's right. Lesbian, not lebian.'

'Eh?'

'Nothing. 'Cos . . . well . . . 'cos I need the rent. That's all.'

'It's at times like this,' says Mum, eyes ablaze, 'that I wish I didn't have crippling arthritis.'

I nod, knowing what's coming.

''Cos at times like this I don't half wish I could knit.'

Which I take to mean her saying, 'Over my dead body.'

TWELVE

I am feeling confused. No change there, then. Putting my disappointment/heartache/heartbreak/balls-aching irritation – whatever you want to call it – with Michael to one side, there are far too many other things buzzing round in my brain and I'm not doing anything proactive to sort them out. With my teacherly head on, I decide to write it all down, so I create a sort of checklist in a new document on my laptop and call it 'The List'.

The List

- Mum won't move out and I want Meredith to move in. Plan of action: talk to Dad; get him to make her see sense. She is now threatening my time in this house. *V. important.*

- Mungo has told me he is in an OR but has since acted all embarrassed in front of me. Plan of action: tell him what happens in the pub, stays in the pub.

- Wendy. Must call back. She often says I never call, so must remedy. Plan of action: call her tonight.

- I want to have sex. Plan of action: join one of those websites. Eurgh.

- Kevin is coming in a week on Friday. I'm not sure why this is bothering me. Well, I do know, but I don't want to think about it. Plan of action: get over it. He's just Connor's dad, and the meeting is important for Connor.

- Call Rita. Plan of action: do I have to? Yes. Soon. She might not have heard from Michael either and could be going out of her mind, though she might tell me he's moved in with Asmaa and I don't want to know.

- Rats in loft?! Plan of action: call Rentokil. Or go into loft. Or ignore. Mum has overactive imagination.

'Hiya, Dad!' I'm full of the joys on the phone, as we've not actually spoken for ages. I'm a bit worried he's not going to be keen on Mum returning to Liverpool, as I imagine he's having a much calmer time of it with her down here moaning at me instead of him. I'm in the bedroom while Mum is out at Zumba.

'Karen, love, how are you? Mum said you're still very, very low.'

'Oh, I'm OK.'

'Karen, you don't have to put on a brave face with me.'

'No, I am, I'm fine.'

'Karen!'

'What?'

'Mum told me.'

'About what?'

'About your . . . dark thoughts.'

'I've been having dark thoughts?'

'You know, and don't think I haven't been there too. Jeez, I've been married to your mother for nearly forty years, but, you know, suicide's shite.'

'I beg your pardon?'

'Topping yourself. Wanting to end it. We all fancy it at some point, but . . . well, you just need to give yourself a talking-to.'

'I don't know what you're on about.'

'You need to sit down, in a quietened room, and think of all the positive things you've got going for you. We could do it now if you want. Have you got a pen?'

'Dad, do you think I'm suicidal?'

'Well, yes.'

'Well, why?'

'Well, 'cos your mum told me.'

'Right.'

'As I say, love, don't be embarrassed. It's nothing to be ashamed of. Mental illness affects something like one in five people. I Googled it. I mean, look at Michael . . .'

Whoa, whoa, whoa, whoa a minute. Mental health issues? Me?!

'What exactly has Mum been saying?'

'Look, she wasn't gonna tell me. I know you swore her to secrecy, but I'm your dad, babe. I love the bones of you.'

Secrecy?

'I made her tell me. I was pissed off that she hadn't come back yet. I told her you've got to learn to stand on your own two feet. And I miss her. It's not good for our relationship, her being away. I was saying all this . . . Oh, don't feel guilty. I'm not arsed really.' He was backtracking now. 'Which is when she explained why it was a bit impossible for her to come back just yet, 'cos of . . . your predicament.'

'I'm not suicidal, Dad.'

'Well, I'm made up for you, love. I'm buzzing you've turned a corner.'

'I never was suicidal, Dad.'

144

'That's the spirit, Karen. Fighting fit. Say it often enough and it comes true.'

'No, I swear on my mother's life. I've not once wanted to kill myself.'

There was a silence on the other end of the phone.

'Your mum said you were like this – in denial about it. I can't say I totally understand it, but I just want you to know it's OK.'

'No, Dad. I'm being serious. Mum's been lying to you.'

'You what?'

'I'm fed up, depressed probably, but only 'cos Michael's buggered off, and that's it really. I don't think my life is over. Well, I do, but only 'cos I'm single and starting again at thirty-six. Not 'cos I wanna slash my wrists or anything. I can't believe she's said this to you.'

'Right.'

'And anyway, if you thought I was mentally ill and thinking of topping myself every five minutes, why didn't you come and visit me? Pick up the phone?'

'Mum said I wasn't to. She said she was dealing with it and to leave you be. Said you'd be mortified if you realized what a fuss it was all creating.'

'I don't know about killing myself, Dad,' I say, 'but at the moment I could willingly kill her.'

'Put her on. I wanna speak to her.' He's sounding furious now.

'She's not here.'

'Shit. Is she coming home?'

'No, she's at Zumba.'

'Y'what?'

'It's like a fusion of keep-fit and dance, I think. Well, that's her description.'

'But I thought she was on round-the-clock suicide watch

with you. Oh, for frig's sake, this is taking the piss, this is. And you're not lying to me?'

'I'm not, no,' I say, with the emphasis on the 'I', meaning someone is and it's not me.

'Dad, she's living the life of Riley down here – out at her classes every evening and then sitting up half the night watching *Borgen* or *The Killing* or *The Bridge*. Give her a subtitle and some Scandinavian knitwear and she's in her fucking element.'

I have never sworn to my dad before and I hope it shows him I'm not inventing any of this. I am incandescent. I cannot believe that my mother – *my mother* – has lied and said I've tried to commit suicide just because she doesn't want to go home and see my dad. Well, that's it – my mind's made up. She is leaving this house as soon as she gets back.

I tell Dad about Meredith wanting to move in, and me wanting her to move in because in the long term I am fearful about keeping up with my mortgage repayments. Dad says it makes complete sense to him and wonders why Mum is so reluctant to return home.

I fantasize about colouring my wrists and neck with ketchup and lying in a pool of my own urine in the kitchen, just to shock her when she gets in later, but I really can't be that mercenary. And I really can't be that arsed.

By the time I come off the phone we have a plan. My poor Dad should not have to be lied to like that. He was clearly very worried about me, but felt he couldn't pick up the phone to see how I was because of Mum's barmy manipulations. And poor me for being tarred with the brush of mental illness – untruthfully – just because Mum's got it cushty in East Ham.

No wonder I made out to everyone that she was dead all those years ago. It was clearly wishful thinking. I spent a childhood mortified by her showing me up, and now I'm to spend my adulthood mortified by her telling everyone I'm going mad? This won't do. This reeeeally won't do.

I toy again with the 'pretending to have killed myself' routine for when she gets back in and decide against it. I've never forgotten that time she and Dad left me with a babysitter while they went out for dinner. I must have been about eight and my babysitter, Bernie from down the road (who can only have been about fourteen), decided it would be really funny to tie me to the rocking chair in the lounge just before they got back from dinner. I too found it unfeasibly hilarious, so when my poor mum and dad walked in, they were greeted by the sight of me rocking backwards and forwards in the rocking chair, tied up, my mouth gagged with a tea towel, sobbing hysterically and screaming, 'Help! Help!'

I have to say I have never seen two more shocked people in my entire life. At the time I thought they were real killjoys for not finding it funny, and sending me to bed early, and phoning Bernie's mum and getting her grounded. Now that I'm older, I completely get that they were acting in shock, and with Mum's advancing years, maybe it's best not to recreate the suicide version of that tonight.

I do, however, go for the softer option. I am determined to ruffle her double-crossing feathers.

By the time she comes back, I am sitting at the kitchen table, a bottle of paracetamol in my hand. I'm staring at it like I haven't known she's come in. I hear her coat coming off in the hall. I hear two Uggs being kicked off – the second harder to remove than the first. I hear the jingle of bangles increasing in volume. Val Carpenter (*sans* Cheeky the Liverpool Bear) is in the building. Actually, she's in the kitchen, staring at me.

'What you doing, Karen?'

'Nothing,' I reply slowly and vacantly. I'm trying to sound like a zombie in a movie. I'm trying to be otherworldly.

'What are they?' She has frozen in the doorway.

I quickly put the pills in the pocket of my cardigan. 'Nothing.'

'What d'you fancy for your tea?'

Mum walks past me and opens the freezer. It's now that I notice her blouse is on inside out. Bless her, was she rushing back to see me?

'I got a lasagne the other day. Thought we could have that with some steamed spinach.'

Oh. This isn't working. She doesn't seem that fussed that just moments ago her only child was sat staring longingly at a tub of pills. Thanks, Mum. So as she fusses around in the fridge, I blurt out, 'Death . . . is the final frontier!'

Mum turns and looks, confused. 'Isn't that space?'

'Who cares . . . when you're clinically depressed?'

'Have you had a drink, Karen?'

'I've never felt more clear-headed in my life.'

Now Mum isn't looking worried, particularly, more quizzical. 'What's going on, Karen?'

I give up. 'I was trying to make out I fancied killing myself.'

'Why?'

'To shock you.'

'Why would you wanna do that?'

'Because I spoke to Dad.'

She gasps. 'I told him not to ring here.'

'I know. He told me.'

She pales. She looks more shocked, come to think of it, than when she found me tied up in the rocking chair all those years ago. Her legs seem to go weak and she lowers herself into the kitchen chair next to mine.

'Oh God,' she groans. 'So he knows?'

I nod. 'Why did you lie to him, Mum? It makes me feel weird. It makes me feel . . . I don't know. Telling lies about me like that, it's . . .'

'Not as bad as when you told your whole class I'd died in a freak tornado at Rhyl Sun Centre.'

'I was about ten. You're fifty-eight.'

'Next birthday!' she says quickly. 'Next birthday,' she repeats, softer now.

'I know things haven't been easy for me, Mum, and I'm dead grateful you came and stayed, but I want Meredith to move in now. I need the rent money or else I'll be homeless.'

Mum nods. Her eyes are miles away. Is she realizing how much she has hurt me?

'I'll go tonight,' she says, nodding more, as if she's had a bit of a convo with herself and this is the decision she and her eighteen other personalities have come to.

'Why have you been putting off the inevitable, Mum?'

'The inevitable?'

'Going home to Dad. I think he's really upset now he knows you've been telling porkies.'

Mum starts chewing her bottom lip. It's quite a babyish move and doesn't suit her.

'I've never once been suicidal.'

She doesn't look too sure. 'I see it more than you.'

'Mum, I think I'd know. Suicidal thoughts, they go on in your head. You don't . . . wear them like clothes, for other folk to clock.'

She looks at me. 'I'm sorry I lied to you, Karen, and I'm sorry I lied to your dad.'

'Well, you haven't really lied to me, so . . .'

'No, I have. Quite a bit, actually. See, I don't really go to Zumba.'

'Your top's inside out.'

'Is it?' She looks. 'So it is.'

'So you've obviously got changed for something.'

She nods. 'Jorgen.'

This throws me.

'*Borgen*?' I ask.

'No, not *Borgen*, Jorgen.'

'But isn't that programme you watch called *Borgen*?'

Mum nods. 'But Jorgen's the reason I watched *Borgen* in the first place.'

'Jorgen's your reason for *Borgen*?'

She nods.

'And who the hell is Borgen?'

'Jorgen!'

'Jorgen.'

'Jorgen . . . is my lover. That's why I don't want to go back to Liverpool. That's why I've stayed so long.'

Oh. I'm a bit hurt by that, actually. She's not been here keeping an eye on me. She's been here because she's been going off for secret assignations with this Jorgen Borgen every Friday *morgen*. Well, every day, actually, though I am quite proud of my rhyme.

Hang about. My mother is seeing someone? *Seeing* someone? Oh. My. God.

She is *seeing* someone.

'Where does he live?'

'Royal Docks. Beckton. I go over on the Docklands Light Railway.'

'How old is he?'

'Age isn't important, Karen.'

I give her a steely look.

'He's thirty-five.'

'He's *thirty-five*? He's younger than me? How did you meet?'

'Online. A website – silvermummies.com.'

I think I have just about heard it all now.

'How long ago?'

'Dunno. Six months? Bit longer?'

'You knew him before Michael . . .'

'Yes. Karen, don't make this about you. I did want to see you were OK. You've been through a terrible thing, a massive shock, but I'd be lying if I didn't say my main reason for being here has been to see sweet Jorgen.'

'Sweet Jorgen?'

She nods, and stands, and touches my shoulder. 'I'll go and pack.'

I nod. She leaves the room. I sit there, and the only thing I can think is . . .

For God's sake, even my *mum* is getting more sex than me.

I am incredulous. Silvermummies.com? I dread to think.

I feel awful. I feel awkward. I want her to go, but I feel bad about making her go back to Dad now, when she hasn't really worked out what she wants, I assume. I trot upstairs and try and do some light-hearted damage limitation, helping her pack, telling her how grateful I am for her being here when I needed it. Even if most of the time she was getting her end away with her very own slice of Danish bacon.

'You could . . . tell Dad I really am mad, if that helps. Then he won't suspect.'

And she freezes with a mauve cardigan, not dropping it into her case. 'Your dad?'

I nod. 'Yes. When you go home. You can tell him I was completely mental. I could phone him now and say I've . . . I've . . . been sectioned, if you like. Then he won't suspect a thing.'

'Karen, I'm not going back to Liverpool. I'm not going back to your dad. When I leave here, I'm going to stay with Jorgen.'

'And what will you tell my dad?'

'I don't know. I've not decided yet.'

'Well, what do I tell him, if he rings here?'

She shrugs. 'Tell him I've gone to stay with Auntie Doreen in Chadwell Heath if you like.'

'But Mum!'

She drops the cardy into the case now. Finally. 'What?'

'That means I've got to lie to him.'

'Well, by all means tell him the truth, if that makes you happy.'

'Making Dad unhappy isn't really where I get my kicks. Unlike some.'

Mum looks at me. 'And what about my happiness? What about me, Karen?'

'I think you take care of that just fine as it is, actually, Mum.'

'If we learned anything from what happened with Michael, it's that life's too short. If you're unhappy, get out. It's never, ever too late to start again.'

I am flummoxed and amazed.

'So what, y-you're leaving my dad?' I gabber, incredulous.

'Karen, I've been living in London for the best part of two months now. This shouldn't be front-page news to you.'

At the doorstep she tells me she's very proud of how I've coped. She tells me she'll call every day, and she reiterates her hope that I'm not a rug-munching lezzer. Then she heads off into the night and I suddenly feel hollow.

Why is life full of all these surprises? I think I've just about got a handle on things and then fate turns round and slaps me in the face and tells me to think a-bloody-gain.

Which I am now having to do.

I just can't ring my dad, much as I'm tempted. It's not up to me to tell him Mum's with a Danish bloke who's *even younger than me*. That's her call. What if it doesn't last? She might go back to Dad and I'd have caused him all that pain for nothing.

I go and run a bath, but don't check the temperature of the water. When I dip my hand in to test it, it's freezing. With Mum's departure, the boiler has gone again.

Oh well, maybe Meredith can mend it. I bet she's really practical around the house.

I call her.

She moves in the next night.

A postcard arrives on Thursday morning.

> Dear Kagsy,
> Sorry for the radio silence. I'm in Canada!! At the last minute my boss asked me to go with her to the Banff TV Festival, so I'm here in the Rockies! And, oh my God, it's gorgeous! And guess what! I've met someone! He's gorgeous and funny and daft and . . . did I mention gorgeous? And loaded? Well, he's not loaded, but he works. So he has an income. So he sometimes picks up the tab for dinner. He works in telly too (met at Fest), so we've stayed on for a few more days to take in the sights. Back next week. Hope you meet him soon. Sorry if you've been ringing non-stop. Phone fucked so have new number. ARRRGGHH!
> Love you,
> Wendy xxx

Even Wendy has a boyfriend. Appears everyone's having a great time except me. And my dad. And Meredith.

Though to be fair, Meredith and I are having a laugh living together, and she has a car, which means I now get a lift to school and it doesn't take half as long as I thought it would. So I can arrive a lot less hassled and take more things than I need to school if I fancy it.

She makes a really healthy breakfast in the morning of porridge (her own recipe) and blueberries, and some sort of weird shakey smoothie thing, so maybe I'll start being a little healthier now too.

She does marking till about nine each night and then we watch telly for an hour or so, bitching about anyone who comes onscreen, making each other laugh.

Life, for the time being, is sweet.

I feel I should phone my dad, though. At least to see he's OK. I know I will have to lie and break it to him gently that Mum has 'gone to stay with Auntie Doreen in Chadwell Heath', but it's her lie, not mine. I will word it in such a way that I can tell myself I'm being honest: 'She says she's gone to Auntie Doreen's. Why don't you ring her mobile?'

That kind of thing.

I pick up the landline in my bedroom, which is when I realize Meredith's already using the phone downstairs. She doesn't realize I'm listening in. And I'm not. I've every intention of putting the receiver down, but then I hear her say, 'Oh, she's definitely giving me the come-on, mate.'

I hear another woman, on the other end of the phone, doing a kind of 'put out' harrumph. I wonder which one of Dee, Dozy, Beaky, Mitch or Titch it might be.

'But I thought she was straight.'

'She is straight,' says Meredith, 'but so's spaghetti till you boil it.'

I freeze.

'She's all over me like a rash. I'm not blind. I can read the signs. And, oh yeah, we might just be acting like best mates now, but you watch. I give it a week. She's putty in my hands.'

Another harrumph on the end of the line.

I feel like harrumphing myself. Loudly. But instead I gently replace the receiver.

And then seethe.

And seethe some more.

Meredith clearly thinks I'm going to be her next girlfriend. I am her spaghetti in human form, or so she thinks.

And in case you were under any misapprehensions, I have nothing in common with spaghetti, or anything else that stops being straight at some point in its life and turns into something else. Something lebian.

Oh *God*. What have I let myself in for?

THIRTEEN

OK, so I've made a bit of a boo-boo. I have invited into my house someone who fancies me and, what's more, is misreading signs that I fancy her. This could be mortifying, except for the one bit of light at the end of the tunnel, which is this: I will never sleep with her. So it's fine really, although I'm currently spending an inordinate amount of time fretting about what exactly it is I've done and which particular behaviours I've displayed that have led Meredith to the conviction that this lady is for turning.

Was it something I did the day we stayed in watching *Mildred Pierce*? We sat pretty close on the settee. Did I unknowingly rub my thigh against hers? Or was it the fact that I was talking about my pegunda? Surely that wouldn't be seen as a come-on, would it? It certainly wouldn't be my first choice of conversation if I went on a date.

'Yup, I'll have the steak Diane and then I simply *have* to tell you about my hairy/hairless pegunda.'

No, that's not my style, and I doubt the morals and integrity of women for whom it would be.

Is it something to do with the way we've been getting on so well? Which we have, I've got to be honest. But I've not noticed her being especially flirty, and I certainly haven't been playing with my hair and sending out telepathic love vibes about wishing I could experience the delights of love in the old-fashioned sapphic way.

Maybe it's the T-shirt I wore last week, with the words 'Make me your bitch, Meredith!'

Actually, I made that up. I don't own such a T-shirt. I'm just at a complete loss as to what it is I might have done that has led her on. And in the absence of any such thang – yes, thang – I decide that I am now living with a lesbian – sorry, lebian – version of Annie Wilkes from *Misery*. I fear that any day now she is going to pounce. Let's just hope there's not a sudden snowstorm and we're cut off from the outside world and she breaks my leg with a hammer and starves me to death until I sign official documents that say I will live as a lebian with her for the rest of my life.

I wish I could talk to Wendy about it, but Wendy has joined that club that everyone else has joined bar me – the Loved-Up Club. And when you're a new member of the Loved-Up Club, nobody else matters.

I can't discuss it with Mum because a) she's in the Loved-Up Club (Danish branch) for the time being, and b) she'd more than likely say something along the lines of 'I told you so.' Which she didn't exactly, but she did seem to be of the opinion 'Where there's lesbians, there's trouble.'

I can't tell anyone at school because they all know Meredith and she's a popular member of staff, and they might be of the opinion that as a newly single nearly middle-aged person, I should maybe, just maybe, throw caution to the wind and embark on a relationship with her as she is so fantastic. She *is* fantastic. I really do like her. I just don't want to have to explore her pegunda, thank you very much. If I am, let's say, going to kiss someone, I want to feel stubble on their face. I'm not into rough sex (although I have to say, I've not really tried it), but I think the roughness of a man's body against a woman's is what I enjoy physically about sex. I'm sure I'm more than capable of developing a crush on a woman, but more than that – actually falling in love and holding hands and finding everything they do completely adorable to the point where you want to take off all their clothes because you're going to find every single inch of them as adorable as their personality – well, I completely get that with blokes, but not with women. And that doesn't make me weird; it makes me heterosexual.

I know what Wendy would say, if I could get hold of her. She'd tell me to sit down with Meredith and talk to her about it – explain gently that I really like her as a friend, but that I am straight to the core and there's no chance of us being anything other than friends. She would probably tell me to throw in the line 'Look, if I was going to sleep with a woman, it would be you, but I'm straight, Meredith, honest to God.' Then I tell myself that a line like that might offer up false hope.

I also know, in the absence of Wendy or not, I will probably never have that conversation with Meredith anyway, as I would find it the height of mortification, and so I decide on a plan of action for how to deal with the situation. I will not *tell* her I don't fancy her. I will *show* her.

And how will I show her?

Well, not, as you might imagine, by vomiting profusely every time I see her and going, 'Oh my God, you repulse me. I'm so glad I'm not a lebian/lesbian.' Or by throwing bricks at the telly every time Sophie comes on in *Coronation Street* and going, 'God, the thought of it knocks me sick. Did you get that, Meredith? Lebianism/lesbianism repulses me.'

I wouldn't be that crass.

Instead I will demonstrate my lack of interest in Meredith by completely avoiding her as much as is humanly possible.

Result!

I put this plan into action by getting up early each morning to go to the gym. (Meredith is impressed. Oh God, I hope she doesn't think I am doing this for her benefit – trying to be like her and get all sporty and wear trainers.) I love my local gym because it's got a really good Jacuzzi. So I go down there, slip into my swimsuit, do three lengths of the pool and then have half an hour in the Jacuzzi watching the breakfast news. I go straight from the gym to school; then after school I have decided I am going to go to the pictures each night. So actually I am turning Meredith's obsession with me to my own advantage. I am going to get healthy (Jacuzzis have got to be healthy. Healthier than sitting drinking in a pub anyway) and cultured (as movies expand the mind). In fact this whole Meredith thing could be the making of me.

At Wednesday's departmental meeting I decide to tackle the fact that I think Mungo is mildly embarrassed about his revelations the other week.

'Mungo?' I say tentatively, as we read through a report that Bashir's social worker has written on what she has discovered at his auntie's place. 'I just want to say . . . what we discussed . . . I don't want you to be embarrassed about what you told me, and I haven't told a soul.'

Liar, liar, pants on fire.

He nods. 'I knew I could trust you, Karen.'

'Well, I'm very hard to shock.'

Again, drench my flaming pantaloons with a 1970s soda siphon. I lie!

'Actually, I was telling Fionnula we'd . . . talked and she was wondering if you were free this weekend to come over for a spot of supper. She makes an amazing spinach pie.'

Spinach pie. Heavens.

'Just us and a couple of pals from Woking.'

Woking. Heavens.

'It'd be really relaxed.'

There's something about the way he says 'really relaxed' that has me imagining Demis Roussos on the stereo, a bunch of car keys in a bowl on the coffee table and the hands of strangers creeping up my inner thigh.

'Oh God, that sounds really nice,' I say, with disappointment in my voice as I continue, 'but I'm a bit tied up this weekend.'

Doing precisely nothing.

'Well, the weekend after, then.'

'You have spinach pie two weekends on the trot?' I say. Why, I had no idea.

But Mungo nods. 'Every Saturday. It's a date, then?'

I gulp and nod. I can't get out of it.

Though a week on Saturday I might just develop a bout of twenty-four-hour flu.

'Can't wait!'

I must, I really must do something about joining one of those sexy websites, or even a dating website. Then, a week on Saturday, I might have a viable alternative to joining in with Mungo and Fionnula's unorthodox lifestyle, I tell myself as I wolf down some muesli on Friday morning. It's ten past six and I'm whacked already. These early starts to avoid Meredith are really catching up with me. Still, I'll be in my favourite Jacuzzi in about twenty minutes. It'll be worth it then.

I just hope I can stay awake long enough for Homework Club tonight, and then the arrival of Kevin, who emailed last night to say he's coming in today for his little chat. I have decided I am not going to go to any trouble by dressing up for him. It's not a date, I no longer fancy him, thanks to his man-slutty tendencies, and actually, he'll probably only be with me for about a zillionth of a second, as Connor appears to have been getting on just fine since his return to school. So, all being well, I'll be able to go to the pictures tonight and then maybe on to an Internet café, where I can set up a profile on www. DoMeNowButDontExpectARelationshipOutOfItCosImOnly InItToGetOverMyEx.com.

It's windy out, rain is pouring, and I remember that today's the day the bin men come. I toy with leaving a note for Meredith (still asleep) saying, 'Please put the bins out,' but she might misinterpret that, thinking what I actually meant to write was, 'Please put the bins out and I'll put out for you tonight,' or some such. So I drag the recycling and normal waste out of their bins in the kitchen, tie them up and head out the front door, where our big army-green Newham council bins sit like cubist plastic hedges before each door.

As I come back in, a gust of wind from the open door shoots down the hallway and various bits of collected dust – that I've not hoovered up – jump into the air. Anything that's not tied down flutters around. It's quite a magical sight, actually, and I leave the door open as I stand there watching the dance. Eventually I close it, and I feel like some mystical witch, walking through the house as the detritus of my life flaps around me, then – as quickly as it started – suddenly settles down.

In the kitchen a receipt-sized piece of paper has landed on the table. I pick it up to inspect it, in case it's something I need to hang on to.

And I get a shock.

Actually, I get the shock of my life.

This is what the paper looks like:

MONDAY TO FRIDAY	302		
B/on	0646	B/off	1505

Train 47

STRD, W	0710
OC	0731
WC	0745
WR	0807

Train 35

WR	1402
WC	1424
OC	1438
STRD	1459

I check the date on it and feel sick. It has last week's date on it.

I sit at the kitchen table and reread it. The paper trembles in my hand as I take in what it means.

I know what 'STRD, W' stands for. It stands for 'Stratford Depot, westbound'. I know what this is. It's a Tube driver's weekly roster. Michael is driver 302. This is his roster, and it is his roster from last week, and it is in my house, and I have no idea why. I have no idea how it came to be here. I recheck the date and make sure it's not from this time last year, but no, it's this year's. How did it come to be here? It makes no sense.

The only explanation I can come up with, and it's one that makes my heart pound in my chest, is that Michael has been in this house in the last week.

He has a key – it would be easy enough for him to let himself in when I wasn't here – and thinking about it, the house is empty every day between half seven in the morning and, say, five in the evening. That's a lot of hours.

Has Michael been back? He must have been. How else would his roster have made it into my kitchen? But what has he been doing here? Maybe he has been getting clothes. I'm so lost in thought I don't hear Meredith coming down the stairs and into the kitchen. I quickly put the roster in my pocket.

'Hello, stranger! How's you?'

I nod. 'Good, thanks. Just off to the gym.'

'Good for you. Hey, d'you know what?'

'What?' I look at her, feigning interest.

'I think your mum might be right. I think you might have rats or something in the loft. Heard some scratching last night.'

I tell her I'll look into it tonight. For now I have bigger things to worry about, so head on out to the gym.

All day long my mind keeps returning to the roster in my pocket and the various scenarios I am coming up with for Michael returning to the house. If only Meredith hadn't come down when she did, I might have nipped upstairs and taken a look in the wardrobe. I bet some of his clothes are missing. I wonder if anything else has gone. I try and work out ways to trap him, next time he returns. Maybe he sits down the road, at a lookout, waiting till I've gone to work. Maybe I need to go out of the front of the house, walk down the street as if nothing is out of the ordinary. Then once I've turned the corner, I need to run round to the street behind me and somehow get into my backyard. In order to do that, though, I need to get through the house behind me. That isn't going to work. I can't knock on their door and go, 'Sorry, can I walk through your house? I want to get into mine the back way and surprise my ex.' If someone did that to me, I'd assume they were a bit bonkers and tell them where to get off. I think. Although now I've thought about it, I decide that if anyone ever does present me with this scenario, I will definitely let them in, even offering to give them a leg-up over the back wall if necessary.

But then I think, Well, maybe he won't come back again. Maybe this was a one-off. Maybe my one chance to nab him has been and gone.

And even if I did 'nab' him, what would I say? Would I really expect him to open up to me if he's not responded to that rather patient card I sent him? If he has thus far offered up not one word of explanation, why would he choose to do so if I cornered him, unsuspecting, in our house?

It's not like I can hold him up at gunpoint, like in some big crime movie, and say, 'Come on, Michael. Spill. Tell me why you jibbed me, or this bitch shoots.'

No. I would never do that. Except perhaps with a water pistol, which wouldn't have the same effect.

I set up Homework Club not long after I joined Fountain Woods. It's something I did at my first school when I realized that a lot of kids, and not just those with special educational needs, were struggling to get their homework done, either because of a chaotic home life or because their parents just weren't up to helping them if they were struggling. Then the kids would come into school and be berated for being lazy, when actually, maybe they had tried to get the work done, but they didn't have enough support or the right setting to make that possible. Anyway, I set up Homework Club for those who want to come to my room after school each day and have an hour in which they can work in a relatively quiet environment, and if they need help, I am on hand to offer it. I can get anything from between three and twenty kids each day. I enjoy helping them. It only adds an extra hour on to my working day, and because everybody knows it's something I do off my own back, if a teacher is off sick and they have to choose someone to cover their lessons, they very rarely ask me. *Plus* it gives me a massive amount of brownie points with the head.

I'm just helping Elizabeth from my class look up some info on oxbow lakes on one of the computers when I realize there is another grown-up in the room. I see his reflection in the window in front of me and turn to see Kevin's here. He must be early.

As if reading my mind, he says, 'I must be early, sorry.'

'Don't be, but don't you dare help any of them. You're not CRB-checked!'

He grimaces and pretends to back out of the room, which makes me and a few of the kids laugh, but then one of the kids calls out a 'hello' to him, and calls him Kevin, and Kevin meanders over and sits next to him and talks to him about what he's up to.

Somehow we end up running Homework Club together for the last ten minutes or so. I'm impressed with how lovely he is with the kids, and how nice his clothes are. And how he fills them. Call me shallow, but whenever I meet anyone, I do a onceover of their outfit and ask myself, Could I live with this look in a life partner? I used to do it all the time when I was with Michael. Michael's fashion is very Fred Perry T-shirts, skinny jeans and trainers. Kevin's is more your baggy jeans and – well, today, anyway – bright red, slightly loose, V-neck cashmere jumper with what appear to be brand-new Caterpillar boots. I'm not usually a big fan of Caterpillar boots – in fact I'm pretty sure the phrase 'I can't bear Caterpillar boots' has come out of my mouth at some point in the not-too-distant past – but these boots he is wearing have the unscruffiness of a brand-new pair. Teamed with the baggy jeans and the red jumper, they lend him an unthreatening air. The air, almost, of an anodyne kids' TV presenter, though that makes him sound a bit wimpy. And those pecs and the thickness of his arm muscles (biceps?) straining at the red cashmere certainly don't say 'wimp' to me.

He has a smallish mouth, slightly downturned, which punctuates the salt-and-pepper stubble, from a few days, I assume, of not shaving. His nose looks like it has been broken in the past (from a batteringly jealous husband of some woman he's slept with, perhaps?), but it's his eyes that are his most striking feature. They're quite small, with creases underneath that don't speak of age but of pain. A beautiful pain. And I can't take *my* eyes off them. They're the palest blue I've ever seen, and when they twinkle, like when he's laughing or interested, or about to crack a joke, then Irish eyes certainly are smiling. For the first time in my life I really get that phrase.

When eventually the kids have gone, he helps me tidy up the unit and we chat as we're doing it. I relay all the information he needs – that Connor has settled back into school perfectly and there is nothing to worry about – and once I realize that, professionally, there is nothing else to speak about, I feel a pang of disappointment.

Remember, though, Karen, this here is a lady's man. He was seeing other women while his wife was dying in hospital. That is not the sign of a decent human being.

I try to match that description of Kevin to the Kevin I see before me – the sweet-natured guy who obviously cares about his son's welfare (if only all the parents were like that), the guy who was conflicted about party platters at the supermarket that day – and I wonder, Is he really a wolf in sheep's clothing?

I am thinking all this, of course, and not saying it out loud, and he takes my silence to be boredom and says he should probably let me get on. Though he then adds, 'Connor's dead lucky having you as his teacher. You're cool.'

Oh my God, he called me 'cool'. Is that really a compliment? I have never told someone to their face that they're cool, even if I've thought it. I wonder if it's just part of his lady-chatting-up shtick.

'Ah, but once you get to know me,' I argue warmly, 'you soon realize that all that glitters isn't gold.'

He laughs. 'I bet that's so not true.'

We head out of the unit together. I'm now wishing I'd made more of an effort with my clothes.

'So what does the weekend have in store for Miss Carpenter?' he asks as we amble through the playground.

'Oh, very little. I'm the most boring cow in the universe. What about you?'

'The same really. Connor's staying at his nan's for the weekend, so I'm kicking around on my own.'

I nearly say it. I nearly say, 'Oh, we should kick around together,' but it feels inappropriate, even if I do know he's a bit of a stud and would probably therefore not be offended or surprised that I'd said it. There's an awkward pause when neither of us speaks. We're at the gates now.

I open my mouth and say, 'Well, it was nice to see you, and thanks for coming in –'

Just at the same time that he opens his and says, 'This is probably bang out of order, but if you fancy some company –'

Then we both shut up.

It has been said.

A line has been crossed, and there's no pretending it hasn't, and there's no going back. I don't know what to say. I know what I want to say; I want to say yes. Yes, sod it. In for a penny, in for a pound. But you know me – I usually screw these things up and say the complete opposite of what I want to say.

Kevin looks gutted. 'Sorry. Me and my mouth.'

I want to say, 'You have a very lovely mouth.'

And thank God I don't say that. Instead I throw caution to the wind and say, 'Yeah. We could do something tomorrow.'

The relief on his face is just joyous.

But he's a dirty old man.

Well, he's not that old, and we're only two people meeting to keep each other company.

He might jump your bones.

Well, wouldn't that be a shame?

What if he doesn't jump your bones? Will you be gutted?

Of course not. Two lonely people, keeping each other company. I don't know how many times I have to say it!

Is it unprofessional? Hooking up with the parent of one of your kids?

No. More professional than hooking up with an actual kid, that's for sure.

He's asking me what I fancy doing. He's suggesting maybe we could head into town.

I tell him yes. I'll meet him outside that theatre where *Singin' in the Rain* is on in the West End. I pluck a time out of the air. Three o'clock.

He grabs my arm, squeezes it, says, 'Excellent,' then squeezes it again and walks off down the road.

His arse isn't bad either.

I decide to miss the pictures tonight and head home. I can brag to Meredith about my date, thus reinforcing my sexuality to her. When I get home, though, she's not in. I put the kettle on and make myself a black Earl Grey. I take the roster out of my pocket and read it for the zillionth time today. Funny. Now I have an impending date with Kevin, it bothers me less that Michael has been home without my knowledge. The longer I sit there, though, staring at the paper, the less comfortable I get. Am I really doing the right thing? Meeting up with the parent of one of my pupils? A guy who, according to his neighbour, puts it about a bit. He seems so nice on the surface, but maybe she's right. Scratch said surface on any bloke and they turn out to be a bit of a bastard.

Then I start fretting about Meredith. Why have I moved someone into the house who is blatantly in love with me and has picked up on lezzy signs in me that I didn't even know I had! And then there's the impending dinner with Swinging Blue Jeans Mungo and Fionnula next weekend. How did I get myself into that mess? Then there's Mum. With Jorgen. And Dad not knowing. And before I know it, my heart is racing and I realize I'm having a panic attack. I stand and pace round the room, taking big gasps of air. Which is when I hear something.

It's something falling over upstairs. Falling over and smashing.

Someone is in the house. No, they can't be.

'Meredith?' I call out, but no reply comes.

Has somebody broken in?

Then I hear something else. A scratch-scratch upstairs. So maybe Mum was right. And Meredith. Maybe I do have rats in the loft. I slowly climb the stairs, trying to be as quiet as I can, waiting to see if I hear the sound again.

I stand on the landing. Nothing. I walk to my bedroom. Behind the door I keep a pole with a hook on the end. I take it back onto the landing and slowly raise it to meet the hook on the hatch that leads into the loft. I unhook it. It falls down and slowly my loft ladder descends.

I don't really want to see any rats. I don't really relish the prospect of coming face to face with vermin. I place the pole back in the bedroom, then return to the ladder.

Would rats really knock something over up there? Something that would smash and make that noise?

Maybe.

I climb the ladder carefully, grabbing on to the cold metal sides, but before I'm even halfway up, I look into the black, black square, the only bit of the loft I can see from here, and I stop. Like *really* stop. I grip on to the ladder for dear life. It feels like my heart has actually stopped beating.

Because I see a pair of eyes staring back at me.

And they're not rat's eyes; they're human eyes.

And I'd know those eyes anywhere.

They're Michael's.

FOURTEEN

I don't know if you've ever bumped into your ex after a month or two of not seeing him, a month or two when he's completely cut you stone dead. No contact, nothing. And if you have been in this situation, I have no idea what you might have done. I would have expected to stand there and talk to him, shout at him, throw missiles at him, Exocets hopefully, but I do none of these things. Instead I scream. A really good scream. 'Piercing' is the only word for it, like something out of a horror film. I scream. Then I run down the stairs. I open the front door and I keep on running. I run down the street. I turn onto the main road and run past the shops. I'm going at quite a speed and have to dodge several startled people coming out of them, or ambling along. Why do people amble? Can't they see I'm . . . I'm . . .

What am I doing?

I don't know.

I don't know why I'm running away from the one person I've been dying to see these past weeks, but I am. And now I have started, I am going to keep on running until I drop down dead. So in a way I'm now dying not to see him.

I must be going mad.

I am running faster than I've ever run before.

I'll tell you something for nothing – I can't keep this up.

I have a pain in my chest. Oh God, I'm having a heart attack. Talk about killing two birds with one stone. I am not only going mad but I am going to die of a heart attack. Physical and mental illness in one fell swoop. Jeez.

But no, it's not a heart attack, I realize. I just have a stitch. I turn through a gate in some railings into the little kids' swing park thing. The feel of the ground beneath me changes; it's softer underfoot now as the turquoise flooring in here is all spongy and bouncy in case toddlers fall off a roundabout or something. It's health and safety gone mad, of course, but right now I don't care. It feels nice. It feels good. And I enjoy the comfort of it as I bend over to get my breath back. I realize I'm making strange whimpering noises as I pant to get more oxygen into my body. I sound like a tennis player at Wimbledon on speed. I stand upright, starting to feel a bit better, the stitch slowly subsiding, and go and plonk myself on one of the swings.

I'm far too big for it, and I wonder briefly if a scary man will come and tell me off – someone from the local council, the swing park's caretaker – but then I also realize that actually that wouldn't be the end of the world. I cling on to the chains either side of me that the seat hangs from to stop myself from falling off. Which is when I see a man coming in through the gate. He's wearing a coat I don't recognize, and his hair is different, but it's him. It's Michael. He's run after me. He's followed me here. His face is weary, though he hasn't broken a sweat. He stands in the gateway and doesn't move forward, probably feeling like I do – that now he's here, he's not sure what he should do, not sure why he's followed me, just like I'm not sure why I ran away. He is waiting for me to speak and I can tell he's scared. Good. He's scared of what I'm going to say. He is fearful I'm going to run over and hit him or something, which is why he's not stepping any further into the swing park.

But I don't want to hit him.

I don't want to kiss him either.

I want to run away again, but I can't, not without pushing past him.

I don't even know why I want to run.

I feel like electric shocks are pulsing through my body. It must be the adrenaline from the run, or the shock of seeing him. I start shaking. It's probably not too evident to other people, but enough for me to try and calm myself with deep breaths.

It's just so strange to see him again. He looks smaller somehow, younger almost, and he's had his hair done like Paul Weller again, which was a mistake all those years ago and is hardly a triumph now. The coat looks like something a Nazi would have worn on a chilly night at Colditz. He has the collar turned up, which lends him an air of severity that doesn't suit him. I look beyond the collar to his face.

Oh God, he looks scared of me.

I don't want him to be scared of me.

Or do I?

No. I don't think I do.

Actually, I'm the one who should be scared of him. Has he been living in my loft? Spying on me? What kind of a freak does that? I should say that. I should be horrible, nasty. I should be a bitch. Call him Anne Frank, the lad from *Flowers in the Attic*, but I doubt he'd get it. I should say something, so I do.

'You've done your hair like Paul Weller again,' I say.

He nods, and then he speaks. It's so lovely hearing him speak, but it troubles me too. I'd almost forgotten how his voice lilts.

I'd almost forgotten the gentleness of his tone, the humility of his attitude, the reassurance of his timbre.

Get me, timbre.

'I always liked it like this, but you didn't. So I've started doing it like this again.'

And it stings, actually.

'I never made you get your hair cut any particular way, Michael,' I say, indignation rising in my voice. 'I never went to the barber's with you and stood over you and said, "Don't make him look like the fella out of The Jam," did I?'

He shakes his head. 'No, but you didn't like it.'

I shrug. It makes the swing shake. 'I still don't.'

Why? Why are we talking about his hair? Why are we talking about something so unimportant when there is so much else to say?

'I like it,' he reiterates, and, possibly sensing I'm not going to hit him, and realizing this might not get as ugly as he'd thought it might, he comes and sits on the swing next to me.

We sit, in silence again. There is so much to say, yet we say nothing. A breeze gets up and a chip paper flutters past us. It's now I realize I am cold. The adrenaline must have been keeping me warm, but that's subsiding and I realize I'm sitting outside in January without so much as a cardy.

'Remember that picnic we had by the swings in Greenbank Park? Back home?'

I don't know why he has to tell me Greenbank Park is back home, but I nod. Now's not the time to be picky.

'And then we lay on the roundabout, pissed, and giggled. Staring at the clouds,' he adds.

Again I nod. Of course I remember. I remember so much. I look at him.

'Did you not go, then? Were you living in the loft all this time?'

He shakes his head.

'Where did you go? Where are you living?'

'Does it matter?'

I kick my feet against the ground, swinging for a bit, less worried about breaking the structure now. Does it matter? I suppose it matters if he is coming back, if this is the first step on the road to a reunion. And then he says it. The two words I've been longing to hear.

'I'm sorry.'

I look at him and immediately tears prick my eyes. They're hot. They make me blink. It's not a full-on sob, but I feel a lump in my throat and am determined I am not going to let him see me cry.

'Why did you go?'

'You know why I went.'

'What did I do wrong?'

'Nothing.'

'I must have or you would have stayed.'

'I've been depressed, Karen.'

'I know.'

I do know. I've always known. And the terrible thing about living with someone with depression is you're so disabled. There is nothing you can do to help them, or that's how it's always felt to me. Or maybe it is just me. Maybe I'm just rubbish at all that. Maybe if I'd been better, if I'd sought more help than I did, then things would have been different. I picture him now, in the midst of the really bad onset, lying on the living-room floor, curled up like a shrimp, sobbing his heart out, his body jerking, and me dancing round him silently trying to work out what to do. If I tried to touch him, he just kicked me away. Swore at me. And there was only so much of that I could take.

That sounds terrible now. It does, doesn't it? It sounds so awful.

I look at him again, and I take a deep breath. 'Are you with Asmaa now?'

He shakes his head. 'I've seen her, but I didn't leave you to be with her. Me leaving bears no reflection on you. You have to believe that, Karen.'

I nod and feel the lump in my throat again. Don't cry. Don't let him see you cry. But the problem is, I'm not sure I believe him.

'Karen?'

I look at him.

'Will you give my mum a ring? She's worried about you. That's all.'

I nod, ashamed that I haven't already. I think he's going to have a go at me about it, but he doesn't.

'So why were you in the loft today?'

It's his turn to shrug. 'It's the warmest room in the house.'

I roll my eyes. This is getting ridiculous now.

'But you don't come back after all this time and go and hide in the loft. Well, you did, but it doesn't make sense. Have you been before? Mum said she heard scratching up there.'

'Oh, what, so I sit up there and scratch, do I?'

'No, but . . .'

'I just wanted to see how you were. I miss you.'

'Well, if you were going to miss me, you shouldn't have gone.'

'We all make mistakes.'

And that hits me. It winds me. I feel I need to bend over again, like when I was trying to get my breath back, but I don't. I stomp my feet on the ground to stop the swinging.

'But I went and that's that. Done now.'

'Are you coming back? Is this some sort of reconciliation?'

'How would that work?'

'I dunno.'

'Would you have me back?'

'I don't know.'

'I think you'd be a fool to have me back.'

'I know.'

And it sort of feels like that's that.

'You got my card, then?'

He nods. 'I saw it, and I know you want an explanation, but I think you already have it, babe.'

Another hit. I'll be bloody bruised at this rate.

'Please.' I look at him. 'Don't call me that.'

He nods, like I've made a fair point, and then he stands. He puts his hands in his pockets.

'Are you going?'

He can hear the anxiety in my voice. He nods. I shouldn't sound so needy, but my head is spinning. Why did he come? Why did he come to see me? Why did he hide in the loft? Why does he want to see me if he doesn't want to get back with me?

'I don't want you to go.'

'I've got to.'

'Will I see you again?'

'Of course.'

Now, that is just plain weird. As if he's stating the obvious. How many times? *None of this is obvious.*

'But just as friends.'

I nod. OK. I can deal with that. I think.

'Is there anyone else?' I ask, and he smiles and shakes his head.

'D'you seriously think anyone'd have me?'

And I chuckle, though I'm a bit hurt, because that makes me sound like the idiot who put up with him. Which actually I suppose I was.

'What about you?'

I give a sarcastic gurn, as if to say, 'Yeah, right.'

'I'da thought they'd be queuing round the block for you, babe,' and then he adds quickly, 'Sorry.'

I can't tell him about Kevin. Or Meredith. Or Mungo, for that matter. It would feel disloyal. Even though he's the one who left me. Up shit creek without a paddle or emotional sat nav.

'I bet there is,' he says cheekily.

'And is it any of your business if there is?'

He smirks and shakes his head. 'I'll be offski,' he says. He's said it to me a million times before, but it never sounded quite so sad then.

I stand. I feel light-headed. I step forward.

What do you do with your ex? Shake hands? Hug? Kiss? He answers it for me. He takes his hands out of his pockets and opens them out. I step forward and he engulfs me in them. I savour the feel of him again. It's nice, nice to be held, but I don't feel any reassurance like I once did. I inhale to smell him, but it must be the coat or something as he doesn't smell how he used to. He smells musty. Yes, it must be the coat. As I pull away, the collar of his coat flops down and I see his neck. There is a fat purple bruise on it. It's too much like a line to be a love bite. Maybe he's been in a fight. He sees me clock it and hastily adjusts his collar so it's hidden again.

'Your coat's vile,' I say, to divert attention from it. Yes, he must have been in a fight.

'I didn't choose this coat,' he says. 'This coat chose me.'

I have absolutely no idea what that means, but it makes me

laugh. He's sneezing suddenly. He pulls out a dusky-pink silky handkerchief with white polka dots on it. Very girly, and so not him. He blows his nose loudly, then returns the hankie to his pocket.

'Real hankies, eh? Very poshe!'

He smiles. 'I'll be in touch, yeah?'

I nod. He's turning to go. I know that hankie from somewhere. Why do I know that hankie? That hankie is important to me, but for now I can't for the life of me think why.

'How?' I gasp. A bit too desperately, actually. Rein that in, Karen! He looks back. 'How will I get in touch? What's your number?'

'I haven't got a mobile now. You know I always hated those things. They give you cancer of the brain.' He winks and heads off.

I watch him go. Maybe I should run after him, beg him to come back for his tea. Or follow him, see where he lives. But I don't feel the compulsion. For some strange reason I'm happy to let him go, drifting off into the rush-hour traffic, the people hurrying home. I feel very calm, God knows why. Somehow, deep down, I know this won't be the last I see of him.

I'd come into Newham General because I was twelve days over-due and was pretty much sure they were going to induce me. I'd had a rough night's sleep and was slightly alarmed by some sharp stabbing pains in my stomach, but as Michael had said, it was probably just 'pre-match nerves'. We were going to have a little girl and we were going to call her Evie. We thought Evie was pretty cool, and it was derived from Eve, who was the first woman to walk the planet – if you believed the Bible. If you believed One Million Years BC, *it was Raquel Welch.*

They were doing some last-minute checks in a tiny consultation room, and I knew immediately that something was wrong from the pained expression on the midwife's face. She excused herself and said she wouldn't be a moment. She exited briskly and I felt Michael squeeze my hand, but I couldn't look at him. I looked down at my swollen stomach, willing Evie to be OK.

'Has she kicked today?' Michael asked in a whisper.

I didn't reply, just stared at my belly, wet with jelly, praying to see some movement. The fact I didn't answer told Michael everything he needed to know, and his hand squeezed mine tighter. My jitters and nerves now quickly turned to panic.

Still without looking at Michael, I said, 'They can't find a heartbeat, can they? I think that's why she's gone to get someone else.'

'Maybe she's just a really shit nurse.'

'Yeah.' I jumped on this hypothesis like a drowning man clinging to a lifebuoy.

Yes. Hoorah. We had worked it out. Trust us to get the completely shit midwife. Oh, how we'd laugh about this one day. When Evie was grown up. At her wedding, her eighteenth or something.

'Yeah, and we got the really shit midwife who couldn't find your heartbeat! God, we panicked, but thank God you were OK in the end.'

And Evie, who I'd decided was going to have lovely red hair and freckles and start a trend for every woman in the country wanting auburn hair, would giggle and clasp the hand of her fiancé and go, 'Wow!'

But when the midwife returned with three other midwives, it turned out that they were just as shit. Not a single one of them could find Evie's heartbeat.

'It's there,' I insisted. 'You're just not doing it right.'

'God, you're all shit at your jobs,' said Michael, desperately wanting it to be true.

'It's there.' I was repeating myself. I knew from my job that if *you wanted something to sink in, you often had to say it more than once. 'Keep on looking. You'll find it.'*

They were looking lost, though. This was the part of their job that sucked. This was the bit of their day that they'd replay in their heads that night when they were home. They'd remember mine and Michael's faces. For a while at least. Our hopeless expressions.

And of course I knew that really they weren't that shit at their jobs. I was obviously just a shit mum. And now I looked at them again, I could see that they weren't all midwives anyway. One of them was my consultant, and another looked a bit doctory. And then they started a gentle chorus of 'I'm so sorry, Karen.'

'So sorry.'

They didn't actually say that Evie had died, but then again, they didn't really need to.

All the time Michael's hand gripped mine. I felt his getting hotter, so it started to slide out of mine, but every time it did, he'd come back stronger and grip again.

'So sorry.'

And with those words, a million planned memories exploded like fireworks in the sky. They burned brightly but quickly. Loud, exciting, scary, but gone in the blink of an eye. No red hair. No freckles. No wedding or boyfriend or eighteenth birthday. Nothing.

I think I went into shock then, as words were said and explanations given as to what would happen next. The general consensus was that it wasn't going to be very nice. It was, in fact, going to be horrendous. They were going to induce me and I was going to go into labour, but I wasn't scared. OK, it was going to be painful. OK, no one had any idea how long it would go on for, and OK, some might say it was a hideous waste of time because at the end of it my baby wouldn't be alive.

But it wasn't a waste of time.

It was worth it.

Because at the end of it, I was going to hold Evie. She had lain there inside of me, part of me, for over nine months, and finally I was going to meet her. I was going to hold my daughter in my arms and tell her I loved her. And then I was going to say goodbye to her.

I have a photograph of Evie. They took quite a few, but this one is the best. She is wearing a pink knitted dress over a white babygro. She has a small white teddy bear tucked under her arm. Apart from a tiny bruise on her forehead and lips, she looks just like any other newborn baby.

Suddenly I remember where I have seen Michael's pink polka-dot hankie before. I had one just like it in Evie's box. I frantically search for it. Has Michael been in and taken it? The box is at the bottom of my wardrobe. It's a big shoebox that I covered in white paper. I pull it out and rip off the lid. Inside I decided to put anything and everything to do with Evie. Anything she came into contact with, it's in here: cards people sent, the order of service for her funeral, the nightie I wore when giving birth, a tiny lock of her hair and the pink polka-dot hankie I used to dry my tears in the days after.

It's there. It's there in the box.

Michael must just have one similar.

I replace the lid on the box, slip it gently back into the wardrobe, as gently as if Evie was in fact in there herself, and slowly shut the door.

I sit and stare at the plastic sunflower by the window. It looks so forlorn, its silky petals drooping. I know how it feels.

FIFTEEN

I'm not meeting Kevin till three o'clock, so I have booked myself in for a Brazilian at one. It's an unassuming little place called Shirelle's Beauty Spa, and is just round the corner from my house on a slightly careworn parade of shops. I'm not sure why I'm doing this – it's not like I plan to be naked in front of Kevin later – but as I'd promised myself, I feel like now is as good a time as any. I dropped by first thing this morning to see if Shirelle could do it then, but the place was locked up. I phoned the number on the front of the shop and a husky-voiced woman (whom I took to be Shirelle) told me she wouldn't be in till one, so here I am.

Don't think about Michael. Don't think about Michael.

As I push open the door, I hear a dog yapping in a back room and the same gruff woman's voice barking back, 'Oh, shut up, Denzil!' and then the beaded curtain behind the reception desk rustles and here she is. Her face is familiar, but I just put that down to her working round the corner from me. I must have seen her at the local shops or the pub or something. Maybe even at the murderous supermarket. I can tell she recognizes me because it's like a penny drops when she sees me and she smiles broadly, revealing the whitest teeth I've ever seen. They make Simon Cowell's look green. I swear on my life, if you can see the Great Wall of China from the moon, then you must be able to see this woman's teeth as well. They're rather at odds with the wrapover cardy and stained sweat pants she's wearing. She also has a bit of what looks like egg mayonnaise on the belt of said cardy. I thought beauticians were meant to wear dentist-style gleaming-white smocks with matching crocs. Shirelle is wearing heeled slippers.

The first thing I smell on her is cigarette smoke, which is pretty off-putting in a beautician. Oh, but I've got that wrong, because she introduces herself as my 'aesthetician' for the day. Aesthetician. Whatever will they think of next?

She leads me down a tatty grey corridor to something she extravagantly announces to be Treatment Room 1. It's like a broom cupboard with a wallpaper table in it. She instructs me to strip completely (I have no idea why. I have only come to get my nether regions sorted), but because she's a little bit scary, I'm completely naked in seconds. She then tells me to hop on the table and squat on all fours with my butt facing her.

She does actually use the word 'butt'.

In fact she says it a few times and instructs, 'Prise apart your butt cheeks with your hands for me so I can get a good look, thank you.'

I'm left thinking, Blimey, this aesthetician didn't go to finishing school. Her voice rasps. In fact, it's not really a voice, just the sound of an ashtray dying.

'Shifty round so I can see your butthole – that's it. Left a bit. Left a— Right a bit. Bullseye. 'Cos I'm gonna start by sorting your butt out.'

Again, not a sentence I have heard that often in everyday life. But who knows? Now I'm single, maybe I will.

Don't think about Michael. Don't think about Michael.

'Cor, you've really let it go down there, haven't you?' she says with a whistle through her teeth before and after. She sounds like she's just caught a glimpse of an overgrown meadow and doesn't know where to start with her Flymo.

Something about this doesn't feel right. Forget the fact that I have never stripped in front of another human being except a) at the doctor's, b) in the changing rooms at the swimming pool, and c) in front of Michael – well, not when I've had bodily hair, let's say – it's just when I pictured myself having my first Brazilian, I assumed there'd be a level of comfort involved.

'D'you want me to bleach that while I'm down there?' she's asking, sounding like her teeth are too big for her mouth. Maybe she got them knock-off.

'Bleach what?'

'Your butt.' As she says it, she sort of taps it with what might either be a finger or the end of a blusher brush. This could be a whole new parlour game: Guess What We're Poking Your Butt With As You Look Away. Not sure it'll catch on, though.

'No, thanks.'

God, was my actual hole jet black or something?

'Won't take long.' Oh God, she is doing the hard sell. 'It's a good colour. Hang on. I've got the wrong glasses on. These are my driving glasses.'

I hear her rummaging about in a drawer, then feel her breathing out over my bum. It feels completely weird and something down there contracts.

'No. Right first time. That's not a bad colour, actually.'

'Just a Brazilian, please.'

'Okey-dokey. I'll just put some nice relaxing music on.'

I'm not sure what your definition of 'nice relaxing music is'. I half expect to hear the sound of babbling brooks or whale music. Instead I have to listen to a Steps album as she gets to work.

I stare ahead of me, trying to ignore what she is doing. On the wall in front of me is a large sepia-coloured photo of Shirelle dressed up in a frilly skirt with a sawn-off shotgun in her hands. She is in fancy dress to look like a saloon-bar girl from a Wild West movie. Underneath in the frame are the words 'Olde Worlde Portraits, Margate.' Not the most obvious choice, I wouldn't have thought, for the wall of your beauty spa, but then it would appear Shirelle is no ordinary beautician/aesthetician. I mean, she has a certificate further along the wall, in a clip frame. It's a bit wonky in the frame, but look, she has qualifications. And there's her name for all to see.

Shirelle Pepper

That rings a . . .

Oh . . . shit . . .

Shirelle Pepper, mother of Keisha-Vanessa, the mother who wrote in to complain about me upsetting her by insisting she pretend her mother was dead.

No wonder she recognized me. We've met at parents' evenings.

Oh, this is mortifying. It is – it's completely mortifying.

What do I do now? She surely thinks I already know who she is. Amazingly, she didn't seem that surprised that I was unfazed about revealing my genitalia to her and practically shoving my butt in her face.

I tell you one thing about Shirelle Pepper, she knows all the words to Steps's back catalogue.

I feel I have to say something, though, otherwise she might think I'm rude.

And I better say something soon, because if I don't, I will obsess about meeting her again at parents' evening and thinking, Oh my God, this woman offered to bleach my bumhole, etc. So I have to block that out with conversation.

'So . . .' I say, sounding, it has to be said, like I am shitting it. Though considering the position I am in currently, it's a good job I'm not. '. . . you like Steps.'

It isn't a question, it is a statement of fact, but she leaps on it as an invitation to spout forth about her favourite supergroup. How she loves 'them Steps' and how she's watching some show on Sky about them reforming and how it always moves her to tears; how she'd like to get her hands on Claire's nether regions and 'strip her right back to basics'.

The more excited she gets as she speaks, the rougher she is with my bits. 'On your back!' she suddenly snarls, and I flip over like a pancake with my legs splayed. I have no idea what she is doing down there, and I daren't look, but when she says, 'OK, I'm gonna go inner lip now,' I close my eyes, bite my (facial) lips and hope to God my parts behave down there.

It is painful. They are the only three words for it.

OK, there are four. It is bloody painful.

Why am I doing this? Kevin is not going to see my lady bits today.

Not unless he gets me really drunk.

No. No, he won't.

All I know is I won't be in a hurry to get this particular procedure done again. Having a Brazilian seems to involve her dabbing on a load of hot gunk from a trolley, sticking rolls of Sellotape all over me, then ripping it off with no thought as to how it actually might make me feel. Which is like someone is peeling me and then dipping me in a bag of salt. As you can imagine, it's not the best feeling in the world. I'm really burning down there when she finally announces she is done.

'You look lovely,' she says, stepping back to admire her handiwork.

'Great,' I say, sliding off the table and limping over to retrieve my clothes.

Surely she should put some moisturizer on or something, anything to take away the pain and soothe the raw skin, but she clomps out saying she needs to let her Denzil in the yard for a wee as she's not had time to walk him today.

I glimpse down briefly, expecting to see that I'm smoother than a billiard ball in my down-belows, but instead I just see that my groin appears to be glowing bright pink, like a sunburned albino. Neon pink or hot pink, and it certainly feels hot. All I fancy doing is finding a bath of ice and lowering myself into it slowly. Ah, the relief! But instead I pull up my thong – why did I wear a thong?! – which really stings, and then slowly peel on my jeans. I feel like there's a foreign object round the back of my knickers, so I unpeel the jeans to check I've not got a sock caught in there, but my jeans and thong are empty. Up they go again and I stagger out to the reception and prepare to pay. Which is when it dawns on me.

I'm pretty sure she's left some wax on my bum cheeks. And why? This is payback. She has done a Brusque Brazilian to attack me for being so unkind and callous to her daughter, and therefore left the job half finished.

But I will not let her think she has won. Oh no!

She's all smarmy smiles when she returns from letting out the dog, and I'm sure she charges me five pounds more than it said on the pamphlet, but I'm not in a position to argue.

Before I leave, I say, 'I'm sorry about the business with Keisha-Vanessa. I really didn't mean to upset her.'

Shirelle glares at me, then shrugs.

'I was just trying to get them to imagine how Connor would be feeling. He's a boy in my class who—'

'I know who Connor is, darlin',' she practically spits at me, 'and don't get me *started* on his dad!'

His dad. His dad with whom I have a date in an hour and a half. What does she mean? Christ, even she knows he's a wrong 'un. Should I say anything? I want to, but then I get a twinge of pain between my legs and decide it's probably better if I just go. Maybe I could subtly unzip my fly on the street and try and get the wind on it, cool it down.

'Well, it was just a misunderstanding and . . . well, hopefully it's all cleared up now.'

Unlike the mess between my legs, I want to add.

'Yeah I got some letter from Miss Thing.'

She means Butterly. I nod and head for the door.

I'm sure I hear her laughing as I leave.

I nearly didn't come on this 'date'. After seeing Michael last night, I just lay on my bed fretting and trying to gain some meaning from it, though I found little. His reappearance brought geysers of emotions bubbling up inside, popping memories into my bedroom like bubbles of hot air. They danced before me, like they were playing on floating television screens. They were all happy memories. First was a party we went to where he did 'London's Calling' on *SingStar* and then we disappeared into a guest bedroom and made out on top of a pile of coats like we were teenagers again. Then there was going to a posh hotel in the West End to see him receive his award for good service from the Underground. He looked so sweet in his ill-fitting suit, and the large African woman who presented him with his certificate flirted with him in her national dress.

For half an hour or so I was comforted and encouraged by the thought that not everything was bad about me and Michael, that not every aspect of our lives was dictated by his illness, but every bubble bursts, and all television sets eventually get turned off, and I was then left deflated, watching the memories fade, replaced instead with the familiar feeling of dread that was my modus operandi for so long. I remembered the days when waking in the morning, I would discover life was all downhill from then on, constantly wondering if I'd ever find a way out from the maze of dread. Well, now I had. So why was I even contemplating seeing Michael again? He was bad news, right? I was resolute. Suddenly my backbone turned to steel. I had to go on this date.

So here I am, waiting outside the Palace Theatre, just before three, to meet a man I hardly know to kill some time and interrupt the mundane predictability of my life at the moment. To mix things up a little and to *stop me thinking about Michael*, even though it's nearly two months since he left. The little I do know about Kevin doesn't bode well. Plus I feel like my bum cheeks have been pebble-dashed with half an altar candle. I hope to God his opening gambit isn't 'Let's go and pull a moony at some people on Leicester Square!' Oh God! Can you imagine? Yes, as long as his opening line isn't that, this could just about be bearable. If it wasn't for the butt thing.

The trees over the road look naked. It's too early for the first green buds of the new year. When a breeze whistles through them they shake, their branches like sinister pointing fingers. The hanging baskets outside a pub nearby lie barren. The only things growing seem to be the weeds pushing up between the paving stones. How hardy they are to survive.

I have a good look at the poster for *Singin' in the Rain* and the big publicity photos that are festooning the building. How ironic – a big, romantic, soppy Hollywood love story and here I am waiting to meet a hot guy who comes from the 'love 'em and leave 'em, especially when your wife is dying' school of romance. I should run, really. If I had any sense, I would just turn round and leg it, jump on a bus, any bus, and get the hell away from Tottenham Court Road, but these shoes are a bit rubbish for running in. Besides, I think I might actually do myself a wax-related chafing injury if I so much as canter right now. As I stand here, I decide I have invented a new word. I will write to the *Oxford University Dictionary*, or whatever it's called, and inform them.

chafinjury: n. an injury caused by chafing: *that bitch did a Brusque Brazilian and shortly I will do myself a chafinjury.*

I like my new word. It's got legs.

So, to avoid a chafinjury, I decide I could just waddle away. That is my only option.

It's a crisp, cold day, but the sun is high in the sky. If I was to say it's like Piccadilly Circus round here, it would be highly appropriate, as the circus itself is only a stone's throw away. It has to be one of the busiest corners of London. This intersection divides the gay streets of Soho to the north-west and Piccadilly Circus to the south-west; Covent Garden's round the corner if you head south-east, and—

Oh God, I see him. He's carrying a massive bouquet of red roses. He's dressed differently, and his face looks . . . What's happened to his face?

It's not him. I'm part relieved, part disappointed. Mr Red Roses walks past and thrusts them in the face of a timid-looking woman in a very loud coat. Maybe she thinks the coat lends her confidence. Unfortunately it just lends her the air of someone with no personality wearing a loud coat. She seems a bit nonplussed about the flowers. I feel like pushing her out of the way and grabbing them like a bouquet at a wedding and—

'Miss Carpenter?'

Oh. I know that voice.

I spin round. Kevin's stood there with a big, goofy grin on his face. It's a grin that says he's a bit excited and a bit nervous. It also says, 'How the hell did this happen, and isn't it just *weird*?' It's a good smile; it's perfect. Surrounding said smile is a bit more stubble than was there yesterday, and correct me if I'm wrong, but the severity of his fringe informs me that he's paid a visit to his local barber this morning. I want to spin him round and check that said barber didn't leave a comb or scissors in the back of his head as payback for some imagined misdemeanour, but maybe that's just the luck of my draw.

'Karen!' he says, now I'm facing forward.

I don't know whether to hug him or shake his hand, but he cuts through my indecision and grabs me and gives me a brief but winding hug. He smells good. His scent is citrusy and sharp and jolts my nostrils. My hands slip down him rather saucily as he's wearing a boxy leather jacket, the colour of a mushroom.

'What d'you fancy doing?' I say as I extrapolate myself from his clutches.

'Well, we could go for a walk,' he offers, knowing it sounds a bit shit, but hey, it's a suggestion. It's not raining, so it's a fair enough idea. I'd've been shocked if he'd suggested a trip to a museum.

I nod like I think it's the best of a bad bunch of ideas, and we start walking down Shaftesbury Avenue towards Piccadilly. We walk at a distance of about a foot away from each other, but sometimes squeeze closer to avoid oncoming tourists, or sometimes lose each other briefly, like when we pass a group of girl guides with Soho maps. We chat casually about what we've done with our days. He has indeed been to 'get his ears lowered' (his phrase for having his hair cut), but I refrain from telling him I've had a Brusque Brazilian. He asks if I've eaten, so I reply, 'Oh, I can always eat,' and he suggests we mozie into Chinatown and grab a bite there. Before we do, though, we stand and snigger at some dreadful caricaturists touting their wares alongside some cashpoints. One quite pretty girl sits giggling, completely unaware that the bespectacled artist has lent her an air of a bloodhound. Someone I take to be her boyfriend stands behind the artist, wetting himself with laughter. We move on.

We turn into Chinatown and it doesn't feel like we're in London anymore; in fact it feels like we're on the set of *Aladdin* and we're venturing into Old Peking.

He hasn't suggested we moony anyone yet. This is good.

There's the ornately jewelled arch rising above us, a statue of a scary smiling lion and at the far end a gaudily coloured pagoda. With the smells of roasting duck, the sounds of sizzling noodles, rows of restaurants and supermarkets, it really feels like another world.

'I speak fluent Cantonese,' Kevin leans in and says.

I'm impressed.

'Really?'

'Nah,' he says, shaking his head. 'I don't even speak Eric Cantona. This one doesn't look too gruesome, and it's got some seats.'

It's only as we're entering this bijou place on the main drag of Gerrard Street, complete with four dead ducks sweating in the window on skewers, like garish Turner Prize bunting, that I realize I've been walking normally since meeting Kevin and have not been aware of discomfort of the cheekage. He must provide the bridge over the troubled waters of my backside. Or maybe, finally, the remaining chunks of wax have dislodged themselves from my derrière and dropped down the legs of my jeans. I don't look back, but if I did, I just *know* there'd be a trail of red spots of wax marking – Hansel and Gretel-like – my route here.

The restaurant, the Smiling Lion – how apt – is a cosy affair where you're nose to nipple not only with each other but with everyone sitting at adjoining tables. Kevin rips the paper covering off his chopsticks as soon as he sits down and starts a display with them not unlike a baton-twirling majorette in Iowa. I feel immediately inept – no change there, then – as I know sooner or later I will have to ask for a fork. Chopsticks have never been my forte. We never ate out as a family, so I never experimented with adventurous cuisines till I left home and went to university. And even then it was only a kebab after a pub crawl. When I went to my first Chinese restaurant, I attempted to use what felt like these two knitting needles to eat with and ended up poking myself in the eye, the neck and the bodywarmer. (It was the 1990s.) While everyone else managed to scrape up fistfuls of noodles, I ate hardly anything, but drank a lot of sake and threw up in the gutter at the end of the night. From then on I asked for a fork and spoon, and wolfed down everything in sight.

I scour the menu, pretending to understand it, but it may as well be in a foreign language to me because— Oh, it's in Chinese. Thought I needed reading glasses then. Kevin tells me to skip to the back, where everything is listed in English. Again, even now, it may as well be in a foreign language, as I don't really know my duck rolls from my chow meins. I know what I like; I just never know what it's called. Kevin sees my glazed look and offers to order for both of us. Who said chivalry was dead? Or is it in fact sexist? He rattles off a list to the hyper waitress, then tells me I'm in for a treat.

'I didn't tell anyone what I was up to today,' he offers up with a grimace, like he's doing something naughty.

'No, neither did I,' I offer back.

'Just wasn't sure about the "Hey, I'm meeting up with Connor's teacher" thing. Wasn't sure it was . . .'

'Professional?'

He shrugs. 'Guess so. And to the casual onlooker it might sound like a date.' He grimaces again.

'Oh, I know. Can you imagine?' I laugh like that would be the most absurd thing in the world. I cover my disappointment well. He laughs.

'And you know . . . Toni . . .' He lets her name hang in the air.

'Yeah. Toni . . .' I let it hang in the air too. 'You must miss her terribly.'

He nods. Is he choked? He looks choked.

'Yeah, it's just . . . completely weird. It's knocked me sideways. This wasn't where I'd planned to be at thirty-five.'

He's younger than me, but I know how he feels.

'Well, I know how that feels,' I say. 'My big long-term relationship . . .'

'Yeah, I heard.'

He heard? How did he hear?

'Sorry?'

'Toni's cousin's Claire?'

'Custard Claire?'

'Yeah.'

'Oh. Did she go to the funeral?'

He nods.

'I didn't see her at the wake.'

'Well, you weren't there that long.' He rightly points out. 'She told me about . . .' his voice drifts off. 'She's got a mouth on her. Not that she was . . .'

I nod. He knows. It's a small world at Fountain Woods. We're interrupted from our mutual 'who'd've thought we'd be single again in our mid-thirties?' chat by a porcelain decanter of sake arriving. I sip some from what is more or less a thimble and am hit by a warmth that seeps through me like rain into roots and makes me relax. Or it would do if my – sorry about this – bum wasn't becoming so itchy. It feels like my cheeks are being welded together.

Kevin starts talking about Toni. And her illness (cancer). And how she bore it (bravely). And how Connor has coped (valiantly). And what he's done with his emotions (hidden them). And what he's going to do with the rest of his life (he doesn't know).

And then he drops the humdinger.

He says, 'Connor's not my son.'

My eyes must be like saucers. Kevin appears to blush. I see a rashy redness creep suddenly across his neck. I don't know what to say.

He continues, 'I can't have kids. Bit of a Jaffa. We were going to adopt, but then Toni fell pregnant.'

'That doesn't make sense,' my eyes tell him.

'Which is when I found out she'd been having an affair with someone from her work.'

Oh God, the poor thing.

'We worked through it. Everyone said I was mad, but I loved her, you know?'

Blimey. Even when he's baring his soul and telling me some brutally hideous things, all I can think is, God, his voice is really sexy.

He sighs. 'Jamie, Connor's real dad—'

'Oh, I'm sure you're his real dad. Changed his nappies, took him out for—'

He cuts in, 'He didn't really wanna know. Till Toni got ill. Since then he's been all over Connor like a rash.'

'That must be awful.'

Just like the increasingly burny sensation in my seat. Er . . .

'Scared I'm losing him, you know?'

I nod. I do know. Well, I can imagine.

'Jaysus. Sorry. First time we've talked properly and I'm banging on about my baggage.'

Before I can answer, our hyper waitress zooms over like she's on roller skates and practically throws ten plates of food at us, as if she's doing it against the clock. She then drops a fork next to my empty bowl like I've asked her for a kidney. (I don't even remember asking for it.) Kevin tells me to try the soft-shell crab. I do. Although it looks unappealing on the plate, like a crab dipped in batter, I bite into it and it is indeed soft and . . . mouthwateringly good.

We both 'ooh' and 'aah' our way through our first mouthfuls. I want to ask him more about Connor and Jamie and Toni, but . . . I can't.

I'm stinging. I'm sorry to be graphic, but as the temperature has risen, so my bum has got more sore and stinging and—

Take your mind off it. Concentrate on the food, Karen. This food is great. Kevin is great. This day should be the greatest of the year so far. I look at my crab and will myself to block out the pain. Right. Move the fork to your mouth. Pop it in said mouth. Chew. Simple.

I do it.

I did it.

I will do it again.

And it's just as I'm taking another bite of this gorgeous bit of soft, dead crustacean that I notice a shadow covering the table. Must be someone standing in the street, peering in or reading the menu displayed in the window. I look up. The person standing there has his face hidden by the menu he is reading. He has his hands in his pockets. The pockets of a German Colditz-style coat. My mouth goes dry. I feel my heart rate quicken. The crab shakes on my fork as my hand spasms with shock. I look back to see if Kevin has noticed my sudden metamorphosis into shaky scaredy lady, but he's too busy dunking his crab in some glutinous dip. I look back to the window, trying to compose myself, but I just see the edge of the coat whipping away out of view. Like the window is a stage and a caped actor has slipped into the wings. It was him. I know it was him. What are the chances that he would just happen to be here when I was on a date? Here of all places? Of all the streets in the whole of London he just happens to be here, outside this tiny restaurant, right at the same time as me? It doesn't make sense.

No, it doesn't. Because let's face it, it probably wasn't even him. Loads of fellas wear German Army coats these days.

Or do they? I look at Kevin's leather jacket tented over the back of his chair. Kevin is talking away, but it may as well be white noise I'm so distracted.

Nobody dresses like a Nazi these days, surely? Except for Prince Harry, and even then that was only for a fancy-dress party.

And this coat was the exact same colour as Michael's.

I tell myself I am going mad. I am seeing things. I didn't even get a look at his face.

Kevin senses something's up. I know this because he says, 'Is something up?'

I fluster a bit and then say I have to go to the little girls' room. I snake through the maze of tables, but with every twist of my body I emit a different kind of an 'ooh' and an 'aah' because now actually moving is painful. Something serious is happening in my jeans, and not in a good way.

What I discover in the toilets is not the chafinjury I anticipated. It's much, much worse than that. I discover that not only are my butt cheeks glued together with red wax, but my thong is glued in the middle of it as well. I try pulling at the wax, but it's too painful. I can't rip it off. What the hell did she use on me? A mixture of wax and superglue? I'm panicking now. I probably have to go to A&E. This is possibly an emergency. Despite never having seen a 'wax in the crack' storyline on *Casualty*, I know that I can't sort this problem myself. I pull my jeans back on and push out of the cubicle. I wash my hands at the sink and look at my reflection in the mirror. And hate myself, because I know what I am going to do next. I dry my hands on an irritatingly weak dryer – may as well just put them in front of a panting dog for all the good it does – then push back into the restaurant. Kevin's smiling over as I snake my way back.

'I ordered more sake. Hope that's OK,' he says with a wink.

Right. In for a penny, in for a pound. I blurt it out. 'I'm really sorry, but I'm going to have to go.'

He looks alarmed.

'Jeez, are you OK?'

'Yes, I just . . . I'm not sure this was such a good idea. I'm sorry.'

Why did I say that? It was a genius idea.

But I can't tell him the truth.

I had a Brazilian this morning and my arse cheeks have

moulded together. I now have to hotfoot it to A&E to be chiselled apart. Lovely meeting you.

Again I say, 'Sorry,' and head for the door. He's up out of his seat, following.

'Well, let me walk you to your—'

'No, I'm fine. Sorry,' and I leg it out onto the street, more mortified than I have ever been in my life. That, teamed with the now excruciating pain, means this is not one of my best days.

Outside on the street, I see a pink polka-dot hankie there on the ground beneath the menu display. I bend – *ouch* – grab it and run.

If I head for Charing Cross Road, I'm sure I can find a cab.

SIXTEEN

From: Kevin O'Keefe Kevok75@hotmail.co.uk
To: Karen Carpenter KCarpenter@fountainwoods.org.uk
Subject: Seaweed?

Hi Karen,

So go on, then, what happened? Did I have seaweed in my teeth? LOL. Listen, I'm sorry you had to get off. And thinking back, I'm sorry all I did was bang on about Toni and Connor. Probably not what you needed to hear on a Saturday afternoon in the town of China. I'm really, really sorry to have put you through all that, but it was nice to see you anyway.

Ah, I feel like I really messed up. Story of my life. Oh well.

You take it easy,

Kevin x

Oh God. He thinks it's all his fault. Of course he does. I feel dreadful.

From: Karen Carpenter KCarpenter@fountainwoods.org.uk
To: Kevin O'Keefe Kevok75@hotmail.co.uk
Subject: Food Poisoning

Dear Kevin,

I'm so, so, so, so sorry about this. You didn't have seaweed stuck in your teeth, and you weren't boring me or freaking me out telling me about Toni and the Jamie/Connor situation. The truth of the matter is, and it's not very ladylike, but as we were sitting there, I started to feel poorly and the next thing I knew I had to run to the toilet to throw up. I had a dodgy croque-monsieur for brunch, and thought it tasted odd at the time, but I was so hungry I devoured it. More fool me! When I came out of the loo, I just knew I had to get to my bed and that's why I scarpered.

I really can't apologize enough and am of course *mortified*, but I truly thought I was going to throw up over you. I've been ill ever since, but I'm sure it will pass. I don't know if you noticed I was a bit distracted during the meal, but that's the reason why. Nothing else! It's all a bit of a mess because I was having such a nice time. Anyway, I'm more than happy to do it all over again – without eating a dodgy croque first – whenever you fancy it. Just let me know.

In the meantime I will of course treat what you told me about Connor and Jamie in the strictest confidence, but it's probably just as well I know, as I imagine it's a lot for him to take in at the moment and he's probably a bit all over the place. No one else needs to know at school, I wouldn't have thought, but it's good that I can keep an eye out for him and make sure he's coping OK. I hope that makes sense? I may be making no sense, of course, as I think I'm a bit delirious after the food poisoning. It's really wiped me out.

Anyway, let me know how you're fixed.

All best, and sorry again,

Karen x

From: Karen Carpenter KCarpenter@fountainwoods.org.uk
To: Wendy Wolverhampton WWolverhampton@wendy.com
Subject: Help

Hi love,

I've tried calling you a few times, but you're just going to answerphone. Are you back yet? I've not heard from you in ages (well, it feels like ages) and was just wondering how you were and how your new love life was going with what's-his-name. Actually, what is his name? I don't think you've said. Is he gorgeous? Is he treating you like a princess? (Kate, not Di. I hope he isn't treating you like Di. That would be a travesty and you'd end up with an eating disorder and do *Panorama* programmes going, 'There were three of us in that marriage,' etc., and look all mad down the camera with too much kohl.) I hope it's going OK, anyway.

You're not going to believe what happened to me today. I had a sort of date with that sexy guy whose wife died and has a kid in my class? The Irish one? God, he's gorgeous, but I screwed up royally by ending up in A&E. Long story, but the upshot is, I have good grounds to sue my local beauty salon, only I won't because the woman who runs it, and who has shit aesthetician skills – word to the wise: apparently, you're *not* supposed to squat on all fours during a Brazilian with your arse exposed – is the mother of one of my kids who has a vendetta against me and I don't want to rock the boat. Anyway, let's just say I now have lots of soothing creams to apply to a certain private area of my body, and I've been sitting on and gaining comfort from a bag of frozen peas for the last hour. The Irish guy (let's call him Kevin, for that is his name) must think I'm completely bonkers.

But hey, maybe I am, because during the little I managed of our meal (have you ever had soft-shell crab? *Hot*), I am pretty sure I saw Michael looking in on the restaurant. What do you make of that? I hope he's not going to start stalking me. Anyway . . .

Please give me a shout. Would love to hear your voice. I've not even told you about Mum and her Danish toy boy (cringe. She's practically old enough to be his *grandmother*. It's disgusting) or my new lodger's crush on me. (She thinks she can turn me. She's no Reese Witherspoon.)

Got to dash. This bag of peas is melting and I need to see if frozen oven chips work just as well.

Love you,

Kags xxxx

From: Wendy Wolverhampton WWolverhampton@wendy.com
To: Karen Carpenter KCarpenter@fountainwoods.org.uk
Subject: Re: Help

Love, it's me.

My God, are you OK? That's awful. I've had loads of Brazilians and never experienced anything like that before. Sue the bitch! The reason you can't get hold of me is I'm in Mauritius. Jake came here on a research trip for a documentary he's making about a murder, so I took some holiday and have joined him. Oh, the luxury. I lie on the beach all day and these divine guys come every hour to clean your sunglasses or offer you cubes of melon on a glass tray. I'm finally reading *Fifty Shades of Grey* and it's depressing me. Is this how far feminism has brought us? Have you read it?

Listen, re: Michael. I'm sure this is really normal. It was probably just someone who looked like him. You're bound to see him everywhere. I'm sure it happens a lot after this sort of thing. Just don't beat yourself up about it, love.

Maybe what you need is a holiday. Oh God, Kags, Jake is So Lovely. We talk about everything and anything, and he's so funny and articulate. His daughter's not very pleased we're together, but you can't have everything. She sounds like a bitch, actually. Refuses to meet me; says I'm trying to take the place of her dead mother. Who died, like, twenty years ago!!! Get over it already!!!! She thinks I'm a gold-digger. (Jake's loaded. Did I say?) Jake's in AA, so my liver has taken quite a rest on this trip. He's amazing. I think he could be the one. A few people assume he's my dad when we're out together, but you know what? Fuck the lot of them. Age is just a number, right? So please don't be too harsh on Val. She's your mother; she deserves some respect.

Love you. Soz, got to go – Jake wants a game of chess.

Mwah,

W x

Chess? *Chess?* Wendy doesn't play *chess*. Strip poker and Twister are much more her thing.

From: Karen Carpenter KCarpenter@fountainwoods.org.uk
To: Wendy Wolverhampton WWolverhampton@wendy.com
Subject: Re: Re: Help

I don't think I made myself clear/explained. Michael came to see me, Friday evening. Too long to go into now, but he apologized and said it was all about his depression. It was a bit weird, and I wasn't as angry with him as I thought I'd be. He's had his hair done like Weller again and he smelt funny.

How old is Jake?

I'm really jealous about Mauritius.

Kxx

From: Wendy Wolverhampton WWolverhampton@wendy.com
To: Karen Carpenter KCarpenter@fountainwoods.org.uk
Subject: Re: Re: Re: Help

He's seventy-two.
Karen, I'm going to ring you.
Stay strong,
  W x

The phone rings. I ignore it because another email pings into my inbox.

From: Fionnula Brookes FionnulaB69@freeserve.co.uk
To: Karen Carpenter KCarpenter@fountainwoods.org.uk
Subject: Can't wait!

Hi Karen,
  Fionnula here, Mungo's wife.
  Karen, I'm *so* thrilled you're going to be joining us on
Saturday for our little soirée. It's a very casual affair and I just
know it's going to be wonderful. Especially with you here as
guest of honour!
  As you know, Mungo and I are both committed vegetarians,
so we won't be serving anything with a face, but if you have
any further dietary requirements, please do let me know. I was
thinking of doing my spinach pie, as it's gluten-free and contains
no nuts or dairy, so that usually covers all bases!
  Now, do you want me to do some matchmaking for you, or
is that too soon? Only, I recently met this really interesting guy
on a Japanese rope bondage and tantra course in Tring who is
currently single and has a really amazing energy. His name is
Lee, though because of his diminutive stature, a lot of people
call him Little Lee. He doesn't mind, honestly! I'm not being

cruel. Anyway, he's really looking forward to meeting you. He
too was raised in a naturist household, so Mungo and I are
sure you'll have *lots* in common.

We usually begin our soirées between seven and half past.
If you're driving, we have the double garage and ample space
on the drive. If you fancy staying over, bring an overnight bag
and prepare to slum it on one of our many futons. (Don't worry,
they're pretty comfy, actually, and really good for a bad back.)

Looking forward to it, Karen. Feels ages since I've seen you
properly.

Love and light,

Fionnula xOxOxOxOxOxOxOx

What?!

From: Karen Carpenter KCarpenter@fountainwoods.org.uk
To: Fionnula Brookes FionnulaB69@freeserve.co.uk
Subject: Re: Can't wait!

Hi Fionnula,

I think there may have been a few crossed wires here
because I don't really remember saying I could definitely come.
Never mind! I've checked my diary and I am free so would love
to join you.

I don't have any food allergies or requirements, and if I'm
honest, I think it might just be a bit too soon to dip my toe back
into the dating game just yet. Though Little Lee sounds lovely.

Don't worry – I won't need to stay over. I won't drink, as
I need to be up early the next morning for an appointment.
Thanks for the offer, though. Maybe another time.

Looking forward to it. Yes, it's been ages.

Karen x

PS I can't drive.

From: Fionnula Brookes FionnulaB69@freeserve.co.uk
To: Karen Carpenter KCarpenter@fountainwoods.org.uk
Subject: Sorry!

Hi Lovely Lee,

Darling, I'm so sorry but that Karen I told you about is being a complete bore and not playing ball. Still, she's a real looker, so at least you can ogle her all night. I know I will be!

I've been trying a few of the techniques from the course out on Mungo this week and edging him. I've also tried it on Joyce next door, and by God, she loves it. Mungo's less keen, but then he's always been pants at relinquishing control. Still, he is keen to work on this, and he loves the edging.

Tring seems but a distant memory now. I really haven't experienced orgasms like it before or since. I miss you.

Love and light,

F xOxOxOxOxOxOx

What?

From: Fionnula Brookes FionnulaB69@freeserve.co.uk
To: Karen Carpenter KCarpenter@fountainwoods.org.uk
Subject: Sorry

Karen,

I mistakenly just sent you an email meant for someone else. Can you do me a *huge* favour and delete it without reading it? It contains some rather sensitive information.

Really looking forward to next Saturday.

Love and light,

Fionnula xOxOxOxOxOxOxOx

From: Karen Carpenter KCarpenter@fountainwoods.org.uk
To: Fionnula Brookes FionnulaB69@freeserve.co.uk
Subject: Re: SORRY

Sure, deleted. All best x

Oh God.

From: Mungo Brookes MBrookes@fountainwoods.org.uk
To: Karen Carpenter KCarpenter@fountainwoods.org.uk
Subject: Hoorah

Hi K,

Fionnula's had a go at me, saying I must have got my wires
crossed about inviting you for the supper/soirée. If I did, then
apologies. See you in school tomorrow, and so glad you're
coming next week. Please don't think anything untoward is going
to happen. I will make sure it doesn't. So don't be scared.

Over and out,

Mungo

Well. That makes me feel *slightly* better.
Oh God. Another ping. Not another mistake from Fionnula?

From: Kevin O'Keefe Kevok75@hotmail.co.uk
To: Karen Carpenter KCarpenter@fountainwoods.org.uk
Subject: Next Saturday

Ah, you poor lamb. Hope you're feeling better soon. God, what a
nightmare. I had no idea – you should've said! Well, that makes
me feel a lot better, and glad it wasn't my baggage-handling
that drove you away.

One thing I never got round to saying is that I didn't tell you the whole truth about where Connor was this weekend. He is at his nan's, but it's *Jamie*'s mum's. Don't ask me why, but Jamie's having him for the next few weekends. I should've put my foot down, but Connor was so keen, and although it hurt like hell, I had to think about what he wanted and he made it clear that's what it was. Jamie looks like the cat that got the fecking cream when he picks him up and it messes with my head, but hey ho. If he's a waste of space (as Toni always claimed he was), I'm sure Connor'll find out in time.

Sorry. Offloading again.

Anyway, what I was writing about was I wondered if you were free next Saturday for a repeat performance. I'm playing footy in the day but can do evening.

Anyway, let me know. Hope all's well with the patient.

Kx

From: Karen Carpenter KCarpenter@fountainwoods.org.uk
To: Kevin O'Keefe Kevok75@hotmail.co.uk
Subject: Re: Next Saturday

Oh God, Kevin, much as I'd like to, I've already said yes to going to my head of department's for dinner that night. I'm dreading it, truth be told, but if I back out, he'll start being all crotchety at work and make my life hell, etc. I can do Sunday? Any good?

Kx

From: Kevin O'Keefe Kevok75@hotmail.co.uk
To: Karen Carpenter KCarpenter@fountainwoods.org.uk
Subject: Re: Re: Next Saturday

Cool. It's a date. Well, it isn't, but you know what I mean.

Till Sunday. I'll email in week with arrangements, etc.

Kxx

Oh well. Looks like my dance card is full next weekend.

From: Wendy Wolverhampton WWolverhampton@wendy.com
To: Karen Carpenter KCarpenter@fountainwoods.org.uk
Subject: Re: Re: Re: Re: Help

Are you avoiding me?
  W x

From: Karen Carpenter KCarpenter@fountainwoods.org.uk
To: Wendy Wolverhampton WWolverhampton@wendy.com
Subject: Re: Re: Re: Re: Re: Help

No, don't be daft. I'm just mad busy.
  Speak soon. Miss you.
    Love to Jake.
      K xx

SEVENTEEN

'You can't *seriously* be thinking of going!' Meredith says, hands on hips in the hall as I try to make my escape.

'He's my head of department,' I insist, as if I have no choice.

'He's a dirty great perv!' she says with an incredulous choke.

It's official. Meredith has turned into my mum. This is exactly what Mum was like that day I was heading to the lezzy-fest in Chiswick. Meredith's lezzy-fest. Oh, the irony!

'He has an alternate sexuality,' I argue.

'Alternative,' she corrects.

'I'm not your student,' I curve-ball, sounding just like a student. She rolls her eyes. 'Anyway, you of all people should have some sympathy for alternative thingamabobs,' I add, my coup de théâtre. I almost take a bow.

Her eyes widen with indignation. 'Karen, do *not* bracket my sexuality with being a dirty great perv. I'm monogamous.'

'Sorry,' I placate, my voice softening. 'What does a lesbian take on a first date? The removal van, I know.'

I love that joke. She told me it, but even that reignites the embers of indignation.

'The old ones are the worst,' she practically spits, but then she shape-shifts to appear more like a concerned friend. It feels fake, like she's donning a plastic mask of a worried face. 'Do you even know who else is going?'

Well, I can hardly say some guy called Little Lee who's into Japanese rope bondage and tantra.

'Of course. Just some other teachers. It's all going to be fine.'

'Until someone slips a Rohypnol in your Lambrini and you're getting spit-roasted on the lazy Susan.'

And that does actually make me laugh, so I tell her I won't be drinking and will be cabbing it home by eleven.

I know what this is all about. She's jealous. She's so into me she doesn't want anyone else to get a sniff of my Kate Winslet-esque beauty. (Yeah, right!) This is why I've not told her about Kevin, or the mysterious reappearance of Michael. This is why I don't tell her anything these days.

'I've got to go, Meredith. Not that I really want to, but Mungo chucked a load of emotional blackmail at me at work and . . .'

And I knew you were having a night in watching telly on your own, so I thought it best to make myself scarce, I don't add.

She nods and rubs my shoulder. I wish she wouldn't do that.

'Well, call me if you feel weird or anything.'

'Thanks, Meredith.'

'Karen, is everything OK?'

'Sure. Why shouldn't it be?'

'No, I just . . . I wasn't sure if . . . Well, you've been a bit distant with me.'

'Oh, I've just been a bit full on with . . . stuff.'

She nods, like she appreciates the tawdry and time-consuming nature of stuff.

And I know that you're trying to get in my knickers, so . . .

'OK, well, girly night in soon, yeah?'

Over my dead body.

'Yeah. That'd be great, actually.'

'Tomorrow?'

'Oh, I can't tomorrow. Meant to be seeing . . . a . . . friend.'

I'd be suspicious if someone spoke so hesitantly to me, but she doesn't seem to pick up on it, though she is interested.

'Oh, who?'

'Just some mate from school. Anyway, better dash. Sooner I get there, sooner I can get back.'

She smiles in such a patronizing way, it's almost like she pats me on the head. I throw myself at the front door, practically tear back the latch and run down the street.

As I walk up Mungo's path, I suddenly wish I'd listened to Meredith. I should've stayed at home and watched rubbish telly with her. So what if she'd pounced on me? All I'd have to do is blurt out, 'I think this will get in the way of our friendship!' or, 'On your bike – I'm not a dyke!' and she'd be embarrassed and then we could return to watching the box. (As long as she wasn't watching my box, if you please.) Instead I'm here, with a bottle of Barolo in my hand when potentially it should be a can of Mace, and my courage is slowly melting into my shoulder bag. What on earth am I doing? The house is a bohemian-looking affair, double-fronted with pregnant bay windows, the bottom right of which is lit up and inside I can see a couple of people standing with champagne glasses and chatting. The woman is wearing a kaftan, the man is wearing a smock of some description, and I suddenly feel very out of place in my skinny jeans and baggy jumper. OK, it's a fair cop – I wanted a look that screamed, 'Out of bounds, swingers. Back the hell off!'

Oh, come on, Karen. Fionnula and Mungo are teachers, just like you. How bad can it be?

I walk up to the front door and ring the crusty doorbell. The door is painted in a very tasteful bandage colour, straight out of a National Trust property brochure, and some of its panes are stained with rich oranges and blues. After a few seconds I see Fionnula in the vestibule, all frizzy hair and smiles. Before I know it, she is clasping me to her bosom and telling me she feels my pain but I'm to leave it at the door. This is an evening of happiness. I am among friends. We are all free spirits here and the house has been cleansed of negative energy and we're in for an evening of camaraderie and love.

O . . . K . . .

Her paw in the small of my back, she guides me through to the living room, where she snatches a glass of champagne from a tray and thrusts it into my hand.

Right, well, I said I wasn't going to drink, but one won't hurt, surely.

It's nice. The cold, dancing bubbles hit the back of my throat, and though I'm still nervous, I decide this evening will not be a chore and that I'll actually have some fun getting to know people who have different interests from me – group sex, for example, possibly even macramé.

Fionnula is an attractive woman, there's no denying it. To say her hair is a little Seventies makes her sound a bit antwacky, but she carries it off with aplomb. Densely gathered fringe over heavily made-up eyes also sounds a little bit Cleopatra as a look, but the frizz of the rest of her do sings Chrissie Hynde, and I tell her so. She's thrilled. She quickly introduces me to Kaftan Woman, who has the eyes of someone with an overactive thyroid, all poppy and starey, like they're made of glass and someone is operating them from the back of her head. Her hair is shortly cropped, though maintaining a light curl. Bizarrely it is dyed orange. She has to be in her sixties, and when she outstretches her hand, I don't know whether to shake it or kiss it. I kiss it – no reason why not – and she seems amused when I bang my teeth on the massive turquoise ring I've thus far not clocked. Her name is Joyce.

Ah! Joyce from next door who likes being tied up.

'We call her Joyce the Voice,' says Smock Man, next to her. 'She's an amazing jazz contralto. You haven't lived till you've heard Joyce scat.'

I know what 'scat' is. Cleo Laine does it. At least I hope she does. I see a microphone on a stand in the corner of the room and hope to God I'm right.

'And this is Sponge,' says Fionnula, by way of introduction to Smock Man.

I thought he was too tall to be Little Lee.

'Gosh, what an unusual name,' I observe. Well, I think I have a point.

He chuckles. 'My real name's Gordon, but I love learning. I'm like a sponge? I soak it all up?'

Joyce gives a very saucy giggle. I notice she has no shoes on. Sandie Shaw, eat your heart out.

She sees me looking and intones, 'I haven't worn footwear since 1997.'

I give her a pitying look, like her feet are too massive for shoes. This disconcerts her. Ah, it is some sort of political statement/choice. So I change my demeanour, give her a mini thumbs-up and say, 'Good for you!' in a weird squeaky voice that makes me sound like one of the dwarves in *Snow White*. I have never spoken like this before, but it lends me an air of confidence. Like I'm saying, 'Look at me. I am at one with myself. So much so that sometimes I do funny voices.' Even though I don't.

Sponge diverts my attention by informing me that he

is a psychic artist. He draws pictures of your dead relatives, basically, based on a feeling he has about you. Joyce tells me she works for a charity with deprived children, snatching my attention back to her. Are they fighting over me?

'Joyce is being very modest. She runs the charity,' says Fionnula, and Joyce gives an embarrassed grimace.

Just then Mungo sashays into the room, stinking to high heaven of cheap aftershave. Fionnula takes a step back.

'Bloody hell, Mungs. Overdone it on the Lynx.'

Mungo blushes and brushes my cheek with his beard by way of a hello.

I say he 'sashays' into the room because he is wearing really hideous hippy trousers, the sort you see on a beach in Goa – dayglo colours, ten sizes too big. I see flip-flops on his feet, and the whole look is set off with a cheesecloth granddad shirt. I see a Brillo pad of orange hair poking out from his chest as he's racily left the top *four* buttons undone.

Fionnula's now passing round some nibbles. She has a plate in one hand housing a bowl of something pink – vegetarian taramasalata – and huge chunks of baguette on a plate in the other. I politely take some bread and dunk it in the rosy gunk, but I misjudge the distance or something because I drip gunk on the carpet and Mungo is sent to get the 2001 Stain Remover.

'Sorry!' I say, and wedge the bread quickly in my mouth. I really have bitten off more than I can chew here.

'It's only a carpet, darling,' says Fionnula.

'And I bet it's seen a few stains in its time!' laughs Joyce.

I almost choke on my baguette chunk. The remaining (vile) gunk is dribbling down my chin. It tastes like wallpaper paste with pink food dye in it.

I feel a hand grip my shoulder, and a deep voice coos in my ear, 'Need a hand with that?'

I turn to my left to see whose voice it is. There's no one there. I look down a bit and see a diminutive chap in a polo shirt and jeans with a twinkle in his eye. He's holding a paper napkin towards me. I can't speak, as my mouth is still working its way through the biggest piece of bread in the world, so I nod and he reaches up and wipes my chin quite forcefully. So much so that I stumble back a bit.

'Whoops-a-diddly-dandy-dido!' I hear Mungo snort, and feel him pushing me upright. Jesus, they're coming at me from all sides. Even Joyce and Sponge jump forward to grab me by the wrists.

My composure recovered, Get Shorty apologizes with a hearty guffaw.

'Lee?' I say to him, through a hunk of carbohydrate, and he nods.

'And you must be Karen.'

He crumples up the dirty napkin and tosses it into the fire.

'Oh, Lee, no, it's artificial!' screeches Fionnula, lurching to the floor and retrieving the napkin when it bounces off the illuminated plastic coals.

Lee grimaces at me, and I hear Joyce jovially echo Fionnula's earlier words: 'Oh, come on, Fionnula. It's only a fire.'

We all laugh. Me possibly more nervously than most.

I see Joyce eyeing me with pert anticipation. Her lips glisten as she licks them, then booms loudly, 'Now, tell me. Did you bring a song?'

I titter, spitting out a bit of bread, then see everyone staring at me. I swallow the last chunk of baguette. It's like swallowing a tennis ball.

As my gullet contracts to squeeze it down, I falter, 'A song?' and give another laugh.

Mungo looks to Fionnula with annoyance.

'Oh God,' she says, 'did I not mention it? We always start the evening off with a song.'

'I don't know if you know this, but I am tone deaf,' I proffer. No one seems to be listening.

My mother would love this. I personally find it excruciating. Joyce is standing in the centre of the room, gripping the microphone on its stand, as Fionnula accompanies her on some sort of electric piano that Mungo and Sponge have dragged in from another room. There's a little loud speaker underneath the piano, and Joyce is currently scatting incomprehensibly to 'Love for Sale'.

I say 'incomprehensibly' because, with no respect to the actual tune, the lyrics now appear to be:

Boo baba da boo boo BOOOOO lo-wo-wo-wo-wo-oooove
Lover lover lover lover love love love LOVE
F-f-f-f-f-f-f-f-f-f-f fooooooooor
Ba ba ba ba dam. Ba ba ba ba dam. Ba ba ba ba d-d-d-
    d-dam.
Shhhh boo boo pee doop Pah! Sha-a-a-a-a-a-le
Poo!

Fionnula is circling her head and hitting any key she fancies on the piano from what I can tell. It's not that she can't play; she played beautifully when Mungo gave us his 'Scarborough Fair'. Suddenly Fionnula lifts her hands dramatically from the keyboard and Joyce pulls a recorder from the folds of her kaftan and starts scatting with that too. In the middle of it, with no rhyme or reason, she stops, keeps the recorder at her mouth and her eyes tight shut, savouring the end of her performance.

I burst out clapping. 'Oh God, that was gorgeous,' I say,

wondering why no one else is joining in. We all clapped Mungo and he was marginally more shit.

'I've not finished,' she hisses, not even opening her eyes.

'Sorry!' I gasp.

Lee gives me a look to say it's all good, and then Joyce starts banging the recorder against various parts of her body rhythmically. Like she's playing the spoons. I've never really 'got' playing the spoons, but at least there are two of them and they create some sort of percussive sound. This just sounds like someone hitting a piece of tubular plastic against their hip, arm and head, which actually is all she is doing. It's not catchy, nor do I think it is clever, but Fionnula starts clapping along in 'time', and soon Mungo follows suit, and then Sponge starts clicking his fingers. I catch sight of Lee, who has tears in his eyes from stifling giggles, and I think, I don't care if he's into Japanese rope bondage – I'm sitting next to *him* at dinner.

Then suddenly Joyce has finished. I know this because she opens her eyes, grins proudly and curtsies. Sponge jumps to his feet, as does Mungo, and Fionnula stamps her feet on the floor like I've seen them do in orchestras after an amazing piano concerto or something. I decide it's safe to clap now, so do, till my hands hurt.

I then have to sit through Sponge singing 'Only You' by Yazoo, a cappella. Halfway through he looks encouragingly at Fionnula and she joins in with some harmonies. Then he looks at Joyce and clicks his finger in her direction and she starts to – *I am not making this up* – beat-box. A sixty-year-old woman in a kaftan beat-boxing. I hope to God he's not going to encourage me to do anything, but yes, he's pointing at me. I've no idea what to do, so I just instinctively whistle. Not quite sure what I'm whistling, but I'm pretty sure it's *almost* in tune. I think I might be harmonizing! Wow, it feels great. I feel so free . . . I feel—

Sponge does a hacking hand motion at his neck while glaring at me and I concede I might not be harmonizing but demonizing, so stop. I feel a bit disappointed, truth be told. I was starting to enjoy myself. I thought I had the music in me.

Then we have to sit through Lee frankly ruining, in my eyes, 'Someone Like You' by Adele. It's awful, though Fionnula's playing's brilliant. Then something weird happens. I forget that he's crap and begin to appreciate the feeling he's putting into it. He might not be singing it, but he's definitely feeling it. And that level of feeling permeates the room. And from nowhere I find myself trying not to cry. And failing. And I burst out crying and run from the room. The hall has many doors. I try a few and eventually find a small room with a toilet in it and hastily lock the door, ram the toilet seat down and hurl myself on it to have a good old bawl.

And of course I know why. The lyrics are all about splitting up with someone, and then that someone has met someone else, and Adele, God love her, is wishing them all the best. Even if, on closer inspection, the lyrics make her sound a bit stalkery because she turned up out of the blue uninvited and . . .

Is Michael with Asmaa? He said he'd seen her, but he's not with her. Maybe he's lying. He didn't deny seeing her. Do I wish them all the best like Adele does? I don't know. I can't even think straight. I can't even get past the idea he has gone and then come back and been so odd and . . . My mind becomes overloaded with too many conflicting thoughts. It's good he's gone. We weren't in a happy place, but I miss him. And now I'm sort of but not really seeing someone else. The father of one of my kids and . . . he's a dirty old dog and I realize now I just want Michael. But he wasn't good for me. He wasn't. So why do I still want him?

I hear a sharp knock at the door. Then Mungo's concerned voice: 'Karen?'

'Yes?' I say, attempting an air of bright and breezy, but sounding just the wrong side of manic.

'Are you OK?'

'Fine! Yes! Won't be long!'

'We . . . thought we might eat.'

'Brilliant. I'm starving.'

I rip off a few pieces of toilet paper and blow my nose.

Oh. So they don't want me to sing.

Jesus. Was I *that* out of tune?

Fionnula's Spinach Pie Recipe

Ingredients:
Flaky pastry
Oodles of spinach
A dash of nutmeg
Four zillion gallons of water

Method:
Make a pastry base.
Stick a load of spinach in it. Pour so much water into it that you create a hosepipe ban. (NB If you want a more right-on alternative, use instead the touchy-feely tears of a thousand bleeding-heart liberals, shed for all the injustices in this world. And possibly the next.)
Sprinkle with nutmeg.
Don't even bother to cook it. Serve it raw. Dare ya!

Well, that's how it tastes to me. Everyone else here is groaning in ecstasy at the deliciousness of it. I have tasted more flavour in a dripping-wet sponge dusted with nutmeg. I'm not really joining in the conversation, which is drifting between the pros and cons of a new type of Percy Pig sweet they've brought out that has no gelatine in it, and the tragedy of Joyce's former neighbour, who has never had an orgasm. I'm pushing my 'pie' round my plate disconsolately, my other hand resting in my lap, when Lee, sat to my left, reaches over and holds my hand.

I look at him, not alarmed per se, as it doesn't feel intimidating.

He smiles and just goes, 'Know you are loved.'

'You don't know me,' I point out.

But he doesn't care. 'The universe knows you, and the universe loves you.'

I'm a bit gutted they don't talk about Japanese rope bondage, or swinging. I'm even disappointed Lee hasn't tried to broach the subject of our supposed shared background in naturism. For the rest of the evening the conversation is jovial but perennially middle-class and – I'm afraid to admit it – veering towards the dull.

It becomes clear that Sponge and Joyce are going to stay over as we sip some hand-blended coffee in the living room. I feel very relaxed and, although this might be the three glasses of wine over dinner talking, decide that Mungo's a decent fella really. He just gets his rocks off by shagging people other than his wife. Mind you, she's no better or worse. And she's a very good pianist. At least they're well matched.

Lee offers to share a cab home with me, as he's going to Islington and claims it's on the way. Before I'm allowed to leave, we have to do a group hug and thank the universe for our health and inner beauty. Joyce runs her fingers down my back and starts massaging the bone at the top of my bum, while Fionnula's incanting on about all the energy she's feeling. It makes me feel a bit queasy, bringing back memories of Shirelle, but before I know it, Fionnula's saying, 'And break the ring!' and hands are removed and everyone steps apart.

Then, of course, I have to kiss everyone goodbye. Mungo is pragmatic with a quick rub of his beard, but Fionnula and Joyce linger a bit too long for my liking. As I head to the door with Lee, Sponge produces a piece of A4 paper.

'I drew this when you were on the toilet. It's a spirit who's been with you twice this evening.'

I can't look at it. That sort of thing might freak me out.

I bumble a goodbye and head out to the taxi with Lee. Again, he holds my hand all the way home. There's nothing sexual in it. I just know he's showing me his deep respect for the universe.

I can't help myself, though.

'Fionnula says you do Japanese rope bondage.'

He snorts, entertained. 'Oh, that!'

'Yes, that!' I chuckle too.

'It doesn't rule my life. It's just something I'm into every now and again. A hobby. Like boating. Some weekends, if I'm not busy, and if I can find a willing partner.'

I give him a look that says, 'That partner is not me.'

'After my wife left me, I realized I'd not had a decent orgasm in years. I'd not explored my own body and my own sensations. I decided from now on I would, and I'm so glad I did. It's not for everyone, and it's a little bit selfish, but after sixteen years with that frigid cow, I thought I was ready for some me-time.'

I nod, kind of knowing what he means. Though I thought it was just women who had crap orgasms.

As we pull up outside my house, I kiss him gently on the cheek.

Well . . . I'm only trying to show him the universe loves him.

Meredith's fast asleep on the couch. Her top is on inside out. It wasn't earlier. Odd.

Once I climb into bed, I get the sketch out of my bag. It's a pencil drawing of a woman, an attractive woman with a shaved head. Beautiful eyes. And I think Sponge is mad. He has drawn me a picture of Sinead O'Connor.

She's not dead, is she?

I take out my phone and compose a text to Michael's mum: **Rita, sorry I've not been in touch. Lots to sort out. Promise I'll speak soon. Sorry for being so rubbish. K xx**

Almost immediately she replies: **No worries. Whenever you're ready. Rita xx**

But I'm not sure I'll ever be ready.

EIGHTEEN

When the phone rings on Sunday morning, I half expect it to be Kevin calling to cancel our second 'date'. I deserve it, for foreclosing on our first one at the Smiling Lion. When I pick up the receiver, though, it's not him – it's Dad.

'Hiya, love. How you diddlin'?'

'Oh, hiya, Dad. Yeah, diddlin' all right, thanks.'

'Is your mother there?'

'Er, no.'

And silence.

'Oh. Has she gone to the shops?'

'Erm, yes. She's gone to the shops for . . . you know . . . things.'

'What, like a Sunday paper? Bacon?'

'That is so spot on, Dad, because before she went, she said – and I'm quoting her word for word here – "Just nipping out for a Sunday paper and some bacon."'

'Right. I'll try her mobile.'

Oh God. What if Jorgen Borgen answers? Danish people might do that, answer each other's phones. I've never seen any of those Danish cop shows, but I bet they do it all the time as a matter of principle. Maybe in Denmark every mobile is identical or it's a courteous tradition.

'Yeah, you could do that, Dad, but I'll make sure I tell her you called.'

Then it transpires that Dad wants to chat. He never wants to chat. Which Dad in the history of the world ever said anything other than 'I'll get your mother' when you rang up? Oh, he's on a roll this morning, asking about the weather, how I'm feeling, if I've seen much of my friends and what Wendy's up to these days. Oh, he's Chatty McFee of Chatsville today, but then I imagine he's probably feeling lonely. He's been on his own since Christmas. Which reminds me of something . . .

'Dad, did you ever speak to Mum about what we were talking about the other day? You know, about her making up stuff about me going psycho?'

'I don't want to get into that right now, Karen.'

Odd. He did the other day. Then I wonder if he did actually speak to Mum and she managed to convince him that she was telling the truth and I was lying and I was always a pill bottle away from topping myself. I bet you that's what she's done. Something's up because I can hear it in his voice. He's being evasive (you can't get more evasive than 'I don't want to get into that right now'), whereas the last time we spoke he was angry and upset. I can't even remember how long ago that was. I know it was before Meredith moved in, but that feels like years ago now. It could only be as little as three weeks. I'm confused.

'You don't still think I'm completely mental, do you, Dad?'

He gives a nervous laugh. 'As if,' he says.

I've heard this particular 'as if' before, though. He says it when Penelope Keith comes on the telly and Mum and I wind him up and go, 'There's your girlfriend, Dad/Vern.'

'Oh, shut up.'

'You do. You *so* fancy her.'

'Oh, as *if.*'

That's how it sounds now – not like a denial but an admission.

He thinks I'm ker-azy!

'Anyway, er . . . I'll give your mother a ring and . . . well, I might come down and see you next week. Got a few days off.'

No. He can't. I must stop him. He comes down here and he'll know the extent of the Jorgen Borgen situation, and how I've lied to cover up for my mother by not saying anything. But then I realize that I'll still come out of it quite well because at least he'll know I didn't lie to him about being psycho, and threatening to throw myself down the stairs all the time or eat a light supper of razor blades and quicklime. He'll hate Mother for that and so mark her down as the Bad Guy and me down as the Goody. Bloody right too.

'I'm . . . really busy with school. Not that it wouldn't be nice to see you.'

'Well, I'm sure we'll sort something out. I'll talk to your mother about it.'

'Yeah. Good idea. Hope you get through to her.'

As soon as I've hung up I quickly phone Mum's mobile and – hey presto – Jorgen Borgen answers. At least I think it's Jorgen Borgen; he doesn't sound particularly foreign to me. In fact he sounds a bit like Guy Ritchie, mockney-wise.

'Hello?' Actually, he's got a lovely voice.

'Hi. Is that Borgen?'

'No, this is Jorgen.'

And I do, I actually say it.

'Ah, good *morgen*, Jorgen. This is Karen, Val's daughter?'

'Oh, hi, Karen. I have heard so much about you. I hope you are good.'

'Yeah, I'm great this *morgen*, *dank* you.'

I really could slap myself right now. I don't even speak Danish, so I don't even know if these are authentic Danish words. I'm guessing not.

'Were you wanting to speak with Valerie?'

'Yes, I would actually. Is she there?'

'She is, Karen, but at the moment she is evacuating.'

I have no idea what this means.

'Evacuating?'

'Yes. On the toilet. As you know, your mother is regular, but she only evacuates twice a week, so . . . she may be some time.'

I did know this, but I usually care to pretend I don't.

'Right.'

I'm in no mood for my mother's toy boy telling me so openly about the bowel movements of his sugar mummy. I beat about the bush no longer.

'Well, can you tell her from me that my dad's been on the phone?' And for emphasis I add, 'You know? Vernon? Her husband?'

'I have not had the pleasure.'

'And he's wanting to speak to her *and* . . .' I even do a dramatic pause '. . . he's threatening to pay a visit next week.'

'He evacuates infrequently too?'

'No. Pay a visit. Come down to London.'

'Oh. I am sorry. When your mother she says she is going to the bathroom, she describes it as "going to pay a visit". Forgive me.'

'No, it's a bit more serious than that,' I say in a contemptuous tone, hoping to shock him, and show I have little respect for him as he's tearing my family apart. I didn't actually realize I felt this way till the words came tumbling out, but now that I've used that tone, I feel immeasurably better. It's a tone I use a lot at work, but in that sphere it rarely improves my mood.

'Of course,' Jorgen Borgen says with a humility that's appealing. I almost feel sorry for him, till I remember. *He's shagging my mother. He is my age. He is not right in the bonce.*

But then I remember. *Wendy is dating a seventy-two-year-old. The world is on its head.*

After hanging up, I try to work out if there are any seventy-two-year-olds out there who I could imagine going to bed with. I wonder if Rod Stewart is that old and decide he's not. I Google Bruce Springsteen. In his sixties. I look up Mickey Rooney, shudder, then decide I was right first time.

The world is full of freaks, and I refuse to be one of them.

But then I think Paul McCartney: would I or wouldn't I?

Well, he's got a sparky personality, and he's not exactly brassic.

I imagine Sir Paul and I having dinner at his favourite veggie restaurant somewhere fancy in Mayfair. We have spinach pie and it knocks spots off Fionnula's mess. We drink vegan wine and I lose my inhibitions and my Oyster card so have to go and stay over on Sir Paul's couch. (NB He is not married in this fantasy.) I curl up on the Terence Conran futon in his box room, but then there is a knock at the door. He comes in, looking down on me in his Deputy Dawg pyjamas. He opens his mouth and I wonder if he's going to sing his bits to 'Ebony and Ivory', but instead he says, 'Karen, I get dead lonely in that bed, you know. Don't suppose you fancy bunkin' in wirr us and making an old man dead happy?'

'Oh, Sir Paul!' I say, peeling myself off the futon and revealing myself naked to him. 'I thought you'd never ask.'

(NB The good thing about a seventy-two-year-old seeing you *sans* clothes, I decide, is that they're so chuffed by your young(er) flesh that even if you have rolls of fat and a welcome mat on your back, they still think you're hot.)

We move into his main bedroom (in my fantasy he has a three-bedroom semi in suburbia. I can't vouch this is 100 per cent accurate), and he lays me down on his black satin sheets, dims the lights, drops his Deputy Dawg pyjama bottoms to reveal his Mull of Kintyre and then aims his remote (that's not a euphemism. The Mull of Kintyre was. This isn't) at his Bose sound system and lowers himself onto me. 'The Frog Chorus' plays in the background as he starts to push himself against me in time to the song.

OK, I've had enough of this. I wouldn't do Paul McCartney, not to the strains of that song. I move on.

It starts to rain and my heart sinks. Kevin and I are meant to be going for a walk in the countryside today. I really wanted the weather to hold up. I realize I've opened my bedroom window to air the room, so I reach up to shut it when I spot something out in the street. A man is sitting on the wall of the house opposite. He's not looking up, but it strikes me as odd. There's the light rain, and his Colditz-style coat is done up to fight off the elements, collar upturned. It's Michael. I step cautiously back from the window, wondering what on earth he is doing here. This is not normal behaviour, surely. You don't just go and sit outside your ex-girlfriend's house unless you're a stalker or you want something from her. If he wants to see me, why hasn't he just rung the doorbell? And now he is sitting there in the rain. I peer between the wall and the curtain and see he is still there, still not looking over at the house, staring blankly at the pavement beneath him. He shakes his head suddenly, like he's having a conversation with himself and disagrees with something.

Oh God, I better go and speak to him.

'What are you doing out here, Michael?' I asked tentatively, not wanting him to snap. He snapped a lot these days. It was a

blazing-hot day – there was no reason why he shouldn't be sun-bathing. It was just odd that he chose to do so on the wall of the house opposite.

'Just thinking.'

'What about?'

He didn't answer. He didn't need to.

'Well, why are you thinking here?'

He looked around himself, as if he was only then realizing the incongruity of his location.

'I was coming back from the park. And I was thinking. And I was a bit knackered. So I thought I'd have a rest here.'

I nodded, then squatted down and touched his hand.

'Why don't you come in with me?'

There was a glazed look in his eyes. He was looking at me, but seeing something much, much further away at the same time. There'd been a gaping chasm between us for a long time now, and it didn't take a genius to work out why. For a second I thought he was crying, but then I realized that the pearls of moisture under his eyes were sweat.

'Come on, come inside.'

He wrapped his thumb over my hand, keeping it there. It was the most he'd touched me in weeks. It sent a jolt of electricity through me and suddenly I wanted to kiss him. I'd not looked at him sexually in such a long time and it felt at once familiar and alien. My breathing deepened, and I scrunched up my hand, tightening my grip on him.

I flicked my head back, towards our house. He breathed in, and without speaking, we stood up. I flitted my eyes down to his chest. He was wearing a thin grey T-shirt that clung to him in the heat. Lines of sweat had appeared beneath his pecs, and his nipples were jutting out above them. He'd worn this T-shirt a million times, but it had never had this effect on me before.

Something animalistic took over and I knew I had to taste him. Something almost masculine flooded over me because I knew I wasn't going to take no for an answer.

He kept gripping my hand as we crossed the road, but as soon as we were inside the hall, I pushed the front door to, pinned him against the wall and started kissing him. He pushed back, clawing at me. We were aggressive, angry; our teeth clashed, and I bit his lip. I pulled up his T-shirt and took his nipple in my mouth and didn't care, I had to bite into it. He squealed in pain, but I wouldn't let go. He pushed me away, onto the stairs, face down. I sensed him jerk down his jogging bottoms. I felt my knickers being ragged off and before I knew it he was inside me. The force was a shock and I felt his fingernails dig into my waist, his bulk, his otherness on top of me. When he pulled out, my body missed him and I wanted him back, deeper. He threw his weight back down on me, and his tongue started exploring my neck as he bore deeper into me. I tried to look round to see his face. His hands were steadying himself on the stair now. I saw his eyes were twisted shut. He didn't take long. He withdrew just in time and I felt him spurt onto my back. He stepped back, into the jumble of jogging bottoms and undies. I looked behind and saw he was attempting to kneel in the middle of the hall. He gave up and just collapsed back against the wall, spent. Which is when I saw he was crying.

We'd not had sex for ages. We'd certainly not had sex like that, where we seemed to be driven by need. I didn't know what the need was. The need to prove we were alive? The need to prove which of us was in charge? In that respect I'm not sure who came off better. So it might have been disheartening in other circumstances that the first time we did it he ended in tears.

His T-shirt was stretched out of shape from where I'd torn at it to bite him. The sleeve was rolled up in an affectation of trendiness,

233

but what it revealed was a stark reminder of the reason for his tears. Tattooed on his bicep was a date. That date of the birth of Evie. Which was also the date of her death. Etched for ever on his skin. And I knew that was why he was crying. Because every time we made love, whatever you want to call it – though there hadn't been much love today – it reminded us both of her. How we made her, and then lost her. I picked my knickers up off the floor, chucked them onto the stairs and crawled across to snuggle up to him. He put his arm round me as he cried his silent tears, and I clung on to his arm, but there was no connection between us. I was right there next to him, but really he was unreachable.

'What are you doing, Michael?'

He doesn't look up. His hair's soaked and looks like he's wearing gel. The coat must be wet too, but close up the pattern is speckled, so it's hard to tell. I may only be wearing leggings and a T-shirt, but I am bone dry because I have my leopard-skin umbrella up.

'It's raining.'

'Is it still raining?' he says in a monotone. I know what's coming next. 'I didn't notice.'

Still he doesn't look up. It's a line from the film *Four Weddings and a Funeral*. I loved it; he hated it. He especially hated that line. Andie MacDowell's stood there in the rain with Huge Grant at the end of the movie in the pouring rain. Their love for each other is so all-consuming that she hasn't even noticed it's raining. Or something like that. Anyway, I always thought it was impossibly moving. Michael just found it nauseating. We had actually rowed about it to such an extent we were never able to watch it together again.

'It's a bit weird,' I point out.

'What's weird? Me sitting on a wall? Nothing weird about

that.' His Liverpool accent sounds stronger. It gets stronger when he's had a drink or when he's angry. He doesn't look particularly plastered, so I'm guessing it's the latter. Either way, this doesn't bode well.

'Well, when you're sitting opposite your ex-girlfriend's house, some might say that's a bit . . . stalkery.'

He shakes his head. 'It's my house too.'

'Then maybe you'd like to pay your half of the mortgage.'

'With what?'

'Er, your wages?'

'You think I still work?'

'You've given up work?'

'I've told you. How many times have I told you? And how many times have you not listened? I'm sick, Karen.'

'Then get some help.'

'I got some help. Fat lot of good that did.'

I'm being sucked back in. I'm being sucked back in to his dramas and crises, and I'm assuming responsibility for them, as if I created them and can therefore make them better. When I can't, and when really they should no longer be my concern. I see a curtain twitch in the window in front of me. The Polish One From Over the Road is peeking out, having a nose.

'The Polish One's looking at us.'

'Let her.'

I've always been a bit mortified in front of the Polish One. During one of Michael's 'episodes' he took to playing loud music in the middle of the night. I always tried to turn it down, but he'd always snap it back up to full volume. The neighbours either side were reasonably understanding when I explained what was going on, though I did swear them to secrecy – Michael would have hit the roof if he'd known I was telling all and sundry what he was going through. Unfortunately the

Polish One From Over the Road stuck a note through the letter box complaining vociferously. As English is not her first language, it was full of spelling and grammatical mistakes. Michael took a red pen, corrected them, then posted it back through her letter box. There'd been a stand-off ever since, and of course because I'm a teacher, I'm sure she assumed it was me who'd been so rude.

'Did you follow me the other week?'

He tuts. 'No. Where?'

'I went for a meal with . . . with a friend and you were looking in through the window.'

He tuts again. He really is behaving like one of the kids. One of the kids when you've caught them out in a lie. 'No. God, you're obsessed.'

The Polish One's front door opens and she pops her head out.

'Everything OK, Karen?'

'Yes, thanks,' I say calmly. 'Won't be long.'

Michael jumps up now and walks off down the road. She doesn't look at him but keeps her eyes transfixed on me. I smile apologetically and then follow him. I hear her door shut.

What am I doing? Why am I following him? I should be getting ready to go and meet Kevin, but instead I'm following my needy ex down the road and I have no idea why.

'Michael! Wait!'

A passing woman looks startled. I shoot her daggers.

'What? Never heard anyone speak before?'

She looks down the street, to where I was shouting, then looks back to me, confused.

'Oh, piss off!' I snap, then hurry on.

I don't even know why I'm so angry.

'Michael, come back! Where you going?'

He stops, looks back.

'You're right,' he says. 'I shouldn't have come. I shouldn't even be here. I buggered off. I've got no right coming back and messing with your head.'

'You'd mess with my head a lot less if you just explained what was going on.'

I've caught up with him now. I put the umbrella over his head too.

'There's nothing to explain. I'm a waste of space. I fuck up everything – everything. I fucked up my life. I fucked up my job. I fucked up our baby and I've fucked up you.'

'God, it's all about you, isn't it?' I half joke, trying to lighten the mood.

'Well, haven't I?' he asks.

Has he? Well, yes, but do I tell him that? What is the protocol here? How honest are you meant to be with depressed exes when they're pushing for how you're getting on now they're gone (but have come back)? I notice his pupils. They're not dilated. Usually when he's taking his antidepressants, his pupils enlarge. It's meant to make you look more sexy when your pupils enlarge, but because I knew the cause, I never could interpret it as exciting. Now, though, well, they just look normal. This too is not a good sign.

'Are you not taking your pills?'

He laughs and looks away. He speaks to the wall beside him. 'Have you heard this?' Then he looks back to me, his eyes now aflame with anger. 'I don't . . . need them anymore, you knob-head.'

Right, that's it.

'Don't call me names, Michael. I didn't put up with it when we were together, and I won't put up with it now.'

Boy, do I really sound like a teacher now. I turn on my heel and head back towards the house. He makes no attempt to retort, or follow me. In the old days he could never let me have the last word. My mum used to advise me, 'Never go to bed on a row,' but that was hard if you'd not factored in Michael's belligerence.

I'm not going to look back. I'm not. I won't give him the satisfaction. I am winning this. I have had the last word. I have stood up for myself and explained where I draw the line, and he will have to accept it, like he never did before.

I hear him shouting, 'You never called my mum!'

I ignore it. At the front door I look back. Michael is standing exactly where I left him, but his demeanour has changed. His eyes are locked on me, and he looks – dare I say it? – hopeful. Excited. Almost as if he is proud of me for standing up to him, as if he's achieved something by doing that. He shoots me a little smile, as if to say, 'Well done.' There is also an air of smugness in that smile. Like something went to plan. Hmm.

He has never let me get the last word in before. And now he has. And it's like he did it on purpose. But why?

He sees that his smile confused me, and immediately he scowls, shoves his hands in his pockets and angrily walks away. As he disappears round the corner, I am left feeling slightly disturbed by the encounter. I put my brolly down, shake off the beads of rain that are clinging to it, head inside and shut the door.

NINETEEN

The smugness of Michael ignites a fierce determination in me. I am going to meet Kevin as planned, and I am going to have a fantastic time with him and not feel guilty about attempting to move on from Michael. There – I've said it. If he thinks he can come back here and mess with my head and try and see if I've still got feelings for him, then he's got another thing coming.

Kevin has come up with the idea of a magical mystery tour. All I know is I have to turn up at Waterloo station at 11 a.m. and wear sensible shoes.

Oh God. Sensible shoes. I want to look all sexy, sophisticated and alluring. How is this possible when you're wearing T-bar sandals? They're sensible.

I did email him and ask him to clarify what 'sensible shoes' means and he replied that there might me some 'country-style walking'. This immediately conjures up images of middle-aged people with fat legs in hiking shorts, chunky fisherman socks and burly boots traipsing, bow-legged, up a hillside with the aid of a stick whittled from the branch of a favourite elm. I find little that is sexy about that, but then I think that Kevin is no country bumpkin, and my hunch is that he'll wear his Caterpillar boots, so I plump for my retro brogues, which I team with skinny jeans. (Wendy once said they make my bum look 'cute'. Cuteness is good, I hope. Mind you, she did say this after a heavy night on the sauce.) I team the jeans with a floaty grey blouse, some noisy jewellery and a matching grey cardy, and stick a cagoule in my bag. Functional but funky is what I'm hoping for. Freaky and frizzy is what I'm trying to avoid. So, in case it rains – and it seems to have done nothing but this year – I pop a grey woolly hat on too. Bad hat hair is probably preferable to the pan-fried curls I get when the do gets wet.

Kevin is indeed wearing his Caterpillar boots when we meet as planned outside Marks & Spencer on the station concourse. They're still remarkably unscuffed. I like the fact that I am getting to know him and so was able to predict something about how he'd look. It's like I know enough to claim some understanding of him, and it breeds familiarity – no contempt. He's wearing jeans (baggy again) and this time a flapping green mod coat that brings me up short because it's the sort of coat Michael used to wear. Well, the sort he wore before he went all Colditz on me. He's laden down with WHSmith bags, so as he throws his arms around me, the bags ricochet round and nearly wind me in the back, which makes us laugh. He tells me he's already got our tickets and we need to hurry. We slide said tickets through the computerized barrier, the gates jerk open, and minutes later we are sitting in the first-class carriage of a train heading for Weymouth. I don't really know where Weymouth is. Kevin informs me we're going to be travelling for about an hour and a half and so to make myself comfortable.

He up-ends the carrier bags onto our table and it's now I discover he has literally bought every Sunday newspaper known to man. I can't believe he has gone to all this trouble, but he shushes me and says you can travel quite cheaply on a Sunday in first class – he just needs to buy an upgrade off the guard when he comes round. As the train pulls out of the cat's cradle of platforms and lines, we settle down with papers and cartons of orange juice, and begin a ninety-minute journey of reading funny stories aloud to each other, pointing out interesting pictures and so on from the various magazines and papers. It feels good. It feels right. It feels like we've known each other for years.

Sometimes I look up over the top of my paper to watch him reading. He bites his bottom lip in concentration and I wonder what it would be like to kiss those lips. Sensing me looking, he flits up his eyes and catches me. And smiles. And I smile back, and we both return to reading our rags. Sometimes I catch him doing it, which gives me butterflies. I have not felt like this in ages. The air is heavy with anticipation, with promise, and I am light-headed, giddy.

I'm even more light-headed, though a lot less giddy, when two hours later we are cycling – yes, *cycling* – down country lanes in the New Forest, of all places. This is the second stage of our magical mystery tour, apparently, though I am so unfit and unused to exercise that I am finding little magical about riding around on a bike in the pouring rain. Thank heavens for the sensibly packed cagoule. I am not a happy bunny, it has to be said, and the more I pedal – seemingly getting myself nowhere – the more convinced I become that this is not a perfect 'date' activity. Even if I do have to put the word 'date' in inverted commas because I can't say hand on heart this is one. My face must have been a picture as we landed in a sleepy place called Brockenhurst and Kevin marched me over to the cycle-hire place that was actually in an old train carriage in the station car park. He had booked in advance, so our bikes were there waiting for us, gleamingly clean in the (then) bright sunlight. Kevin laughed and assured me we'd only be riding for half an hour or so. I hate the phrase 'or so': it usually means double/treble/quadruple that. Once again I am proved right, as we have been cycling for the best part of fifty minutes – I've checked my watch. Also, as soon as we left the cycle-hire place, the heavens opened. Rest assured I am not convinced that outdoor activities are a good look for a date if there is the possibility of it pissing down.

It turns out Kevin's a really proficient cyclist who works out or goes to the gym. I know he was playing football yesterday, so either way he is in decent shape and therefore much fitter than me. He keeps cycling on ahead and then having to stop and wait to let me catch up, so the majority of our time is being spent apart and not communicating. He's pushing on at some speed, in his own little world, leaving me to observe and admire the scenery alone. Yes, OK, it's very pretty – there are lots and lots and lots of trees, and we have seen ponies strutting their stuff along every lane we've been down – but surely it would look nicer from the inside of a hire car, with windscreen wipers and a tax disc adding to the view. At least then we'd be able to chat, make each other laugh, just like we were doing on the train. It's hard to make someone chuckle when all you can see is their backside bouncing up and down on a bicycle seat. OK, so I'm making that sound like an attractive prospect, but because of the inclemency of the weather, believe me it's not. There may as well be people lining the route with buckets of cold water and chucking them over us, it's that wet.

I toy with the idea that maybe a tandem would have been a better option, but even then we wouldn't have been able to communicate, because the idea of speaking at the moment is beyond ridiculous. I am panting like Pavlov's dog and sweating like the Child Catcher in a crèche. I amuse myself briefly with the idea that maybe I could invent a communication system for hardy cyclists. Right now Kevin could have fibre-optic lights sewn into the back of his coat and he could flick a switch on his handlebars that would light up various spelled-out messages in the fibre optics, saying stuff like:

WE'RE TAKING THE NEXT RIGHT.

Or:

GET A MOVE ON, YOU LAZY ARTICLE.

Or:

STOP OGLING MY ARSE, LADY!

I say I amuse myself with this, but the amusement is only fleeting, because unless I think about anything other than the effort I am putting in to actually get these pedals to go round and get the wheels spinning, I immediately slow down and Kevin becomes a speck on the horizon.

After nearly giving myself a heart attack pushing my way up a hill on a bend, I find Kevin at the top of the slope, waiting at a track that turns off into the trees. When eventually, eighty-five years later, I catch up with him, he nods down the track and says, 'Mind if we have a look down here?'

I look at the sign at the side of the track. It says, 'Three Hills Campsite.' I nod, still unable to speak, my chest rising up and down, and doing an awful interpretation of a heaving bosom on speed. I manage to get some of my lost breath back as we head down the track, as it's flat and Kevin goes really slowly. We've entered a tunnel of tall trees, so it's quite dark, but it's OK, as it's nice to be dry and sheltered from the rain.

I wonder what's so interesting about seeing a campsite. And then I realize. Oh my God, this is so embarrassing. Has he hired a caravan for us to . . . I don't know . . . do stuff in? I'm not looking forward to this. I guess it knocks spots off renting a sleazy motel in the middle of the day for an afternoon of friskiness, but a caravan? Really? Right now I need luxury. I need somewhere to bathe, to change into something slinkier or warmer, and preferably some champagne on ice. I can see none of these things on offer here. Also, nothing about Kevin's behaviour or demeanour has intimated that this is what he's after. Yes, there was a bit of light eye-flirting on the train, but we've not really spoken since then, and getting sweaty on a bike isn't the sort of foreplay I'm familiar with.

Suddenly the trees part and we are looking at a very ordinary campsite. Thanks to the rain, everyone must be indoors. There are, however, a smattering of caravans dotted about. Some of them appear to be permanent, as they have decking around them; some seem to be visiting. I wonder which one ours might be, and desperately look for one that might have a luxury bathroom and possibly an escalator to a penthouse suite. I see none.

I look to Kevin, wondering what he is going to say. Is he going to point to one in particular and say, 'To be sure, there is our mobile love palace'?

In his defence, I have never heard him use the phrase 'to be sure', to be sure.

When I crook my neck, I see that he seems different. The sparkle has gone from his eyes. He looks crushed.

'Are . . . are you OK?' I venture.

He takes a deep breath, staring straight ahead at the caravans, exhales loudly, then shrugs.

'What is it? Kevin?'

'Sorry, Karen. This is a bit unfair.'

'Why? What?'

He's working up to say something. What can it be? It's just a smattering of caravans.

'This is where I used to come with Toni, when Connor was little. I've not been back since . . .' His voice peters out and he doesn't have to explain what he means.

I nod, to show I understand, but I'm not sure exactly how I feel. Should I feel touched that he's brought me to his and Toni's old haunt? Jealous? Angry? I don't know. I suppose her loss is part of him, so maybe it's OK. Still feels weird, though. I reach out and rub his arm, the way many have done to me these past few months. His coat is soaked through.

'God, this was so stupid,' he says. 'I don't know what I was thinking.'

'No, it's not – it's fine,' I argue. 'Just as long as you're OK.'

'I honestly didn't choose coming here 'cos of . . . all this. I just . . . I wanted us to have a gas and . . . and I know the area and . . .'

Of course he knows the area. He came here with his wife.

'. . . and I know it's dead nice and . . . the scenery and . . . I felt I could show it off to you. I didn't really think.'

'It's fine,' I insist, though I can't help doubting his thought processes at the planning stage.

'We always came in the summer, so it was never pissing it down.'

I giggle, to show it's fine.

'It's all gravy,' I venture. Now he laughs.

'I hear Connor saying that. I have absolutely no idea what it means. Do you?'

I nod. 'Never use a phrase you don't understand.'

'What, like the FTSE 100 Index? I think I'll go to my grave not knowing what that is.'

The way he speaks his 'think' sounds like 'tink' and I find it impossibly cute. If you can call a man in his mid-thirties 'cute'. 'Cute' implies Disneyesque cartoon baby elephants with big ears and adorable smiles that blow rainbow-coloured bubbles in the air every time they giggle. Kevin is far from that.

'It means it's all good,' I say proudly. God, it feels cool to be down with the kids.

He suddenly puts his arm round me and drags me into him. It's a bit awkward, as there's his bike between us, but I don't resist.

'Jesus, Karen, what am I even doing? I think I'm going mental.'

There it was again. Tink.

'Toni's not even cold in the ground and here I am carrying on like . . . like she wasn't even here.'

Oh God. He's talking like we're dating. Like properly dating. I'm not sure how I feel about that.

'I think you're a great girl, and I'd be lying if I said I didn't fancy the bollocks of you, but I'm a bit of a basket case, truth be told.'

'That's OK,' I butt in gently. 'So am I.'

'I know we're not planning on getting married or anything, but . . .'

'I know. We've not even kissed or anything.'

'No, I know. Oh, don't listen to me. I talk shite. I do like you. I just don't know if . . .' and he sighs and gives a little groan. Because he's still got his arm round me, I feel it reverberate through my body. 'Jeez, I'm jumping the gun a bit here. Sorry.'

'No, it's . . . good to know where we stand. Or where you see it developing. All I'd say is, we shouldn't run before we can walk.'

'Well, at the moment we're standing in a muddy fecking campsite getting pissed on by God. Come on, let's get to the pub and have something to eat.'

Fortunately the ride to the pub only takes about ten minutes.

It's not a pleasant journey because now we've been stood still for a while, so the sweat on my body has gone cold, accentuating the chill of the rain on my clothes and hat and hair. The pub is warm, luckily, and there's even a roaring fire in the next room as we sit down to eat. Kevin is the most relaxed I've seen him as he sups from a pint of local bitter (I plump for half a Guinness) and starts to tell me his life story. It's weird. It's like because he let his guard down at the caravan site, because he gave me a glimpse into how he was feeling, because he has shown me a weakness, we've moved somewhere else.

He tells me all about his upbringing on a farm in rural West Ireland and how he loves the outdoors and hates living in London, especially Fountain Woods, where every house is the same. How his childhood dream was to be a movie star, but that never quite worked out. How he has always had a good singing voice and sang at all his family weddings and funerals – if there was a party, basically, he was wheeled out – but how he never really followed it up, as his dad was a builder and from an early age he forced him to bunk off school and go and work for the family business. Then he fell in love with Toni when she came over to work as a receptionist in a nearby hotel, and when she said she was going back to England, he didn't tell his parents and ran away to be with her. His parents didn't speak to him for ages, even boycotting his wedding. Ironically they got back in touch when they heard that Connor had been born, not realizing of course that he wasn't really their grandson.

He tells me how he worked on building sites when he first came over, and Toni worked at various posh hotels on Park Lane, and they hardly ever saw each other because of their long hours and differing shifts, which is why it was easy for her to have the affair. Then Kevin decided to set up his own building firm and work for himself. He tells me the business has done OK, but he's had to lay a few fellas off in the last year or so and now tends to do smaller jobs or just hire his mates on the odd job, whereas they used to be permanent staff. He says he and Toni lived in a nice big house up until three years ago, when they had to downsize to Fountain Woods because of the credit crunch. He has two sisters, Coleen and Bernadette – at this point I ask hilariously if they've ever released a record called 'I'm in the Mood for Dancing'. He practically spits out his pint, he laughs so much. Then he talks about how he feels about Connor being with Jamie, and how it's killing him, and how alone and scared he feels.

'What are you scared of?' I ask.

He looks at me. 'Losing him.'

I shake my head. 'You're not gonna lose him.'

He doesn't look convinced.

'You're amazing and funny and caring and . . . everything he needs.'

'Ah, a vote of confidence.'

Though I'm not sure where 'amazing' came from.

'And if he does decide to live with Jamie, I'll give him detention every night for the rest of his life until he realizes he's making a complete and utter prick of himself.'

Kevin nods. He sees this could work. We chuckle.

'But I really don't think it's going to come to that.'

We both have scampi and chips. It's a million times nicer than when I ate out with Mungo the other week, and a zillion times nicer than Fionnula's spinach pie, but maybe it's the company. And the Guinness. And the roaring log fire.

Actually, it's not roaring; it's crackling. It sounds nothing like a lion.

'Anyway, listen to me, banging on,' he says, reaching out and rubbing my hand. 'I'm not the only one who's lost someone special, eh?'

I nod, but I don't want to spoil this. This is . . . gravy . . . just the way it is.

'D'you mind if we don't talk about that?' I ask.

'Sure. Your wish is my command.'

We eat in silence for a bit. I've asked for some tartare sauce and the barmaid brings it over suspiciously, like I've asked for a gram of cocaine.

'Karen?'

'Aha?'

'You know when we get back to London later?'

'Aha?'

'What would you say to, like . . . coming and staying at mine the night?'

Wow.

I wasn't expecting that.

He sees my amazement and reads it as horror. It's not horror. I just don't know what to say. Part of me wants to scream, 'Yes, yes! Take me on your dining-room table, you gorgeous hunk of a brute!' but another part of me whispers, 'I don't think I'm ready. I know it's daft, but I don't think I'm over Michael yet.'

Then the other part of me overrules the whole shebang, reminding myself that I have been exercising for the afternoon and will be all sweaty and smelly.

'I don't mean shagging,' he says.

And now that the chance has been grabbed from me, it's what I want more than anything in the world. Who cares if I smell? He'll have running water. He's a builder. He'll have a bath, won't he?

'I just . . . don't wanna be on my own tonight. I'm fed up of being on my own.'

I nod.

'No funny business,' he adds. 'Just . . . what do you call it? Thingy.'

'Frottage?' I ask, then immediately regret it.

'Spooning,' he says.

I nod. Of course. Spooning. Why didn't I think of that? Do I have a one-track mind?

'Would you actually say the word "yes", Karen? Or else I won't believe my luck.'

'Spooning?' I'm confused.

'No. "Yes."'

'Sorry?'

'Will you just say "yes"? Please?'

Oh. I get it now.

'Yes, Kevin. I'll come and stay.'

'Brilliant,' he says, and I see the twinkle return to his eyes. And then he says it again for good measure. 'Brilliant.'

It's only on the train home that I remember that of course this could all be a line. This could be Kevin's shtick. It's only now I remember what I was told at the wake about him having a different woman round every night while Toni was dying in hospital.

I could quite easily get out of this. There's a whole hour and a half on the train for me to say, 'D'you know what, Kevin? I've thought about this and I don't think it's a good idea. I don't think either of us is in the right place just now for this kind of intimacy.'

But I don't. And I'm not going to. Because right now that Kevin doesn't seem real. The one before me, slightly broken and battered, seems genuine. And even if it is his shtick, I've bought it. Even if it is a line, I've gobbled it up.

Besides, I don't want to be on my own tonight either.

I've had no signal on my phone in the New Forest, and once our train leaves the greenery and hits the greyness of Southampton, a few texts come through from Mum. She wants me to call her. Needs to talk about something Dad said. I decide it can wait till tomorrow.

I'm still not willing to so much as spoon him when I've spent the afternoon working up a sweat and cycling for so long that my jeans and knickers have wedged up my backside to more of an alarming degree than when I went to the Smiling Lion, courtesy of Shirelle, so I come up with a plan and he buys into it. From Waterloo we are going to head back to my place, where I am going to jump in the shower, change my clothes and pack an overnight bag and all the stuff I need for school in the morning. I ignore the possibly feminist thing of insisting we don't stay at his, but at mine instead, but only because I can't be doing with Meredith knowing what is going on. Besides, it means I can have more of a lie-in in the morning. OK, so I'll have to wait till the coast is clear before leaving his house in case any of the kids from school see. A thought hits me . . .

'Oh God, Connor's not coming home tonight, is he?'

Kevin shakes his head. 'Jamie gets to drop him off at school.' Then he rolls his eyes.

OK. And relax.

And panic again. Because when we get back to East Ham, Meredith is home. I really did think she was going to be at her Sunday-afternoon netball practice. She is lying on the couch watching reruns of *The L Word* on cable when we tiptoe in. She jolts upright, recognizing Kevin immediately.

'Mr O'Keefe!'

'Ah, Miss Penrose.'

'You . . . know each other,' I say, because I'm quick like that, and always say the right thing, natch.

'Connor's in the year seven football team,' Kevin explains to me.

'Have you . . . had a nice day?' she asks, her voice so full of alarm and anxiety that she sounds like Minnie Mouse.

'Great, thanks, yeah,' says Kevin.

'I thought you were going out with an old school friend,' Meredith says. She really has turned irredeemably into my mother.

'Yes, I was,' I say. 'Kevin and I were at school together.'

'Really?' she says, not believing me for one second.

We both nod at her and she shifts on the couch, straightening out her shell suit bottoms.

'Oh. I didn't realize.'

I smile, like I'm so scatty I forgot to tell her I knew one of the parents outside of school.

'Yeah, I lived in Liverpool for a while when I was a kid,' says Kevin, running with this, not realizing Meredith has seen right through it. 'After all, it's the capital of Ireland.'

'Karen, could I have a quick word with you in the kitchen, please?'

'Yes, Mum,' I say. It's a genuine mistake. I quickly correct myself. 'Meredith.'

I look to Kevin and tell him to take a seat, then follow Bossy Pants into the kitchen, where she shuts the door.

'That's Connor O'Keefe's dad,' she whispers.

'I know.'

'What are you doing with him?'

'We just went for a bike ride in the countryside.'

'You picked him up at his wife's funeral?'

'Oh, shut up, Meredith. It wasn't like that.'

Don't get jealous, I want to add, but don't.

'Well, what *was* it like?'

'I dunno. We're just . . . two lonely people trying to . . . find our way through this mad, mad world, I guess.'

Yes, I really did say that. Please don't ask me why.

'And when did you start sounding like a crap 1970s ballad by Leo Sayer?'

'Meredith, this is none of your business. There's no law against it. Anyway, I haven't got time for this. I need to pack an overnight bag.'

'You're going to sleep with him?'

'Not that it's any of your business, but actually . . . we're going to spoon.'

She looks like she is going to be sick.

'It's all very innocent,' I add.

She is catatonic with shock. I really don't get what the biggie is.

'Oh, get over yourself, Meredith. It's not like he's a kid.'

'What if Ethleen finds out?'

'It's none of the head's business, and even if she did, we're both grown-ups.'

'I think it's disgusting,' she says defensively.

'I'm tired of being on my own. He's tired of being on his own. We're just going to . . . spend the evening together. He's nice.'

'Karen, I don't think you're in your right mind. I've been worried about you for a while and now you're just going to pounce on the first guy who crosses your path?'

OK. That stings. I could quite happily slap her now.

'Well, putting aside my obvious mental health issues – thank you for your concern, by the way – what am I meant to do? Wait? For what? For bloke number two? Three? Four hundred?

Or sit here pining and waiting for Michael to come back? Hmm?'

She rolls her eyes. 'This is exactly why I'm worried. You keep going on as if—'

I butt in, 'Meredith, I really don't have time for this. Maybe I am making a huge mistake, but it's my mistake and not yours, and you really don't need to worry. OK?'

She nods. Eventually. I smile, open the door and head out.

It's all terribly teenage when we get to Kevin's. A lot of eggshells are trodden on as we overcompensate for our nerves with uber-politeness. We sit and watch a bit of telly, but choose to sit on adjoining settees rather than risk the embarrassment of being in close proximity, even though we are intending on sharing a bed. The house is spotless and I wonder if Kevin had planned all along to invite me back, or whether he just has cleaning-related OCD. Either way I don't really mind. I'd half expected a woman-free bloke to live in a pigsty, but I was almost tempted to ask if I should take my shoes off when I walked in. It's of course different being here today, just me and him, instead of the last time I was here, when the place was packed to the Ikea rafters with mourners.

I can't concentrate on the television programme, as I'm taking in everything in the room. The mock-Georgian mantel-piece houses an artificial fire not dissimilar to Mungo and Fionnula's. Above it is a simple mirror, which I wonder if I'll be checking my make-up in in the morning. The large flat-screen telly sits in the corner on top of a cabinet of piled-up DVDs and Xbox games. I can see the controls for a Wii too. Underfoot are some kind of wooden floorboards that look too old to be original to the house and are stained an almost cherry colour. All the furniture is white – the sofas and the meringue of an armchair. The only bits of colour are the Union Jack cushions, which strike me as odd for an Irish guy. Maybe they were Toni's choice. A long, thin window looks out over the street of similar Toy Town houses, and nestled on the windowsill are a handful of framed photos: Connor in his primary-school uniform, Toni and Kevin on their wedding day – he has a Nineties curtains hairdo, and she's got massive hair. I think he looks much better now, like he's grown into his looks, but my eyes keep returning to Toni. She was undeniably pretty, but I can't help wondering if she was having her affair when the picture was taken. Kevin's not mentioned any of that today, and it has felt impolite to enquire, even though I'm desperate to know what really happened, and how he really felt, and if he really forgave her, and how he took her back, or even if he kicked her out in the first place. I'm also intrigued to know if he . . . I dunno . . . punched this Jamie one in the face in the local pub, the way they would in *EastEnders*. I know I shan't ask him any of this tonight. Tonight we can pretend that neither of us has baggage and just enjoy the presence of another human being.

He offered me wine, but I didn't really want it, so we're sat here sipping from massive mugs of tea. The clock's ticking by and I wonder what is a sensible time for two grown-up lonelies, struggling to find their way through this mad, mad world – I have grown to like this phrase and may put it on my passport as my occupation – to go to bed. Eleven? Twelve? I don't want to be drinking tea into the early hours when I've got to be up for work.

Fortunately Kevin starts doing some rather loud yawning, and a bit of stretching of arms and feet, then just looks at me and says, 'Shall we?' and I nod.

I head into the bathroom to clean my teeth and wash my

face. I look around the room. It's also clean, so again I wonder whether he was expecting my visit or if he's impressively domestic. The products are all masculine, the telltale signs of a man and boy living together: razors, face wash, a bottle of Matey. Above the bath there is a poster for a movie from years back with Helen Mirren hugging some bloke. Maybe that was Toni's taste. Mind you, everyone loves Helen Mirren, I think, as I slip into my nightie. Yes, I've brought a nightie. That makes me sound a bit like my mother – or does it? Maybe she wears a baby-doll these days with Jorgen Borgen clawing away at her – but actually, it's one I bought myself over Christmas. It's from Marks's and it's from their posh trendy range and looks more like a stripy summer dress than a nightie. Oh. On second thoughts, maybe he'll just think I've put a new frock on for bed. I plan to say, 'This is a nightie, by the way,' when I enter the bedroom, but as I do, I find that the lights are on so low I can hardly see a thing.

'Have you got a torch?' I whisper, and he giggles. He turns the lights up a bit – they must be on a dimmer switch – and I see he is wearing pyjamas. Phew. I was a bit worried he'd be stood there starkers with his Mull of Kintyre hanging out for all the world to see.

He slips away to the bathroom. I hear him lock the door, as I did, but then I hear him having a really noisy wee. Gosh, that's so not romantic. I look at the double bed and wonder which side Kevin likes to sleep on. As I always used to sleep on the left with Michael, I decide to ring the changes and hop in on the right. Then I worry that, God knows why, Kevin might think that makes me right wing, so I shufty over to the left. Then I decide that's ridiculous and shufty back over to the right. I lie there waiting, hearing everything that Kevin is doing through the wall: cleaning his teeth, gargling with what I assume is mouthwash. Then I hear the click of the lock. I close my eyes, feigning sleepiness, and then feel the bed shift and the temperature rise as he climbs in next to me. We both lie stock still for a while, and then I feel him moving closer. He slips an arm round my waist and I turn my back to him to spoon. I push myself against him. He tucks his arm further round my waist. I worry that soon I'll feel an erection pressing into the small of my back, but I don't. Hmm, what's that all about? Doesn't he fancy me? With his other hand he gently strokes the top of my head. I've always found this incredibly relaxing and the next thing I know . . .

I wake up. Sunlight is streaming through the white blinds on the bedroom window. I am alone in the bed and I sit up, disorientated at first, as I've not seen this room in daylight. I can hear Kevin pottering downstairs, a kettle boiling. I look to the bedside cabinet. The digital alarm clock says it's twenty-five past seven. I suddenly remember it's Valentine's Day next week and wonder if I'll be spending it with Kevin.

Getting ahead of myself there.

Can't even remember the last time Michael bought me a card.

There are some books on the floor by the bed and I pick one up to see what Kevin is reading. It's one of those American self-help books. It's called *Moving On: Saying Goodbye to the One You Love*. I open it and a bookmark falls out. Then I discover it's not a bookmark. It's a driver's licence. I see Kevin's face and nosily read the name on it.

Except it's not his name.

It's his face, but this driver's licence says it belongs to Steven McIntyre.

What?

Behind it is another, slightly bigger card. Again the name Steven McIntyre. No picture this time. And the words on this card make me tremble. It's a membership card for the IRA. That's bad. Is it still bad? They kill people, right? Or did they? Or are they now members of Parliament? Or is that Sinn Fein? Oh God. Something's not right here. Steven McIntyre. I look again at the picture on the driving licence. It's definitely Kevin.

Then the words from the wake, from the Deirdre Barlow-glasses woman come back to haunt me. They ring in my ears like tinnitus: 'Watch that one. He's not all that he appears.'

I put the cards back in the book, snap the pages shut and return it to the floor.

TWENTY

Ten minutes later I am doing the walk of shame, hurrying along a pavement in last night's clothes, although really, I have nothing to be ashamed of. I didn't cop off in some seedy nightclub after a vodka-fuelled session; this was planned. We didn't even 'sleep' sleep together. And yet . . . and yet . . . shame seems to be gripping me by the throat and choking me.

Steven McIntyre, IRA. Steven McIntyre, IRA, I think to myself as I rat-a-tat along in my a-bit-too-racy-for-school high heels. I stop. Was I rude back then? When I hurried out with startling urgency, he looked so shocked. Like he'd done something wrong.

Oh yes, you've done something wrong. You've murdered innocent children . . . I think.

Maybe he hasn't. But the IRA . . . yes! They used to set off bombs and kill people, and weren't allowed to go on the news without their faces being pixelated and someone dubbing their voices. For ages I thought all terrorists must've become terrorists because they had such weird faces and clumped themselves together with other equally weird-looking people. I also thought they all spoke cleverly, adopting a trick of moving their lips but having the words come out in a slightly delayed way. Till one day my dad explained it was a television trick and the voices were done by actors. In fact, Mum liked to guess which actors they used for the dubbing. Unfortunately her knowledge of Northern Irish performers was hardly extensive, so she'd either say, 'That's Jim McDonald from *Corrie*!' or, 'That's Liam Neeson!' or, 'That's thingy from *Emmerdale*, putting one on!' (I'm assuming she meant the accent.) But still. The IRA! They were really bad years ago, although I know they'd always say it was because the British had gone over there and invaded their country and hung out on street corners shooting people and stuff like that.

I really should learn more about Irish history.

Had there been any clues? Of course! That poster in his bathroom of Helen Mirren hugging someone. *Some Mother's Son*. It was a film about the IRA. I'm pretty sure it was about the hunger strikers. Blimey, no wonder he had a poster up of it on his toilet wall. It was probably seeing that that inspired him to join the Irish Revolutionary Army. Or is it Republican? Oh, it's one of those political thingamajigs.

And to think he had me fooled! To think I had him down as . . . well . . . as . . .

Where did I think his politics lay? Has he ever really discussed what he thought of politicians or the history of Ireland? If I was to be really honest with myself, politics hadn't crossed my mind while I'd been with him, which feels pretty at odds with the discovery that actually he is . . . well . . .

What is he?

An IRA member/soldier living in mainland Britain with a false name.

A trained killer with a new identity who has spooned me, and who I might just have hacked off with my blustering 'God, Kevin, I'm really sorry. I've just remembered an early staff meeting I've got to go to . . . No, don't bother to see me out.

You carry on making bacon sandwiches . . . No, I don't need a lift. I really have to leg it. Bye!'

Oh my God. What if he's ordering my execution right now?!

A car drives past me, pretty fast actually, and I scream and duck behind a parked car, convinced the passenger window is going to whoosh down and a machine gun zoom out and perforate me. As the car zooms past, though, and no assassination takes place, I see that the car is actually a dayglo-pink mini-van with the words 'Hair by Sonia' written on the side. OK, so maybe an assassin might not be driving around in something that screams for attention like that. I stay hunched down because I see a dark car approaching, slowly, like it's looking for something, like it's locating its target. It's a posh sports car. It looks as incongruous as a bejewelled elephant on this ordinary street. It suddenly stops. I try to lower myself nearer to the pavement in an attempt not to be seen and then shot. Why was I so rude to Kevin? He's done me no harm. OK, so he didn't tell me he had Mafia links. Ish. And now look how he is repaying my slight. There's going to be blood on the paving stones and it's going to be mine. Whatever happened to a good old-fashioned horse's head on the bed?

The passenger window lowers and I feel an ice-like grip tightening around my heart. I go light-headed. The grit of the pavement digs into my knees. I want to close my eyes, but for some reason I can't stop cricking my neck in the most awkward manoeuvre possible to try and get a glance at the car. Once the window is down, I hold my breath. Here comes the gun. Here it comes. It'll be here in a minute. But . . . well . . . no gun comes.

Instead I see a familiar face poking out of the window.

Meredith.

Meredith???

Is Meredith in the IRA too? Oh God, it doesn't bear thinking about. She must be a member of the New Zealand branch.

But hang on, that doesn't sound very . . . plausible. Does it?

The car stops outside Kevin's house and then zooms off again. Passing me. Not killing me. No guns. Nothing. I continue kneeling, confused, which is when I realize I have seen that sports car before. Every day at work. It stands proudly in the car park at school, saying, 'I have more money in the bank than is absolutely necessary.' I know it well, and the sticker in the back window that says, 'If you can read this, thank a teacher.' I always want to add another: 'If you can't read this, blame a teacher.'

That car is Ethleen's.

Meredith is in Ethleen the head's car, kerb-crawling outside Kevin's house.

This can only mean one thing. And I don't like or understand it.

Meredith has been on the phone to our boss and told her all about the fact that her housemate/landlady has spent the night spooning with the father of a student, and Ethleen is so panic-stricken or fascinated by it that she has jumped in her car, driven to my house, picked up Meredith, then wazzed over here and paused outside the House of Spoon to see if they can witness first-hand our debauched cutlery-imitating behaviour.

The car drives off. I duck again so as not to be seen by my traitor.

I am incensed. How dare she? How *dare* she get straight on the phone and tell her what I'm up to in my personal life? I don't text Ethleen every time Meredith's out with Dee, Dozy, Beaky, Mitch and whatever they're called. And why?

Because it's none of her bloody business!!!!!

I hear footsteps. I'm so incensed I've forgotten they could

belong to my killer. I look round, still kneeling on the ground, to see a girl from year seven hurrying past with two pints of milk. It's too early for her to be going to school. She must just be running an errand for her mum. Oddly, she doesn't look that perturbed to see me crouching beside a car.

'All right, Miss?'

'Hi, Shenille!'

She scurries away and I stand, then hurry on towards the school. I get my phone out and compose a text to Meredith. **WHY ARE YOU DOING THIS?** I write in big, shouty capital letters. **IT'S NOT LIKE I'M BONKING A SIXTH-FORMER**. Then I angrily press send.

Thirty or so seconds later I get one back as I practically trip down the road in my anger: **Where R U?**

I turn a corner to see the front of the school. And get another shock.

Standing beside Ethleen's car in the car park are not only Ethleen and Meredith (Meredith is looking at her phone, clearly waiting for me to reply), but also my mum and . . .

Oh. My. God.

My dad is there too!

My *dad*!

I panic. Something is wrong. They must have invented a new law that says you can't hang out with kids' parents when you're a teacher. They're going to make out I'm inappropriate and I'll be all over the tabloids for having groomed Kevin into making him take me on a countryside bike ride and then share a bed – no kissing. It is ridiculous, but why else would they be stood there having what looks like an urgent conversation? I don't take a step further. I edge back to observe them from round the corner. I glue my body to the brickwork of the Who'd've Thought It? and wonder what on earth they're up to. Should I go over? What could they want? Why is the sight of seeing my own mum and dad, along with my housemate and my boss, making me feel so anxious? Why has my dad come all the way from Liverpool to be standing in a school car park before eight o'clock in the morning? Just then my image of them is distorted as another car pulls up outside the school gates. A man jumps out and heads towards them. Meredith's introducing him to everyone. He turns. I flinch.

It's Kevin. He's in on it too. But in on what? Is there some massive conspiracy going on behind my back?

I feel sick. I don't understand anything anymore.

And even though I know I should go over there and ask them what the *bloody hell it is that they want . . .*

I don't. I turn and run. And run. I am scared to find out what they want. Or what they want to tell me. Or what they want to accuse me of.

I am not a bad person. I try not to be horrible to people. I try to do as it says on my living-room wall: 'Work hard and be nice to people.'

I am the Good Person of East Ham. I was nice to Kevin, and he was nice to me. Is that a crime? OK, so I didn't know what his political allegiances were, but I'm pretty sure the IRA are probably quite decent these days and do party political broadcasts and the like. Nick Clegg might even be a member.

Yes, I know this is ridiculous, but I'm panicking. But that's OK because the panic makes me run faster. For a second I think that all professional runners should get panic attacks. It'd shave seconds off their personal bests, though it might make for uncomfortable TV viewing as they hyperventilate on the starting blocks and knock back Rescue Remedy at a rate of knots or breathe into brown paper bags.

I jump on a bus.

After the bus I jump on a Tube.

After the Tube I jump on another bus.

I run. I walk. I run again, then stop and catch my breath and soon I am home.

I could collapse I feel so exhausted. That is probably the most exercise I've done in years. I may as well have run a marathon.

And I feel so silly, so small, bunking off school at the age of thirty-six, with no idea why. Just an irrational fear that maybe they're all out to get me, but with absolutely no notion as to what they're going to get at me about. I close the front door and put on the chain, hoping that now, finally, I will feel safe. But I don't. Once again I feel panic rising in my chest, but as soon as it starts, it evaporates, because I see a familiar figure descending the stairs. Warmth floods over me as I see Michael smiling at me. I know he is going to make everything all right.

Is he?

I hope so.

Oh, but the last time I saw him we had that little spat and . . .

'Are you going to be nice to me?' I ask quickly, spitting the words out conspiratorially like that Resistance woman in *'Allo, 'Allo!* who used to say, 'Listen very carefully. I shall say zees only wance.'

He nods.

'Oh good. 'Cos I'm having a really weird day.'

'Why don't you come up to the bedroom and put your feet up?'

Now listen, I'm not daft. I know that usually when a man asks you upstairs to the bedroom, it means only one thing. He wants to do the furtive fandango with you, particularly if he's your ex. But I know that's not on the cards right now, and somehow I know he's right. I need to retreat to the comfort of my bedroom to escape the strangeness of what's going on outside, out in the big, bad world. It's like I'm in a sci-fi film. Maybe it's the end of the world and someone forgot to tell me. Nothing out there is making sense right now.

Out there. Suddenly my life has taken on two dimensions: stuff that happens Out There (bad/weird) and stuff that goes on In Here (good. Well, OK anyway). When did that happen? Just this morning? I think so, but I can't really remember. I'm so tired.

Once I get to my bedroom, Michael is over by the window, his back to me. He draws the curtains and then flicks the lights on low. I kick off my shoes and flop onto the bed, exhausted. I should really be questioning him about why he's here, how he let himself in. I should really be telling him to take a running jump, but I've had a shock and for some reason it just feels right and I don't want to ask him anything in case it makes him want to go. It must still be early. I don't even know if school's started yet. I should really have phoned the office to let them know I was going to be sick, but even the fact that I've not done that doesn't bother me. They probably don't want me there anyway. It looked like they were all about to gang up on me outside the gates: my parents, my housemate, my boss and my co-spooner/terrorist one-night stand (no sex). The only person who isn't ganging up on me is Michael.

He's moving around the bedroom tidying things away for me, putting all my shoes in a corner, picking up a few open books and putting them on my bedside cabinet. He drapes a scarf across the top of the mirror over the fireplace. Then he turns and smiles at me and encourages me to get some sleep. He sits on the end of the bed and squeezes my ankle. Not that I'm particularly aware that this is a well-known procedure for encouraging people to sleep. His weirdy Nazi coat flops open and I see that purple bruising on his neck. It still shocks me.

'How did you get that?' I ask.

He pulls the lapels of his coat to and shakes his head. 'Don't you worry about that.'

'Why are you here?' Oh God. I said it.

'I knew there was something not right.'

How? How did he know?

'Did Meredith tell you?'

He sighs.

'What did she say? I don't know what it is that I've done wrong. I'm not sure why Mum and Dad were at the school.'

Suddenly out on the street we hear a screech of brakes as a car pulls up abruptly outside the house. We both look to the curtains, as if magically we'd be able to see through them. When seconds later we hear the key go in the lock downstairs, my anxiety floods back.

'I think you're about to find out,' says Michael.

He looks to the door and his expression of alarm engenders a new thought: What if the people out there are pissed off with what's going on in here? What if they've found out I've seen Michael and that is what's causing them alarm?

Have I told anyone that Michael keeps coming back? I might have told Meredith, but I'm not sure. I definitely told Wendy, but I've not seen Wendy for ages, not since she beggared off without so much as a by your leave after meeting her septuagenarian Lothario, and it's not like she's here today. In fact, she was conspicuous by her absence outside the school.

No. It must be something else. And I don't want them knowing about Michael. Michael's my secret. I mustn't let them know about him. They'd think I was mad, letting him back in when he's caused so much pain.

I put the chain on the lock when I came in, so whoever is trying to get in downstairs can't open the front door. They're banging their body weight against it in an attempt to break the chain.

'You could just go and let them in,' suggests Michael.

I look at him. Is he mad?

'But they haven't rung the doorbell,' I say. 'For all I know it's some mad rapist.'

For a second I get even more confused. For a second I see the Nazi-ishness of Michael's coat and think I'm Anne Frank hiding away in her attic and the Germans are coming to get her. But I'm not.

Who am I?

I am Karen Carpenter, the girl with the stupid name whose boyfriend left her and . . .

Someone weightier has thrown themselves against the front door and I hear the chain break and the door burst open and someone fall in. Then I hear Dad's voice: 'Karen?'

Oh God. Why does he sound as scared as I do?

I hear various footsteps downstairs, then some coming up the stairs. I jump off the bed and lock my door so they can't come in.

More calling: 'Karen? Karen?'

I look to Michael, then motion to the wardrobe. He frowns, but my desperate look tells him he has no choice.

'I don't want them knowing you're here. That's the last thing I need,' I say in a bit of a stage whisper.

It's then I hear Mum's voice through the door, obviously speaking to someone else.

'She's in her bedroom. She's talking to herself. What did I tell you?'

I watch Michael climb into his side of the wardrobe and pull the door shut. I look back to the bedroom door. I take a deep breath. I turn my lips into a broad smile. I grab the lock, unlock it and open the door.

Mum is standing on the landing, looking anxiously towards me. A fearful smile is frozen on her face. Dad is coming up the stairs.

'All right, Karen, love? How you diddlin'?'

'Dad! Hi! What are you doing here, and why have you broken my chain?'

I push through them, heading for the stairs. Maybe if I can make a run for it, I can get out of the house, but Meredith is at the bottom of the stairs.

'Oh, we just wanted a chat with you, love,' Dad's saying.

'Meredith!' I say, all surprised. I look at my watch. 'Shouldn't you be at school?'

'Shouldn't you?' she says forcefully.

'Oh, I was just about to ring in, actually. Feeling a bit peaky.' Damn, I can't make a run for it.

I know, I know. It's madness. Why would I want to run away from my parents?

I decide that if I head downstairs, the parents will follow me and then be less likely to discover my ex-boyfriend lurking in the wardrobe, so I sweep downstairs, my hand on the banister, all crinkly-eyed smiles and beaming grins. Really I should be wearing a straw hat and a crinoline to finish off the look, and be uttering, 'Fiddle dee dee!' in a Deep South accent. As I get to the bottom of the stairs, Meredith intercepts me. She doesn't quite administer a roundhouse kick to my face, but she may as well do. She grabs my wrist and holds on to me.

'Get off me.'

'Where are you going?'

'To get my phone to ring in sick.'

'You don't need to. You just need to talk to your mum and dad.'

'About what?' I emit with a girly giggle. 'This is ridiculous!'

Not half as ridiculous as I sounded emitting that girly giggle. Meredith looks past me to the stairs, where Mum and Dad are now galumphing down after me. They must be exhausted, all this running about. God, what has Meredith told them to warrant them legging it around the East End of London at this time on a Monday morning? It's completely unfair at their time of life.

I take advantage of her distraction, looking up the stairs, and duck underneath her arm, forcing her to squeal as I bend her wrist into a painful cat's cradle. I grab the handle on the front door, pull it open and run.

I seem to spend my life running out of this house, escaping the bizarre. Now more than ever. As soon as I step outside the house, I see an unfamiliar car parked there, its engine running, the back passenger door open, a man in the front seat I don't recognize. He's looking at me, though. Who is he? I make to run past the car but feel Meredith launching herself at me from behind. She rugby-tackles me and pushes me up against the car. I hit cold metal with my cheek and bang my ribs.

'What are you doing?' I scream. 'That *hurts*.'

'Don't overdo it, Meredith!' I hear Dad calling, coming out of the house.

'She's a lesbian,' explains Mum, following him, and for some reason I know exactly what she means.

Next thing I know, Meredith is bundling me into the car. Like I have no say in the matter. I stumble onto the back seat and look at the man in the front. I check out his jacket. It's tweed. Not exactly a man in a white coat.

'Are you a psychiatrist?' I ask.

Just then Mum opens the front passenger door. 'No, this is Jorgen.'

Dad is clambering in too, beside me.

My God. It's Jorgen Borgen Stick It Up Your Horgen, I think. I may actually say it out loud because I hear Mum going, 'No, Karen, just Jorgen,' as she sits up front next to him and slams her door shut with some force. Wow, she seems angry.

Just Jorgen, eh?

I am reminded of an advert from my childhood for a juice that had no pips or crap in it and I sing the jingle for everyone: 'No pips, no powders, no preservatives, Just Juice!'

Then I laugh. Doors have shut and the car is moving now. I am hemmed in between Meredith, who's now on my left, and Dad on my right. I look to him.

'You know about Jorgen?'

He nods curtly.

'Are you fuming?' I ask.

'Not now, Karen.'

'Where are we going?'

'All will become clear eventually,' says Mother cryptically from the front seat.

'Am I being sectioned?' I ask.

'No,' says Meredith.

'Should you be?' asks Mum.

I don't answer that.

'I don't know what I've done wrong. What's this about?'

'Try not to worry, love,' says Dad, and gives my arm a squeeze.

'You told Wendy you'd seen Michael, didn't you, love?' says Mum, turning to look at me. She sounds sympathetic.

'I'm sorry,' I say.

'I'm sure it's a perfectly natural reaction,' Jorgen suddenly pipes up in his telly Danish accent.

My immediate thought is to say, 'Who asked you?' but when I realize he's being supportive, I warm to him briefly. Then I hate him again.

'Er, thanks for splitting my family up, by the way,' I hiss at him.

He looks unperturbed, from what I can see in the rear-view mirror.

'They do not look particularly broken up to me, Karen,' he insists. I decide to ignore him. He looks quite handsome from the back. Except that he has a beard. Not that I can see this from behind. I just catch a glimpse of it from the side. He has freckles, sandy hair. He's wearing a tweedy Barbour jacket, the sort designed for men to go shooting in, but now appropriated by trendy types who hang out in Hoxton, or want to give the impression of hanging out in Hoxton. I'm not a big fan of beards. Everyone's got them these days, even women.

'Have you seen Michael?' Mum asks.

'No,' I lie, taking my eyes off the Bearded One.

Mum looks to Dad, shakes her head and turns back. 'Why haven't you spoken to Rita?' Mum says, checking her nails now.

'I don't want to.'

'She loves you,' adds Mum.

'If I don't want to speak to her, I don't have to,' I insist. 'Michael left me. If she wants to take his side, she can.'

And Meredith, Dad and Mum all appear to sigh in unison.

'What?' I shriek, but they ignore me. I turn to Dad. 'How did you get to London so quickly? Have you seen the time?'

'I came last night,' he explains. 'I've been worried about you.'

'Oh, because *she* –' and here I indicate Mum '– reckons I'm all dark and suicidal, and I'm so not.'

'No, because of the Michael thing.'

I don't like where this is going, so I side-swipe him with a quick 'I found out this morning that my new boyfriend's in the IRA.'

'IRA?' asks Meredith. Oh, so suddenly she's got a voice.

'Yes,' I say. 'It stands for . . .' and then my voice trails off, as I'm still not sure what it stands for exactly.

'He's not from Northern Ireland,' Meredith points out, as if that means anything.

'It's far too soon for you to have a boyfriend,' Mum says.

'Let he who is without sin cast the first stone,' I say pointedly, giving both people in the front of the car daggers.

'Anyway, you're a grass,' I tell Meredith, wanting to sting her. She doesn't respond, so I explain. 'Telling thingy, Ethleen.'

Again, no response. God, she's hard-faced. I hear a clicking noise and try to locate it.

Jorgen's got the right indicator on. We're waiting for the traffic to clear on the right. When eventually it does, we sweep round and through some wrought-iron gates. As I bump into Meredith and quickly remove myself from her grassy touch, I recognize the gates and suddenly realize what this is all about.

This is about me being a bad mother.

Oh God.

Moments later I am walking down a gravel path. Mum and Dad have an arm each and I am being cajoled against my will. Meredith and Jorgen have stayed in the car. Either side of us there are row upon row of gravestones.

'This is about me not visiting the grave, isn't it?' I venture.

I've not been to Evie's grave since Michael left. I know it's unforgivable, I know it's inexcusable, but I've just not been able to face it. I have left my daughter all on her own and for that I am deeply ashamed. I used to come every Saturday, spruce up the flowers, have a little chat, but since Michael left, I've not wanted to.

'I've just not been able to face it since Michael left.'

'When you say "left", what do you mean?' asks Mum as we hurry along.

'You know what I mean.' I am sounding surly. I am surly. Probably because I am embarrassed.

'I don't,' she insists.

'He walked out on me.'

'He walked out on you and what did he do?'

I don't want to answer that. I change the subject.

'This is about Evie, isn't it?'

I'm a bad mother, you see. So rubbish at being a mum that I couldn't even keep my baby alive inside me, and even more rubbish now that I've not visited her grave for months. As I said, inexcusable.

But they don't answer.

We veer left down a path of more modern graves. Blocks of dark grey granite lying on the grass like little statues of discarded phone books. Polished circles of silver at the top with holes in like old telephone dials, some with flowers in. And then we stop. And I look down. And I see those all-too-familiar words:

EVIE CARPENTER-FLETCHER

And the date. The date that is inked on Michael's skin. There are fresh flowers poking out of the silver circle. Mum must have put them there. God love Mum.

'I'm sorry,' I say again, almost inaudibly. I want to cry but find that I can't. I am too scared. What am I scared of?

But it appears I am mistaken: this is not what they have brought me to see. Gently they pull and push me a foot to the left. I don't want to look down. Why should I have to look down? Because . . . because . . . this is what I'm scared of.

'Karen,' Dad says gently, and he motions to the ground.

OK. I look down.

Another discarded phone book. Fresh flowers again. The stone is still new, sparkling. I'm not sure if it's because of the quality of the stone or if it's been raining.

And then I see the words, chiselled into the stone. And I am even more ashamed.

MICHAEL FLETCHER
1976–2012

The fear, the shame, it all gets too much. Reality hits me round the face, and as I recover from their sting, the tears fall.

They have brought me to Michael's grave.

TWENTY-ONE

Mum is shouting at the receptionist at the GP's surgery. Usually I wouldn't mind – as a breed, I find them just a bit to the right of Jabba the Hut. Or is it Attila the Hun? Either way, today her remonstrations leave me a bit mortified and I go and sit on one of the plastic sofas in the waiting room and flick through a nearby *OK!* magazine. I try to drown out her cries of 'The doctor's expecting her! She needs help!' I feel all eyes in the waiting room on me. 'She might need sectioning!' I bristle, but the eyes look away and I turn the page.

I curse that there is a leak in the roof and the rain is getting in; the page beneath me is becoming sodden. Then I realize there is no leak. What's wetting the shiny paper is my tears.

A minute or two later, with an efficacy unheard of in GP's surgeries, a few people come out of doctors' rooms and the receptionist says I can see Dr Bhatia. I head to the nearest open door and feel Mum grabbing my arm. I look at her, startled.

'What?'

'You're not coming in too.'

'Oh, yes I am. Goodness only knows what claptrap you'll tell the doctor.'

The way she keeps saying 'the doctor' puts me in mind of

Dr Who. It's incredibly annoying. I shrug her off and insist, 'I'll see her on my own.'

I push her away with some force. She falls backwards into a spinning display of pamphlets, a bit like the sort that would house greetings cards in a corner shop, and before she can get it or herself up again, I hurry in and slam the door.

A middle-aged Asian woman is sitting in a sari doodling on a notepad with the name of what looks like a logo for the morning-after pill on the top when I sit down and smile.

She looks up. 'Wodda madda wid you?' she says with a thick Pakistani accent.

'Sorry?'

'Wodda madda wid you?'

'Well,' I say, not sure how to reply, 'I was rather hoping you might be able to tell me that.'

Suddenly the door swings open. Bloody Mother! Before I can say anything, she announces, 'That's not Dr Bhatia – that's a locum. Come on, next door.'

I get up.

Mum can't help shouting at the locum, 'My daughter needs professional help!'

The locum continues to doodle.

Dr Bhatia has a kindly face, and a nicer sari than the locum. Plus she doesn't doodle. I can't stop crying and she doesn't seem to mind. I've lost the will to argue with Mum and she is now sat next to me, voice raised again.

'She needs professional help!'

'I know, Mrs Carpenter, and I'm going to make sure she gets it.'

'She needs sectioning!'

I can't be bothered to argue. Maybe I do. Maybe if they take me to a mental home, I can just sleep and ignore all the horrible things going through my head.

'I don't think she does,' Dr Bhatia replies. 'Not from what you've told me already.'

'What's she told you?' I gasp between sobs. She passes me a box of tissues. I take one and pass the box back, but she waves it away with her hand, clearly thinking I might get through the lot.

She doesn't answer my question but instead says, 'I think you could benefit from some grief therapy, to help you process your feelings.'

Right.

'What you're experiencing is something sometimes called "abnormal grief reaction".'

Oh God, I'm abnormal. I knew it.

'But I don't like that term. I prefer "complicated grief".'

'So she doesn't need sectioning?' Mum jumps in.

'No,' says Dr Bhatia, with more than a hint of exasperation. 'She has been functioning normally, functioning well. I just feel something is blocking her grief.'

I expect Mum to be cross, but what she actually looks is relieved.

'What has she told you?' I ask again, quieter, as if I don't think she'll ever answer. I know it's not that important, yet I know I need to hear the words because I can't actually voice them myself. Not right now. And that's not just complicated; it is abnormal. Dress it up how you like. I'm a freak.

Dr Bhatia clears her throat. 'She told me that your partner committed suicide in December . . .'

The words hit me like a bullet in the chest. They do – I actually feel winded. I hunch over, gasping.

'. . . and that since then your coping mechanism has been to . . . well . . . to pretend that he didn't, that he just left you. This is not unusual.'

She carries on. She's talking about how a middle-aged businessman might lose his job yet pretend to his family he's still at work and leave the house at half eight in the morning and head for the commuter train, briefcase in hand . . . but eventually I stop listening. She's told me something I already knew, but it still overwhelms me. That's how I feel, overwhelmed. Michael didn't leave me. Well, he did. He walked out on me, but he walked out on me, then took his own life. And although I know this – of course I know this – I have buried the information for so long, hidden it away in one of the drawers in my brain, marked 'Too Painful to Deal With', that hearing it now is like hearing it for the first time. I have been lying. I have been lying to myself, to everyone. I've been saying that Michael has just gone somewhere else and isn't interested in me, when actually, the truth is far too excruciating to even consider. He is dead.

When we eventually leave, with an appointment booked with a clinical psychologist in a few days' time – apparently Mum has had me on a waiting list for over a week and there's now a vacancy – I am crying a little less. Plus Dr Bhatia has convinced me that I'm not mad, which is good. I've just been doing some mad things, which is less good.

What of course I haven't told her is that Michael is currently hiding in the wardrobe at home. I must get back there and tell him. But tell him what? Tell him he's dead? Oh God, he's going to be devastated. But . . . if he's dead . . . how can I have been having conversations with him? How can I see him? He held me. I touched him. I smelt him. He looked after me. I try to bury these thoughts, for fear that Dr Bhatia's diagnosis might actually be wrong. That it's not just mad things I've been doing; that I've actually lost the bloody plot.

Michael's not there when I get back. I pretend I need a lie-down, which isn't far from the truth, but when I open the wardrobe doors, he's nowhere to be seen.

Of course he's nowhere to be seen. He's dead.

But he was definitely there, this morning. He was. He talked to me. He was there.

Maybe I just imagined him.

I didn't realize what a good imagination I have.

I found him in the loft. I ran away from him.

He followed me to the swing park. He followed me on my date with Kevin. He sat on the wall opposite.

Or did I imagine all that? Was that as much a pretence as the laughable one that all he did was walk out and move on?

I feel completely desolate. I can't even cry now. I lie on the bed and feel so hollow I'm not sure I am human. I can't be this hollow and still have vital organs inside me. It's like I've only just discovered he's dead. I don't want him to be dead. Don't get me wrong – many's the time I've lain on this bed and wished he wasn't here, but now he isn't, and there's a finality to it, it's almost unbearable. No, scrap that – it *is* unbearable. I have wandered around for the last few months pretending everything was fine, insisting on it, when actually it wasn't, and now I am exhausted. I have expended too much energy on sidestepping conversations so that no one would mention Michael's death. Sometimes it was easy. No one likes to talk about death, much less so suicide. There's a stigma attached to it. But the constant fear of confronting it, and the active subject-changing, and the desperate deployment of euphemisms have completely worn me out.

If I had any more energy, I would feel relieved – no more lying, no more pretence, no more madness. Truth and honesty from now on – but I can't. I can't feel positive or hopeful or like there is light at the end of the tunnel. Because none of that takes anything away from the awful truth about Michael's departure that thus far I've been avoiding.

I might have felt better if I'd been honest with Kevin. When he acknowledged that I'd lost someone like him, I just batted it away, reducing it to something inconsequential, on a par with 'Oh, it didn't work out.' How many times recently have I said, 'Oh, can we talk about something else?' I might even have gained some common ground with the secretary from school. I couldn't understand her reaction to his leaving, like it hadn't happened; it had left me cold. And yet she was behaving eerily similarly to me, making out everything was OK when in fact she was crumbling. As was I.

Mind you, at least I didn't kill Michael.

I didn't need to. He killed himself.

Oh, here they come again. The tears. This crying doesn't feel normal. It's like it's emanating from my core, whatever my core is, coming from deep inside me and spreading out in convulsive waves, causing my whole body to judder with each seal-like bark. My skin tingles as if it's been peeled away and the atmosphere is piercing it with electric currents in time to my barks and convulsions. The actual crying bit, the tears, seems secondary to the jerking pain, which I'm powerless to stop. I fear I'll never stop. I fear I might die like this. It must be taking up so much energy. And indeed it does. And eventually I'm too wounded by it to continue. And I lie there, heroin-numb.

The clinical psychologist I'm to see works from the front room of her semi-detached house in the far reaches of East London, which is a bit of a schlep on the Docklands Light Railway, but apparently she is going to make me better, so frankly I'd be happy to hotfoot it to the moon if it meant I was to get some sort of resolution to this mess I've created. I know I am going to like her, I just know I am. And why? Because her name is – get this – Roberta Flack.

When Dr Bhatia first mentioned her earlier this week, I remember thinking, Ooh, I've heard of her. I wondered if she was one of those psychologists who pop up on telly, interpreting the body language of contestants on *Big Brother*. I always like those psychologists, and they're more often than not quite trendy and wear blouses that make me go into chat rooms to try and find out where they came from. When I Googled the name, though, I realized that Roberta Flack is the name of some singer from the 1970s. Now, unless Ms Flack has had a change of career, which, according to Wikipedia, she hasn't, then my Ms Flack will also have had a lifetime, or a childhood at least, of mickey-taking about having the same name as a 1970s pop star. This is kismet. This was written in the stars. I am so excited about meeting her that I almost forget the reason why I'm there when she opens her front door to me.

OK, so it's not the 1970s singer, famed for hits like 'Killing Me Softly'. I know from Google that that lady is black, and this lady is so pale she actually looks a bit crepuscular and corpse-like. How apt that she deals so much with grief. She's seen it from the other side, I titter to myself as she shows me through to her light, bright front room. She smiles questioningly, as if encouraging me to share the joke. So I blurt out something about us both having the names of 1970s singers and she smiles and nods.

I talk a little bit too much before she interrupts with: 'Actually, Karen, we only have fifty minutes, so it might be better to limit our discussion to the real reason you're here – to work through your complicated grief.'

I nod courteously and settle down on a nice big leather armchair.

'Actually, that's my seat.'

I get up again quickly and she points to a couch with scatter cushions on it. They have famous paintings cross-stitched on them. I clock Munch's *The Scream* nestled between Gainsborough's *The Blue Boy* and the *Mona Lisa*, and turn *The Scream* round to face the other way before sitting demurely on it. I think this is what's expected. I'm certainly not the sort to kick off my slingbacks, put up my feet and open a bag of crisps like I'm watching *The X Factor*. She sits opposite me and places her hands in her lap. She's wearing some smart capri pants in olive green, matching Birkenstocks and a very pretty grey cardigan. I'm almost tempted to take a picture on my phone and then do some research online when I get in. Her hair is cut in a smart bob, dyed red, and she could be any age from late forties to mid-fifties. She's still very pale, though – that's not changed in the last few minutes. A silence pervades the room. Fortunately she breaks it.

'So, Karen, maybe you'd like to tell me why you've come here.'

And so I tell her. About the day at the cemetery. And how I'd been fooling myself that Michael wasn't dead when he was, and how I'd been pretending to others that he'd just left me, and how I'd seen him and he'd—

Damn. I promised myself I wouldn't say that!

Her eyes immediately fire up and her body language changes, sitting bolt upright in the chair. You don't have to be a *Big Brother* psychologist to tell that *this* psychologist knows a mad one when she sees it. She interrupts me.

'You've seen him?'

I nod and offer nothing more.

'In your dreams?'

I pause, then shake my head slowly. 'In a sort of . . . day-dream, I suppose.'

She slouches down again. Maybe not as mad as she'd hoped.

'It is very common, and a very normal part of the grieving procedure, to see the dead person in your dreams.'

I brush over this and twitter on for a bit longer, till the words run dry and I feel I've said enough, or possibly too much. I tell her about Evie. Immediately she straightens herself in her seat again, like she's just heard the juiciest bit of gossip. She wants to know how I coped after Evie died and I bluster a few words. We're not here to talk about Evie.

God, I'm crying *again*.

We're here to talk about Michael.

'In order to understand your reaction to Michael's death, we will need to explore how you grieved for your daughter and how you coped in the aftermath.'

I blow my nose, and she says something about talking about Evie next week.

'This might be painful for you,' she goes on, 'but I'd like you to tell me how you discovered that Michael had died.'

I nod. I can do this. I know I can do this. I can tell her. It's not like she can tell me. I nod again and then realize I'm nodding incessantly like Woody Woodpecker hammering a tree. Then I dissolve into a tsunami of tears. She cocks her head on one side and, without even looking at her trousers, irons out an imaginary crease with her fingers. And between sobs, gasping for breath, I tell her.

I tell her how I came home from work and found the letter

on the kettle. How it said that he'd left me and not to try to find him, how I was better off without him. How I was devastated and tried calling him, only to discover he'd left his phone in the kitchen drawer. How confused I was that he appeared not to have taken anything with him apart from his laptop. And then how a few hours later I had been lying on my bed, catatonic with shock, wondering if I should tell someone, but thinking no, as he might come back tomorrow, when the phone rang. The landline. I grabbed it, thinking it was him. Only it wasn't. It was Rita, his mum, and she had some terrible news. How a woman walking her dog late at night had found Michael. He had hanged himself from a tree in Central Park – Roberta looked confused by this, so I explained it's the name of our local park – and how he'd left a note in his pocket saying to contact her, so the police had. And how I'd dropped the phone and run out of the house and run and run and run to the park to see if I could find him. To see if I could see him. To see if the police had got it right or got it wrong. To tell them they must have. As I got there, though, I saw an ambulance driving away without its lights flashing, and a police car driving off. And I just stood there, dazed.

'What did he do with the laptop?' she asks. And I actually laugh. I do. I find it funny that after telling her the most tragic thing in my life, she's homed in on the one thing a lot of people have asked as it is so bizarre.

'Turned out he'd given it to a friend at work because she needed a new one.'

She nods. That makes sense. (Completely ignoring the fact that maybe I needed a new laptop. Even though I didn't.) Then she asks me to describe how I felt when I was standing in Central Park. I can think of only one word: confused.

'What were you confused about, Karen?'

Isn't that completely obvious? Maybe not.

'Well, you know . . . how one minute he was there, then the next minute he wasn't. And how he'd just said he was leaving, nothing else. And how he'd told them to contact his mum and not me. And how I'd not even seen him and yet I was supposed to believe he was dead.'

She nods, her eyes narrowing as if she's picturing me stood there in the park. I feel a desire to tell her what I was wearing, make something stylish up to impress her, but then I decide that's inappropriate.

'And I thought it was typical. That even though he'd died, I felt like the last person to know.'

'Why was that typical?'

'Oh, it's just a feeling I often had, that he would talk to other people about . . . stuff, but not me.'

'What sort of stuff?'

'Erm . . . his feelings, I guess.'

'Did you ever see him dead?'

It takes all my will not to start crying again. I shake my head. 'I didn't want to. Rita said there was a mark round his neck. She said the funeral parlour had put loads of make-up over it so you couldn't see, but I couldn't look. I've not told anyone this before. I knew everyone'd kick off if I didn't go and see him in his coffin, so I went on my own. I sat in the room with him on my own, but I didn't actually look into the coffin. I wanted to remember him how he was.'

She nods. She nods well. It's a brisk, efficient nod. I may try and ape it later in front of a mirror.

'Tell me about a time when you were happy with Michael, a recent time. Have a little think.' Again she brushes down her slacks.

Slacks. I'm turning into my mother. I'll be shoving my

hand up a glove puppet soon and invading my local primary schools.

I think.

And I think some more.

And then I remember.

We'd gone to the Thames Barrier Park. Michael loved it there. He also loved the fact that someone from his work, some gay fella called Jayson (who they called Gay Jayson, inventively and not in the slightest bit reductively), had gone to Sitges for ten days and left his Staffordshire bull terrier, Mama Cass, with Michael (and, as a result, me too) in his absence. I ambled along, dragging my heels on the gravel path, enjoying the sensation and noise, like a big kid with autumn leaves, as I watched Michael sprinting round the park with a big stick in his hand, Mama Cass following, barking, loving the game. Michael threw the stick. I saw it sailing through the air. Cass stopped barking and chased it, grabbing it up from the grass and then whooshing away, wanting Michael to chase her, which he did. I half expected him to start barking then. The pair of them disappeared round the other side of the ornamental hedges, clipped into the shape of waves, that dissected the centre of the park and I smiled to myself. For once I allowed myself to feel content. We felt like a normal couple on days like this. I wanted to say 'normal family' – me, Michael and Mama Cass – but she was only on loan. That's how Evie had felt, actually. Like she'd been on loan to me. Like something or some-one more important than me – God perhaps, although believe me, I was never a God-botherer – had preordained that she'd just live in my womb before going somewhere else. Somewhere fabulous. Somewhere like this park, perhaps, which had higher levels of fabulosity than most of the places round here. I looked ahead of me, at the silver armadillos of the flood barrier in the

Thames glinting in the sun as if encrusted with diamonds. I breathed in the fresh, crisp air of the dry autumn day and for the first time in ages felt . . .

D'you know what? Life is pretty good.

I hated thinking like that. It usually signalled things were going to get much, much worse. But the big black shadow over our lives, Michael's depression, had seemed to fade to grey a bit lately. He'd been on some new pills for the last few months and – touch wood – they seemed to be helping. The doctor said he had something called reactive depression, in as much as he'd reacted to Evie's death in this way.

I heard Mama Cass barking, so knew that Michael must have had control of the stick again. He ran out in front of me, the dog bouncing after him. He swivelled round and threw the stick towards the river. It spun through the air, only Michael's throw must have been stronger than he'd bargained on, because it flew over the fence and into the river with a satisfying splash. Cass ran towards the railings and for a horrible moment I thought she was going to jump over into the water.

'Cass! No!' shouted Michael, running towards her.

Mama wasn't stupid, though. She just stood in front of the railing, staring at the river, emitting little whines of frustration, her eyes focused on the exact spot where the stick broke the water, no doubt.

I caught them up. Michael looked round and smiled. 'She knows where it is, but she can't get it, bless her. I know how she feels.'

And he threw his arm round me and drew me in for a hug.

An act of physical affection. So few and far between these days. I savoured it as we both looked out over the river.

'Why d'you like it here so much?' I asked.

He sighed. 'I like the drama of it.'

'Of what?'

'I like the idea that the barrier's there to hold back a flood, stop us all from drowning. Every time I look at it, I see it in action. Some massive biblical flood, and the gates shutting, and I don't know if I'm dead or alive.'

'You're weird.'

'Yeah, but I'm on tablets.'

And we laughed.

'Put your hands in my pockets.'

I looked at him, confused.

'Put your hands in my pockets.'

So I did as I was told. He was wearing his big green mod parka thing. He liked to think he looked like something off the poster for Quadrophenia, bless him. He used to call it the Weller. Now he'd rechristened it his Dogwalking Coat. This was so that when Mama Cass returned to Gay Jayson, he could go all mopey around the house and be placated only by a visit to Battersea Dogs Home, where we would not be allowed to return empty-handed.

He placed his hands on his head. We would have looked a bit odd if there'd been anyone else in the park, but it was always quiet here, him with his hands on his head, me up close and personal with my hands in his pockets. I could feel his cock getting hard through the denim of his jeans as he pushed himself into me.

'Dirty bastard,' I said with a wink.

He giggled in a really filthy way.

I liked it.

'What's in my pockets?' he whispered mysteriously.

'A gun?' I joked. 'Or are you just pleased to see me?'

'Feel.'

'What?'

Was he initiating sex in a public place?

'In my pockets, you dirty cow.'

289

I felt around. I felt a piece of paper in the left pocket. It felt like a receipt. He arched his eyebrows like a two-faced Roger Moore, and I pulled out the paper.

It was small. The size of a receipt. But I saw now it was a purple Post-it note folded up. He loved Post-it notes. Whenever he thought of a job that needed doing, like replacing a light bulb, he'd make a note of it on a Post-it and stick it on the fridge.

On the front of the note he'd written, 'Karen.'

'It's a question,' he explained.

I knew what it was going to say once I unfolded it. He would have written, 'Can we get a dog?'

I rolled my eyes. He may have been winning me over.

'Read it,' he encouraged.

I opened it. And got the shock of my life. Two words and a question mark: 'MARRY ME?'

I burst out laughing. And so did he.

'Where did that come from?' I have to say I was astonished.

'Ryman's.' He winked.

I poked him playfully on his chest.

'You know what I mean.'

He had never expressed much of an interest in the institution of marriage, usually quoting the Groucho Marx quip about who wants to live in an institution . . .

'Think about it,' he said, and I couldn't say fairer than that. 'Come on, Cass.'

He turned and walked back onto the grass, heading for the wavey hedges. Cass followed him obediently, no doubt hoping for another game of fetch the stick.

I watched him go, then looked back at the note. I cleared my throat and called after him, 'Yes!'

He turned back, burst out laughing, then carried on walking.

I followed him. It wasn't the most romantic of moments, really. I felt like one of those women in Muslim countries who has to walk a few steps behind her husband. Was I doing the right thing? Did I really want to be married to him? Was I really that happy? For now I didn't care. For now my feelings on the matter were unimportant. What was promising was that he was thinking of something in the future, something positive. Finally I thought he must be turning a corner. This Post-it proposal meant that he was getting better.

Roberta looks soothed, like my little story was a nice relaxing bath with some Jo Malones burning on the side. She even sighs in a post-coital way, but then notices I look less happy.

'How does that memory make you feel?'

I shrug. 'OK, but . . .'

'Yes?'

'It was the calm before the storm, because that night something dreadful happened.'

She doesn't ask anything. I assume she is waiting for me to explain.

'It was about a woman called Asmaa.'

She takes this in, nods, waits, but I say nothing. I feel hot tears pricking my eyes and try to fight them back. She's still waiting.

So I tell her about Asmaa.

TWENTY-TWO

I am feeling brave when I return home, so I bypass Mum, who's incinerating some chicken kievs in the kitchen, and head up to my room. I can hear Dad in the bathroom having a bath, the water swishing, and him humming 'Is This the Way to Amarillo?' in fits and starts. I'll worry about their bizarre marriage in a moment, but first I shut the bedroom door and sit on the bed, facing the wardrobe. I take a deep breath, then kneel on the floor and open the left-hand door. Michael's side. His shoes and trainers stand in neat piles on the floor, and beneath a pair of slippers is a fading yellow folder. I pull it out, dislodging the slippers. I quickly return them to their OCD-ish neatness, then sit back on the bed. I open the folder and pull out the sheets of paper inside.

The first is a letter from his union explaining that they will accompany him to the coroner's court when he is giving evidence at the inquest. I put it to one side. The next sheet is a print-off from the Internet, a piece from an online newspaper that is local to East Ham. The headline reads, '**Woman Under Tube Was Outpatient.**' Hardly the catchiest one ever. Beneath the caption there's a photograph of a woman in her mid-twenties. It's her. It's Asmaa. I read on about how she was originally a medical student till she was blighted by depression and had to be sectioned; how she got better, but the depression came and went. When leaving an appointment at the local mental health clinic, she had headed straight for the Tube and thrown herself under the next train. The piece says both the driver and the Underground workers who helped the police retrieve her had been offered counselling. I wish there was a photograph of Michael. Not because I particularly want to see his face, but because that would have meant that readers of the article would have known she wasn't the only victim of her depression.

I remember so vividly how he came home early that night and lay on the bed, still in his uniform. He never came home in his uniform. Although he explained in short bursts about the 'one under', he hadn't gone into too much detail, and I hadn't wanted to push him.

And that was it. Asmaa was the straw that broke the camel's back. Down he sank yet again into another depressive episode. I couldn't reach him. He was given a month off work because he was having trouble sleeping. He spent his nights in the spare room and was hollow-eyed each morning and looked like it was him who was dead and not her. He became slightly obsessed with her. He found an 'RIP, Asmaa' page on Facebook and would scour it regularly to see what her friends had posted. He found out where she lived and would go on pilgrimages to her block of flats and leave flowers outside. He wrote to her parents expressing his sorrow. They replied and he met them for coffee. God knows what they talked about – he wouldn't tell me. As I say, he reverted to being distant. He had been so crushed by our baby dying all those years before and now he felt like he had actively killed someone. He never returned to work. Beneath the print-off from the Internet, I find the letter her parents wrote to him, apologizing for what their daughter had put him through.

I place the papers back in the folder. I go to return it to the wardrobe, but I don't know whether I should. What do I do? What do I do with all his things? What do I do with his Asmaa folder? It's of no use to anyone else. I decide to place it on the dressing table and the move feels bold, brave. Like I'm changing something, altering the status quo. As if I am admitting he is no longer here so has no say over where things live. This is my space now, and if I wish to keep the folder there, I will. If I wish to throw it in the bin, I will. I won't, though. It's such a vital part of who Michael was, towards the end anyway.

Mum calls up the stairs, 'Karen? Tea'll be five minutes, OK?'

'OK,' I call back, and feel thirteen again.

Mum and Dad sit in terse silence over tea. Dad's in Michael's old dressing gown. Mum has her coat on the back of the chair, as if to say, 'As soon as this bloody meal is over, I'm getting out of here and running into the arms of Jorgen Borgen.'

So, what's going on with them?

I ask them. 'What's going on with you two?'

Mum slices into some boiled (yes, boiled) parsnips and looks confused, as if it's perfectly normal for them to be sat here chewing the (boiled) cud when we all know really she'd rather be with Wallander on the other side of town.

'We're helping you get through a difficult time,' Dad says. 'As a family.'

Mum nods and pops some parsnip into her mouth. Even she must think it's hideous.

'But . . . what about Jorgen?' I ask.

'What's important, Karen . . .' Mum insists, slicing into her Kiev. Garlicky gunk pops out of it like a squeezed spot '. . . is making sure you're OK. OK?'

'OK,' I say, with a heavy heart.

Mum looks to Dad. 'OK?'

He nods. 'OK.'

And then, after a bit, he adds, 'These parsnips are minging, Val.'

She steels herself, pulling herself up to the fullest height she can muster in my, it has to be said, pretty low kitchen chairs, and says, 'If you don't enjoy my veg, Vern, feel free to cook for yourself once in a blue moon.'

'Oh, I've been cooking for myself all right, Val.' There is a definite hint of menace in his voice. I quite like it. It shows her behaviour means something. 'Every day since you left me.'

She titters. She titters badly. For some reason it puts me in mind of a French and Saunders sketch. I see them in crinolines. 'Well, there's a first. I'm amazed you're still standing.'

After a pudding of Viennetta and fresh pineapple – not the most obvious of combinations – Mum grabs her handbag and tells me she'll see me tomorrow. Then she disappears into the night to go and see Jorgen Borgen How Often Do You Play the Mouth Organ?

I persuade Dad to have a little drink with me. We sit in the living room with the fire on, and he has a whisky, while I have a Tia Maria with ice. We put the telly on, to give the feeling that this is a normal evening, and that one of us isn't mortified about having a bonkers-ish reaction to her fella stringing himself up from a tree in the local park, and the other isn't fuming that his missus of nearly forty years has run off with a younger model with a difficult-to-rhyme name. I surreptitiously glance over to

Dad and see he's circling his glass in his hand, like they do in the movies when they want to look pensive. I wonder if that's clever acting in the films, that they've seen it done in life so are imitating it for art, or whether Dad has seen it happen in films and is therefore aping it now to help himself think.

I'm working up to ask him how he is when he looks over and says, 'How are you, love?'

Oh. He got there first.

'Bit mortified, actually,' I admit.

He turns his mouth upside down and wobbles his head from side to side, like he's weighing that statement up and coming down on the side of 'You have every right to be, fruitbat.'

Must be the warm Tia Maria, but I find myself expanding, as if he requires an explanation, though none was requested.

'Mortified that I've been lying to everyone. I'm not mortified that . . . that I've not been coping with Michael's death . . . but to go around lying . . . I'll have to face everyone and tell them I was lying.'

'They'll understand, love.'

Let's hope so.

Ethleen has given me a week off to sort myself out, get my head round recent events. She says I can take more if I want to. Originally I just wanted to keep it to the week, but the more I think about it, the more I'm dreading seeing everyone and having to explain that yes, Michael is really dead, and my claims that he just left me were complete balderdash.

There's also the small issue of facing Connor when I go back in. Two issues there, I remind myself. One: will his dad have told him that I took his mother's place in their bed one night and spooned? And two: does he know his father has a false identity? I try to put these worries to the back of my mind, something of course I am very adept at. Instead I turn my attention back to Dad. He's finishing off saying something. I've no idea what. I just hear him say, 'And that can only be a positive thing.'

I nod, a bit like how I remember Roberta Flack nodding. Then I say what he always taught me to say if I'd not understood what another person had said or was stuck for something to say.

I say, 'Watch your language!' and then emit a hearty chuckle.

He looks incredulous. I take another swig of my Tia Maria, and he says, 'Karen, have you got any idea what I just said?'

Well, it's pointless arguing with him. He's the inventor of Watch Your Language.

I shake my head.

He rolls his eyes. 'I said, the thing about admitting Michael's gone is that now maybe you can start visiting our Evie's grave again, and that can only be a positive thing.'

'Oh yes. Deffo,' I say, and am then embarrassed that originally I'd said, 'Watch your language.'

'Anyway, how are you?' I bat back.

He shrugs.

Part of me wants him to say nothing. That's what dads are meant to do. They're meant to be stoic in the face of great emotion and never crack their shells. I want him to push me away, insisting he's 'fine, fine. Don't you worry about me' type thing. I don't know that I could cope with a touchy-feely dad. He's never been one of those and it'd feel weird, him starting now. Like he was only doing it because I was a borderline nutter and he felt he'd created that. I sit there, partly wanting to know how it must feel to lose the love of your life after all these years (although some might say I have an inkling what that is like) and the other part's screaming, 'Say nothing! Bitch don't wanna know!'

Instead he just says quietly, 'Well, it's not the first time, you know.'

'No, I don't know. Know what?' I ask, horror creeping into my voice. It rises like scales on a piano. Good job I didn't say any more words or I'd have hit top C.

He carries on, 'Well, it goes back as far as the market.'

'Garston Market?'

'Yeah, she was giving the bloke off the misshapes stall the glad eye. Trevor, his name was. All tattoos and gobshite. She put on half a stone with all the freebies he was feeding her.'

'Did she go off with him?' Again my voice is rising.

I certainly don't remember her being absent from my life if she did.

Dad shakes his head. 'I gave her an ultimatum. Leave the stall or I'm leaving you.'

I am the epitome of gobsmack. I had *no* idea. All this was going on under my nose as I was growing up and I didn't have a *clue*.

'I mean, I didn't want to leave, love. I didn't wanna leave you, that's for sure.'

I look touched and relieved, even though I'm not, but I'm sure it's what he wants to see. I'm more fascinated by what I think is coming.

'So when she became the ventriloquist, when she tried to launch her performing career . . .'

The one that bombed, I want to add, but don't.

'. . . she was doing that to . . .'

'To distance herself from that Trevor knob,' I finish for him.

Dad nods. ''Cos I told her, it's him or me.'

I'm quite impressed, I have to say.

But then I wonder, How did big, butch, law-laying-down

Dad go from that to this – this 'put up and shut up' person I see before me today, while Mum's probably, as we speak, falling into the arms of— God, the name Jorgen's annoying.

Neil. From now on I will call him Neil.

''Course, she was a shite ventriloquist, so that didn't last long. Then we found out Trevor had married a Brazilian, so I let her go back to the market.'

I can't help it. Whenever I hear the word 'Brazilian', I still clench my buttocks. Damn you, Mrs Pepper!

'Have there been . . . other ones?' I ask tentatively.

'Oh, yes,' he says almost immediately. 'And after a while I . . . stopped caring and . . . turned a blind eye.'

He continues, and I continue to be amazed by what I am hearing. There are words. Lots of words. And names. A veritable phone book of names. (Well, three, but this is my *mother* we're talking about.) Basically, the gist of what he's saying is, 'Your mother's a slut.'

Tonight my dad looks like a deflated old man. The red hair of his youth has given way to a sandy-grey colour. Even his freckles have faded. The man always seen at parties in his sheepskin coat, jangling keys in his pocket and making off-colour jokes has gone, the life sucked out of him, and in his place is a crumpled mess with skin like crêpe paper. It looks so thin it might tear at the slightest touch. Surely he used to have thicker skin than that?

'Why d'you stay with her?'

He looks down to his drink, like that's the million-dollar question.

'Well, they always fizzle out. Then she comes back, tail between her legs. Ever so nice then, she is.' He clears his throat. 'I don't usually get to meet them.'

I nod. It must have been weird meeting J— *Neil*, then.

'I had this uncontrollable desire to throttle the Danish bastard.'

And for a second, the sheepskin jacket is back. And I feel bad. He wouldn't have had to have met – oh, OK, I can't help myself – Jorgen Borgen Not to Be Confused With Piers Morgan if he'd not felt the need to come down here and stage an intervention with Mum. So it's my fault they met.

'I'm so sorry you had to see him,' I say, and I mean it.

'It's not your fault, love. It's your mam who's the nightmare. You're chicken feed compared to her.'

For some reason this makes me laugh. Well, I know the reason. The reason being that in the last week I have probably come the closest I ever will to having a nervous breakdown/ going a bit mental and yet even then I'm not as much of a nightmare as my mother. Dad smiles. It's nice when he does that. Makes me feel everything's going to be OK.

'Dad?'

'What, love?'

'Do you believe in ghosts?'

He thinks. I like this about him. He doesn't have a knee-jerk response to anything. He thinks, considers, then gives his opinion.

'Dunno.'

I like this less about him now.

Then he elaborates, 'I've never seen one, like. Your auntie Margaret has.'

Auntie Margaret's done everything. She's like Gina from science. If you've got a cough, she's got secondary cancer. I remember being very excited as a child because on the way to the baths, in my dad's car, we had to slow down to let someone cross the road and it was the woman who played Nellie Boswell in the sitcom *Bread*. Dad had beeped his horn and she had waved and that was it, but I couldn't wait to tell anyone who crossed my path after that. And everyone was of course impressed and envious and made me tell them the story again and again and again in case I'd missed anything out.

Apart from Auntie Margaret.

We were in her kitchenette at the time. She always called it her 'kitchenette' even though it was anything but small. She was dragging on a menthol cigarette ('Like smoking a Polo, Karen. Wait till you're old enough to try it,' she used to say) and she looked down at me from the high stool next to her breakfast bar and said, 'Nellie from *Bread*?'

'Uh-huh. We actually saw her.'

'Nellie from *Bread*, you say?'

'Yeah. On the zebra crossing by the Abbey Cinema.'

'Nellie Boswell, yeah? The actress who plays her?'

Oh God. Even I knew she was gearing up for something.

'Yes.' The impatience in my voice rang out like a bell.

Auntie Margaret nodded her head and stubbed out her cigarette. 'Don't talk to me about Nellie from friggin' *Bread*,' she said. 'I only know her bloody mother.'

'Go'way. Do you?' chimed in Mum as she wandered in rubbing Atrixo into her hands. Her and Auntie Margaret were always doing things to their bodies, beauty-wise, when they got together.

'Oh yeah. Her real name's Jean Boht, and her mother's called Shona, and she's always coming on my book bus.'

Then she went on and on about what Shona Boht was like. She was very put out when I dared to ask, 'Does anyone call her Show Boat?'

Auntie Margaret looked at me and continued to go on about Shona Boht and her dicky hip, and how she only had the one hand, and that hand had six fingers on it.

'Still, saves her a fortune on nail varnish, eh, Val?'

And Mum had nodded sagely from the other side of the breakfast bar.

It was only when I was a teenager that I saw an interview with the actress from *Bread* and she talked about her upbringing in Liverpool, and about her mum. I forget now what her name was, but:

1. She wasn't called Shona, and
2. She was a recital pianist. *With two hands.*

I was quick to point this out to Auntie Margaret next time I went round. At first she called me a liar. Then after a while she came up with the excuse that Jean Boht was disablist and embarrassed of having a one-handed mother and so was lying. Mum bought the story. I didn't. I took everything Auntie Margaret said from then on in with a huge dose of salt.

'Yeah,' Dad was going on, 'she reckons she used to see a ghost when she was a volunteer at Speke Hall. Said she seen a white lady in the tapestry room.'

'That's racist,' I say, and we both giggle.

'Why d'you ask?' Dad probes.

'Oh, nothing.'

'Have you ever seen one?'

Should I? Should I tell him about Michael?

'Sometimes I think I see Michael.'

Dad thinks about this. I can tell he's trying to work out the best thing to say without upsetting me. I hate putting him in this position, so I backtrack quietly. 'But it's not him.'

And he looks so relieved.

So, the only person I know who claims to have seen a ghost is the one member of my family who tells tall tales. This doesn't bode well. Am I the only person in my family to have experienced this phenomenon? Or am I, as I am beginning to suspect, just a bit crazy? Did Michael really come and see me, or did I just conjure him up in my mind's eye to further my pretence that he hadn't really died? At the moment I just don't know. If he was there, though, and I'm not going mad, then maybe I need to find him again somehow.

But how do you go about finding a ghost? I never sought him out before; he always came to me. I have no idea how I am going to do this.

And the more worrying thing is, if I just imagined him, I must be going mad. Because he was so real. It's not like I begged and begged for him to come and see me, and so magicked him up. I didn't really want him there half the time.

I have a few more days off before I return to school, so decide I will spend them wisely, looking for Michael. If he won't come to me, I'll go to him. And if I can't find him, then it's clear I am losing it, or was losing it, or have lost it. Whatever 'it' is. It is probably my sanity.

I go to all the places I feel were special to him, and where he might be likely to be hanging out. Not that I'm sure ghosts hang out. Even thinking it makes me feel demented, so of course I don't tell anyone this is what I'm doing. I just say I'm going for long walks, as exercise is bound to help me at the moment. No one argues. Well, Dad doesn't argue, and he's the only one who seems to be hanging around (not in a ghosty way) at the moment. Mum's forever rushing round to Jorgen/Sharon Horgan after each hideous tea, and Meredith has decided to go and stay with a friend while Dad's here. I'm a bit perturbed by this. If she fancies me that much, why isn't she hanging around (not in a ghosty way) to check I'm doing all right?

Wendy drops by unannounced one evening just as we're

clearing the dinner plates away (breaded turkey steaks with fresh asparagus) and is full of apologies for being a 'crap friend' and tells me she's 'back now' and she's 'going to be there' for me 'every step of the way'. Then in the next breath she's whipping her iPad out and showing me photos of all her recent trips with Jake. Jake doesn't look too bad for his advancing years, it has to be said, but there's no denying the pictures of them together look like she was on holiday with her DILF of a dad. Not that I want to do any rudies with him; it'd be like cosying up with an inappropriate uncle. Jake dresses well, from what I can tell by the designer trunks he's sporting around the pool, and he's very at home with an orange juice.

I, of course, rave on about how hot he is as if she's showing me pictures of Jake Gyllenhaal or something, and she doesn't read my insincerity at all, which is a relief. But I can't help but feel slightly antagonistic towards her. I love her – of course I love her; she has been my closest friend for aeons – but each time I look at her sun-kissed forehead I can't help but see the word 'Grass' written across it in peach lipstick. Why did I tell her I'd seen Michael? Why did I have to open my big bloody mouth? If I'd not told her in that email, she would never have become concerned and spoken to Mum or whoever about it. And then I wouldn't have been found out. And then I could still be floating along atop my cloud of denial. I liked it up there. It made more sense than the hole I find myself in now, questioning my own sanity, wondering what the hell actually happened each time Michael showed his face. Believing he is dead stings like nettles, all over, like I'm walking through a field of them, but knowing I spoke with him, was held by him . . . and not being able to work out how that happened . . . well . . . I could do without that. And I blame no one else but Wendy here.

She can see I'm distracted. She can see I'm not really listening as she gabbles on, glass of Merlot in her hand in the lean-to, and when she finishes a sentence and I say, 'Watch your language,' she looks hurt.

She lets silence fill the room, then leans in to me. 'Have you had any more . . . sightings?'

I freeze. I can't tell her the truth, surely. Maybe if I was honest with her, though, she might be able to help me.

'Of Michael,' she adds, in case I'm too stupid to work it out.

Slowly I shake my head. A smile creeps across her face, like she is completely relieved her best mate isn't b-b-b-bonkers.

'I'm sure part of the problem . . .' she carries on. Oh God, she's going to analyse me. Why do people think they've got carte blanche to analyse me? I have Roberta Flack for that, thank you very much, '. . . is that you didn't go to the funeral.'

'I did go to the funeral!' I spit back. She looks unnerved by my vehemence. 'I just didn't go inside.'

I ask her to leave. She fears she's done something wrong, but I pretend I am tired and emotional and need to sleep, so she says she'll get a cab on the street and eventually wends her merry way, saying she's going to Jake's in Hampstead and he'll foot the taxi bill. Bully for her.

Of course, Wendy is right. It was a crystal-clear day. It was cold, I remember, because standing outside the church, my breath turned to vapour in front of my face when I breathed out. Wendy stood with me by the open door as we listened in. I'd refused to go in. I said it would be too traumatic and I'd sit at the back in case I wanted to flee. No one was happy about it. His mum said it was disrespectful. I remember screaming at her, 'Well, it was disrespectful of him to bloody well kill himself, Rita!' The memory of it now fills me with shame, but I knew why I was doing it. By not being there . . . well, by being there and not being there at the same time, listening to it like a radio play, a thought was forming in my mind: This is so much easier to deal with if I just tell myself he left me. This is someone else's funeral. This is some other Michael. The details of his life are strangely familiar, but they've made a mistake. This is not him.

And so it continued, the thought pattern in my head. I didn't care if his workmates thought I was mad – Wendy insisted they didn't. Wendy insisted they understood. I don't know, maybe they did, but this was the easiest way of coping for me. He didn't die; he just left.

I wait till she has been gone twenty minutes – can't risk bumping into her in the street when I've said I'm off to bed – then put a coat on and quietly leave the house, shutting the door softly so Dad, from his bed, won't hear. It's night-time; it's dark; ghosts are always coming out in the dark.

I walk to the park. I find the tree where it happened. He's not there. I take a taxi to the Thames Barrier Park and tell it to wait, but then discover the park is closed. I peer through the railings to see if I can see him. He's not there either. I spend a fortune getting the cab to take me to Whitechapel. Then I scour the streets looking for the entrance to the disused Tube station. I can't find it anywhere. I ask a few homeless people if they know where it is. They seem quite keen to know themselves – sounds just the place for them to spend the night, underground and warm. They help me look, but really I have no idea what we're looking for. In my head the door is a magical, mystical thing in luminous paint with roses growing round it and someone who is half human, half goat playing the pan pipes outside it, bewitchingly. Amazingly there is no one fitting this description in Whitechapel tonight. And by the time I give up the ghost –

oh, the irony! So that's what that phrase means! – my homeless friends are really pissed off with me. I dangled a carrot and then stole it away from under their noses. I'm half inclined to invite them back to stay at mine the night, but I'm just not sure how I'd explain it to Dad.

When I'm home, I do some research online and discover that where the original entrance was is now a garage. I feel I am on to something because in one of the Google searches the station is listed as one of the 'ghost stations of London'. Of course a ghost would live there! And he'd probably have company with people who died in the Second World War in some air raid or something! It makes complete sense!

I head to the garage the next day. My plan is to pass myself off as someone inspecting the cars for sale, pretending I'm interested, but all the time be scouring the showroom and forecourt for my magical, secret door. Salesmen will harangue me to see if they can sell me anything and I will make non-committal noises about 'just looking' and 'not sure yet'. Then I will see the door and will ram-raid it with one of the cars and leg it down the stairs. Oh yes, this is perfect.

Except when I get there, I can't even find a garage. Was that webpage out of date? I see many shops. I see this is exactly where I was looking last night. There is a takeaway place specializing in chicken (I dread to think what sort of chicken), a mobile phone shop, a cheap clothes shop, but no garage. And no magicky door. I want to see a magicky door!

Were these shops here all those years ago when Michael brought me here? The buildings look too old to be new. I don't want to ask anyone, though. I'm worried that even by asking about the disused Tube station, they'll know I'm looking for a ghost and send for the men in white coats. I trudge down the road in a foul mood. It's starting to rain. Great. And I didn't even bring an umbrella. Cue frizzy hair, no doubt. What is it with this year? Is it the wettest on record? It's almost March. I thought April was meant to be the showery month. Or did Bambi make that up?

Some flats over the road have scaffolding round them and green netting all across. The scaffolding has made a tunnel over the pavement. I dart through the traffic and take refuge in the tunnel for a bit.

Some workmen are in the road, painting an Olympic symbol in the bus lane.

This rain shows no sign of abating.

It's heavy. Before I know it, there are about twenty of us under the scaffolding. It's like an air raid and we're huddled together till it passes. I decide to ask some of these people if they know how I can find the Tube station, but as I open my mouth to say it, something weird happens.

Really weird.

Like completely weird.

I hear a voice. A voice I recognize. It says one word.

'Karen?'

And I know immediately who it is.

OK, he says a couple more words. Well, four to be precise.

'Karen, is that you?'

I turn and I see, sheltered in the tunnel alongside me, none other than Kevin.

TWENTY-THREE

No. This can't be happening. This is weird, too weird. I came here looking for Michael and instead I've . . . conjured up *Kevin* instead? No. *No!* I look away, then look back. He's still there, seemingly a little bewildered.

Bewildered? He should try being me for a bit!

And oh God, I've conjured him up and for some reason my brain has made him even better-looking than usual: new haircut, more stubble, paler skin, making the eyes look more piercey. I'm not totally bananas about his 'hi-vis jacket and battered jeans' look, or the light dusting of talc on his face. Has my brain decided that he too is a ghost, and is that the best my brain's make-up team can come up with?

I look away again. Then he will dissolve in the rain, I just know it. The rain will wash him and his talc away. I watch the rings being painted on the road. Lovely Olympic rings.

But he says it again: 'Karen?'

Other shelter members are looking round now. A black guy with a gold tooth looks warily behind me, then at me, and says, 'Is he giving you grief?'

'Is there someone there?' I ask urgently. He looks again, now thinking I'm mad, then nods again.

'Karen, it's me, Kevin,' he insists behind me.

'He's called Kevin,' says the black guy.

'I know,' I admit, for I am not deaf.

OK, so he's real, but even so, this is just too crazy for words. To go looking for the dead one and find instead the alive one, in a part of London that has no proper link for either of us . . . I look back at him. How did he get more gorgeous in the past few weeks? How? How is that humanly possible? It's not fair. Why can't I get more gorgeous, incrementally, week by week? Bloody hell, by the time I'm sixty, I could be Angelina Jolie. I fluster, unsure what to say to him, because I don't actually believe he's there by his own free will. This must be something that's going on in my head, whether other people can see him or not. And because of this – it's all about me – I really have no idea what to say to him. I must say something, though.

And so I say the first thing that comes into my head, the thing my dad taught me to say when stuck for social discourse.

I say, 'Watch your language!' then turn on my heel and run.

And here I am again, running, with no idea where I'm going but with a huge determination to escape some sort of perceived threat. I hear him running after me and calling out my name. It seems to dissolve in the rain. I know I can't keep this up for ever – I'm getting out of breath, and running in this weather is hazardous; I'm sure I'm going to go flying soon. This is pointless. Completely pointless. I may as well give up and give in to it. So I do. I slow down, from a sprint to a canter to a stroll, and then he's there, alongside me.

'Why do you keep running away?'

It's a fair enough question, but then mine that follows is too.

'What are you doing here?'

'Talking to you.'

'Here. In Whitechapel.'

'I'm working here. The flats back there. We're doing some renovations for the housing association that owns them. It's not the sort of thing I want to do, but it keeps things ticking over.'

OK, that makes sense.

'So this is just a coincidence?'

'What, that we've bumped into each other? Well, what other reason would there be?'

I'm sounding mad. I back-pedal. 'No, I'm just . . . Oh, I dunno.'

He stops walking, which makes me stop walking. We're both drenched. It reminds me again of that scene from *Four Weddings*. Only now if one of us proposed and they didn't know it was bucketing down, they would indeed be certifiable. I realize the talc on his face is on his clothes too, and it's dust from plastering.

'Why do you keep running away from me?' he asks again.

I don't want to have this conversation. I am embarrassed and squirmy. I've lied to him. OK, so he's lied to me too (IRA, name and so on), but right now that's less important than the fact I know he's spoken with Meredith and all that lot and . . .

'Will you just leave me alone, Kevin? If Kevin is your name.'

'What d'you mean? Of course Kevin's my name.'

'Oh, don't worry,' I cut in. God, he's a good actor, I'll give him that. He looks genuinely perplexed. Years of practice, no doubt. 'You're not the only one who's lied.'

'I've not lied. I've been dead straight up with you.'

'Well, I haven't.'

'Why? What's gone on?'

OK. Truth time. Time to face my fears and . . .

'My boyfriend didn't leave me.'

311

He nods. Everybody nods. He doesn't nod as well as Roberta Flack. This nod is more 'I have no idea what you're on about', whereas hers is 'I totally get you.' I prefer hers.

'He died, and I never told you.'

He nods again, but doesn't look too shocked.

'I'm sorry,' I add as an afterthought.

'I know.'

He knows I'm sorry?

'What?'

'I know he died. I've always known.'

He has?

'Claire told me.'

'Claire? Custard Claire?'

'Yeah. I thought everyone knew. I didn't realize it was a secret.'

'It's not a secret, but . . . well, didn't you think it was weird I never mentioned it?'

'No. I just thought you weren't ready to talk about it.'

Oh. Right.

'Which is a shame, 'cos I felt it was something we might have in common. I just didn't wanna press you.'

Oh. *Right*.

'You never lied to me, Karen. You never said, I dunno, he's still alive and living in . . . Mortlake.'

Mortlake? Why is he saying Mortlake? Have I got to go there to locate Michael's ghost? Where the hell is Mortlake?

'You were just a bit . . . evasive if he came up in conversation.'

Oh.

'And I did think it was weird you referred to him as your "ex".'

So I didn't lie to him outright. I was just . . . evasive. Evasive

I like. Evasive I can deal with. And as he says the words and I allow them to sink in, it's as if a weight has been lifted from my shoulders. Literally. I feel lighter. I feel myself rising, growing taller, as if I'm being pulled up like a marionette on invisible strings. I feel amazing, actually. I'm almost levitating. So maybe I didn't lie to everyone. Maybe I was evasive instead. I'd not looked at it like that. Suddenly my return to school feels far less intimidating.

Maybe it'll seem like more of an 'I wasn't ready to talk about it before, but I am now' type thing.

His phone bleeps. He gets it out of his pocket and checks something on the tiny screen.

It might be someone from the IRA. The whole 'renovating flats' thing might be a cover.

He looks back up. 'The lads are wondering where I've got to.'

I gulp. The lads. I can't let him see I know his secret.

'When did I lie to you? I've never lied to you.'

I shake my head. Pointless getting into that now.

'Oh, I just . . . You didn't. You didn't. I'm . . . projecting, probably. Anyway . . .'

'Karen, can I see you again?'

'NO!'

Jeez, I really did scream it. What a plum! He takes a step back, like my breath has blown him away. I speak more softly now, lying.

'I just . . . I'm not in the right headspace. Does that make sense?'

Actually, that's not so much of a lie.

He lets out an ironic laugh. 'Oh yeah, it does. Listen.'

And he hugs me. I don't want him hugging me. I freeze. And

313

get more wet from him being wet. For God's sake, get off me, IRA Man!

'If you change your mind, or you're feeling ready, give us a call, yeah?'

'Of course!' I giggle, pushing him away. He goes to peck me on the cheek, but I duck out of his way and run off down the street.

I don't even say goodbye.

On the Tube home I think about the word 'ex'. Maybe it is inappropriate to use about Michael. What word do you use when your partner has turned in on himself, left you out in the cold, then gone and killed himself? 'Partner' implies you did everything together. I'm not sure we did. 'Ex' implies you split up. We didn't, not really. How should I word it in future? 'My fiancé who killed himself'? And then I realize there's one word I can use that implies nothing. I can just call him Michael.

When I get home, I do something I've not done for a very long time. I log in to Facebook. My page appears before me. My face smiles back at me from a photograph taken on a school trip to Mont St Michel a few years ago. I see I have thirty-six messages waiting for me. I ignore them and in the search box at the top I type in, 'RIP, Michael Fletcher.' I am redirected to another page, where I see Michael's face smiling back. He looks so happy. He's wearing a Christmas party hat and has been caught mid-laugh. I've not seen the picture before and it floors me. It floors me that he is laughing. And not with me. It floors me that he had a life beyond this house, sometimes. The page, I know, was set up by some of his workmates as a virtual book of condolence. I scan through the members of the group looking for the name Laura. I click on the name Laura Grace and up comes another page. It has to be her. She has burgundy hair. I don't bother adding her as a friend, but instead click on the box marked 'Message', and I write. I eat humble pie and I write.

On my third visit to Roberta Flack she has introduced something new to her front room: an extra chair.

'Are you expecting someone?' I ask brightly as I wander in, turn the cushion with *The Scream* on it back to front and plonk myself on the sofa. I like this sofa now. It's relaxing. It's my friend. It welcomes me with open arms (once *The Scream* is reversed) and says to me, 'You'll be OK here, Karen.'

'It's for an exercise.'

Keep fit? I wonder. What's she going to have me do? Jump on and off it balancing a phone book on my head? Or better still, some massive tome about psychotherapy and counselling? *The British Register of Shrinks*? That's really going to help my complicated grief!

A bit of the way into our session she explains the presence of the chair, and invites me to imagine that Michael's sitting in it. She asks me to speak to him about my feelings, about my thoughts on his death and about our relationship. I look quickly back to the chair, hoping this will be the moment that he reappears, dramatically, filling the gap between the armrests, but he's not there. Disappointment crushes me, but I take a deep breath. I can already sense that this could be a good thing. Because he might actually be listening. Maybe he's hiding in the chimney. Maybe in a room above, with a floorboard dislodged so he can eavesdrop. Maybe he's in the front garden, listening in through a grate or air vent I cannot see. If I can just speak up a bit, he will hear me.

When I open my mouth, though, I find it's hard to speak loudly when you're feeling emotional. I'm shaking, something I'd not anticipated. I take a deep breath, and another, stemming a rising panic in me. Why am I feeling like this? Why can't I control my feelings and just . . . bloody talk as if Michael is here?

I take another deep breath and slowly but surely the words start to come. And eventually I become coherent. And once I get into my stride, I wonder whether I'll actually ever stop.

God, Michael. I'm so angry with you at the moment. I think I've been angry with you for years. When Evie died, and you became depressed, it's like I wasn't allowed to grieve for her properly, because you'd sunk so low, and one of us had to carry on and get things done – pay the bills, make the tea. One of us had to keep going. Which meant you could sink as low as you wanted 'cos I kept picking up the pieces. You ceased to function. And although I totally understood why you went like that, it stopped me going like that, and some days I wanted to. Some days I wanted to just curl up in a ball in the living room and scream and kick things, but you were doing that, so I couldn't. It's like . . . every time I felt a wave of grief rolling over me I had to fight it with all my might and stop it drenching me, dig my nails into the sand so it didn't sweep me away, and that was exhausting. And left me feeling numb. And people thought I was coping amazingly. My big fear was that people might think I didn't care. I did care. I just couldn't collapse with that care like you.

There was a woman a few streets away. Do you remember? You couldn't bear to look at her, because we had similar due dates and . . . well, you felt she was rubbing our nose in it when she walked down the street with her pram. I became a bit obsessed with her. I comforted myself with the scenario that she had our baby. There'd been some hideous mix-up at the hospital and one day soon she'd be back with us. Complete bollocks, of course, but those fantasies kept me warm at night. I even picked out a knitted coat for her from that little boutiquey baby clothes place in Covent Garden and left it on their doorstep. I never saw the baby in it, but I like to think she wore it a lot. And looked pretty in it. I like to think it was her best outfit. I knew it was mad, but I was so looking forward to her starting school, growing older. To me, it didn't feel like rubbing my nose in it. Each day was one step closer to everyone realizing the mix-up and her being returned to us. Even if that day would never really come.

And then one day: disaster. You came in from work and said you'd seen a removal van outside their house. I ran round in my slippers and saw a sofa being loaded into a huge van. I asked the driver where they were moving to. He just replied, 'The country.'

I was furious. I kicked one of the tyres on the van. He gave me a piece of his mind and then I scarpered. You were delighted. You hated seeing their happiness. It put your unhappiness into stark contrast.

I stop and take a sip from the small bottle of water I've brought with me.

Roberta grabs her chance. 'Talk to him about his death, how that's made you feel.'

She flicks me a nod. Her nod. And I find it so gratifying I can't wait to carry on, but I fear I'm going to sound like a scratched CD.

'I'm really cross with him about that too,' I say, like it's a bad thing.

'Tell him,' she encourages.

Oh God. He's never going to come back if I'm honest. It's one thing having a go at him about the aftermath of Evie, but about this? I'm not sure I want to do it. I go from 'gung ho' to 'oh no, no' in a matter of seconds.

But then I think, Well, he might not be coming back. He might not have been there in the first place, you mad bitch. So in for a penny, in for a pound.

How dare you?

My voice is quiet. But I amaze myself with the sudden surge of anger I feel.

How dare you kill yourself? How dare *you!*

Oh God. It's like someone's lit a touchpaper inside me and the flare is about to shoot off into the sky. I try to keep a lid on it, my temper, but it's hard. I see Roberta's eyes aflame also, dancing with excitement that I am showing my true colours. Here we go, then.

I stuck by you. All that time. You withdrew from me, you stopped loving me, and I stayed. I stayed because I thought I'd get you back, that one day your illness would be cured and we'd be OK again. Jesus, I only agreed to marry you because I thought it was a sign things were getting better. And then bloody Asmaa had to go and kill herself. And then you became more interested in her than in bloody me, you bastard!

She's liking the swearing – I can tell – but I'm not doing this for her now.

I've felt so alone for years and years, and that's your fault. And now I feel stupid 'cos I should have left you years ago. And I didn't because, d'you know what? I'm a decent person. I'm nice. I'm not so bloody selfish that I don't consider other people's feelings. And you didn't. You never did. Well, you used to – that's unfair – but in the last few years you didn't. And certainly you didn't when you hung yourself from that bloody tree.

I'm not even looking at her now. I'm staring at that chair, quelling a huge desire to get up and kick it. Where is this coming from?

I've felt so alone and now you're gone. It's like nothing's changed. Even though everything has. Because it feels like I've been mourning our relationship for ages. It's like you started to vanish as soon as Evie died. And you kept on vanishing. Bits of you. Like the Cheshire Cat. Only your grin didn't stay – your grim outlook did, pervading every corner of the house. And then you'd come back. New pills. For a bit. But then you'd go again and that's why I'm all fucked up. And haven't been able to tell people, or talk about it, because it's embarrassing. I was useless to you as a girlfriend. I was that crap that you stopped loving me – everyone could see that. You made no pretence of being nice to me in front of anybody towards the end, and now you've paid me the biggest disservice by bloody topping yourself. Now everyone probably thinks, What a waste of space. Couldn't stop him killing himself? It must be something she did. She must be partly to blame.

And maybe they're right. 'Cos much as I feel angry towards you, I feel guilty. I'm sorry. I'm sorry I couldn't help you. I wanted nothing more in the whole wide world than for you to be happy. And you couldn't be. And I was the person you allegedly shared your life with. I should have been able to make you feel better. I should have been able to stop you killing yourself. I should have. And I'm sorry I didn't. And couldn't. I really am sorry.

Whereas originally I feared I might never shut up. Now I simply can't go on because tears are blocking my speech. I clench my fist to my mouth, wanting to punch myself in the face to stop me, to shut me up. Hot tears bubble from my eyes and I'm making the most inhuman sound. I want to run, but I don't. I shake so much I fear the couch will move. I want to scream. Surely if I scream, that will get rid of all this weird, wired energy inside me. I scream, but it stops nothing. Still the tears fall. Still I shake. And I keep saying, again and again, *I am so sorry.*

Eventually I calm down. As has happened before, my body slowly stops shaking and a numbness washes over me. It's like a hot flush, seeping from my head to my toes, and it's comforting.

Like a warm electric blanket. I don't know if it's a blood rush or my body reacting to the shaking, the screaming, but it's like I've been injected with a sedative. I feel the neck of my blouse sticking coldly to my neck, wet with tears. Suddenly the couch feels so comfortable I want to lie back and sleep. And never wake up? No. I do not feel like that. I may be upset, I may be all over the place, but I will never attack like with like. I am not depressed. I will not allow myself to be. I will get through this. I want to come out the other side and be normal.

In the following days I know I've blown it. He's never going to come back now. After years of bottling up stuff that I wanted to say, I've let it out into the open and it's probably wafted on the ether to him and he's heard it. So why should he want to see me again now? He was the one in distress and what's my reaction? *It's all about me!* No. If I was him, I'd wash my hands of me. I decide I don't like this grief therapy nonsense. I'm not sure it's giving me many answers. I'm not sure it's meant to, mind you, but all the same it only feels like semi-closure. I'm getting a lot off my chest, which is good, I guess, but not getting much back. Then again, how much can you actually get back from a dead person? Very little, I guess. Roberta is adamant I will get there eventually, and see, reap and acknowledge the benefits. I'm not so sure. If anything, it's making me feel even more guilty. Guilty I'm expressing my selfishness when he was only ever ill.

'I remember when Mums died, bless her, I don't think I actually cried for a good twenty years,' Mungo says while tucking into a kumquat in his office.

We've decided to do our departmental meeting at lunchtime to give us a free evening. I've brought in a salad I picked up from Pret as a treat. He seems to have brought in food that can only be eaten as if performing cunnilingus. He's telling me how he coped when his mum died when he was about ten.

'I went into "looking after Dads" mode. I'm sure it's perfectly common, but it did mean I constipated myself of all emotion until I met Fionnula. She was my emotional laxative, I guess.' And he licks the inside of a passion fruit lasciviously. 'I remember once she gave me this hot-finger massage. We were in a caravan in Mevagissey at the time and oh, the release. The stuff that came out of me.'

I'm slurping on a coconut smoothie and feel a bit sick.

'I thought I'd never stop crying.'

And relax. I can't face any more smoothie, mind.

'Do you call your mum "Mums" and your dad "Dads", Mungo?' I ask, unsure if I've heard him right.

'You know me, Karen. Never conventional.'

I have decided I like Mungo. It was wrong of me to judge his personality based on the fact that he often teams open-toed sandals with grey socks. That is the behaviour of a shallow person, and I've decided I don't want to be that type. It is right to judge the same personality based on his 'emotionally monogamous but sexually promiscuous' thing, but I've decided I like him all the more for that. Although he doesn't broadcast it to the nation – imagine that on *The Chris Evans Breakfast Show*: 'And coming up we have Mungo, who's going to tell us what it's like to be a swinger!' – his proclivities impress me, in as much as he is cocking a snook at society and ploughing his own furrow. Or someone else's furrow, come to think of it. Quite a lot of other furrows, probably. I should take inspiration from this and find the courage to care less about what other people think.

Not that anyone's been too judgemental since my return to school. The kids have no idea why I was off, obviously, and have given me the nickname Sick Note, which I quite like. And whereas as a child I used to think that all grown-ups knew everything kids got up to, I'm not so sure it's the same the other way round: Keisha-Vanessa never mentioned my Brazilian as administered by her mother all those weeks ago, and Connor has never mentioned the fact that I have stayed in his house in a spooning situation. I've gone into his file on the school computer system and looked up all his notes from his primary school and this one, searching in vain for some info on a name change or the fact that he has a false identity. I could find nothing. So goodness only knows what's gone on there. I certainly don't know, and I don't really like to think of it. I did like Kevin. I don't spoon with just anyone, particularly so soon after my boyfriend dying – even if I was in denial at the time – but whenever I think about him, an alarm bell rings in my head. It's a really loud siren. And I know where I've heard it before – it's the sort that sounds when a bomb goes off. A bomb planted by the IRA.

OK, I don't really have any idea whether sirens go off when a bomb explodes, but in my head, right now, they do. Anyway, it doesn't take a genius to work out that something's not quite right there. He's trouble. With a capital T. I have had a narrow escape.

Meredith's still staying with her 'friend', just till Dad goes home, which will probably be this weekend. It's my birthday on Saturday (whoopee doo) and he reckons he'll hang on for that, then get a coach back to Liverpool on Sunday. Meredith can then move back into the spare room.

I'm a bit put out, truth be told, and unimpressed with old Meredith. I know I wasn't exactly over the moon about her being completely obsessed with me and moving in with me so she could pounce, but why did she flee so quickly? And why didn't she pounce? I know I was hardly ever there, and always keen to avoid her lesbeterian clutches, but she didn't so much as graze the hem of my nightie if we passed on the landing. Call yourself a predatory lez? Yikes. I've known amoeba with more backbone. And now she's obviously diverted her affections to someone else. It's very frustrating for me. I thought I looked like Kate Winslet. What's the matter with me now?

Maybe she thinks I should have been sectioned. Maybe she thinks I'm an out-and-out mad woman of Shallot. I guess that would be enough to put you off someone. They're a fickle breed, PE teachers. If I ever see her putting a penny in the slot of someone collecting for a mental health charity, I'll say one word to her, and one word alone: *hypocrite*.

I have asked her about this new 'friend' and I'm pretty much sure she's changed her name twice. The first time it was Eileen, said with a stutter, like this: 'E-e-eileen'. To the rhythm of 'Come On, Eileen' by Dexys Midnight Runners. Then the next time I ask about Eileen, she looks blank and says, 'Eileen?'

I go, 'Duh! Your girlfriend?!'

'Oh. You've remembered it wrong. Her name's . . . Ivy-Jean.'

Now excuse me, but I don't think I did mishear, because I remember thinking the way she said it fitted the rhythm of 'Come on, Eileen'. And anyway, who on earth is called Ivy-Jean? It's too Nancy Drew for my liking, but then I always suspected her of being a bit like that. Maybe she's American. From Noo Yoik.

I realize I am distracting myself, displacing my brain. It's something Roberta says I am good at, as if I needed telling. She says if I become aware of it, I should try and think about Michael. She also says this weekend might be tough, as it will be the first of my birthdays since he died. I tell her I've often felt quite lonely on my birthday due to Michael's emotional absence, but she claims forewarned is forearmed. She also thinks I need to mark his death somehow. She thinks this may help. She asks if we marked Evie's death in any way other than the funeral and the grave. I tell her we did.

Michael used to like talking to her through my tummy, and till we knew if she was going to be a boy or a girl, he used to call the baby 'Sunshine'. I worried that sounded like it was a boy, so he changed it to the more generic, in his eyes, 'Sunflower'. I worried this sounded a bit too girly, but he resolutely refused to change it again for fear of confusing 'Sunflower'. So when she died, he hit upon the bright idea of planting a sunflower in a tub in the backyard. He made a cloche for the burgeoning buds as they crept up using the cut-off neck of a bottle of tonic water. And lo and behold, like our very own beanstalk, one sunflower grew and grew, its face chasing the sun as its yellow petals burst forth, and it stood there like a big, shiny aciiiid face, serene against the shabby grey bricks of our backyard.

But then disaster struck. We were a bit green about being green-fingered, and after several weeks of majesty overnight the sunflower wilted, collapsed, went dark brown and died. Honestly, it looked so forlorn, like it had been assassinated. The seeds that dropped from its humongous face created such a mess on the ground. Like it had been shot. It was horrific. We hadn't realized they lasted for such a short space of time, and it was more than a little ironic that this was how we'd chosen to celebrate Evie's existence – also too short – on this planet. We read up on the plant then and discovered that if you planted the seeds out again, more would grow next year, but it seemed cruel, taunting. Like Mother Nature was rubbing our predicament, and hers, in our face. Michael said he needed to think about it.

The next day he came in from work with a four-foot-high

plastic sunflower with silky petals. He arranged it in a waste-paper basked stuffed with crêpe paper in our bedroom. A more permanent memorial.

I've never liked artificial flowers. I don't think they look quite right. I didn't like the appearance of this and it proved to be a bugger to clean. I sucked up one of its petals when attempting to clean it with the Dyson. I dutifully stuck it back on with superglue and Michael was none the wiser, but I couldn't tell him how unattractive I found it. It was far too important to him. Every morning he would get up and say, 'Morning, Sunflower!' and wink at it. Some mornings I would too. Some mornings I still do.

But a way of remembering Michael? A toy railway round the backyard perhaps? Get someone to paint a mural of Paul Weller on the back of the house? Wendy suggests planting a tree somewhere when we talk one night on the phone. Then there is a cavernous silence. And she apologizes.

I'll have to give it some more thought.

In the meantime there's the small matter of my birthday to get through.

The night before my birthday, before going to bed, I check my Facebook. I have thirty-seven messages. I open the newest. It's from Laura. I read it, then get out my phone to call her.

TWENTY-FOUR

I lie in bed not wanting to get up. Three things are playing on my mind:

1. It is my birthday.
2. I am having a surprise party, and
3. Today I am going to find Michael (I've decided).

OK, let's get the first two items out of the way.

There are few things in life (well, apart from the events that led up to number three, of course) worse than a surprise party. But even worse than that is discovering you're having a surprise party and having to pretend you know nothing and act all surprised when you turn up to it. Particularly today, because today I can't. Be. Bothered. Or, if I'm going to nail my true Scouse colours to the apathy mast, I can't. Be. Arsed.

I was hoping I'd wake with a modicum of enthusiasm, that I'd see the light dancing through my curtains, the petals of the sunflower dancing in the breeze where the sash doesn't shut properly, and be full of the joys, but no. Nothing. Just a familiar sense of dread. I rarely enjoy being the centre of attention, and I'm certainly not relishing being so at the moment, when my skin feels thinner than usual and my moods have a tendency to fluctuate all over the place.

Now, on to the 'finding Michael' thing. This does get me quite excited, so much so that I actually deign to sit up in bed. I pull my knees up to my chest and rest my head on them. Well, on the duvet, but you know what I mean. I want to believe it. I want to believe that today I will see him. In fact, I'm kind of banking on it.

Before I can think too much of my adventure into contacting the unloving, however, there is a tentative tap at the door and Dad tiptoes in and presents me with breakfast in bed. Well, he gives me a cup of tea and a breakfast cereal bar because he claims he saw an advert in which soldiers ate them before marching for miles. I'm touched, and feign smiles and giggles well as I open my card – clearly bought from the local garage, and meant for a boy: it features a speedboat and a moustachioed man in shades on the boat in a Seventies tracksuit drinking a glass of champagne. Oh, the glamour! – and my present: thirty pounds in WHSmith vouchers. I'm not bonkers about stationery, but I'm sure I'll find something. He looks chuffed that I look chuffed, but it's not a smile on my lips; it's a desperate gurn to stop myself from saying, 'I know about the party,' and, 'I am going to find Michael today.'

How do I know about this surprise party that I'm not meant to know anything about? Blame my mother's booming voice, as per. She was over the other night, and while she was making the tea, I slipped away to my bedroom to fashion the fluff from my belly button into figurines of well-known ice skaters. OK, that's a lie. I came up here just to sit on my bed and take cover from a monumental row. It's getting to something when you're in your mid-thirties and your parents choose to tussle verbally in your house.

I could hear Dad telling her she was 'making a holy show' of herself, and Mum saying he wouldn't know her clitoris if it came up to him and slapped him round the face and said, 'Hi! I'm Clitoris! What's your name?' and then Dad repeating that she was 'making a holy show' of herself. Then Mum cranked up the volume and I heard her throw something in the kitchen, possibly a Le Creuset pan, as it made quite a loud crack, possibly against a wall, then I heard her say he'd been 'frigging useless with organizing this surprise party'. Then Dad hushing her with 'Shut up or our Karen'll hear' and Mum rejoindering with 'You make me sick' and him replying, 'I keep trying to help, but you and that Meredith have got it all stitched up between you. Nice one!'

So then I knew, and I still know. I've been tempted many times to sit Mum down and say, 'Please. No party, surprise or other,' but she's been hard to pin down, rushing in, throwing the tea on, then rushing out again with the air of a 'synchronize watches!' character from a spy film. I toyed with asking Dad to intervene, to stop this madness, but knew without asking that Mum would be furious with him for piddling on her chips. She'd probably accuse him of telling me about the party just to ruin things for her. Meredith has studiously avoided me all week, and I couldn't be bothered/arsed to enter into conversations with her where I had to pretend I had no plans for my birthday and to have her making out, nonchalantly, that she was busy Saturday.

Now, I have to get out of the house today. I am not going to find Michael here.

I tell Dad I want to go out for the day to gauge his reaction.

'OK,' he's saying, 'but when will you be back? Be good if you were back by five.'

I say, 'Five will be fine,' and make out I assume Mum is cooking me a birthday tea.

He agrees eagerly, claiming, 'Yes, that is exactly what she is doing.' He then enquires where I'm going.

I say, 'Just out.'

He assumes I am going to spend my vouchers.

I tap them excitedly. 'Yep, can't wait! I'm really looking forward to Mum's birthday tea,' I lie, overegging the pudding of deceit somewhat.

He looks at me like he can smell a rat. Then I grimace, making out I was joking, and he relaxes. Phew.

Two hours later I'm with Laura on Whitechapel Road.

'I love what you've done with your hair,' I gush, and she looks genuinely thrilled. I do actually, in a Mrs Slocombe in *Are You Being Served?* kind of way. The tight-knit curls have gone and in their place is a burgundy swirl of candy floss, and I can't tell whether it's a wig or a weave or the real thing. 'Listen, I'm sorry about the other week. Whenever it was. When I brought that card.'

'I know, babe. You said in your message, is it. You musta been fackin' all over the place, you get me?'

I like the way she speaks: part Essex, part Jamaica, part indecipherable. Her teeth are perfectly white. I want to hate her for this, but can't, as she's being so sweet.

'Yeah, I was a bit.'

'Michael was always so nice 'bout you.'

'Was he?'

'Sha'ap . . .' course he was! Always gan' on aba' what a brilliant teacher you was, is it.'

'Oh, that's nice.'

She is opening a door with a big set of keys. She makes me promise not to tell anyone where the secret door is, in case loads of people want to come and hang out there. Personally I don't think this is likely, but I am not going to argue with her today. As we're descending the stairs, I decide to come clean.

'Laura? Do you believe in God?'

'Too bloody right, you get me?'

'What d'you think happens to you when you die?'

'Sha'ap, you worried about Michael? He'll be fine, babe, is it.'

'Yeah, but what if he's not? I mean, do you believe in ghosts?'

'Sha'ap, it's my favourite film.'

'What is?'

'*Ghost*.'

'Oh yeah. Patrick Swayze's well fit, isn't he?'

'He's dead, babe. He was in that *Dirty Dancin'* 'n' shiz, in it?'

'I know. Anyway, what would you say if I told you . . . I'd seen Michael.'

She doesn't speak immediately. I sense a frisson of alarm.

'He's dead.'

'As a ghost. If I'd seen him as a ghost.'

'Sha'ap.' Then as an afterthought she adds, her voice getting wary, 'What you bringin' me down here for?' She stops mid-stair.

We must be about halfway down. There's no daylight, but I can still make out her face. The temperature has dropped, and I can hear the plink-plonk of dropping water.

'Laura, stay here if you want and I'll go on my own. You'll probably think I'm mad, but . . .'

Her breath goes funny. Like she's working up, very slowly, to scream, but then she sneezes. It scares the living daylights out of me.

'Sorry, babe!' She goes about finding a tissue to blow her nose, which she does melodiously. Joe 'Schnozzle' Durante would've been proud to make a sound like that. She's avoiding eye contact with me. She thinks I'm mental, but I can't help myself. I don't care. I'm excited. I'm about to see him, I know I am. This is where he's going to be – he is!

'I've seen Michael a few times. I don't know if he's . . . a figment of my imagination or if he's a ghost, but I want to see him again.'

She takes this in, looking at the ground. Then she looks up and attempts a smile. 'Down here, is it?'

'Yes. Many years ago he brought me here. We had an adventure. We drank lager and made love.'

She makes a funny noise, a bit like someone not knowing where to put themselves when Barbara Windsor's bra flies off in a Carry On.

'This is where I think our baby was conceived.'

'May she rest in peace,' she says quickly, like an over-enthusiastic nun.

'Yes, may she rest in peace. Now I've got it into my head that Michael's down here.'

She makes the funny noise again.

'So maybe it's better if I go on my own.'

Oh good. She looks so relaxed now. Like she's being saved a huge job. Like we're in an office and I've offered to count up all the pencil sharpeners and see if they need replacing.

OK, so that's a rubbish analogy, but *I'm excited. I may not be thinking straight.*

'You won't do no vandalism?' she says, pulling her hair back cautiously.

'I won't do no vandalism.'

'Is it?'

I'm not sure how to answer that. I'm not even sure it's a question, but I reply, 'Is it,' with a shake of my head.

'I could get into trouble if they knew I'd shown you round, you get me?'

'I get you. I really get you, and I appreciate you helping me.'

'I thought you wanted a trip down Memory Lane, is it.'

'I'm sorry, but it's kind of like that as well.'

'I'll stay here,' she says, like she's the second in command on an expedition to discover the North Pole and she's hanging back here in case of casualties, letting the braver of us go on and pierce the ground with my flag.

'OK. I mean, he might not be here.'

'Is it.'

I squeeze her arm, then continue down the stairs, glad to be shot of her. I light the torch app on my phone to help illuminate the way, though there are some low-level lights on either side of the stairs. It all smells so familiar. Olfactory recall, I believe it's called. And because of the familiarity, I know I am on to something here. It gets colder. I don't remember it being this cold. I feel I am getting closer to him. I'm a kid again, and this is a game, and someone is calling, 'Warmer, warmer . . .' with every step, and as soon as I get to the little room downstairs, they're going to cry, 'HOT!'

They are.

I know they are.

I, Karen Carpenter, am never wrong.

Oh shit. I'm always wrong.

They don't cry, 'HOT!' They don't cry anything. When I reach the bottom step and can't go any deeper, the familiar room opens itself up to me with the beam of my torch app. It's bigger than I remember, but he's not here. Is he hiding?

'Michael?'

Come on. He's got to answer me soon. He must be hiding.

He was not a figment of my imagination. He was a ghost. A real, live ghost. Well, a real, dead ghost.

I search for the light switch and can't find it. I push through to a small corridor down the back. Is this the way he brought me to that other room where the people hid out in the war? I see the banister of the stairs mounting the wall at an angle. I remember that. I'm in the right place. I find the room. Exactly as we left it last time. The funny-shaped air vent. The bench. Poles coming out of the wall. But again, this room is empty. I was so, so sure he would be here. If he's not here, I don't know where he could be. I call his name again. It echoes oddly, like I'm in the smallest room in the world. I hear a rumbling noise and the ground shakes and I realize a Tube is passing on the other side of the wall. He's going to come out. He's going to step through the wall dramatically as the noise engulfs me. I'm almost faint with excitement.

But the noise abates. It slowly dies away. The vibrating beneath my feet peters out too. And with it the hope in me also starts to fade.

I say it again. Almost a whisper. 'Michael. It's me. Please. Where are you?'

I hear a scratching behind me. I turn, shine the torch in the direction from which it's coming. I get a shock and scream.

A rat is staring at me. Black. Eyes like they're lit up. Oily. Like a small cat. Sat there looking at me. My scream frightens it and it scurries off.

Disappointment crushes me. I sit on the bench. He is not here. I have been pinning my hopes on . . . but . . . he's not . . .

Maybe he was never here.

The seat is wet. My bum is getting cold and sodden.

Maybe we were never here.

I jump up. I know. I can find proof we were here. I scour

the walls with my torch. He wrote on this wall. He wrote our initials. In a loveheart. I will find it, and by finding it, I will have found a little piece of him. Proof. Proof that I am not going mad. And then it will be like he is here.

I can find his writing nowhere. It's gone, vanished, washed away by the falling condensation down the brickwork of this underground cave.

I suddenly feel very alone.

And it hits me. He's gone.

And I'll never see him again.

'You've got to come,' Dad hisses, looking down on me as I lie on the bed.

'Yeah, well, I'm not.'

'Your mother'll kill you if you don't. Look, she's booked a table at . . . at . . . an Angus Steakhouse.'

'Why would I wanna go to a shitty old Angus Steakhouse anyway?' I snarl like a teenager.

I know he's lying about the steakhouse. At least I hope he is. I hope they haven't organized the surprise in one of those.

'You know what your mother's like!' he argues.

Oh, I've had enough. I wave the white flag.

'Dad, I know there's a surprise party –' his eyes widen with fear '– but I'm just not in the mood. I can't. Be. Arsed.'

'Who told you?' He plonks himself on the bed.

I'm a bit worried he's going to start crying. I sit up. 'Don't make me go, Dad. I'm sorry if you've gone to a load of trouble.'

'Oh, sod that, love. I've not done anything. Not been allowed. It's all your mother's doing.'

'Is it really in an Angus Steakhouse?' It's impossible to hide the horror in my voice.

He shakes his head. 'I've got to take you to the Who'd've Thought It?'

Blimey. Which is worse? Oh, the imagination of Mum and Meredith, planning my party in the pub nearest to the school.

'Oh well, I'm definitely not going, then.'

'Why not?'

''Cos it's vile. Have you seen their soft furnishings? It's like being in an episode of *George and Mildred*.'

Dad looks away from me. I know what he's going to say. He's going to say I can suit myself. He'll no doubt enjoy telling my mum that all her hard work has gone to nothing. He looks back and I'm waiting for him, a delicious smile on my face, but his look is steely. He even points his finger at me.

'Now listen, you. I never put me foot down, ever, but you are going to that party whether you like it or not.'

Oh God. You could knock me down with a feather.

'There's a load of people in that pub who think the world of you, who love you. Now, I know Michael went on a downer and killed himself, and I'm sorry about that, I really am, but he's dead and they're not. They've not abandoned you, so why abandon them?'

I can't answer that. He's being so . . . un . . . Dad.

'So get in that bath, put your glad rags on and slap a smile on your face, you miserable mare.'

I have never in my life been spoken to like that before. Not by my *dad*.

It's hilarious.

I burst out laughing. And he playfully slaps me. But misjudges it. And hurts my leg.

But I forgive him.

Even though I know I'll have a bruise later.

*

335

'*SU-U-U-RRR-PRI-ISE!*'

Party poppers go off. Music starts to play. A mass of people cheer and I stammer in my rehearsed way, 'Oh my God! What a *surprise!*' and add in mock annoyance to my dad, and to Mum, who's looming with a glass of something bubbly for me, 'Oh . . . *you two!*'

And then laugh. And take the something bubbly.

I am the consummate professional. When you're a teacher, you become adept at leaving your feelings at the door and turning in the performance of your life in front of a class of braying brats. Pointless letting them see that you've gone over your overdraft limit or had a row with your head of department or . . . oh, I don't know . . . been unable to locate the ghost of your dead ex. So I turn on the Hollywood smile and the Liverpool charm and float from person to person saying, 'Hello,' and, 'Thank you,' and, 'No, I had no idea.' It's good to take my mind off what happened in the abandoned Tube station. Or what didn't happen, to be more precise. And instead of feeling impossibly crushed, I feel buoyed by the warmth and laughter around me. I could float like the balloons clustered around the top of the bar.

I notice there is a sign above a buffet table in the corner that reads, 'HAPPY BIRTHDAY, KAREN,' though I can see – with my teacherly eye – that whoever made the sign ran out of space, so the 'N' of 'KAREN' is half as wide as the other letters. Cards are thrust into my hand, presents pushed to my chest. I gush 'Thank you's and 'You needn't have bothered, really's and 'Oh God, I can't wait to open it's with a maintained level of excitement that, although forced, sounds impressively genuine, I have to admit. I feel like I'm on a reality show, performing a task. *You have to get through this party making out you're having the best time*, and I succeed. With flying colours.

I pile my presents up at one end of the buffet table that has been cleared for that very job and wonder if people think I'm actually forty today and not boring thirty-seven. Why such a fuss? The food is standard Mum fare: curled ham sandwiches, salmon-paste finger rolls, bowls of Wotsits, Iceland vol-au-vents . . . A massive spinach pie in the centre of the table flamboyantly fanfares that Mungo and Fionnula must be here, and indeed they are. I see them joking in the corner with a red-faced Jorgen. Oh blimey, she's brought him. What do I tell people?

Meredith's poking me in the ribs and asking if I really had no idea they were planning the party of the year. My instinct is to reply, 'Don't big up your part!' but I refrain and give her a hug and squeal my delight, before she drags me off to see Dee, Dozy, Beaky, Mitch and Titch, who are all wearing T-shirts with an image of the singer Karen Carpenter on, which I realize is meant to make me feel touched and amused, and so I am. And Ethleen's with them, and she too is wearing a matching T-shirt, which makes her tits look all pointy and is no doubt giving the girls a thrill. I think it's odd she's joined in their T-shirt japes, but ignore my surprise as she hands me a beautifully wrapped box, which is so gorgeous I have to open it there and then. I look at the card on it. Beautiful handwriting, like calligraphy – Ethleen's trademark. But the words don't make sense.

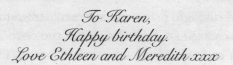

To Karen,
Happy birthday.
Love Ethleen and Meredith xxx

'Oh, you clubbed together!' I smile, wrong-footed, and see a nervous look dart between the two of them. Then, as I rip open the leopard-print wrapping paper, to reveal a jewellery box, I see that Meredith has her arm round Ethleen's waist. And is fondling her bum with her fingers, while her thumb is hitched *inside* the top of her jeans.

There's a necklace inside. It's a pretty, dainty thing in silver with a 'K' hanging off it.

As I stammer my gratitude, they know what I've seen.

Meredith blushes. 'Karen, I've been meaning to tell you.'

Oh *no*. I am gobsmacked.

'I've left Dick,' says Ethleen, and the lesbians laugh.

'She really has gone off Dick,' one of the others titters, and they titter in unison like a million Muttleys.

'Dick and I haven't seen eye to eye for some time,' adds Ethleen.

Ah. Eileen. Ivy-Jean. Ethleen. Erm . . .

Meredith and Ethleen are now an item, and I am the last to know.

Oh, and I am mortified. I heard her on the phone saying she fancied someone, someone straight, and I thought it was me. And all along . . . it was *Ethleen*? Heterosexual, happily married Ethleen?

So that's why she's been telling Ethleen stuff about me, and that's why she was in Ethleen's car that day.

Oh, it's really lovely. It's so sweet!

I think.

The dirty *cows*.

But even though I am amazed and embarrassed that I was so self-centred I thought Meredith only had eyes for me, I hug them and tell them I love them. Then as I part from a hug with Ethleen, I joke that 'You better watch where you put your hands, you big lezzer!' which makes the others howl, but Ethleen fluster. And I giggle to show I was joking. I put the necklace on to show willing, then realize my glass is empty.

As I head to the bar, I pass Mum and Jorgen laughing and joking with Mungo and Fionnula, and see that Little Lee is with them, though there's no sign of Sponge or Joyce. More hugs. More kisses.

And Mum says, 'Mungo's been telling us all about . . . some of their hobbies.'

'Yes,' agrees Jorgen. 'It's really fascinating.'

'Don't be getting any ideas, now!' I joke nervously, but Mum's smile makes me wince and I head off to the bar.

I feel a tap on my back and turn round to see Little Lee beaming up at me. He asks how I am and for a moment I'm vulnerable. Then I take a deep breath and tell him I'm coping. I explain I've been having counselling, and how I'm more positive about the future, and he tells me he is pleased. And that if I ever fancy trying Japanese rope bondage, I should give him a call. I tell him I'll bear it in mind. It's odd, making small talk in a pub against a backdrop of a rather loud rendition of a Simply Red song I can't stand, when that small talk is about bereavement and loss and . . . well, bondage. But that just about sums my life up, I suppose. I kiss Lee fondly on the cheek and edge my way to the bar, squeezing between some teachers I can't really stand but who have no doubt turned up for the free food and because they've heard I've been down and need cheering up.

The barmaid is cracking her knuckles and hacking up some phlegm as I arrive to be served.

I'd know her anywhere. My buttocks clench involuntarily.

'Oh, Shirelle. You not working at the salon anymore?'

She shakes her head as she gets me another glass of fizz. 'Some bastard customer tried to sue me. Said I practically give her a . . .' She turns to another barmaid. 'What's the word, Jamelia?'

'Cliterectomy,' Jamelia says, backcombing her hair with an

Afro comb, no doubt flicking dandruff into people's drinks on the bar.

'Cliterectomy,' nods Shirelle, nonplussed, then does a 'would you believe it?' shrug as she passes me my glass.

'It's polidical correctness gone mad,' adds Jamelia.

'Thassright!' agrees Shirelle.

I take a swig of my drink and turn to see Custard Claire heading over. My, this is a social whirl! More kissing. More hugs. She hands me her present and card, and accompanies me to the table to put them there for later. Which is when she hands me a second present. A bottle wrapped in crêpe paper, and a card.

'Oh. Who's this from?'

'Kevin,' she says, sounding a bit embarrassed.

Oh.

'O'Keefe?' she adds, by way of explanation.

'No. Yes. No, I know who Kevin is.' She can see by the face I'm pulling that I'm awkward, and in case she doesn't get the message, I say, '*Awkward!*' really loudly and she looks perplexed.

'Why?'

'I don't really want anything to do with him.'

'Why? He's been through what you're going through. Sort of. You've got loads in common.'

'Yeah, but when his wife was dying, he had, like . . . loads of different women back to the house.'

I say it quite gossipy, though, as I'm now on my second drink. Claire looks really perplexed now.

'When Toni was dying in the hospital,' I explain, sure that will clarify things.

'She didn't die in no hospital, Karen. She died at home. And

the only women what come round his house was the Macmillan nurses.'

Oh.

Oh shit.

'Who told you that?' Claire sounds murderous.

'Oh, er . . . someone at the party.'

'Which party?'

'Toni's wake. I think she's a neighbour. Big glasses.'

Claire is now furious. 'Oh, Dirty Gertie. She's a piece o'
work, Karen. Always had the hots for Kevin, and fuming he
never saw his way clear to flirting with her. Take no notice of
that poisonous witch. I'll fuckin' 'ave her!'

Right.

Oh God.

Oh, but then . . .

'Also' – and I lean in as if this is pretty major gossip. Which
it is – 'he's not who he says he is.'

Claire shunts her head back like my breath smells. 'Are you
on drugs, Karen?' she says, incredulous.

'No!'

'Well, what you bloody on about, then, you nutter!'

So I tell her. About Steven McIntyre. And the IRA membership card. And the poster. And she thinks. Long and hard. I
can practically see the cogs whirring in her brain. And then
her face cracks. And she laughs. Long and hard. At one point I
fear she's having a hernia. She has to cling on to me for support.

'What? Claire, what?'

And then she tells me. And I want the ground to open and
swallow me up. As I stand there in stunned silence, her laughter ringing in my ears, I see the door open and hope it might
be Kevin who's coming in. Instead I see Wendy. She waves over.

She looks great. I wave back, still dumbfounded by what Claire has said. I see an old man, quite nattily dressed, follow Wendy in. I wonder briefly if he's got the wrong pub, or hasn't realized this is a private party, and then I realize. It's Wendy's boyfriend.

TWENTY-FIVE

I lie in bed, warm and fuzzy with drink and spinach pie and Black Forest gateau. I hear Dad pottering in his room, packing to return to Liverpool tomorrow. I think how valiant he was in the face of Mum's behaviour tonight, parading Jorgen around like he was her new puppy from Battersea, offering everyone a quick pet and a stroke. How composed he'd remained. Till we were leaving, and I heard him say menacingly to Jorgen, 'I give it six months, you Norwegian nonce,' and Jorgen looked shocked and stammered that he was Danish, but then he had to go because Mum was calling him to an awaiting taxi. It's a wonder Dad didn't punch him. Oh, to have his patience. But maybe we're all always waiting for our lost loves to come back. Even if having them back isn't the best option in the world, and they're not even right for you. I confuse myself with this line of thinking, then decide not to lose any more sleep over it. If it's a trait that runs in the family, fine. It shouldn't really affect me. Mum might, one day, return to Dad. Michael will never return to me.

Maybe I should try and find Dad a girlfriend. I'm surprised Wendy wasn't all over him like a rash.

I toy with sending Kevin an email, apologizing for my behaviour, but decide it can wait till the morning. I cringe with embarrassment when I think about him. Oh well. Maybe I was stupid for a reason. Maybe I misunderstood because that is what needed to happen. Again, not going to lose any sleep over that.

I remember Little Lee getting in the cab with Mum and Jorgen, but comfort myself with the fact that they must have just been giving him a lift home. They must have. They must . . .

I realize I'm fighting sleep. I enjoy drifting in and out of consciousness. I wonder if I should get up and go to the loo – I did drink more than usual tonight – but sleep is too attractive right now, too comforting. I give in to it.

I wake and think the lights are on. I'm sure I switched them off. Then I see that the curtains are open and moonlight is casting a silvery glow over the room. The sash of the window is up. I know I didn't leave it up, but I also know why it is. My eyes seek him out and he is stood there, in the corner of the room, next to the wardrobe. His side of it is open and he has a holdall in his hand. His clothes rail is empty.

'Just came for my things.'

I sit up. I feel wide awake. I no longer feel drunk. In fact I've never felt so alert, like every nerve in my body is pulsating, wildly alive.

'Are you cold? I can close the window?'

I shake my head. He comes and sits on the bed. He takes my hand.

'Are you a ghost?' I ask.

He thinks. 'Possibly. Not sure. I think so.'

'Why are you here?'

'Well . . .' he struggles for the right words '. . . I think this is it.'

'Time to go?'

He nods. 'Yeah.' Then he grimaces, like he doesn't want to. I return the grimace. I don't want him to either, but know he has to.

He goes in a drawer. He pulls out a work roster and the hankie I found in Chinatown. I'd put them there for safe keeping. He tucks them in his pocket.

'I came looking for you,' I say, trying to convey in those few words how hard I tried.

'I know.'

'Oh God, Michael, there's so much I want to say, but, well, now you're here, it's all gone out of my mind.'

'I know, babe. Try not to worry about it.'

OK. I won't.

But he carries on, 'I just want to say, before I go . . . I . . . I'm sorry.'

I nod. OK. It's nice to hear, though I think he's said it before. Then I realize he's not said it before when I've been in a position to appreciate it.

'I know you think I didn't love you, that I fell out of love with you, but I didn't.'

I gulp. He's saying something lovely, but it pierces me with a hot pain. Salt stings my eyes.

'I fell out of love with the world, with living. You could never rescue me from that, and I'm sorry you had to try.'

It is, it's so lovely, and yet it's like a scalding iron on my stomach. I could double over, it hurts so much.

'You were the only person I ever truly loved, apart from my mam, and you know how she did my head in. The only reason I put her contact details in my pocket was so that she'd get the news and not you. I wasn't really thinking straight, babe, but I was trying to protect you, in my own stupid way.'

I take a deep breath; maybe that will make the pain go away.

'I'm sorry I was so selfish over Evie and didn't appreciate what you were going through. And I'm sorry it's left you in a bit of a mess. Anyway, that's about it really. Except . . .'

I breathe out.

'. . . I don't want you to be sad. Well . . . I am a bit of a selfish bastard, so, like, be sad for a bit, but don't let it stop you living. You deserve to be dead, dead happy. You're brilliant. And beautiful.'

'Oh, shut up,' I say gently. Never good at taking compliments. Even from a dead man.

'Well, you are, and I'm just a knobhead, so . . .'

So? So what? What does he mean?

He lifts the holdall from the floor and puts it on his knee.

'Will you come with me? A bit of the way?'

This is unbearable, but it has to be done. I hoick my legs out of the bed and tell him I'm going to put on my dressing gown. When I have, I turn and see he's standing by the open window. I slip on some old trainers that don't need lacing up.

'Oh, just one thing, Michael.'

He turns, wondering what I might want.

'D'you mind if we go through the front door?'

'Sorry.' He moves away from the window. 'Force of habit.'

I turn the handle on my bedroom door, careful not to make any noise that might wake Dad, and we head downstairs.

I have no concept of time as we walk the deserted street. The streetlamps are off, but the whole area has taken on a surreal quality with the strength of what, I can see now, is a full moon. It's cold. Michael takes my hand as if this might warm me. We stop so he can rebutton his army jacket, then carry on. We don't speak as we walk, and I'm not sure where we are heading. He seems to know, so I just let him lead me. Eventually I ask what I've been burning to know.

'So what happens when you die, then?'

'I think I'm about to find out. There's been quite a lot of hanging about so far. Queuing, doors slamming in your face, some people being helpful, others not. A bit like getting a new passport.'

This had happened to us before, years back. We'd forgotten to renew our passports and had booked a week in Spain. We'd had to queue for ages, begging men in suits to try and get it all done quickly. Faceless men, characterless rooms, never-ending corridors.

'Do you know someone called Toni?' he suddenly says.

God, that's weird. What do I say?

'Yes,' I answer, but he doesn't want details.

'She says . . . to tell you . . . he's OK. Does that make sense?'

I nod. It does.

'What's she like?' I say, not sure why I'm asking.

'She's nice. Her hair's still growing back. Looks a bit like Sinead O'Connor.'

Sinead O' . . . ?

Ah. The picture. The picture from the spinach pie party. It makes sense now. Everything does. But how is that possible? None of this is, yet somehow everything feels so right. I get a sense that I'm walking towards the edge of the world. That should scare me, but strangely I feel safe. I could literally fall off, spin into space, but know I won't, as Michael is here to protect me.

We're in the park now, I see. I don't remember us coming in, but it doesn't perturb me. Moonlight filters down through the branches of the trees. They look like bony fingers, I think to myself, and suddenly I realize where we're heading. Maybe that should scare me, but for now it doesn't. A faint mist has descended and wraps round our feet like dry ice. Somewhere an owl hoots.

'It's very Disney,' I joke, and his hand tightens round mine and I know he thinks it's funny.

We stop. Oh God.

'Is this it, then?'

He doesn't answer. He's looking straight ahead, not at me. I look to see what he might possibly be staring at. Ahead, near the trees, is a bench. Sitting on the bench is a child. It looks sunny over there. How is that possible?

'Come on,' he says, and we walk forward.

As we get closer, I see there is a little girl sitting on the bench. She must be about five or six, and she's radiating so much light. She's reading a book with pictures in it. She's wearing a duffle coat. She looks up. She has the prettiest face. Freckles. I can see her eyes are green, and her hair, curly as anything, is the most beautiful shade of red, like a sunset. She smiles at me and I know immediately who she is. I run to her and hug her, picking her up and swinging her round. She chuckles and I smother her in kisses. I am warmed by her light.

'Oh, you're such a beautiful little girl!'

Her laughter is like sweet music. It's as loud as an orchestra. It echoes round the park and I feel so joyous, so proud. She's warm and smells of honeysuckle, summertime. Then I see Michael looking sadly on and realize it's time to say goodbye. I slide her back to the ground. She runs and gets her book.

'Come on, Sunflower.' Michael says, and stretches out his hand.

She hurries to his side. I walk over and kneel, facing her, head to head.

'Now, you be a good girl and always keep an eye out for Daddy, right?'

She nods.

I envelop her in a hug and kiss her curls, then let her go again. She looks up to Michael. He has a tear in his eye. I stand. He buries his head in my shoulders and I feel he's trying not to cry. I have to stay strong. I tell him I love him and give him an extra-hard squeeze. He no longer smells musty. He smells like him again. He's wearing the peppery aftershave I bought him for Christmas but ended up not giving him. I step back.

'I love you,' I say. And I mean it.

He swings the holdall over his shoulder then bends to pick up Evie. She nestles into him, the book still in her hand, like she might fall asleep in his arms. I hope she does. Her glow is fading.

What do you say? What do you say when you know you're never going to see someone again? It all sounds so pathetic and banal and mundane. Words aren't enough.

And in that moment I realize we don't need words.

He gives me the fondest smile.

'Come on, then. Let's go,' he whispers, and Evie smiles.

He gives me one last wink, then turns and walks towards the trees.

I try my hardest to concentrate. I drink the picture in, desperate to remember every last detail: his slightly lolloping gait, balancing the bag and our daughter, her wrestling slightly in his arms to get more comfortable. Then he stops. He looks back. He looks scared. I give him an encouraging look and think so, so hard, *Come on. You can do this.*

He gathers himself up to his fullest height, suddenly looks fearless and proud. Evie waves sleepily. Then he turns and walks off into the trees. Evie slumps, limp against him.

I have an urge to follow them, find out where they are going, but I know it's not my time yet.

The mist seems to rise the further they walk from me. Eventually it swallows them and I am just stood looking at moonlit trees.

I pull my dressing gown to me, freezing suddenly, and look about myself.

Did that really just happen?

Did it?

It did. I know it did.

I am a woman. In a park. In the dead of night. In her dressing gown. But I no longer feel confused.

---

4 December 2012

I write on the rice paper with silver marker pen. I write gently, not too much force, scared of ripping the fragile sheath. Kneeling on the grass my knees are wet, but these are old jeans, so it doesn't matter. My message written, Kevin passes me the next billowing piece of rice paper. I write my second message and draw a sunflower.

I look up. I'm ready. Kevin holds out his hand and helps me to my feet. The night air is cold and our chimney breath dances in the air.

'There's no breeze. Does it matter?' I ask, but he shakes his head.

'Which d'you want to do first?'

'Can we do them both together?'

He's unsure. 'Might be easier to do them separately.'

The Chinese wish lanterns were his idea. He and Connor did one for Toni on her anniversary, and it felt right to do it today, a year after Michael went.

'Do Michael's first,' I suggest, and he takes out a cigarette lighter.

I hold the bamboo frame of the first lantern as he lights the flammable material in its base. Immediately the white paper illuminates and expands. A magic cube of light. He looks at me. He smiles, his face lit by the lantern. He takes hold of the other side and we lift it so it obliterates our faces.

'Let go,' I hear him say. I do and the lantern floats effortlessly up into the inky-black sky.

'Now Evie.'

We do the same with the second lantern, then step back, necks cricked to the sky. Kevin puts his arm round me.

I thought I might cry. I could, but the sight is too beautiful. If tears come, they will be tears inspired by wonder and awe. The lanterns float higher and higher, one higher than the other, Michael leading the way. They're like moonlit swans soaring silently ahead. At one point the crescent moon looks like their distant triplet sister. They head to our right, westward, like they're following the path of the Thames. Like sedate shooting stars, majestic galleons sailing on – to where, I do not know – carrying their wishes with them. Will they fly to heaven, or will they simply evaporate into the ether? Who can tell? Who knows the secrets of the universe? Who wants to?

We stand there, wishing, praying, hoping, happy, until they're so high and so far away that eventually they just leave pinprick white spots on the inside of my eyelids.

They have gone.

Kevin pulls me to him and kisses the top of my head.

I have done it. I have marked Michael's passing. And Evie's. I feel numb but serene. As serene as the lanterns as they glided into the clouds.

I put the marker pen in my pocket. Kevin puts the lighter in his and we head back to his car.

Before leaving the park, I take one last look at the armadillos of the flood barrier. In the dark it looks like they're sleeping. It would have been wonderful if they'd been awake and raised for the occasion. Michael would have loved a biblical flood, but life has a way of not working out the way you expect it.

'What d'you want to do?' Kevin asks quietly.

I turn to him and smile.

'I think it's high time we went back to yours and watched *Some Mother's Son* on DVD,' I giggle.

He laughs his head off. 'It's embarrassing!'

'No, come on, I want to see how rubbish you were as an extra.'

He's still laughing. 'Can't we go for a Chinese? There's a really good one by London City Airport. You can watch the planes taking off.'

'Then we'll go there and get a takeaway. Come on, I've seen your props. Now I want to see your one and only film appearance.'

'I was shite. They had to tell me to stop looking at the camera.'

'I don't care,' I insist.

We snake through the bushes that lead from the park to the car park.

He opens the passenger door for me and I clamber in.

Before he shuts the door, he asks, 'How you feeling?'

'Not bad.'

'Good.' And he slams the door shut.

Connor is staying at Jason's tonight. Connor who is not best pleased that his dad has started seeing his form tutor. Connor who blushes every time I dare to look at him in class.

As Kevin slides into the driver's seat, I feel a wave of panic.

This happens sometimes. I've learned to live with it, aware that it's just my body's way of reacting to all the changes I've been through. Sometimes I think I'm going to go home and find Michael sitting at the kitchen table, furious that I've betrayed him, but the panic lasts for a shorter time each time it visits. I allow it to wash over me, then drain away, and I reassure myself as we head back towards Kevin's that in a minute I will feel safe again.

I focus on the Olympics 2012 sticker on the dashboard. It's fading now. I remember how we drank wine and scoffed pizza throughout the opening ceremony as we watched it on my telly, sporadically shouting things out like, 'Oh, look! The suffragettes!' or, 'Oh my God, is that J. K. Rowling?' and, 'God love the NHS!' It was the first time we kissed. It was like . . . like the show had been put on especially for us.

And even though it was a while ago now, the memory warms me like a pashmina. I look away from the sticker and smile at Kevin, but he's concentrating on driving.

As we're pulling into the car park of the Chinese place, I think I see the lanterns in the sky, but it's a plane coming in to land at City Airport. I wonder if the passengers have seen the glowing cubes on their descent.

I am going to have fun tonight. We will get nice food, then watch a good film, and then later on we will go to bed and spoon. All we ever do is spoon, Kevin and me.

OK, so sometimes I lie.

I must do something about that.

If you enjoyed
The Confusion of Karen Carpenter,
why not try JONATHAN HARVEY's debut novel,
All She Wants

'Utterly original, sharply written and very funny.
I laughed, and then I laughed'
JOJO MOYES

'A mad-cap, laugh-out-loud rollercoaster of a ride
through the life of an actress/soapstar, with an
unexpectedly tender sting in the tail'
MARIAN KEYES

There are some things in life you can always rely on. Living in
the shadow of your 'perfect' brother Joey, getting the flu over
Christmas, and your Mother showing you up in the supermarket.

Then there are some things you really don't count on happening: a good dose of fame, getting completely trashed at an
awards ceremony, and catching your fella doing something un-
mentionable on your wedding day.

This is my story. It's dead tragic. You have been warned . . .

Jodie

Xx

Read on for the first chapter

PROLOGUE

1994

We must have looked an odd sight, the three of us: me, Our Joey and Mum, scuttling along the pavement of an industrial estate in South Liverpool carrying deckchairs and packed lunch boxes in the middle of December.

'Jodie, your shoes are really getting on my tits,' moaned Our Joey.

'Don't say tits, Joey,' Mum said sternly.

'Why not?'

He knew why not. 'It's not becoming of an eight-year-old.'

'Can I say it?' I asked. I was ten. AKA dead grown-up.

'No.'

Our Joey tried again. 'Jodie, your shoes are really getting on my *nerves*.'

He meant the noise they were making. I'd recently looped some *Friends* fridge magnets into the laces of my shoes, so with every hurried step I took, Chandler and Joey clunked against my burgundy patent leather T-bars.

The air was heavy with the acrid tang of chemicals wafting on the breeze from the Mersey. We passed the cigarette factory where Mum worked. We passed the boarded-up bank. We passed the faded old sign that said, 'Welcome To Liverpool, A Socialist Council', onto which someone had graffitied 'anti' before the 'socialist' and then crossed out the 'ist'. Hilarious. And then suddenly Mum stopped, snapped her deckchair out and sat down. Me and Our Joey followed suit, and wondered what on earth was going on.

We appeared to be sitting outside some gates. There was a barrier that looked like it might go up to let traffic through, a glass-fronted booth with a security guard in it and two brick walls on either side. It looked just like the entrance to Mum's work, except there were a few purple flags on each side of the gates, which I felt was a bit showy offy for a factory.

'Mum? Why are we here?'

'Shut up and have a sandwich, Jodie.'

I opened the red plastic *Friends* lunchbox I held in my shivering hand and prised apart the Slimcea slices within to inspect their contents. Tuna paste. I pulled a face and looked at Mum. She smiled apologetically.

'I haven't had time to go up Kwik Save,' she explained.

I rolled my eyes and shut the box in disgust.

'Where are we, Mum?' moaned Our Joey, toying with the clasp on his Polly Pocket lunchbox. 'I don't understand.'

Mum allowed herself a mischievous chuckle and my heart sank.

'This, kids,' – I rolled my eyes again and tutted. I wasn't a kid. I was TEN – 'is where dreams are made!'

I looked at her like she was mad.

Let me explain. This was meant to be a Big Day Out for us. It was the school holidays, and to spare us the monotony of just 'playing out' each day, Mum would occasionally wake us up with the thrilling announcement, 'Right! We're having a day . . . *out*!' At which me and my brother would squeal, jump like lemmings from our bunk beds, then run to the bathroom to wash and brush our teeth together, fizzing with excitement. We did everything together, me and Our Joey, bar going to the loo. Mind you, we did that too sometimes, just to wind Mum up.

'Get out of there, the pair of you! It's not natural!' she'd holler, banging on the door. 'If you're showing each other your bits, I'll hit the roof,' which, bearing in mind she always wore impossibly high heels, was not outside the realms of possibility. Though she needn't have worried. We never showed each other our bits. For my part I'd already seen Sean McEvoy's todger when he waggled it around in show-and-tell, and whenever I mentioned fannies to Our Joey he went a bit pale, said, 'I feel sick,' and waggled his hand around, which was drama queen sign language for 'change the subject'.

Anyway. Where was I? Oh yes! Big Days Out. So there's me and Our Joey, full of the joys of spring, or summer, or Christmas, or whichever half-term it might be. But then, within an hour or so, as reality set in, we'd become less enamoured with what constituted Mum's idea of 'a holiday in a day':

One day in the summer holidays we went to watch the planes take off at Liverpool Airport.

One day in the Easter half-term we got a train to Southport to go and see some red squirrels in a forest, only instead we found a trampy bloke playing with himself and ended up catching the first train back. When Our Joey asked Mum what he was doing, she kept saying he was 'very itchy'.

Another day Mum took us to the local cats' home to stare at a bunch of moggies lying behind Perspex. At the end of the visit me and Our Joey wanted to take one home, but Mum claimed Dad was allergic.

So as you can imagine, my hopes weren't high for this

particular day out. Especially as we were sitting in deckchairs outside a factory three bus stops away from home.

However, the next thing she said made my heart literally skip a beat.

'This, kids, is where they film *Acacia Avenue*.'

'WHAT?!' That was me and Our Joey speaking in unison.

We looked at each other, then peered back at the gates. It was now I realized that written on the purple flags on either side of the gates were the words 'Crystal TV'. I had seen those words before. They came up on the telly at the end of every episode of our favourite soap opera.

Every Monday and Wednesday *Acacia Avenue* was religious viewing in our house. Me, Our Joey, Mum and Dad would sit watching it through a fog of smoke, courtesy of the free cigarettes Mum got from work, Mum and Dad sucking away like they were getting the elixir of youth from every little drag; me and Our Joey hacking our guts up and wafting the smoke away dramatically. We were completely gripped when Nona Newman from the corner shop began her illicit affair with Harry from the factory behind her street-sweeper hubby Tex's back. And there was that heart-stopping moment when Tex saw Nona's handbag on the back seat of Harry's Ford Capri. But when he referred to it as 'My Nona's handbag', Our Joey hit the roof.

'It's not a handbag; it's a clutchbag!' he screamed, knocking some Wotsits onto the carpet and getting an arched-eyebrow glare from my dad. It really wasn't becoming for an eight-year-old boy in Liverpool to know the difference between a handbag and a clutchbag. Our Joey caught the glare, looked wounded and muttered to himself, 'Any idiot can see that.' Mum seemed to consider this, then nodded her head in agreement. Not knowing what to say, Dad just pointed to the Wotsits on the floor and Our Joey curtly picked them up.

Our Joey and me used to play *Acacia Avenue* in the bedroom of our dormer bungalow. My dressing table became the counter of the Sleepy Trout pub and I was sneering barmaid Sorrel while Our Joey was her ditzy sidekick Cheryl. Together we'd serve imaginary pints of bitter to a selection of Barbies, Tiny Tears and teddy bears. Sometimes our back garden became the avenue itself and we'd re-enact one of the catfights that regularly ensued after kicking-out time. Mum and Dad had often commented that it was filmed 'just down the road', but I'd never quite believed them. To me it was a real world, real life; it just happened to take place inside a box in the corner of our lounge with really little people twice a week.

'Can we go in and look?' asked Joey, peering at the security guard.

'No.'

'Ah, go on, Mum,' I joined in.

'No, Jodie. It's against the law.' And she clicked out the nib of her twelve-colour biro and started having a crack at a word-search in her *Puzzler* magazine. I looked at her, and in that instant decided she was the most brilliant, most lovely, most beautiful mum in the whole wide world. For once I thought it was fab the way she thought she looked a bit like Princess Di, side-flicking her hair accordingly, peeking out from behind her bottle-blonde fringe with an air of coyness that didn't quite suit her. I thought – possibly for the first time – that it was great she still took care of herself and her figure and that, at the grand old age of thirty-two, she still got wolf whistles whenever she passed a building site. 'Best legs in Liverpool,' my dad always said. I looked at them now, resplendent in their morello cherry woollen tights. I'd always been slightly mortified by her propensity to show them off all the time by wearing skirts that were far too short for her, but today I decided she had every right. Those legs were just so . . . leggy. Both of them. So why not wear miniskirts at the really old age of thirty-two and make a show of yourself and your family? She was my mum. She could do anything she wanted. She had brought me and Our Joey to *Acacia Avenue*!

I looked at Our Joey and it seemed like he was having similar thoughts. His little snub nose with the smattering of freckles – which I had too but covered in the powder from Mum's compact whenever she wasn't looking – rose skyward, like one of the Bisto kids smelling something wonderful on the other side of the gates. It was as if the magic of *Acacia Avenue* was wafting towards us in a glittery line of fairy dust, completely blocking out the smell from the factories. His green eyes, which I hated with an envy only a sibling can understand – one of mine was blue, the other brown; I was a freak – were half closed in an affectation of contentment that he usually only saved for the Eurovision Song Contest and whenever Madonna was on *Top of the Pops*. While I watched him, his eyes flicked open like a startled china doll as a shadow crossed our path. Someone else had joined our party.

A fat man in a dirty parka with matted fur trim and a plaster on his glasses was standing nearer the gates than our deck-chairs. He had a camera in one hand and an autograph book in the other. At first I thought he was the trampy bloke from the forest near Southport, but when Mum gave him a cheery, 'Hiya!' I thought he mustn't be. There was definitely something weird about him, though. If he lived on our street, Mum would probably have told us to hurry past his house whenever we went by. The fat man nodded and started flicking through his autograph book.

'Who's that?' asked Joey. But Mum gave him one of her looks, so he tutted and looked away, muttering, 'Well, you were talking to him,' under his breath.

The fat guy had a weird habit of licking his thumb and turning the pages of his autograph book quickly, almost tearing the paper in his brusqueness. I could tell he was showing off, so I ignored him. I saw Joey looking at the weird guy, so I coughed and he looked at me.

'He loves that book,' I said quietly, cocking my head in the direction of the fat bloke.

Joey giggled. 'I know.'

'He's made up with it.'

'I know.'

'He's like, going with it.'

'I know.'

Our Joey could hardly get his words out because he was laughing so much. I loved it when I made Our Joey laugh. But then we jumped as Fat Bloke said something.

'How long you been here?' he was talking to Mum.

'Just got here, love.' Mum was calling him love. I looked to Our Joey.

'She fancies him,' he mouthed to me and I giggled.

'Seen anyone?'

'Not yet, love.'

And because she said love again, me and Our Joey creased up. Mum gave us a look, so we settled down.

'I've seen them all here,' the bloke carried on, and reeled off a list of names that meant nothing to me but everything to my mum, because she oo'd and ah'd throughout the extensive list. When he finished she took a cigarette out of her handbag and lit up, like she did after a good movie or a long phone conversation. She breathed the smoke out of her nose like a dragon and shook her head, impressed. I was just about to ask her who all those people were when Fat Bloke jumped to attention and Mum swivelled her head to look down the street. I looked. Our Joey looked.

A car was approaching. I'm not sure what sort of car it was – I've never been into cars – but it was black and the windows were black, too. Fat Bloke was getting very excited, hopping from one foot to the other like some sort of sumo morris dancer.

'It's Yvonne Carsgrove! It's Yvonne Carsgrove!' he squealed. 'That's her car, I'd know it anywhere!' Mum stood up, letting her *Puzzler* fall into her deckchair.

'Go'way, you're joking!' she was getting excited, too. She flicked her ciggie into the road and reflicked her hair with her hands. 'Get up, kids!'

Kids! I was TEN! I got up anyway as the black car slowed down as it approached the gates. Fat Bloke was waving at it like we were stranded in the desert and he was flagging down the first vehicle in ages that might take us to the next town. As the car ground to a halt – it had little choice as Fat Bloke had flung himself into its path, so it was either stop or the fat guy gets it – the driver's window lowered. I looked in.

All I could see was a head. Not severed or anything, but a woman's head. She had a fur hat thing on and *massive* sunglasses. And it wasn't even sunny. For a second I thought it was Shirley Bassey, because that's what she looked like on the back of one of my dad's LPs (the one that described her as 'the Lily of Tiger Bay'), but as Fat Bloke was rushing to the open car window waggling his autograph book in this vision's face, I realized it must be someone from *Acacia Avenue*. But who? He thrust the book through the open window and I saw the vision scribble something inside.

Mum started poking me. 'Say hello, Jodie!' And she pushed me forward. Our Joey fell in alongside me; she must have been poking him, too.

'Who is it?' Our Joey asked.

Mum rolled her eyes like he was stupid. 'It's Nona Newman!'

I gulped and looked again. Could it really be? No! Nona Newman? The lady who worked in the corner shop who'd had an affair with the factory foreman behind her street-sweeper husband's back? That wasn't Nona Newman. Nona Newman was dead ordinary looking. She worked in a shop. She wore a mac when it rained and always moaned that she 'didn't have enough money for a pair of shoes that wouldn't let the rain in'. Why would she be driving round in a big black car, wearing fur hats and sunglasses? Nona was a bit . . . dull. So dull me and Our Joey used to row over who would play her when we were playing corner shop in our bedroom. But this lady. Well, this lady looked like a star!

'Excuse me, Nona,' I heard Mum saying. 'Only these are my kids. Our Jodie and Our Joey. And they're both big fans of yours.'

At which the vision slipped off her sunglasses to reveal that – oh my God, Mum was right – it was indeed Nona Newman. She smiled. We both stood there in stunned silence. She was a lot bigger than when she was in the corner of our lounge.

'But he said your name was something else,' I said, confused.

The vision smiled, like a kindly teacher who was going to teach you a big word you didn't understand but they did and they loved showing off about it.

'Darling, I'm an actress. My real name is Yvonne, but I play Nona. It's my job.'

I nodded.

'Kids, eh?' Fat Bloke muttered. Nona shot him a look of contempt, which made me warm to her.

'Anyway,' said Nona. She sounded posher than she did on the telly. 'Have you two cherubs decided what you want for Christmas yet?'

I had. I'd written to Santa and asked for a night of passion with Joey from *Friends*. I had no idea what it meant, but I'd heard Mum's friend Maureen saying she'd had a night of passion with Ged from the Elephant and not to tell their Tony. Something told me that if I said this now Mum'd protest that it wasn't becoming of a ten-year-old, so I just shook my head and shrugged. Our Joey stepped forward and opened his mouth. Surely he wasn't going to tell her the truth, was he? He'd confided in me only the night before that all he wanted for Christmas was a horse-riding Barbie. He'd sworn me to secrecy over it, because if anyone found out he would a) get his head kicked in, and b) get his head kicked in again. But he opened his mouth and instead of telling the truth and saying, 'I might only be eight, but I'm the biggest poofter on the block and would therefore like a horse-riding Barbie with a poseable body and moveable arms,' he said:

'All I want for Christmas is a kiss from Nona Newman.'

Oh God. I actually felt physically sick. My brother, much as I loved him, and much as he was kind of my best friend in the whole wide world, always knew which buttons to press to get people on his side. I knew now that Nona Newman would be putty in his hands.

And indeed she was. She stretched out both her arms – no mean feat through a car window – and beckoned my little brother towards her with a very theatrical cry of, 'Come here, my little soldier!' Which he did. Though how many soldiers were known to skip rather than march I didn't know. Mum was bubbling with excitement and pride as she watched her youngest being kissed by none other than Nona Newman. Problem was, Our Joey was a bit too tiny to reach up through her window.

'Lift him up, Mum,' Nona encouraged. Mum stepped forward and hoisted Our Joey aloft so he came in line with Nona's lips, and when she eventually put him down again he had an orange lip mark on his forehead. I jealously saw that she was now holding his hand through the window. It looked quite awkward, but neither of them seemed to mind. She had this weird black velvet coat thing on with a wizard's sleeve effect, which would have looked hideous on Mum or me, but sort of worked on her.

'What do you want to be when you grow up, kid?' Nona asked.

'Like you,' he bleated. And again I felt sick. He didn't want to be her. He wanted to be Madonna in her 'True Blue' outfits. But Nona nodded as if it was perfectly normal.

'Well, kid. If I can offer you one piece of advice, it's this.'

I glanced over at Fat Bloke. He was seething with jealousy. Nona Newman had obviously never kissed him or given him advice. Mum was almost crying by now.

'What, Nona?' asked Our Joey. Blimey, he was on first-name terms with her now.

'That's not her real name!' barked Fat Bloke. 'That's her character's name. Her real name's Yvonne Carsgrove. God! GET IT RIGHT!'

Mum looked like she might punch him and said, 'All right, Tubby love. Wind your neck in!'

Nona clasped Our Joey's hand so tight I could see the colour draining out of his knuckles, then she offered her words of wisdom.

'Reach for the stars, kid. But remember, be nice to the people you meet on the way up, coz you only meet the same people on the way back down. OK?'

Our Joey nodded, though I could tell he had no idea what she was on about. Mum was nodding her head vehemently, as if she'd been entrusted with the meaning of life itself. I saw her lips move as she mouthed the words back to herself, in case she was asked to repeat it at a later date.

And then Nona's hand slipped away from Our Joey's and disappeared back into the car. As the colour returned to Our Joey's hand, so the window silently slid closed and the car started up again. Nona Newman/Yvonne Carsgrove drove through the gates into Crystal TV and Our Joey stood on the pavement gloating like the cat who'd got the cream.

We hung around for another hour. A few cars came and went, but no one else stopped to say hello and Fat Bloke was convinced they were 'only extras' – whatever that meant – then when it started to rain Mum decided it was time to go home. As we dragged our deckchairs to the bus stop Mum kept wittering on about what a special day it had been and how lovely Nona Newman was. Our Joey kept his mouth shut, which was almost more irritating than if he'd not shut up about his 'special moment'. I thought he was still gloating until he said, 'Nona Newman's breath smells of poo.'

'Joey!' snapped Mum.

'What?'

'That's very unbecoming!'

'Why? I never said shite!'

'JOEY!'

We carried on walking. God, the deckchairs were heavy.

'Nona Newman was lovely to you and that's how you repay her? Joey McGee, I am disappointed in you. Very disappointed in you. You had to go and spoil an otherwise perfect day.'

As we waited at the bus stop, Mum took out a cigarette and lit it up. Again the dragon nose. She saw me staring and smiled. I smiled back.

'Mum?'

'What?'

'When I grow up,' I said, 'I'm gonna be an actress. And I'm gonna be in *Acacia Avenue*.'

Mum chuckled, letting the ciggie hang out of the corner of her mouth as she looked in her handbag for her little compact mirror. She got it out and checked her face.

'You daft sod,' she said, but she said it fondly.

I looked out at the empty street. There was nothing to be seen for miles but factory gates and boarded-up buildings. And I thought, Why not? It was only three bus stops away. Why shouldn't I? The teachers at school were always asking us what we wanted to be when we grew up. Everyone else in my class used to say they wanted to work at the ciggie factory like their mams and dads, but I was going to be different. From now on I'd say I was going to be like Nona Newman and be an actress in *Acacia Avenue*. What was so weird about that?

And maybe, if I wished for it hard enough, one day it would actually come true.

ONE

2012

Keep it all in, Jodie. Keep it all in. Deep breaths, you're going to be fine. Just get through this and then the rest of your life can begin.

I opened my eyes. I'd arrived.

The noise from the screaming fans outside the Royal Albert Hall was so high-pitched I thought my eardrums might explode. Thank God I wasn't epileptic or the constant flash of paparazzi bulbs would surely have sparked a seizure. I squinted my way through the melee, convinced that every picture being taken would show me blinded by the glare, a hostage seeing daylight for the first time. It had only just stopped bucketing it down, so with every step my heels dug further and further into the squidgy red carpet that felt like it was actually sucking me in. What a great look. Jeez. What was I doing? Pressing grapes or arriving at the National Soap Awards? Hands punched forwards from the barriers on either side of the carpet, waving scraps of paper, autograph books, pens and camera phones. It would have been quite scary if I wasn't so dazed.

'Jodie! Jodie! Over here, Jodie!'

I turned towards the voice and stopped side on to the

cameraman, maintaining the fixed smile I'd had on my face since stepping out of the limo.

'You look gorgeous, Jodie!' someone screamed.

And so would you, I thought, if you'd spent three hours in a hotel room being primped, plucked and backcombed to within an inch of your life. I'd had little say over my look: Crystal TV provided the hair and make-up artists and some top designers had donated the dress and jewellery for free publicity. They'd delivered a van load of stuff to the hotel, and me and my fellow cast mates had fought over who'd wear what. I'm not saying blood was drawn, but a couple of the girls had had to lie down with steaks on their eyes for half an hour afterwards.

Our producer Eva had been adamant that I should look as unlike my character Sister Agatha as possible. And as Sister Agatha was a nun I'd ended up wearing what can best be described as a dwarf's tinfoil hankie with gladiatorially laced high heels. Setting off the look was a diamond-encrusted headband with matching bracelet. I looked like an anaemic Tina Turner entering the Thunderdome.

'We love you, Sister Aggie!' someone screamed.

'Bless you, my child!' I giggled, before being herded inside by an overenthusiastic runner who got her clipboard caught in my bracelet.

'Sorry, Sister.'

Blimey. Even when I was wearing little more than tit tape, people still thought I was a nun. I looked again and saw that it wasn't a runner but our press officer, Ming.

(Ming rhymed with Sting. Yes, I'd made that mistake, too. She was Chinese, but sounded like Cilla Black.)

'Ming! How many times? I'm not a nun. I'm an actress

who *plays* a nun,' I said as she did a fetching 'disentangling a clipboard from a bracelet' dance I'd not seen before and wasn't likely to ever see again.

'Oh, gerrover yourself, Jodie, am only pullinya leg. Now there's looooadsa press hoove gorra lorra questions for you. Come on chuck. And DON'T mention the war. Please.'

(OK, so I'm exaggerating her voice, but she was totally annoying.)

OK. The war. I wasn't to mention what I'd done only this morning. And if anyone did ask, I was to answer with a polite, 'Not now, sorry . . .'

'I'm warning you, Jozie,' Ming said as she thrust me forward, 'you've shown us up enough these past twenny-four hours.'

Anyway. I wasn't going to let someone as energy sucking as miserable Ming spoil my fun tonight. I was determined this was going to be the best night of my life. And that included the night I'd found back-to-back reruns of *Hart to Hart* on some cable channel *and* a twenty pound note down the back of the settee.

I, Jodie McGee, had been nominated for Best Actress at the National bloody Soap Awards. *ARGH!*

It was pandemonium in the foyer. Ming pushed me through a cattle market of emaciated babes in too much make-up and too little clothing and identikit muscled hunks bursting out of their dinner jackets. God, I wanted a drink. I had promised myself I wouldn't touch a drop till after my award was announced. I was 90 per cent sure I wouldn't get it and that heifer from *EastEnders* would, but I thought I'd better steer clear of the sauce just in case.

Ming steered me into a side room, which had a bank of besuited and be-ballgowned radio and TV journos penned in behind a cordon, cameras and microphones at the ready.

'Remember,' Ming whispered in my ear, 'there's no competition between us, *Corrie* and *EastEnders*. There's a lorra lovintharoom.'

I rolled my eyes, stepped into the pen and beamed at the gurning simpleton from *On the Sofa with Colin and Carol*, who'd decided to dress as a big bar of pink soap for the occasion.

'Everybody, look, it's Jodie McGee who plays Sister Agatha in *Acacia Avenue*!' She beamed into the camera, then turned to me with all the fluidity and grace of the tin man. 'So, Jodie, can I just say you look amazing.'

I fluttered my eyelashes and shot a 'What, these old rags?' grimace to camera.

'Thanks . . .' But I couldn't remember her name. I couldn't say Gurning Simpleton, so I just gurned back at her and said it again: 'Thanks,' which made it sound like I was being uber sincere. Back of the net!

'So, Jodie. Great piece on *Brunch with Bronwen* this morning. You've had a lot of hits on YouTube already. Have you got the police involved yet?'

'No comment. Sorry.'

She could see it would be like getting blood out of a stone, so . . .

'So, Jodie. Who's going to win Best Actress?'

'Well' – damn, if only I could remember her name – 'it's a really tough year and a really tough category, but I thought Colette Court was *to die for* in those wonderful rape scenes.'

Oh God. Did I really say that? Gurning Simpleton was poking me with her mic again.

'So the rivalry between *Corrie*, *EastEnders* and *Acacia Avenue*, that's just something that's made up by the press?'

I smiled my best Sister Agatha beatific smile and suddenly remembered the interviewer's name.

'Stephanie. Colette Court and I really are best buddies.'

The words almost choked me. I was desperate to add, *Even if she does sound like a block of flats.* I clocked Gurning Simpleton frowning and miming a hacking movement at her throat.

'OK, can we re-record that?' she said to her cameraman, then looked to me. 'My name's Penny?'

Suitably humbled, or at least pretending to be, we continued.

Twenty minutes later I was in the bar.

'It's not going your way. I know it's not going your way. Don't ask how I know.' Eva Hart the producer of *Acacia Avenue* (AKA my boss) took a big swig of her champagne and my balloon of pride was burst. She'd poked it with a pin, and now she was poking me with a finger. What was it with all the poking tonight?

'OK, you dragged it out of me. Lisa in the office's boyfriend knows someone who knows someone who actually does thingy.' She snapped her fingers, searching for the word. 'ENGRAVES!' she screamed. 'He engraves . . . the awards. He's an engraver; he does ENGRAVING. And she swears blind he had to ask if there was one or two 'L's in Colette. What do you think of THAT?'

Eva had a very annoying habit of shouting words she wanted to emphasize. I shrugged coyly.

'She was really good at getting raped.'

Eva practically spat out her champagne.

'BOLLOCKS! She was just lit well.' I didn't dare disagree. This was my boss after all. She leaned in conspiratorially.

'Anyway, fuck Colette Court. I've got big plans for you, Jodie. Big, big plans. The writers heart you. They do – they HEART you. And they have got VERY big plans for Sister Agatha.'

'Ooh, that sounds fun. Like what?'

Eva leaned in even further. 'I suppose you've heard there's a serial killer hitting the Avenue?'

I had. It was all we'd discussed in the green room for weeks. Rumours were spreading like wildfire about who'd be killed off. Every day a cast member would come in to work and be convinced they'd seen an early draft of a script in which they were for the chop, or someone else was for the chop. Maybe if I won the award tonight I'd be saved the chop.

'Well, people have been talking.'

Eva's eyes narrowed.

'Shit! Did anyone from *EastEnders* hear?' She looked around furtively as she raised her champagne flute to her lips. 'Who told you we were planning a serial-killer story? Who's leaking stuff to the actors? Oh, this won't do, this WON'T do.'

'No, Eva, I didn't know for—'

'I can't possibly tell you who's going to be the killer or who's going to be KILLED.'

'Eva, no one's leaking stories.'

Eva rearranged the collar on her electric-blue Bacofoil two-piece.

'Suffice it to say I want you in my office tomorrow at TEN,' Eva continued.

'Eva. About this morning. When I was on *Brunch With Bronwen*. I—'

'Don't piss on my chips, Jodie! We'll discuss it tomorrow at TEN.'

Ten? Blimey, I'd better not have a hangover and oversleep, I thought. Getting back to Liverpool for ten meant getting a train at some ungodly hour. Was it even worth going to bed?

'We're gonna make sure Sister Agatha keeps on growing and stays right at the heart of the show as an FCC.'

'FCC?'

'Front Cover Character. I want you on all of them, darling, ALL of them.'

'OK, Eva. Great.'

But how would I be at the centre of the show? Were they going to make *me* the serial killer? Or have me bumped off by said killer? I started to shake with nerves. Just then Eva's handbag vibrated and she yanked out her phone. She jabbed it a couple of times, then threw her head back and guffawed.

'Look at that. Look at THAT.' She shoved her phone in front of my nose. 'Aren't my kids ADORABLE?'

I really wanted to push her away from me and say, 'Actually, can I just have five minutes? I've been really looking forward to tonight. It's a really big deal for me to be nominated for this award and yet you've just told me in no uncertain terms that I haven't won it. I just need five minutes to process that. Plus you're confusing me with your serial killer musings . . .'

But instead I was looking at an image on her phone of three toddlers holding up a sign saying, 'We Miss You, Mummy'. They weren't adorable, even if Eva had signed them up with a kiddies modelling agency, but then I wasn't really the maternal sort. I got into trouble last year when a former cast member paraded her new baby up and down *Acacia Avenue* to adoring wails from present cast members about how cute and angelic-looking he was. I spoke before I thought and said, 'Ooh, isn't she fat?', which triggered the former cast member to burst into tears and run to the green room, clutching her baby to her bosom.

On the back of that I guessed honesty wasn't the best policy with my boss. Eva's kids were very important to her. I knew every mother would say the same about their kids, but Eva had adopted hers from Lithuania. It had been all over the papers at the time because Eva was in her early sixties, so her biological clock had ticked itself out decades earlier and no British adoption agency would touch her with a very long bargepole. Plus she was single, all of which meant she was the devil incarnate as far the press was concerned. Eva was, in her own words, 'a ball-busting media bitch who took no prisoners,' so I heard myself saying, 'God, Eva, I want your kids.'

'You can have them. An episode fee each. Only KIDDING!' And she poked me again. I'd been Eva'd.

'I think you've done something really amazing there, Eva.' I smiled and she smiled back.

'I've got it all, Jodie. Got it all. And I just wanna share it with someone, you know?'

She had lowered her voice and in that moment she sounded almost human. But then she saw someone more important than me and sprinted over to speak to them.

Left alone in the melee, I looked across the room and saw none other than Colette Court sweep into the room in lots of mushroom-coloured tulle, a tiara perched on her jet black beehive, looking like the queen of all she surveyed. And with that lazy eye she surveyed a lot. I smiled and when I thought she was looking over at me I raised my glass of orange to her, which is when I realized she wasn't looking at me, she was looking at a tray of mini burgers, which were heading her way on the arm of a spotty-necked waiter. She appeared to snort the lot. One minute the tray was full; the next it was empty and Colette Court was chewing away like Ermintrude the cow in *The Magic Roundabout*. A voice cooed in my ear, 'I know, babe. How does she stay so slim? She totes has an eating disorder.'

I looked to see who it was. It was my best friend on the show, Trudy. She laughed her head off to show she was being sarcastic, then pecked me fondly on the cheek.

'You look fabulous, babe.'

'Thanks, Trude.'

'Who cares what the papers say? I think you dress really well.'

She cocked her head to one side and rubbed my arm.

'Everyone's saying you haven't won, babe,' and then she quickly added, 'I'm just saying coz I'm your friend, babe. Don't want you to be too disappointed if you don't.'

I gulped and realized I wanted to cry. I looked around the room. Was everyone laughing at me for coming this evening?

I'd looked forward to this night for ages. I was going to be the first person to win Best Actress at the National Soap Awards and then go on to win an Oscar. Fat chance of that now.

I know it sounds daft. But I once met a gypsy in Blackpool who told me that one day I would win an Oscar. Mum reckoned Our Joey had put her up to it, but I had an inkling Gypsy Donna Marie could see the future.

'Anyway,' added Trudy. 'It's the taking part that counts, babe.'

I was starting to cry.

'I have to go the toilet,' I said.

And I legged it.

I sat on the loo for what felt like an eternity and quietly cried my eyes out. I went to text Stu, then realized I couldn't. Not any more. Then I heard some rustling in the cubicle next to me and wondered if it was Colette Court from *EastEnders* chopping out a line of coke. Rumours abounded that she had a drug problem, though I found it hard to believe: she certainly didn't have the figure of a drug addict. Not that it did her any harm – audiences loved her, presumably unthreatened by her ample shape. Just then I heard Eva's voice.

'Can you put me on speakerphone, Ivanka? I want to sing them a LULLABYE.'

Oh no. My boss was phoning her kids from inside a toilet. I heard Eva strain quietly then start to sing, 'Hush, Little Baby, Don't You Cry'. As she did I heard something falling into water.

Oh God. My boss was singing her kids to sleep while taking a dump. I felt sick. Talk about multitasking. I got up, flushed, unbolted the door and went out to do some damage-repair to my panda eyes. Trudy stood by the basins, touching up her lippy.

'Isn't Stu with you tonight?' she fished.

'No.'

'Why?'

'Did you not see *Brunch With Bronwen*?'

Trudy looked at me. 'God, babe. I've watched it like eighty times on YouTube. So it was true?'

'Well, I wasn't making it up.'

She rubbed my arm and cocked her head to one side again.

'Oh, babe. It was really brave of you to try and have a boyfriend who wasn't in the business. But, babe, people like us aren't meant to date civilians.'

She turned back to her other best friend, the mirror, and added, 'So, did he find out about your little . . . affair and stuff?'

I was about to argue with her – I had not been having an affair – but before I could say anything she was talking again.

'You know what you need, babe?'

I chuckled and examined my chest in the mirror. 'A boob job?'

Trudy laughed. 'Apart from that, babe!' And she opened her massive handbag. I peered inside. It was completely full of miniatures. (Drinks. Not miniature anything else, like miniature furniture. That would have been weird.)

She winked at me.

'A drink.'

I smiled. Maybe she was right.

An hour later and boy was I feeling a lot better. I think I'd had five miniatures by then. Or maybe six. Enough to feel nice and warm. Like on Christmas Day. But a nice Christmas Day. Not the sort of Christmas Day where your husband beats you up or your dog eats the turkey. You know, the sort of Christmas Day you might get on *Acacia Avenue* – a nice nostalgic Christmas Day where you've got all the presents you want and you've eaten too much turkey and the dog doesn't fart and your boyfriend isn't, like, 'Give me a blow job during *Victoria Wood*,' etc., 'Coz it's, like, women's comedy and it'll help me get into it.'

Like go fuck yourself, Stu.

And then I remembered. I wasn't with Stu any more.

God, this was a long night. And the seats were really uncomfortable. I was wedged in between that new girl who played the chip shop assistant with OCD whose name I could never remember, and the sweet one who played tearaway Asian teenager Supjit (I was convinced Supjit was a made-up name, invented by lazy/racist storyliners). There was a tribalistic feeling in the hall, with each quarter of the stalls area holding cast members of the different soaps, penned in like horses on slaughter day, each team power-screaming for their representative nominee as the names were read out. It was getting so heated I half expected to see loo roll and chairs come flying above our heads every time *Acacia Avenue* was namechecked.

I felt my mobile pulse in my bag and pulled it out to check for texts, hoping against hope that it might be from Our Joey.

But no, it was from Jason, who played Dodgy Rog, *Acacia Avenue*'s much loathed drug dealer.

Nice rack.

I looked round and saw him sat a few rows behind. He winked and took a swig from a bottle of lager he'd snuck in. I shook my head playfully, then turned back round to see Trudy mouthing, 'D'you want another absinthe?' I didn't realize how good I was at lip-reading till then and nodded eagerly. She handed me another miniature and I unscrewed the top and glugged it greedily. This stuff was great: it had almost made me forget all my worries over the past few weeks and the upcoming serial-killer story. They were just announcing Best Storyline. As *Acacia Avenue* was declared victorious for its 'evil Pippa escapes from prison and pretends to be her nice identical twin (with tragic consequences for the Nandras)' storyline, the entire cast and crew leapt to their feet in a frenzy of self-congratulation. Cameras zoomed up the aisle towards us and I found myself performing for them, suddenly bursting into tears with pride. The two actresses on either side of me caught on quickly and followed suit. It had the desired effect: a camera jabbed in our faces, beaming our tears into millions of living rooms. Eva, some of the writers and the actresses who played Pippa and Feroza Nandra practically flew towards the stage, with Eva screaming, 'Can you BELIEVE this? This is SO deserved. SO deserved,' to the wrong area of seating. She was shouting it to *EastEnders*.

'Well done, guys. Well DONE, guys!'

She clearly hadn't put her contacts in. When she reached the stage she screamed into the mic, 'GOD, YOU GUYS GET IT RIGHT SOMETIMES! WOWZER!'

I thought I might be a little bit tipsy because I started to zone out and wonder if Stu might be watching me. Yeah right, Jodie, dream on. If he was watching this, he'd probably be sticking pins in a doll of you. I tried to think of something else.

I wondered if Mrs Mendelson might be watching. Mrs Mendelson was my drama teacher in the 90s. She ran the Myrtle Mendelson School of Drama and Disco, South Merseyside, with a rod of iron and a well-oiled metronome in a couple of rooms above a betting shop two nights a week and all day Saturdays. I was her star pupil. No mean feat when, according to Mrs Mendelson, 'South Merseyside is a breeding ground for stars. They've all come from here. Smile!'

At which point her thirty eager students, standing straight backed in rows of five facing her, smiled as though we were on dangerously strong anti-depressants.

'And . . . Look worried!'

The thirty wannabes switched from beaming grins to furrowed brows and lip biting in an instant.

This was one of Mrs Mendelson's techniques: instant emotion.

'You never know when you're going to be called upon to instantly emote. When you are arrested on *The Bill*, when you have to choose which conjoined twin to lose on *Casualty*, even selecting a sweet at The Kabin on *Coronation Street*. Will you have hours to get into character and practice 'the Method'? No. You will have to instantly emote. And . . . be scared!'

The furrowed brows gave way to wide-eyed terror, hands jumped to faces. I whimpered out loud like a kicked puppy.

'Very good, Miss McGee. Never be frightened to make a noise. They can always switch the boom off if they no likey. And relax!'

We relaxed. Mrs Mendelson grabbed her stick and crab-walked to the toilet. This was a little ritual of hers: disappearing to the ladies' room every twenty minutes with her lorry-sized handbag to 'powder my accoutrements'. She was a strange woman, Mrs Mendelson, with her victory-roll hairdo and clip-on earrings that looked like sucked boiled sweets. She had a habit of unclipping them during a lesson and then putting them back on later without so much as a glance towards a mirror, leaving the earrings at mismatching levels on her ears. She always spoke as if playing to the back row, and had a habit of rolling her Rs so aggressively that strangers passing the Myrtle Mendelson School of Drama and Disco, South Merseyside, might have mistaken it for machine-gun fire. She would return from the toilet cherry red of face, having secretly knocked back some vodka from a hip flask. After each comfort break she'd flop into a chair, come over a bit misty-eyed and regale us with tales of her life in weekly rep in the 50s and how Sir John Gielgud once made a pass at her then boyfriend when they were in *Salad Days* in Chipping Norton. I loved these tales and would hurry home to repeat them at the dinner table to Our Joey and Mum and Dad. I was really good at taking her off, so even though the family rarely met Mrs Mendelson, they felt they knew her intimately.

I hoped she could see me tonight and be proud. Purists might have poo-pooed her instant emotion technique – I could hardly imagine Fiona Shaw employing it when performing *Medea* – but on a soap like *Acacia Avenue* it was an invaluable tool. I had a reputation at work for being able to cry buckets on cue. When the writers saw how good I was they started writing tears into nearly every episode. Sister Agatha was frequently sobbing over the Godlessness of the world, or her ill-fated kiss, and in a recent episode I'd even had to bawl about finding some litter on *Acacia Avenue*, whilst uttering the immortal line, 'Why, dear Lord? Why do they do it?' The memory made me shiver.

Trudy slipped me another absinthe and again I found my mind wandering back to Stu. In the big scheme of things I should have been married by now. I should have had seven children, three dogs, annual holidays somewhere fancy and a macrobiotic chef. Instead I was twenty-eight, and already washed up and over the hill. I felt like crying.

Suddenly I was being nudged. The Supjit girl leaned in.

'You next, Jodie. Good luck!'

I appeared to have slumped down in my seat. I could see two Trudies and they were both mouthing, 'You OK, babe?'

I tried to sit up. Straight back, eye on the sky, as Mrs Mendelson used to say. Some cheesy pop presenter walked onstage and said, 'And now the award for best dramatic performance by an actress. Let's have a look at the nominations.'

For some reason, I started to giggle uncontrollably.

extracts reading groups
books new
competitions
discounts extracts
competitions
books
new
events books
extracts
new titles reading groups
interviews
discounts
new books events
events new
discounts extracts discounts
www.panmacmillan.com
extracts events reading groups
competitions books extracts new